THE
WHOLE ART
OF
DETECTION

THE
WHOLE ART
OF
DETECTION

LOST MYSTERIES OF

SHERLOCK HOLMES

LYNDSAY FAYE

The Mysterious Press
New York

First Grove Atlantic hardcover edition: March 2017

Published simultaneously in Canada
Printed in the United States of America

FIRST EDITION

ISBN 978-0-8021-2592-7
eISBN 978-0-8021-8936-3

The Mysterious Press
an imprint of Grove Atlantic
154 West 14th Street
New York, NY 10011

Distributed by Publishers Group West

groveatlantic.com

17 18 19 20   10 9 8 7 6 5 4 3 2 1

This collection is dedicated to
my late Uncle Michael, who gave me my first copy of
The Adventures of Sherlock Holmes.

Contents

PART IV: THE LATER YEARS

THE
WHOLE ART
OF
DETECTION

PART I

BEFORE
BAKER STREET

The Case of
Colonel Warburton's
Madness

My friend Mr. Sherlock Holmes, while possessed of one of the most vigorous minds of our generation, and while capable of displaying tremendous feats of physical activity when the situation required it, could nevertheless remain in his armchair perfectly motionless longer than any other human being I have ever encountered. This skill passed wholly unrecognized by its owner. I do not believe he held any intentions to impress me so, nor do I think the exercise was, for him, a strenuous one. Still, I maintain the belief that when a man has held the same pose for a period exceeding three hours, and when that man is undoubtedly awake, that same man has accomplished an unnatural feat.

I turned away from my task of organizing a set of old journals that lead-grey afternoon to observe Holmes yet perched with one leg curled beneath him, firelight burnishing the edges of his dressing gown as he sat with his head in his hand, a long-abandoned book laid upon the carpet. The familiar sight had grown increasingly unnerving as the hours progressed. It was with a view to ascertain that my friend was still alive that I went so far against my habits as to interrupt his reverie.

"My dear chap, would you care to take a turn with me? I've an errand with the boot-maker down the road, and the weather has cleared somewhat."

I do not know if it was the still-ominous dark canopy that deterred him or his own pensive mood, but Holmes merely replied, "I require better distraction just now than an errand which is not my own and the capricious designs of a March rainstorm."

"What precise variety of distraction would be more to your liking?" I inquired, a trifle nettled at his dismissal.

He waved a slender hand, at last lifting his dark head from the upholstery where it had reclined for so long. "Nothing you can provide me. It is the old story—for these two days I have received not a shred of worthwhile correspondence, nor has any poor soul abused our front doorbell with an eye to engage my services. The world is weary, I am weary, and I grow weary with being weary of it. Thus, Watson, as you see I am entirely useless myself at the moment, my state cannot be bettered through frivolous occupations."

"I suppose I would be pleased no one is so disturbed in mind as to seek your aid, if I did not know what your work meant to you," I said with greater sympathy.

"Well, well, there is no use lamenting over it."

"No, but I should certainly help if I could."

"What could you possibly do?" he sniffed. "I hope you are not about to tell me your pocket watch has been stolen, or your great-aunt disappeared without trace."

"I am safe on those counts, thank you. But perhaps I can yet offer you a problem to vex your brain for half an hour."

"A problem? Oh, I'm terribly sorry—I had forgotten. If you want to know where the other key to the desk has wandered off to, I was given cause recently to test the pliancy of such objects. I'll have a new one made—"

"I had not noticed the key," I interrupted him with a smile, "but I could, if you like, relate a series of events which once befell me when I was in practice in San Francisco, the curious details of which have perplexed me for years. My work on these old diaries reminded me of them, and the circumstances were quite in your line."

"I suppose I should be grateful you are at least not staring daggers at my undocketed case files," he remarked.

"You see? There are myriad advantages. It would be preferable to venturing out, for it is already raining again. And should you refuse, I will be every bit as unoccupied as you, which I would also prefer to avoid." I did not mention that if he remained a statue an instant longer, the sheer eeriness of the room would force me out of doors.

"You are to tell me a tale of your frontier days, and I am to solve it?" he asked blandly, but the subtle angle of one eyebrow told me he was intrigued.

"Yes, if you can."

"What if you haven't the data?"

"Then we shall proceed directly to the brandy and cigars."

"It's a formidable challenge." To my great relief, he lifted himself in the air by his hands and crossed his legs underneath him, reaching after he had done so for the pipe lying cold on the side table. "I cannot say I've any confidence it can be done, but as an experiment presented to the specialist, it has a certain flair."

"In that case, I shall tell you the story, and you may pose any questions that occur to you."

"Take care that you begin at the beginning, Watson," he admonished me sternly, settling himself into a comfortable air of resigned attention. "And provide me with as many details as you can summon up."

"It is quite fresh in my mind again, for I'd set it down in the volumes I was just mulling over. As you know, my residence in America was relatively brief, but San Francisco lives in my memory quite as vividly as Sydney or Bombay—an impetuous, thriving town nestled among the great hills, where the fogs are spun from ocean air and the pale amber light refracts from Montgomery Street's countless glass windows. It is as if all the men and women of enterprise across the globe determined they should have a city of their own, for the Gold Rush built it and the Silver Lode built it again, and now that they have been linked by railroad with the Eastern states, the populace believes quite rightly that nothing is impossible. One sees quite as many nations and trades represented as in London, all jostling each other into a thousand bizarre coincidences, and you would not be surprised to find a Chinese apothecary wedged between a French milliner and an Italian wine merchant.

"My practice was based on Front Street in a small brick building, near a number of druggist establishments, and I readily received any patients who happened my way. Poor or well-off, genteel or ruffianly, it made no difference to a boy in the first flush of his career. I'd no long-established references, and for that reason no great clientele, but it was impossible to feel small in that city, for they so prized hard work and optimism that I anticipated sudden successes lay every moment round the next corner.

"One hazy afternoon, as I'd no appointments and I could see the sun lighting up the masts of the ships in the Bay, I decided I'd sat idle long enough, and set out for a bit of exercise. It is one of San Francisco's peculiar characteristics that no matter in what direction one wanders, one must encounter a steep hill, for there are seven of them, and within half an hour of walking aimlessly away from the water, I found myself striding up Nob Hill, staring in awe at the array of houses.

"'Houses,' in fact, is rather a misnomer; they call it Nob Hill because it is populated by mining and railroad nabobs, and the residences are like something from the reign of Ludwig the Second or Marie Antoinette. Many are larger than our landed estates, but all were built within ten years of the time I arrived. I ambled past a Gothic near-castle and a Neo-Classic mansion only to spy an Italianate villa across the street, each making an effort to best all the others in stained glass, columns, and turrets. The neighborhood—"

"Was a wealthy one." Holmes sighed, hopping out of his chair to pour two glasses of claret.

"And you would doubtless have found that section of town appalling." As he handed me a wineglass, I smiled at the thought of my Bohemian friend eyeing those pleasure domes with cool distaste. "There would have been others more to your liking, I think. Nevertheless, the villa was a marvel of architecture, and as I neared the crest of the hill, I stopped to take in the view of the Pacific.

"Standing there watching the sun glow orange over the waves, I heard a door fly open, and turned to see an old man hobbling frantically down a manicured path leading to the street. The mansion he'd exited was built more discreetly than most, vaguely Grecian and painted white. He was very tall—quite as tall as you, my dear fellow—but with shoulders like an ox. He was dressed in a decades-old military uniform, with a tattered blue coat over his grey trousers, and a broad red tie and cloth belt, his silvery hair standing out from his head as if he'd just stepped from the thick of battle.

"Although he cut an extraordinary figure, I would not have paid him much mind in that mad metropolis had not a young lady rushed after him in pursuit, crying out, 'Uncle! Stop, please! You mustn't go, I beg of you!'

"The man she'd addressed as her uncle gained the curb not ten feet from where I stood and then all at once collapsed onto the pavement, his chest no longer heaving and the leg which had limped crumpled underneath him.

"I rushed to his side. He breathed, but shallowly. From my closer vantage point, I could see that one of his limbs was false, and that it had come loose from its leather straps, causing his fall. The girl reached us not ten seconds later, gasping for breath even as she made a valiant effort to prevent her eyes from tearing.

"'Is he all right?' she asked me.

"'I think so,' I replied, 'but I prefer to be certain. I am a doctor, and would be happy to examine him more carefully indoors.'

"'I cannot tell you how grateful we would be. Jefferson!' she called to a tall black servant hurrying down the path. 'Please help us get the colonel inside.'

"Between the three of us, we quickly established my patient on the sofa in a cheerful, glass-walled morning room, and I was able to make a more thorough diagnosis. Apart from the carefully crafted wooden leg, which I reattached more securely, he seemed in perfect health, and if he were not such a large and apparently hale man I should have imagined that he had merely fainted.

"'Has he hurt himself, Doctor?' the young lady asked breathlessly.

"Despite her evident distress, I saw at once she was a beautiful woman, with a small-framed figure and yet a large measure of that grace which goes with greater stature. Her hair was light auburn, swept away from her creamy complexion in loose waves and wound in an elegant knot, and her eyes shone golden brown through her remaining tears. She wore a pale blue dress trimmed with silver, and her ungloved hand clutched at the folds in her apprehension. She—my dear fellow, are you all right?"

"Perfectly," Holmes replied with another cough which, had I been in an uncharitable humor, I would have thought resembled a chuckle. "Do go on."

"'This man will be quite all right once he has rested,' I told her. 'My name is John Watson.'

"'Forgive me—I am Molly Warburton, and the man you've been tending is my uncle, Colonel Patrick Warburton. Oh, what a fright I have had! I cannot thank you enough.'

"'Miss Warburton, I wonder if I might speak with you in another room, so as not to disturb your uncle while he recovers.'

"She led me across the hall into another tastefully appointed parlor, this one decorated with paintings of desert landscapes I thought must have depicted the American South, and fell exhaustedly into a chair. I hesitated to disturb her further, and yet I felt compelled to make my anxieties known.

"'Miss Warburton, I do not think your uncle would have collapsed in such a dramatic manner had he not been under serious mental strain. Has anything occurred recently which might have upset him?'

"'Dr. Watson, you have stumbled upon a family embarrassment,' she said softly. 'My uncle's mental state has been precarious for some time now, and I fear recently he—he has taken a great turn for the worse.'

"'I am sorry to hear it.'

"'The story takes some little time in telling, but I will ring for tea, and you will know all about it. First of all, Dr. Watson, I live here with my brother Charles and my uncle the colonel. Apart from Uncle Patrick, Charles and I have no living relatives, and we are very grateful to him for his generosity. Uncle made a great fortune in shipping during the early days of California statehood. My brother is making his start in the photography business, and I am unmarried, so living with the colonel is for the moment a very comfortable situation.'

"'You must know that my uncle was a firebrand in his youth, and saw a great deal of war as a settler in Texas, before that region was counted among the United States. The pitched fighting between the Texians—that is, the Anglo settlers—and the Tejanos so moved him that he joined the Texas Army under Sam Houston, and was decorated several times for his valor on the field, notably at the Battle of San Jacinto. Later, when the War Between the States began, he was a commander for the Union, and lost his leg during the Siege of Petersburg. Forgive me if I bore you.'

"'Not at all.'

"'From your voice, I do not think you are a natural-born American,' she added with a smile.

"'Your story greatly interests me. Is that his old Texas uniform he wore today?' I asked.

"'Yes, it is,' she replied as a flicker of pain distorted her pretty face. 'He has been costuming himself like that with greater and greater frequency. The affliction—for I do not know what else to call it—began several weeks ago. Indeed, I believe the first symptom took place when he changed his will.'

"'How so? Was it a material alteration?'

"'Charlie and I had been the sole beneficiaries,' she replied, gripping a handkerchief tightly. 'But now, his entire fortune will be distributed amongst various war charities. Texas War for Independence charities, Civil War charities. He is obsessed with war,' she choked, and then hid her face in her hands.

"I was already moved by her story, Holmes, but the oddity of the colonel's condition intrigued me still further.

"'What are his other symptoms?' I queried when she had recovered herself.

"'After he changed his will, he began seeing the most terrible visions in the dark. Dr. Watson, he claims in truly passionate language that he is haunted. He swears he saw a fearsome Tejano with a pistol and a whip threatening a white woman, and on another occasion he witnessed the same apparition using a bayonet to slaughter one of Houston's men. That is what so upset him, for only this morning he insisted he saw a murderous band of ghosts brandishing swords and torches, with the identical Tejano at their head. My brother believes that we have a duty as his family to remain and care for him, but I confess Uncle frightens me at times. If we abandoned him, he would have no one save his old manservant. Sam Jefferson served the colonel for many years—as far back as Texas, I believe—and when my uncle built this house, Jefferson became the head butler.'

"She was interrupted in her narrative as the door opened and the man I knew at once to be her brother stepped in. He had the same light brown eyes as she, and fine features, which twisted into a question at the sight of me.

"'Hello, Molly. Who is this gentleman?'

"'Charlie, it was horrible,' she cried, running to him. 'Uncle Patrick tore out of the house and collapsed. This is Dr. John Watson. He has been so helpful and sympathetic that I was telling him all about Uncle's condition.'

"Charles Warburton shook my hand readily. 'Very sorry to have troubled you, Doctor, but as you can see, we are in something of a mess. If Uncle Patrick grows any worse, I hate to think what—'

"Just then a great roar echoed from the morning room, followed by a shattering crash. The three of us rushed into the hallway and found Colonel Warburton staring wildly about him, a vase broken into shards at his feet.

"'I left this house once,' he swore, 'and by the devil I will do it again. It's full of vengeful spirits, and I will see you all in Hell for keeping me here!'

"The niece and nephew did their utmost to calm the colonel, but he grew even more enraged at the sight of them. In fact, he was so violently agitated that only Sam Jefferson could coax him, with my help, toward his bedroom, and once we had reached it, the colonel slammed the door shut in the faces of his kinfolk.

"By sheer good fortune, after some cajoling I persuaded him to take a sedative, and when he fell back in a daze on his bed, I stood up and looked about me. His room was quite Spartan, with hardly anything on the white walls, in a simple style I supposed was a relic of his days in Texas. I have told you that the remainder of the house also reflected his disdain for frippery. The wall-facing bed rested under a pleasant open window, and as it was on the ground floor, one could look directly out at the gardens after turning about and blinking oneself awake.

"I had turned to rejoin my hosts when Sam Jefferson cleared his throat behind me.

"'You believe he'll be all right, sir?'

"He spoke with the slow, deep tones of a man born on the other side of the Mississippi. I had not noticed it before, but a thick knot of scarring ran across his dark temple, which led me to believe he had done quite as much fighting in his youth as his employer—or worse, been somehow brutalized during the period before the harrowing conflict which ripped the nation asunder to end the slave trade.

"'I hope he will recover from his present attack quite soon, but his family would do well to consult a specialist,' I replied. 'He is on the brink of a nervous collapse. Was the colonel so fanciful in his younger days?'

"'I don't rightly know about 'fanciful,' sir. He's as superstitious a man as ever I knew, and more afeared of spirits than most. Always has been. But sir, I got a mind to tell you something else about these spells the colonel been having.'

"'Yes?'

"'Only this, Doctor,' and his low voice sank to a whisper. 'That first time as he had a vision, I set it down for a dream. Mister Patrick's always been more keen on the bogeymen than I have, sir, and I paid it no mind. But after the second bad spell—the one where he saw the Tejano stabbing the soldier—he went and showed me something that he didn't show the others.'

"'What was it?'

"He walked over to where the colonel now slept and pointed at a gash in the old uniform's breast, where the garment had been carefully mended.

"'The day Mister Patrick told me about that dream was the same day I mended this here hole in his shirt. Thought himself crazy, he did, and I can't say as I blame him. Because this hole is in exactly the spot where he dreamed the Tejano stabbed the Texian the night before. What do you think of that, sir?'

"'I've no idea what to think of it,' I replied. 'It is most peculiar, but surely it must prove to be a coincidence.'

"'Then there's this third vision,' he went on patiently. 'The one he had last night. Says he saw a band of 'em with torches, marching toward him like a pack of demons. I don't know about that. But I sure know that yesterday morning, when I went to start the fire in the library, half our kindling was missing. Clean gone, sir. Didn't make much of it at the time, but this puts it in another light.'"

Sherlock Holmes, who had changed postures a gratifying number of times during my account, rubbed his long hands together avidly before clapping them.

"It's splendid, my dear fellow. Positively first-class. The room was very bare indeed, you say?"

"Yes. Even in the midst of wealth, he lived like a soldier."

"I don't suppose you can tell me what you saw outside the window?"

I hesitated, reflecting as best I could.

"Though I wish I could furnish you with a clue of some sort, there was nothing outside the window, for I made certain to look. Jefferson assured me that he examined the grounds near the house after he discovered that the firewood was missing and found no sign of unusual traffic. When I asked after an odd hole, he mentioned that a tall lilac had been torn out from under the window weeks previous because it blocked the sunshine, but that cannot have had any bearing. As I said, the bed faced the wall, not the window."

Holmes tilted his head back with a light laugh. "Yes, you did say that, and I assure you I am coming to a greater appreciation of your skills as an investigator. What happened next?"

"I quit the house soon afterward. The younger Warburtons were anxious to know what had transpired in the sickroom, and I comforted them, saying that their uncle was asleep, and unlikely to suffer another such outburst that day. Then I assured them all, including Jefferson, that I would return the following afternoon to check on my patient.

"As I departed, I could not help noticing another man walking up the side path leading to the back door. He was very bronzed, with a long handlebar moustache and unkempt black hair, and he was dressed in simple trousers and a colorful but roughly woven linen shirt of the kind that the Mexican laborers wore. This swarthy fellow paid me no mind, but walked straight ahead, and I seized the opportunity to memorize his looks in case he should come to have any bearing on the matter. I did not know what to make of the colonel's ghostly affliction, or Jefferson's bizarre account of its two physical manifestations, but I thought it an odd enough coincidence to note.

"The next day, I saw a patient or two in the afternoon and then locked my practice, this time hailing a hack to take me up Nob Hill. Jefferson greeted me at the door and led me into a study of sorts, its tall shelves stacked with gold-lettered military volumes and historical works. Colonel Warburton stood there dressed quite normally, in a grey summer suit, and he seemed bewildered by his own behavior the day before.

"'It's a bona fide curse, I can't help but think, and I'm suffering to end it,' he said to me. 'There are times I know I'm not in my right senses, and other times when I can see those wretched visions before me as clear as your face is now.'

"'Is there anything else you can tell me which might help in my diagnosis?'

"'Not that won't make me out to be cracked in the head, Dr. Watson. After every one of these living nightmares, I've awakened with the same pain in my head, and I can't for the life of me decide whether I've imagined the whole thing or if I really am haunted by one of the men I killed during the war in Texas. I can't pretend as I'd be a lick surprised to learn I'd done someone a terrible wrong back then. Affairs were that muddled, and the lands under such bitter dispute, and for such surefire reasons on both sides, you understand—I've no doubt I came out on one or more of the wrong Tejanos, men who were only thinking to protect what was and always had been theirs. So much bloodshed in those days, no man has the luxury of knowing he was always in the right.'

"'It does indeed sound as if the past preoccupies your thoughts excessively. I am no expert in disorders of the mind,' I warned him, 'although I will do all I can for you. You ought to consult a specialist if your symptoms persist or worsen. May I have your permission, however, to ask a seemingly unrelated question?'

"'By all means.'

"'Have you in your employ, or do any of your servants or gardeners occasionally hire, Mexican workers?'

"He seemed quite puzzled by the question. 'I don't happen to have any Hispanos on my payroll. And when the staff need day labor, they almost always engage Chinese. They're quick and honest, and they come cheap. Why do you ask?'

"I convinced him that my question had been purely clinical, congratulated him on his recovery, and made my way to the foyer, mulling several new ideas over in my brain. Jefferson appeared to see me out, handing me my hat and stick.

"'Where are the other members of the household today?' I inquired.

"'Miss Molly is out paying calls, and Mister Charles is working in his darkroom.'

" 'Jefferson, I saw a rather mysterious fellow yesterday as I was leaving. To your knowledge, are any men of Mexican or Chileno descent ever hired by the groundskeeper?'

"I would swear to you, Holmes, that a strange glow lit his eyes when I posed that question, but he merely shook his head. 'Anyone does any hiring, Dr. Watson, I know all about it. And no one of that type been asking after work here for six months and more.'

" 'I was merely curious whether the sight of such a man had upset the colonel,' I explained, 'but as you know, he is much better today. I am no closer to tracing the source of his affliction, but I hope that if anything new occurs, or if you are ever in doubt, you will contact me.'

" 'These spells, they come and they go, Dr. Watson,' Jefferson replied, 'but if I discover aught, I'll surely let you know of it.'

"When I quit the house, I set myself a brisk pace, for I thought to walk down the hill as evening fell. But just as I began my descent, and the wind picked up from the west, I saw not twenty yards ahead of me the same sun-burnished laborer I'd spied the day before, attired in the same fashion, and clearly having emerged from some part of the Warburton residence moments previous. The very sight of him roused my blood; I had not yet met you, of course, and thus knew nothing whatever of detective work, but some instinct told me to follow him to determine whether or not the colonel was the victim of a malignant design."

"You followed him?" Holmes interjected with a startled expression. "Whatever for?"

"I felt I had no choice—the parallels between his presence and Colonel Warburton's nightmares had to be explained."

"Ever the man of action." My friend shook his head. "Where did he lead you?"

"When he reached Broadway, where the land flattened and the mansions gave way to grocers, butcheries, and cigar shops, he stopped to mount a streetcar. By a lucky chance, there was a passing hack, which I hailed, and I ordered the driver to follow the streetcar until I called for him to stop.

"My quarry went nearly as far as the waterfront before he descended, and in a trice I paid my driver and set off in pursuit toward the base of Telegraph Hill. During the Gold Rush days, the ocean-facing slope had been a tent colony of chilenos and peruanos. That settlement intermixed with the lowest hell of them all on its eastern flank: Sydney-Town, where the escaped Australian convicts and ticket-of-leave men ran the vilest public houses imaginable. It is a matter of historical record that the Fierce Grizzly employed a live bear chained outside its door."

"I have heard of that district," Holmes declared keenly. "The whole of it is known as the Barbary Coast, is it not? I confess I should have liked to see it in its prime, although there are any number of streets in London I can visit should I wish to take my life in my hands. You did not yourself encounter any wild beasts?"

"Not in the strictest sense; but inside of ten minutes, I found myself passing gin palaces that could have rivaled St. Giles for depravity. The gaslights appeared sickly and meager, and riotous men stumbled from one red-curtained den of thieves to the next, either losing their money willingly by gambling it away, or drinking from the wrong glass only to find themselves propped insensate in an alley the next morning without a cent to their name.

"At one point I thought I had lost sight of him, for a drayman's cart came between us and at the same moment he ducked into one of the deadfalls. I soon ascertained where he had gone, however, and after a moment's hesitation entered the place myself.

"Dull light shone from cheap tallow candles and ancient kerosene lamps with dark purple shades. Losing no time, I approached the man and asked if I could speak with him.

"He stared at me silently, his dark eyes narrowed into slits. At last, he signaled the barman for a second drink and handed me a small glass of clear liquor.

"I thanked him, but he remained dumb. 'Do you speak English?' I inquired finally.

"He grinned, and with an easy motion of his wrist flicked back his drink and set the empty glass on the bar. 'I speak it as well as you, *señor*. My name is Juan Portillo. What do you want?'

"'I want to know why you visited the Warburton residence yesterday and again this afternoon.'

"His smile broadened even further. 'Ah, now I understand. You follow me?'

"'There have been suspicious events at that house, ones which I have reason to believe may concern you.'

"'I know nothing of suspicious events. They hire me to do a job, and to be quiet. So I am quiet.'

"'I must warn you that if you attempt to harm the colonel in any way, you will answer for it to me.'

"He nodded at me coldly, still smiling. 'Finish your drink, *señor*. And then I will show you something.'

"I had seen the saloon keeper pour my liquor from the same bottle as his, and thus could not object to drinking it. The stuff was as strong as gin, but warmer, and left a fiery burn in the throat. I had barely finished it when Portillo drew out of some hidden sheath a very long, mother-of-pearl-handled knife.

"'I never harm the colonel. I never even see this colonel. But I tell you something anyway. Men who follow me, they answer to this,' he said, lifting the knife.

"He snarled something in Spanish. Three men, who had been sitting at a round table several yards away, stood up and strode toward us. Two carried pistols in their belts, and one tapped a short, stout cudgel in his hand. I was evaluating whether to make do with the bowie knife I kept on my person, or cut my losses and attempt an escape, when one of the men stopped short.

"'*Es el Doctor!* Dr. Watson, yes?' he said eagerly.

"After a moment's astonishment, I recognized a patient I had treated not two weeks before even though he could not pay me, a man who had gashed his leg so badly in a fight on the wharf, his friends had carried him to the nearest physician. He was profoundly happy to see me, a torrent of Spanish flowing from his lips, and before two minutes had passed of him gesturing proudly at his wound and pointing at me, Portillo's dispute had been forgotten. I did not press my luck, but joined them for another glass of that wretched substance and bade them farewell, Portillo's unblinking black eyes upon me until I was out of the bar and making for Front Street with all speed.

"The next day I determined to report Portillo's presence to the colonel, for as little as I understood, I now believed him an even more sinister character than I'd first suspected. To my dismay, however, I found the house in a terrible uproar."

"I am not surprised. What had happened?"

"Sam Jefferson stood accused of breaking into Charles Warburton's darkroom with the intent to steal his photographic apparatus. The servant who opened the door to me was hardly lucid for her tears, and I heard cruel vituperations even from outside the house. Apparently, or so the downstairs maid said in her state of near-hysterics, Charles had already sacked Jefferson, but the colonel was livid his nephew had acted without his approval, theft or no theft, and at the very moment I arrived they were locked in a violent quarrel. From where I stood, I could hear Colonel Warburton screaming that Jefferson be recalled, and Charles shouting back that he had already suffered enough indignities in that house to last him a lifetime. Come now, Holmes, admit to me that the tale is entirely unique," I could not help but add, for the flush of color in my friend's face told me precisely how deeply he was interested.

"It is not the ideal word," he demurred, sipping his wine. "I have not yet heard all, but there were cases in Lisbon and Salzburg within the last fifty years which may possibly have some bearing. Please, finish your story. You left, of course, for what gentleman could remain in such circumstances, and you called the next day upon the colonel."

"I did not, as a matter of fact, call upon the colonel."

"No? Your natural curiosity did not get the better of you?"

"When I arrived the following morning, Colonel Warburton as well as Sam Jefferson had vanished into thin air."

I expected this revelation to strike like a bolt from the firmament, but was destined for disappointment.

"Ha," Holmes said with the trace of a smile. "Had they indeed?"

"Molly and Charles Warburton were beside themselves with worry. The safe had been opened and many deeds and securities, not to mention paper currency, were missing. There was no sign of force, so they theorized that their uncle had been compelled or persuaded to provide the combination.

"A search party set out at once, of course, and descriptions of Warburton and Jefferson were circulated, but to no avail. The mad colonel and his servant, either together or separately, voluntarily or against their wills, quit the city without leaving a single clue behind them. Upon my evidence the police brought Portillo in for questioning, but he provided a conclusive alibi and could not be charged. And so Colonel Warburton's obsession with war, as well as the inscrutable designs of his manservant, remain to this day unexplained.

"What do you think of it?" I finished triumphantly, for Holmes by this time had leaned forward in his chair, entirely engrossed.

"I think that Sam Jefferson—apart from you and your noble intentions, my dear fellow—was quite the hero of this tale."

"How can you mean?" I asked, puzzled. "Surely the darkroom incident casts him in an extremely suspicious light. All we know is that he disappeared, probably with the colonel, and the rumor in San Francisco told that they were both stolen away by the Tejano ghost who possessed the house. That is rubbish, of course, but even now I cannot think where they went, or why."

"It is impossible to know where they vanished," Holmes replied, his grey eyes sparkling, "but I can certainly tell you why."

"Dear God, you have solved it?" I exclaimed in delight. "You cannot be in earnest—I've racked my brain over it for all these years to no avail. What the devil happened?"

"First of all, Watson, I fear I must relieve you of a misapprehension. I believe Molly and Charles Warburton were the authors of a nefarious and subtle plot which, if not for your intervention and Sam Jefferson's, might well have succeeded."

"How could you know that?"

"Because you have told me, my dear fellow, and a very workmanlike job you did in posting me up. Ask yourself when the colonel's mental illness began. What was his initial symptom?"

"He changed his will."

"It is, you must own, a very telling starting point. So telling, in fact, that we must pay it the most stringent attention." Holmes jumped to his feet and commenced pacing the carpet like a mathematician expounding over a theorem. "Now, there are very few steps—criminal or otherwise—one can take when one is disinherited. Forgery is a viable option, and the most common. Murder is out, unless your victim has yet to sign his intentions into effect. The Warburtons hit upon a scheme as cunning as it is rare: they undertook to prove a sane man mad."

"But Holmes, that can scarcely be possible."

"I admit that fortune was undoubtedly in their favor. The colonel already suffered from an irrational preoccupation with the supernatural. Additionally, his bedroom lacked any sort of ornament, and young Charles Warburton specialized in photographic technique."

"My dear Holmes, you know I've the utmost respect for your remarkable faculty, but I cannot fathom a word of what you just said," I confessed.

He laughed. "I shall do better, then. Have we any reason to think Jefferson lied when he told you of the ghost's earthly manifestations?"

"No, but nevertheless he could have meant anything by it. He could have slit that hole and stolen that firewood himself."

"Granted. But it was after you told him of Portillo's presence that he broke into the photography studio."

"You see a connection between Portillo and Charles Warburton's photographs?"

"Decidedly so, as well as a connection between the photographs, the blank wall, and the torn-out lilac bush."

"Holmes, that doesn't even—"

I stopped myself as an idea dawned on me. Finally, after the passage of many years, I was beginning to understand.

"You are talking about a magic lantern," I said slowly. "By God, I have been so blind."

"You were remarkably astute, my boy, for you took note of every essential detail. As a matter of fact, I believe you can take it from here," he added with more than his usual grace.

"The colonel disinherited his niece and nephew, possibly because he abhorred their mercenary natures, in favor of war charities," I stated hesitantly. "In a stroke of brilliance, they decided to make it seem war was his mania; they would not allow him to so slight his kin. Charles hired Juan Portillo to appear in a series of photographs as a Tejano soldier and promised that he would be paid handsomely if he kept the sessions secret. The nephew developed the images onto glass slides and projected them through a magic lantern device outside the window in the dead of night. His victim was so terrified by the apparition on his wall, he never thought to look for its source behind him. The first picture, threatening the white woman, likely featured Molly Warburton. But for the second plate . . . "

"That of the knife plunging into the Texian's chest, they borrowed the colonel's old garb and probably placed it on a dummy. The firewood 'disappeared' so that a number of men could assemble, farther off on the grounds, to portray rebels with torches. The lilac, as is obvious—"

"Stood in the way of the magic lantern apparatus!" I cried. "What could be simpler?"

"And the headaches the colonel experienced afterward?" my friend prodded me.

"Likely an aftereffect of an opiate or narcotic his family added to his meal in order to heighten the experience of the visions in his bedchamber."

"And Sam Jefferson?"

"A deeply underestimated opponent who saw the Warburtons for what they were and kept a constant watch. The only thing he stole was a look at the plates in Charles's studio as his final piece of evidence. When they sent him packing, he told the colonel all he knew and they—"

"Were never heard from again," Holmes finished with a poetic flourish.

"In fact, they found the perfect revenge." I laughed to think of it. "Colonel Warburton had no interest in his own wealth and took more than enough to live from the safe. And after all, when he was finally declared dead, his estate was distributed just as he wished it."

"Yes, a number of lucky events occurred. I am grateful, as I confess I have been at other times, that you are an utterly decent fellow, my dear Doctor."

"I don't understand," I said in some confusion.

"I see the world in terms of cause and effect. If you had not been the sort of man willing to treat a rogue wounded in a knife fight who had no means of paying you, it is possible you would not have had the opportunity to tell me this story."

"It wasn't so simple as all that," I muttered, rather abashed, "but thank—"

"And an admirable story it was, too. You know, Watson," Holmes continued, extinguishing his pipe, "from all I have heard of America, it must be an exceedingly fertile ground for men of mettle. The place lives almost mythically in the estimations of most Englishmen. I myself have scarcely met an American, ethically inclined or otherwise, who did not possess a certain audacity of mind."

"It's the pioneer in them, I suppose. Still, I cannot help thinking that you are more than a match for anyone, American or otherwise."

"I would not presume to contradict you, but that vast expanse boasts more than its share of crime as well as of imagination, and for that reason commands some respect. I am not a complete stranger to the American criminal."

"My dear fellow, I should be delighted to hear you expound on that subject," I exclaimed, glancing longingly at my notebook and pen.

"Another time, perhaps." My friend paused, his long fingers drumming along with the drops as he stared through our front window, eyes glittering brighter than the rain-soaked street below. "Perhaps one day we may both find occasion to test ourselves further on their soil. I should like to have met this Sam Jefferson, for instance. He had a decided talent."

"Talent or no, he was there to witness the events; you solved them based on a secondhand account by a man who'd never so much as heard of the science of deduction at that time."

"There are precious few crimes in this world, merely a hundred million variations upon a dozen or so themes. I have thought of categorizing them into a monograph at some point, to aid assiduous officers of the law in identifying what type of mischief they are facing. Some of these inspectors wouldn't know a Spanish Prisoner scheme from an involuntary manslaughter, I fear."

Laughing, I remarked, "To think I imagined it might confound you—how very callow of me."

He shrugged. "It was a fetching little problem, however, no matter it was not matchless. The use of the magic lantern, although I will never prove it, I believe to have been absolutely inspired. Now," he proclaimed, striding to his violin and picking it up, "if you would be so kind as to locate the brandy and cigars you mentioned earlier, I will show my appreciation by entertaining you in turn. You've come round to my liking for Kreutzer, I think? Capital. I must thank you for bringing your very interesting case to my attention; I shall lose no time informing my brother I solved it without moving a muscle. And thus, my dear Watson, we shall continue our efforts to enliven a dreary afternoon."

The Adventure of the Magical Menagerie

It has long been a dictum of my internationally celebrated friend Sherlock Holmes that work is the best antidote to sorrow. As his biographer, therefore, I have been given occasion to wonder whether the almost superhuman effort he himself expends over his cases is relevant to this credo. When at work, he is an indefatigable automaton: dashing hither and thither consulting all relevant parties, weighing the value of data to hand provided by the police, and more often discovering clues everyone else has overlooked. When idle, however, he is a listless creature, hollow-eyed to a degree which ever causes me the deepest sympathetic consternation.

Perhaps the maxim and the man have no literal relation to one another. Holmes has many times accused me of owning too poetic a nature for my own good; were I to broach the subject with him, howsoever obliquely, he would lift an icy brow while inquiring whether I was not a trifle feverish and suggesting I lie down. And yet, so mournful does he appear when inactive that I shall never rule out the possibility of some tragedy having befallen my friend. It remains to be seen whether he shall ever give his tongue-tied sorrows leave to speak, as it were, but I can state with personal assurance that his adage is wisdom and, on March the 15th of 1897, he proved it to me.

As was usual during that season, I had a letter from Mrs. Cecil Forrester, a former client of my friend but, far more important, the former employer of my late wife. Mary had for years worked as a governess before we wed, and had been far better disposed to that difficult work than some, for her nature was so tender and gentle that even the most colicky newborn would settle into her arms and coo like a dove.

This facility of hers had been treated by the Forrester household not with cold approval but with heartfelt affection, particularly by the wife, who called Mary her "darling girl" and shared every intimacy of co-habitation and companionship with her. The two had remained devoted to each other even after our wedding separated them geographically, just as I continued to join in adventures with my vastly more eccentric friend, and Mrs. Forrester each March since 1894 had written me a heartfelt missive suggesting that if I ever needed an audience for my reminiscences, she would prove not only a devoted listener but a willing participant. It was typical of Mary's closest friend that she should not abandon me following our shared bitter loss, and whenever in Mrs. Forrester's company, I thought with warmth how glad I was that Mary may have been poor when we met save for the mysterious pearls that were her inheritance, but nevertheless was perfectly comfortable in her situation.

Unfortunately, Mrs. Forrester's well-intentioned overture ever filled me with harrowing dread of our postman, Mr. McPhail (who deserved no such sentiment, as he was a florid, jolly fellow with four children and a fifth on the way). When the letter addressed in her handwriting arrived I was alone at Baker Street with a vexing case of catarrh—still in my dressing gown, my chin and hair in a pitiable state, all my handkerchiefs soiled, staring at untouched toast and the film of white clouds pasted over the sky beyond our window. On the two other occasions when I had received this apparently annual correspondence, Holmes and I had both been from home; since his miraculous return, he had been the most sought-after man by the police and the most loathed by the underworld in the history of England, and I had been at his side all the while.

Holmes, however, had gone to consult with his brother Mycroft over some abstruse encoding work at Whitehall regarding which he could tell me nothing whatsoever; I was alone. I was, in addition, irrationally petulant over the fact. It would be the basest self-flattery to suggest that this was due to mere illness, for I am no stranger to physical hardship. The sea of melancholy in which I was floating had soaked me to the bone. By the time I heard my fellow lodger's brisk step upon the stair and his lean form had burst into the room, scattering his beloved latest editions as if he were a potentate showering the masses with gold, the skies beyond the window had darkened to the somber bluish coal of twilight's end, and the fire had died untimely. I was spread lengthwise upon the settee patently doing nothing whatsoever, to my own considerable disgust.

Sherlock Holmes whistled, his grey eyes pinned to one of the newspapers. "Dear me. A fiver says you and I will be called to the Norfolk coast over this business of the Viking manuscript, Watson. A complete eleventh-century ballad cycle discovered just when the Earl is rumored to be selling half his securities? The mind balks at such felicitous coincidences. At least the barometer suggests we'll have no difficulty in traveling there. The nine-twenty-three express from Charing Cross ought to do nicely, though I suppose there is no use in getting an early start when I don't yet know which party involved will inevitably consult me."

When I merely coughed, he glanced up, taking in the scene with his usual lightning precision. Admittedly, genius was not required to create a narrative from the rapidly dimming room, the dismal condition of the fire I had neglected, the supply of kerchiefs, my own state of undress, and the letter which I had slid unopened onto the mantel so that I might glare at it unreservedly. As Holmes himself would put it, the greenest C Division constable would have solved the mystery quick as blinking.

My life is one of perpetual surprises. Whatever I had expected to happen next, I did not expect Sherlock Holmes to tilt his chiseled features as if in thought, slap the newspaper against his hand, drop it with its brethren upon the rug, and quit the room.

When I heard his bedroom door shut, I confess my already hunched shoulders slumped fully into the cushions. The combination of sorrow, sickness, and idleness had already so depressed my spirits that this latest development suggested I give the entire day up as lost and hope for an improved tomorrow. By the time I had determined to do just that, however, Holmes was back, now clad in his blue dressing gown, with its ties valiantly fluttering as he announced, "I will not tolerate this sort of abuse."

My bleary eyes widened to saucers as he briskly opened the scuttle and stoked up the blaze. That task finished, he donned his slippers and whirled about seeing to various lamps until our parlor glowed as yellow as the inside of an egg.

"What abuse might that be?" I rasped incredulously.

Guilty as I already felt over my own black humor, I supposed that he meant the dark, chilly, and altogether inhospitable atmosphere to which I had subjected him. Instead of answering, however, he flung himself out of the room with fully as much alacrity as he applies to unidentified footmarks.

This rankled tremendously. However insalubrious Holmes found Baker Street that day, surely I found it trebly worse. I was about to quit the sofa in favor of demanding satisfaction of my friend when he returned bearing the ever-tantalizing tin box which houses reports of his earliest cases. This he dropped to the floor so disgustedly that Mrs. Hudson must have supposed the sky was falling.

"It absolutely will not do, Watson," Holmes declared imperiously. An instant later he had sunk neatly behind the box, in one fluid movement crossing his legs as if he were a Buddha presiding over a temple. "Even men whose time is of less value than my own prefer to be engaged upon work related to their actual vocations—one does not enlist the secretarial services of costermongers or the nautical skills of ornithologists. Speaking directly to this principle: I am a consulting detective, not a secretary for a third-rate shipping concern."

I regarded him in no little awe. "What on earth are you on about?"

His hand waved in an impatient spiral before lifting the box lid. "Athelney Jones has lost the paperwork regarding a shared case. Naturally he has. The man ought to be daily congratulated for selecting the correct left and right boots for his respective feet. Now he needs to write a secondary report, and of course, *I* could tell you at once that the business hinged entirely upon the fellow's having had a twin brother in the diamond cutting business, but surely you'll agree Inspector Jones owns considerably more energy than acumen."

When once Sherlock Holmes has embarked upon his tirades, those not enthralled despite their customary verve and nuance could no more stop them than they could a charging elephant. My money, in fact, should be upon the gargantuan mammal's being felled long before my friend wearied of invective. I watched as he rummaged through the box whilst muttering in his rapid tenor, "Pointless waste of a perfectly pleasant evening. Is it to be my job to file the Yarders' paperwork now, after solving their cases for them? That was Gregson . . . this one Hollingberry . . . Heavens, Doctor, but we spend a great deal of our lives with Lestrade. . . . Ha, Jones!" His face fell immediately, however. "Confound it, this is a Jones case to be sure, but it's one from before your time which introduced me to Old Mr. Sherman. Come to think of it, the matter must hold some interest for you—you surely remember Sherman's dog Toby, from the business of Jonathan Small and the Morstan treasure."

Holmes's steely eyes swept up to mine. "Should you like me to recount the case for you? Supposing you're not too done in."

When I realized precisely what my friend had just orchestrated, I confess I was forced to clear my throat for reasons other than illness. He knew all about poor Mrs Forrester's yearly letter commiserating over Mary's—née Morstan's—passing; in one fell swoop, he not only had said in his peculiar sideways fashion that he knew why I was so low, but had offered an obvious way to honor my late spouse without any maudlin sentiment entering the picture, nor any work on my part other than to sit back and listen.

"You are altogether extraordinary," was my answer when I could speak.

Holmes formed a sudden acute interest in the mantel clock. "If you prefer—"

"I should prefer nothing more in the world! Let us hear it."

Still he hesitated, uncharacteristically doubtful of his own scheme. "It's not too late to make it to Covent Garden if you dress quickly, and *Aïda* is supposedly—"

"Heavens no—my nerves are as tight as your fiddle strings and my bones ache whenever I shift a muscle. Bring me a little brandy and lemon if you would, and tell me how you came to meet that remarkable Sherman fellow."

Wordlessly, though his brow cleared, Holmes hopped to his feet and took his time in procuring a pair of toddies. I was quite myself again when he returned, settling on a cushion with his back to the sofa and his long legs stretched before him as he flipped through the case file.

"Well, then. I have mentioned," said he whilst lighting his pipe, "that in the period before I found myself possessed of a biographer to trumpet my name, I spent much of my time in the British Museum. They were good days, but they were, as was quite usual for me, rather solitary and desultory. You know that, saving yourself, I have no knack for camaraderie, but far more vexing was the fact I had no template of consulting detectives before me so that I might follow their course of study. It was a pretty conundrum which went hand in glove with inventing my own profession. You see, I'd no idea what sort of information would prove essential in future. Anyone who observed me there might have told you I was an intellectual wastrel, or else a helpless idiot, for I skipped from topic to topic like a butterfly, memorizing mammalian footmarks and types of rope and the Thames's tidal schedule. I often wearied of being cooped up indoors, and that is when I hit upon creating a comprehensive mental map of London's streets."

"I perennially wonder how you formed one in the first place, let alone keep it up to date."

The detective's eyes twinkled mischievously. "If you prefer that I learn the solar system . . ."

"Good Lord, no. We should have perished several times over if not for your knowledge of winding little crevices. Pray go on."

"I was memorizing Lambeth in April." My friend's voice had grown almost wistful; he has an iron nature, but if there is one subject upon which he speaks romantically, other than music, it is London, for he adores the place. "The sawyers' mills, the barges bobbing on the bloated river, the stately pleasure gardens, Westminster Palace looming across the water. I had good reason to focus upon that area. According to the papers, a disproportionate number of robberies had taken place there recently and, as a fledgling investigator, I wanted a look at the houses which had been targeted.

"I walked past each in turn—Union Road, Larkhall Lane, Gaskell Street. They were quite innocuous dwellings, with freshly doused steps and budding flowers in the window boxes, modestly well-off but far from wealthy. Noting the dearth of scratches around the door locks, I inferred that the cracksmen involved were far from inexperienced. But this seemed a futile enough lead, and I had no pretext to offer the residents when requesting an interview. It was trying, Watson. Save for the fact I felt about these crime scenes as a child would staring at sweets through a window, I could do nothing but play the gawking loafer."

"A part which has availed you well since, at the least."

"True enough. Just a moment. You know how I loathe dining on Tuesdays—ought I tell Mrs. Hudson it shall be hot soup for you at eight? Capital. Anyhow, I had moved along and canvassed most of Vauxhall when I arrived at the queer address to which I sent you for Toby. The road was Pinchin Lane, and the most extraordinary commotion was occurring outside number three.

"'You daren't cross us, Tom Sherman! Let us in!' a great brute of a fellow boomed as he shook his fist at the dingy red brick building. A little ginger-headed chap huddled close by, and something about him seemed equally menacing even as he cringed. The pair of them appeared coarse and cruel in a way that the merely impoverished never do despite all of them being customarily clad in the same rough wool and thick-soled boots.

"'This 'ere wiper says you'll not cross me neither!' the resident of the first floor shrieked from above, waving a brown burlap sack in his fist. 'This wiper is a particular friend o' mine, d'ye hear me? None closer! He's as good as me brother! And he'll be biting the pair o' you in the face if you don't shove off. I'll drop 'im on yer pates quick as blinking!'"

Laughing heartily at my friend's mimicry skills, I took a sip of hot brandy and lemon. The fire crackled nicely by now, and—owing to the fact that Sherlock Holmes almost never bothers with such mundane activities as lighting all the lamps—the room seemed in its subtle difference of illumination to have an almost theatrically homelike effect. I settled farther back into my nest of cushions and adjusted the afghan over my legs.

"Old Sherman and his bag of 'wipers,'" I reflected. "I remember it as if I'd met him yesterday."

"Piquant, is it not?"

"Decidedly. I'd never seen such a display in my life."

"I'll admit that when I sent you to him, knowing your spirit of adventure as I do, I hoped you'd be treated to the usual performance."

"Very kind of you. Although when he threatened to throw serpents on my head, he at least did me the gentlemanly courtesy of offering to first count to three," I added, chuckling.

"*You* may well laugh, my dear Watson," Holmes returned with feigned asperity. "*You* had my name to offer as a password. Here *I* was, an aspiring detective stumbling upon a live housebreaking. Were I to walk away, I should never regain my confidence. Were I to approach, vipers would fall from the very heavens."

My friend Sherlock Holmes, who pretends to fear nothing between Southwark and the Sahara, almost visibly cringes at the mere mention of snakes. He reserves the word itself for the most vile of epithets directed at the most degraded of criminals. On the unforgettable occasion when we kept vigil at Stoke Moran, I quite feared that the strain before he finally glimpsed the swamp adder would do him permanent mental harm. When he did spy the venomous creature, he lashed at it as if a demon had been loosed from Hell itself and he were trying to drive it back again. I would twit him over this quirk, but, as it is endearingly uncharacteristic, I instead keep my peace.

I observed, "Of course you approached them."

Holmes tapped his pipe stem against his prominent chin as he smiled at the memory. "Naturally. It was irresistible. The creeping little chap, I soon learned, went by Jack o' the Devil for his scarlet pate, and the gigantic lout was called Plaid Charlie. So many different plaids never have I seen on a single man at once, Watson—waistcoat, trousers, jacket, tie, all different colors and patterns to boot—and he weighed at least three stone more than I ever have. He also wore a cracked bowler over bushy black side-whiskers, and, when he saw me, he grinned as if happy at the chance of a fresh fight.

"'What's this, then? A toff on the lookout for a free hiding?' he leered, showing rather less than a perfect roster of teeth.

"'Oh, I beg your pardon,' said I. 'I merely lacked a plaid undershirt, and wondered whether you might assist me in procuring one.'

"As Plaid Charlie's nostrils flared like a bull's, I studied my options other than pugilism, and my eyes lit upon Old Tom Sherman hanging out of his window. He's a gaunt chap, you'll recall, and seemed composed of sticks and strings, with a much-pleated neck like a leathery curtain and spectacles tinted an eccentric shade of Prussian blue, though his hair back then was a sandy brown color. Then I spied the display upon the lower story and gaped at the taxidermy in various stages of slaughtering one another. The panorama was violent, delirious, like nothing I'd ever imagined. You saw it for yourself—within the dried moss and grasses and tree branches was set a mongoose killing a snake, an owl sinking its claws into a stoat, a ferret carrying a baby rabbit."

"Yes, and a hawk snatching up a pretty blue and green lizard of a species I've never seen in any museum. It did seem a more exotic ode to Nature's whims than I should have expected in that oddly whimsical house."

"Quite so." Sherlock Holmes set his pipe aside on the case file and drew one leg up with his hands clasped around his shin, reminiscing. "Well, I asked myself whether I was a detective or a toff, as Plaid

Charlie would have it, and I chose the former, asking Old Sherman his name and why these men were troubling him."

"'They're both blackguards, that's why!' Sherman howled. 'Troubling decent folk is a blackguard's stock in trade, innit now? That there's Plaid Charlie and Jack o' the Devil come to do me injury, and I a civilized naturalist defending me 'ome!'

"'Oh, how cruel to say that!'

"Jack o' the Devil finally spoke, removing a filthy beaver hat to reveal more of his fiery hair and an extraordinarily broad smile. I've scarce ever encountered such a repulsive individual, Watson, and you will concede that I meet more than my share of that sort. His voice was highly unnerving—a mixture of the pleading and the invidious, grating through his throat—and he bowed repeatedly up and down. He meant the motion to be coaxing, I imagine, but in fact it was intensely disturbing. I was reminded of a wicked marionette with a tuft of red yarn attached to its wooden pate and a queerly wide grin painted across its face, bobbing about a miniature stage.

"'Don't even think that, Old Sherman, for all yer old partner wants is a word or two. Don't break me 'eart so, I beg. 'Tisn't Christian of ye.'

"'This man is your partner?' I called up, attempting not to note how loosely Mr. Sherman held his bag and the prisoner within.

"'Former partner!' shrieked the proprietor. 'The wretch was sacked! The villain was sent packin' and I meant it to be fer good and all. Watch the wiper, for 'ere she comes!'"

My friend smiled ruefully. "At this juncture, Watson, matters were growing a trifle unfriendly, and nary a constable in sight. As I had been memorizing less than harmonious neighborhoods, I was armed with a weighted stick, and thus I decided that the best course would be to adopt a more forceful manner."

For my own part, I failed to picture Sherlock Holmes as anything less than forceful, but bade him continue.

"'You are obviously unwelcome,' I called out. 'Be off before I whistle for reinforcements—I am a plainclothes detective inspector, and were I not already engaged, I should have you in darbies.'

"'Oh ho!' cried Plaid Charlie. 'You, a 'tec! And I'm Mary Magdalene!'"

"As you can imagine, Watson, it was immensely flattering that, even at such an early age, no one could possibly confuse me with a Yard inspector. The memory still gratifies me. But while I thanked him in my heart, I sought to lend my story some credence and nevertheless advanced, my walking stick at the ready.

"'I've business of my own to see to,' I repeated to Plaid Charlie. 'However, I observe that, while your attire is sagged at the knees and elbows and your boots are cracking, your cravat is made of fine silk and fastened with a Celtic-patterned gold tiepin matching the description of an item stolen from Exton Street not two days hence. Your cowering companion, despite his similarly shabby togs, is wearing ivory kidskin gloves which I should wager have been worn twice at most, if the cleanliness of the fingertips is any indication. Given the evidence against you, I suggest you bless your maker for a few more days of freedom and get out of my sight.'

"'What if,' Plaid Charlie snarled, 'we thought that snuffing yer lights 'ere and now was a better lay, you scrawny jack?'

"At this time, he deemed it best to take a swing at me. I've no doubt he could have taken my head clean off, Doctor, save for the fact that I had been studying defensive techniques, and that large brutes often severely underestimate their opponents; for the first time, I congratulated myself on my choice of at least one of my studies, for aptitude with a singlestick proved then and there to have been a prudent selection. A snapping block with the cane followed by a left hook and then a sweep under his leg laid him out in the street. But I knew it could not be for long and glanced back to find Sherman. He stood in the now-unlocked doorway wildly beckoning me to come inside.

"This seemed wisdom despite my callow hubris, so I dashed for shelter. As I went, however, I heard a terrible hissing voice calling, 'Your name then, Inspector, for this affront will haunt you.' It was Jack o' the Devil, and a shiver runs through me whenever I recall it.

"Stopping on the threshold, I lit on the name of the only detective inspector I had ever consulted with and cried out, 'You'll rue the day you crossed Athelney Jones!'"

Holmes paused in his narrative, either because his sense of timing is so apt or because I was laughing so hard I could scarce breathe—laughter which turned quickly into wheezing, which led to coughing, which led to some concern on my friend's part. The fit would not seem to pass, but I could not regret it, so preferable did the ache in my lungs feel to my former sullen misery. Water was fetched, and sipped.

"My God, it's priceless. How old were you?" I managed finally.

The faint flush which praise always brings to Holmes's thin face had appeared. He resumed his perch on the floor before my knees and rested an elbow on the settee's edge with an impish twinkle in his gaze.

"Twenty-two. Ridiculous, was I not?"

"I shall defer answering. Come, what did you think of Sherman's shop?"

Holmes shook his head. "You've seen that magical menagerie, Watson. It had not changed in the interim and still has not to this day. All the walls were lined with cages, a veritable zoo, and several of the beasts within reared up at the appearance of a stranger. The tables were littered with the macabre tools of the taxidermist—sewing needles and skinning knives and mysterious awls—and the air was pungent with chemicals and manure, but for all these defects it was incongruously cheerful. Well, perhaps some would not say so. Still, my young self was rather taken with the place. Perhaps I thought it as odd as I was. I recall a monkey chattered from the rafters, disturbing the dozen or so plumed birds who also resided there, a pair of conjoined twin weasels bared their teeth and hissed as one at me, and what appeared to be a tamed fox shied away upstairs at my approach.

"'Where, then, is the viper?' I asked with due caution after Sherman had bolted us safe within.

"'Cor, he's only a corn snake—there's no harm in 'im, sir, no harm in the world. 'E's as gentle as that wee bunny yonder. And I'd not risk 'im harming 'imself in a fall fer all the world. But if you wave a wiper, it gets 'em to thinking, supposing as they try to muscle you, eh?'

"It was on my lips to question this reasoning further when a stair creaked from on high and a small woman—very small, almost a child's size, but well over forty years in age—came shuffling down from the living quarters. She was dressed as plainly as Mr. Sherman, with a cloud of auburn hair streaked with grey and gleaming brown eyes, and she held in her arms a beautiful mottled spaniel pup.

"'It's all right, luv,' Mr. Sherman called to his wife, for so she was, 'you can come down. It's safe enough now, and the door bolted and all. This young inspector 'ere drove the wolves away.'"

"There is a Mrs. Sherman?"

"No, but there was." Holmes cast a glance to ensure I was at ease; I smiled encouragingly. "You would have liked her, Watson. In any case, the pup she was holding had escaped and was sniffing my trouser legs and boots, doubtless learning as much as it could of the streets I'd been walking for hours, when Mr. Sherman remarked, 'You don't look like any policeman as I ever saw, sir. But you'll be wantin' to know what that row signified?'

"I succumbed to base temptation and said yes, and here is what Old Sherman told me: Jack o' the Devil had once been his assistant at bird-stuffing. As repellent a man as he was, he was deft at the work, and business was thriving enough to make him quite valuable. Old Sherman had something of a reputation for dramatic staging, which led to both local and mail orders. Whenever a request came in for a fowl, Jack would do the more menial dressing with tremendous skill and speed, and Old Sherman—who really is something of an artist, Watson—would arrange and put the finishing touches on the pieces.

"When Jack o' the Devil took up with Plaid Charlie, a known cracksman, Mr. Sherman didn't like it, but he could hardly tell his assistant who to share a pint with of an evening. So he clucked and hummed but said nothing to the purpose. Then the single treasure the Shermans owned other than their exotic animals, a diamond brooch passed on from Mrs. Sherman's mother, went missing. Old Sherman decided he'd had quite enough and sent Jack o' the Devil packing. Now it seemed that Jack would not be shaken off and wanted his position back, and I had interrupted what must have become a violent altercation."

I listened, rapt. "Did you decide to pursue the sinister connection between Jack o' the Devil and Plaid Charlie?"

"Excellent hypothesis, but wrong: I lingered. You know how reclusive I am, but the dog had taken a liking to me—whining and pawing and generally making a spectacle of herself. After bragging for ten minutes that Molly the spaniel already had the best tracking nose in London despite her youth, Mrs. Sherman would not allow me to depart before I had taken tea. They were poor in funds despite their revenues on account of the veritable zoo they maintained, but they laid out a feast of tea cakes and some very passable Darjeeling and I found myself loath to deny them. In fact, I confess I stayed still longer talking of obscure byways in biological science with Mr. Sherman, and then the training of tracking dogs with Mrs. Sherman, and when I departed I left my address, though by then I was too ashamed to leave my name."

"Do you know, I *would* have liked Mrs. Sherman," I decided warmly. "Go on, old fellow. The next day you began your campaign?"

My friend's eyes shone with mischief. "The next day I was knocked up by the police at my lodgings in Montague Street because Plaid Charlie had been murdered the previous night."

Gaping at him, I lowered my brandy to my lap. "Good heavens, Holmes! *Your* lodgings? Whatever for?"

"You see, they had already taken a culprit for the murder into custody." Holmes's expression was as aloof as a statue's, but his entire torso wriggled with anticipation. "The suspect stridently insisted that he was innocent, and that the only man who could help to save his character was Inspector Athelney Jones. So who should arrive at my wretched little hovel but . . ."

"Inspector Athelney Jones and Mr. Sherman!" I exclaimed, and then we both collapsed into laughter once more until we had quite exhausted ourselves.

"Oh, you can't imagine it, Watson," Holmes crowed, sweeping his arms wide. "It was *delicious*. I only wish you could have been present. There were my seedy digs, with their chemical apparatus, a bed, a desk, a wardrobe with two suits in it, and a chair, and there was poor Mr. Sherman and an apoplectic police inspector.

"'What's this, now!' Jones cried. He was only slightly thinner then, Watson, and his face already as red and shiny as an apple. 'Oh, here's a fine business! I arrest a fellow for murder, and I have *my* name thrown in my face!'

"'Let me—' I began.

"'"Athelney Jones," he says! "Athelney Jones will set it right!" Then I ask him to *describe* this Athelney Jones, and—'

"'Just a moment—'

"'A moment, my eye, Sherlock Holmes! Then he says he has the *address* of this Athelney Jones, and—'

"'I can explain everything!'

"'Explain impersonating a police inspector you've met once in your life, and harassed with your crackbrained theories no less!' he cried. 'Oh, ho, ho! Now, *here's* a pretty business!'

"'This gentleman was being threatened by one of the cracksmen you are seeking in Lambeth, Inspector,' I attempted. The odds were against me, Watson, but this time the fates blessed my enterprise and I was able to complete a few sentences. 'I intervened, and as they fled, I shouted that they would rue the day they crossed Athelney Jones. So you see it is actually quite a flattering mistake.'

"'Is this true?' the policeman demanded of Old Sherman.

"I won't pretend I wasn't quaking in my boots a bit by this time, Watson. But Mr. Sherman said yes, there must have been some error, and when he winked at me, I understood that the kind old fellow had thought me only an eccentric good Samaritan, never a policeman at all. He had merely played along with the ruse out of a reluctance to insist on my real identity after I had helped him. Inspector Jones walked up and down booming and flailing his arms a while longer before he finally turned to speak with a constable and I had the chance to corner Sherman.

"'I'm innocent as snow, but I dread to say where I was last night and there's no one as witnessed me anyhow,' the poor soul whispered. The shadows beneath his blue glasses were dreadful to look at, my dear fellow, and his steady artisan's hands were all atremble. The change that had been wrought in him from the time of our pleasant impromptu tea the day before was most alarming. I could tell the man honestly feared for his life, and when I think of Jones's acumen, not to mention his bluster, I cannot fault his keen instinct for self-preservation. 'You're a right sharp young lad. I 'eard what you said to those villains about the crib they done cracked. God knows we're strangers, but I've a feeling about you, a feeling it's 'ard to put into words fer all I'm old enough to be yer father. Please, fer 'eaven's sake, try to solve this or I'll swing for it.'

"It had been so long since I'd sat down to a friendly table with anyone, Doctor—come to think of it, it must have been since college, and my brief acquaintance with Victor Trevor before he went abroad to try his luck at tea farming in faraway Terai—that I never considered refusing, nor stopped to warn myself that an utter greenhand could potentially have done poor Mr. Sherman more harm than benefit. I was all eagerness, arrogance, and optimism. Of course I promised him I should do all I could, and after Athelney Jones had wagged his finger in my face a few more times, and bullied poor Old Sherman into a police wagon, I was off like a rabbit."

"To Sherman's?"

"No, to the news-agents' at the corner." Holmes shrugged sheepishly. "I hadn't the money to subscribe to every edition then, and so had no notion what the true facts of the murder were, and I'd no desire to listen to another word of Jones's unparalleled poppycock. Briefly, the case went as so: Plaid Charlie was found knifed in his rooms. The knife was peculiar, the sort used for delicate work with wild game, and had 'Sherman' carved on the handle. The word 'VENGEANCE' had been scrawled on the wall above, and a stuffed rat was left on the dead man's chest. It did not take Athelney Jones long to knock up the neighbors and learn Old Sherman was threatened that day, and the inspector drew his version of the natural conclusion."

"But that's entirely preposterous. Why should—"

"Oh, I know," he assured me, chuckling. "Then I raced to find Mrs. Sherman. She related the following conclusive facts, though she was so upset at first I could hardly understand her. First, that Plaid Charlie had been not merely a cracksman but a notorious fence of stolen gems. Second, that Mr. Sherman had been passionately poring over his records of late to see where the birds Jack o' the Devil worked on had been delivered. And third, that there had been another house broken into the night before. So now you must see everything."

I did not, but the atmosphere was so congenial, I felt in no hurry. Sherlock Holmes often sat up all night untangling the threads of a problem—why should not I follow his expert example? My friend smoked placidly, and I watched giddy sparks fly away up the flue, and I had just despaired of the attempt when I cried, "By Jove!"

"I ought not to be so free with my methods," Holmes affected to grouse. "I shall be out of a profession."

I sat up fully in my excitement, gripping his sinewy shoulder. "Plaid Charlie needed a better way to rid himself of recently stolen jewels and hatched a scheme with Jack o' the Devil to sew them into taxidermy."

Sherlock Holmes fairly beamed at me. "Go on."

"They then waited until the stones were thought forever lost and acted as cracksmen, taking a number of items so as not to arouse suspicion when the real object was the decorative bird. And Old Sherman was right. It was Jack o' the Devil who stole Mrs. Sherman's brooch," I continued breathlessly. "He sewed it into another bird before he lost his position."

"I shall not contradict you."

"Mr. Sherman had been trying to discover its whereabouts and foolishly made his own first attempt at housebreaking, likely because he knew his story preposterous on the face of it and feared to peach on such a dangerous duo to the Yarders. That is the reason he was loath to give you an alibi. He had wanted his wife's keepsake back but was embarrassed of his method—telling the truth only meant confessing to a second crime."

"And?" my friend prompted, waving his pipe in enthusiastic circles. "Who in fact killed Plaid Charlie?"

"Well," I puzzled, reclining again, "it must have been Jack o' the Devil, fabricating evidence which pointed to Old Sherman, but why?"

"Ah." Holmes nodded. "Because he supposed that with her husband in the dock, Mrs. Sherman would lose her livelihood, and would hire him back, enabling him to hide his plunder in the fowl again. The man was utterly mad, Watson—killing Plaid Charlie was proof of it. He wanted to become the greatest fence in London and so slaughtered his favorite income source without even blinking. His nasal, grating voice, that leering smile like a gash, the endless servile ducking—he is the seventh most abhorrent man I have ever put behind bars."

"What did you do?" I asked avidly.

"Nothing of consequence." My friend affected complete nonchalance. "I tracked Mr. Sherman's path the previous night with Molly the spaniel."

I held up my hands. "Just a moment—you mean to tell me that after Sherman had already left his house thousands of times, Molly could trace only the most *recent*—"

"Oh, she could have, undoubtedly—but she didn't." Holmes smirked. "I provided a reverse demonstration, as I thought the good Inspector Jones might appreciate a dramatic conclusion, and I was already developing something of a taste for them. We started at the house Sherman had broken *into* the night before, with one of his boots—it was child's play for Molly to trace his steps backward and discover the stolen bird hidden at the rear of the shop. I whisked off the tarp he had hid it in, opened the carcass, found Mrs. Sherman's brooch, *et voilà*. Alarms for the murder and the theft happened five minutes and two miles apart, so Old Sherman's alibi was proved."

"Wonderful!" I marveled. "But how did it turn out?"

"Rather splendidly. I was able to cause Jack o' the Devil's arrest and subsequent prosecution—his cockiness was so absolute, he had neglected to notice blood on his own clothing, and Molly the spaniel handily proved he had been in Plaid Charlie's rooms the night previous, which added a bit of circumstantial reinforcement if nothing more. Athelney Jones called me a lucky young rake and told me to join the Yard to learn my craft, which offer I declined. Old Sherman was charged with housebreaking; when we returned the repaired bird, that was reduced to trespass, happily. I visited his jail cell as quickly as I could and told him everything.

"'Oh, bless you!' he cried, wringing me by the hand. 'You've cleared my good name, sir.'

"'I cleared it a trifle,' said I, dubiously.

"'Now, never say as Old Sherman don't know a friendly turn when it's done 'im. I'll have six months' stint at most, likelier four. What's your real moniker, lad?'

"'Oh, I beg your pardon. Sherlock Holmes,' I answered. 'And forgive me for—'

"'Not another word about that!' he exclaimed. 'Whatever I can do for you in future, Mr. Sherlock Holmes, I shan't 'estitate a single tick o' the clock. And you'll 'ave as many lessons in zoological anatomy and naturalism as that great brain o' yours can sponge up, by God, for who can say what use such might prove to a criminologist? I'll teach you everything I know, lad, and gladly too.'

"'Shall you?' By this point, my dear fellow, I confess myself to have been somewhat perplexed. 'But you're impris—'

"'I'll not 'ear a single syllable against it!' he shrieked. 'Ye've done a service, ye have, ye noddle-headed thing, and ye'll take some hearty home-cooked meals and a serving of education fer it if me wife and I have to shove it down yer scrawny neck like I'd stuff one o' me dressed weasels, so 'elp me.'

"So there you have it, Watson. Old Tom Sherman taught me everything I know about practical naturalism as applies to detection after his parole, his wife taught me all about canine tracking and training and made us tea on countless occasions, and whenever I need a dog's nose, I have the very best in London at my disposal."

We fell into a comfortable silence, Holmes meditating upon the last of his smoke rings and I upon the ceiling.

"Holmes, was Molly the spaniel Toby's mother?"

"Grandmother," he corrected.

"Did Jones take the credit?"

"Of course. It was in all the papers, but I was quite content with adding another obscure branch of knowledge to my rainbow array of studies."

Another thought occurred. "Who helped Mrs. Sherman with bird-stuffing while her husband was incarcerated?"

"How the deuce should I know?" he retorted, and then stretched extravagantly and rolled to his feet.

"It *was* you," I accused him, chuckling.

My friend said nothing, and said it with his back turned to me, which was every bit as good as an affirmative.

"What fresh work have we tomorrow?"

Holmes lounged at the mantel refilling his pipe, and his languid expression brightened instantly. "Oh, you've just reminded me, I've a lovely problem for us tomorrow. Come to think of it, we're lucky the Viking manuscript lot are dragging their heels so dreadfully. Are you well enough to be ready at half ten? Someone has been anonymously mailing Lady Marianne Chandler a lock of hair every day for a fortnight—and according to her letter, each lock is from a different person. She insists every individual cutting is entirely unique and is needless to say quite disturbed in mind over it. Of course, the regular force can do nothing in the absence of any crime, so she has turned to us to study over the collection. Picturesque, don't you think?"

"It is." More meaningfully I added, "Thank you. For the story, and for the work."

Sherlock Holmes's deep-set eyes narrowed as he frowned. "Not at all."

"Come now, Holmes. I may not be a detective, but it is obvious what you were just doing."

"And what I was doing was nothing significant." He lifted one shoulder coolly. "I can offer only the sole anodyne which brings me such vivid scraps of relief from the doldrums—a crime to solve or accounts of crimes past. Twisted puzzles, shocking revelations, a solution tied up with a ribbon and placed in a tin box. A slender consolation indeed. Surely my personal choice of distractions is ludicrously inadequate under the circumstances. Is it not? Well, well, never mind answering that. I shouldn't, if I were in your place. As regards your own situation, you know I have no experience of such emotions, and thus would be the worst candidate on earth to entrust with your confidences. I can now ring for your soup, and there my usefulness ends."

Sighing, I finished my brandy. I wanted to contradict him, for he was egregiously wrong on two counts. First, he was not the worst person on earth to trust with confidences, for he never pitied the giver of them, only listened with focused impatience or silent sympathy, which is why such a hubbub of strangers continually clattered up and down our staircase begging for his help. He was, in fact, the foremost keeper of confidences in London—and he had created the profession, no less. Second, be the person a mother, a brother, a sister, a friend, or some other beloved ghost, I by 1897 knew him to be mistaken in suggesting he lacked for feeling entirely.

The discussion ended there, however; Sherlock Holmes rang for my soup and then launched into a detailed and lively account of Lady Chandler's mysterious follicular woes. So I poured us more brandy and held my peace as ever on the subject of his own sorrows, and the letter which had started it all sat forgotten on the mantelpiece next to my friend's jackknife.

The Adventure of the Vintner's Codex

During the lengthy period when I lodged with my celebrated friend Mr. Sherlock Holmes, our habit by common consent was to celebrate the holiday season in as quiet and Bohemian a manner as possible. As our establishment was a thoroughly bachelor one, we had little use for the more frivolous trappings of Yuletide, and my companion—when not frenetically engaged upon some dark and enigmatical criminal investigation which would drag us both into most un-Christmas-like environs—had a marked tendency to indolence during the winter months. The ennui which has always plagued him in the absence of brainwork was not, I fear, ever any lessened by grey skies and the soot-blackened snow beneath our sitting room window. Nor could I fail to notice that he made extra use of his Baker Street Irregulars as the banks of the Thames crusted over and made scavenging perilous, continually sending the urchins on petty errands and paying them at double rates during the storms. I myself have on occasion found London a strain upon the senses during its darkest months and had cause to reflect that, for a man of my friend's minutely pitched sensitivities, the bleakness of its icy Decembers must have been grating in the extremest degree.

During one such period, upon New Year's Eve to be precise, I was returning home after a well-bundled evening constitutional and found myself veering in the direction of the dim and cozy wineshop we frequented in Marylebone Road. Though the hour was early enough yet that the skies gleamed a clear eggshell blue, the wind bore sharp fangs, and the holiday revelers were largely at home before their punch bowls or else in pubs before roaring hearthstones. The streets were therefore all but barren despite the festive date, and I slipped a coin into the tin cup of a bearded beggar as I turned the corner, feeling pensive and a trifle outside myself in the eerily calm thoroughfare. Stepping into the muted light and warmth of Eaker's Festive Spirits revived me somewhat, and Mr. Eaker was his usual ebullient self, but I failed to linger there, instead selecting my purchases and at once making my way back to Baker Street, taking care not to slip on the slick cobbles in my renewed haste.

It had been a circuitous outing which was of absolute necessity upon my part and which Holmes had dismissed with the barest flick of his agile fingers when I suggested it to him. He had not, I believe, quit the flat in some five days, having taken up semipermanent residence before the fire with his tobacco and his articles, interrupting himself only so far as to fling annoyingly peaceful pages of newsprint into the flames or to recline with an expression on his aquiline face of the utmost listlessness. When I poured tea, he drank it, and when I urged food upon him, he caustically suggested I volunteer in a soup kitchen so as to satisfy some of my more irritating quirks of nature outside the house. None of these signs were the least encouraging. I was, in short, growing concerned for his health, and it was this worry which propelled me back up our staircase with more alacrity than my chilled form would otherwise have attempted.

"I've been round to Eaker's for a bottle of Imperial Tokay, and he assures me that this is the specimen required to toast the coming year properly," I called from the doorway. I hung my hat upon its peg as I stamped, urging the blood to return to my extremities. "I must say, it's appropriately dusty. We'll lose no time in testing its reputation—just after I've polished it, I think. My gloves are positively filthy."

When I turned round, the sight I had for days been half-dreading and half-expecting met my eyes. Holmes stood at his desk, long limbs wrapped in his oldest dressing gown, holding the polished morocco leather case I could never glimpse without experiencing the strongest urge to throw it out the window, as it contained a tiny medical syringe used exclusively for unhealthful substances. Its loathsome shape never made an appearance when Holmes was working or in good spirits; its shadow haunted me, however, every time he slipped into despondence. Upon his glancing at me, my friend's eyes narrowed appraisingly, lending to his countenance that aloof and uncannily calculating expression which inevitably causes one to feel like a particle trapped in one of his microscope slides.

"For heaven's sake, my dear Holmes," I protested, setting the bottle heavily upon our sideboard.

"Apologies, but to what exactly are you referring, my good man?" he replied lazily.

"I should have thought that was obvious."

"Come now, I am no clairvoyant—spell it out for me."

"I refer to the clear indication that you are about to embark upon an activity which will only chip away at the very characteristic that makes you unique."

"Everyone is unique, surely."

"Not the way you are," I insisted, and for some reason the assertion, though admittedly ill-phrased, altogether pained me.

"You've just delivered the exact dictionary definition of the word 'unique,' I hope you're aware."

"Holmes, it's New Year's Eve."

"Watson, despite the fact you have chided me in the past for having deliberately erased facets of everyday living from my mind to make room for bicycle tire patterns and odorless fatal poisons, I assure you that I can read a calendar."

"You are deliberately needling me."

"It isn't my fault that you're uttering a string of obvious non sequiturs. I suppose next you're about to observe that that is a wicker-backed armchair."

I took a calming breath. "Fine. May I request that you refrain from dosing yourself?"

"Oh, come, it isn't as if I've any choice in the matter!" he cried. "For weeks now, nothing has taken place in this wretched city of any appreciable interest, never mind a genuinely stimulating effect upon the faculties. These people wandering aimlessly about beyond our windows—think of the nefarious schemes, the harrowing choices, the miraculous happenstances that ought to take place hourly in a city of millions of beings crammed up against one another, and so far as I can tell from the latest editions, their imaginations extend no further than to marry each other, assault each other, or otherwise degrade each other. Where is the scope, where is the creative spark, what is the *point* of a proficiency like mine if it cannot be put to any *use*?"

"It has been invaluable in the past and it will be again soon. You must trust in this, and have a little patience, Holmes."

"Patience?" he scoffed. "I am unique, you tell me, and more so than everyone else—which is a grammatical impossibility, by the way, and I have heard rumor that you dabble in published prose from time to time, but never mind—very well, I am unique. If my fate is to be caged indoors staring at household furnishings, utterly sterile news reports, and an Army pensioner reading yellow-backed novels a child would dismiss as overly sensational, allow me at least some clarification of my thought processes."

My jaw tensed, but I soldiered on. "Setting aside the rest, which doesn't bear discussion, temporary clarification of your thought processes with after-effects of gradual but sure damage hardly seems to me the best method of ringing in the New Year, particularly in the case of a man who lives by his legendary wits," I replied tartly, stung despite my familiarity with Holmes's black humors. "But in any case, I'll leave you to it. Apparently the respective vistas within our parlor have grown equally distasteful to the pair of us, so I shall take myself out of the picture and solve both of our problems simultaneously. A happy New Year to you."

As infrequently as Holmes and I quarrel, and as comprehensively as I esteem my distant and masterful friend, I was in that moment desirous of nothing more than sharing a quiet pint with a fellow creature better suited to polite conversation and seasonal cheer. It felt nothing like a retreat, but rather like a tactical decision to approach the fray from a position of greater advantage and at a more salubrious time. In fact, I was already returning my hands to my dirtied gloves, wondering whether I should patronize one of our local watering holes or hail a cab to escape the tedium of our niche of Westminster, when a commanding tenor halted me.

"Stop."

I hazarded a glance back. Holmes was staring speculatively at the wine bottle, arms crossed and his head proudly tilted to one side like a sleek raven's. Since I could not imagine what he was about to say, I waited in silence.

"Eaker's supply of Imperial Tokay is superior to most, but the best I ever encountered was hand-selected by a wine merchant named Vamberry. He sold remarkable vintages and indeed shipped them the world over. The highest potentates of no fewer than ten sovereign principalities consulted with him when seeking rare specimens for their private collections."

"Yes, doubtless the wine likewise fails to meet your high standards. Good night, Holmes."

"He was robbed of a beautiful set of Medieval sheet music illuminations, the pride of his life, indeed the most precious objects on earth so far as he was concerned, and he asked me to find them."

"How very fortunate for you, if not for him. If you'll excuse me—"

"Would you like to hear about it?"

My temper had been tested so far already that I might have taken umbrage at this laughably transparent ploy to lure me into the role of captive audience, a mere prop for my friend's considerable ego, had it not been for two things. First, I can never elicit accounts of Holmes's cases prior to our acquaintance save when he is in a particular frame of mind, and such tales interest me extremely. When I ask to hear about them, he is as shy and elusive as a sheltered maiden, and when I least expect the miraculous to take place, he will launch into accounts of his fledgling career that are every bit as rousing as the finest adventure tales at which he so openly sneers. Whether he is truly reticent or deliberately coy I do not know, but the effect is identical: I thrill at the mere thought of those lost tales. As for the second factor, Holmes replaced the morocco case in the desk drawer and banged it shut, striding to the sideboard and pulling two wineglasses from the shelf. He dangled them by their stems, watching them catch the firelight whilst wearing an uncertain expression that looked very odd on him.

"I should prefer not to lose your company, provided you can tolerate mine," he said quietly.

"Tolerating you is a skill at which I'm rather deft." I slowly drew off my gloves again, for while my friend is often so abrasive, he is seldom so aware of the fact. The mere cognizance that he had all but driven me out of my own flat on New Year's Eve was a sign of improvement, and I cherish such budding suggestions that spring will come as it always does. "I can at least assure you that an account of your early work would be very tolerable indeed."

He ventured a flicker of a smile which failed to reach his eyes. It was, once more, better than nothing. "You're far too kind."

"Nonsense. You already know that I love to hear of your first cases."

"No, I meant that sentiment in the general rather than the specific sense. But my blushes. I did gather that you enjoyed them."

"They're very engaging. That is, provided you don't plan to reduce the anecdote to a dry mathematical diagram, or a lecture in Latin on the practical application of logical abstractions, I shall be content," I teased, settling into my armchair.

This time his smile, though rueful, was lingering. "A touch, a touch, I do confess it, Watson. Well, we shall see what I can do to spin a yarn for my own biographer. Make yourself comfortable, and thaw your feet, and I'll present to you the facts of the case."

Passing me a now-full glass of Tokay, Holmes curled himself into his own chair like a diffident feline. He balanced the measure of golden liquid upon his knee and peered into it as if divining a fortune. When he finally took a sip, his face cleared a little in surprise. I was, I confess, amused.

"It may not be from this Vamberry chap's establishment," I ventured, savoring the complexity of the flavor coating my tongue, "but it will serve."

"By Jove, it certainly will."

"Mr. Eaker insisted that it was a superb selection."

"I shall pop round tomorrow and clean out his remaining stock for us."

"That would be admirable," I owned, knowing an apology when I heard one. "You were telling me a tale, however."

"Yes, of course." He cleared his throat, ever the showman. "After I left college, as you know, I had it firmly fixed in my mind that I should make my living solving the conundrums which so often seem indecipherable to the earnest but unimaginative men of the Metropolitan Police."

"And with some success from the outset."

"Some. Unfortunately, no one had ever heard of me, and my researches hardly fattened my bank account, so that by the time you met me—the case in question took place mere weeks before, in February of eighteen eighty-one—my financial outlook was less sanguine than a gentleman likes to contemplate. It had, in fact, reached the level of personal embarrassment."

"You'll recall I was in similar straits myself."

"Yes," said he, the ghost of an impish light dawning in his grey irises. "Forgive me for mentioning it, Watson, but your skills as a medico were rather wasted upon mending aged handkerchiefs."

"Of course you noticed that," I sighed.

"It was no reflection on your neatness, merely one upon your indifferent thread choice. My own stabs at frugality would have been hardly less obvious to the trained observer. In any case, a fellow who fancies his digs a private practice likes to have a small selection of spirits on hand, for himself as well as his clients, and I soon identified Mr. Uriah Vamberry as the most reasonably priced vendor in the area despite his fame. Every month or so, I would pay him a call, and after several such occasions he came to take an interest in me. I suppose I must have been a bit of a melancholy figure, callow and bookish to a fault, and old Vamberry often engaged me upon the subject of my highly eccentric lines of study."

"If you bothered to answer, you must have liked him."

"I suppose I did." Holmes swirled his wine, pondering. "He loved music and the rare, mysterious artifacts associated with song. Whenever I spoke of my violin dabblings, he became particularly voluble—his prized possession was a Medieval musical codex in six pages, embellished in the most fantastical array of peacock greens and purples and sapphires, meticulously framed and kept in the back room away from harmful light, hung above the rarest of the distilled spirits as if crowning the collection. The inking was phenomenally detailed, and the gilt work dazzling. It notated a *rondet de carole* by none other than Adam de la Halle and, though dated in the fifteenth century long after his death, was of such exquisite rendering that I never set foot in the shop without devoting a few minutes of my own attention to Vamberry's prized possession.

"He would have intrigued you, Watson. He was a cunning little chap, stooped over as if he were perennially inhaling the essence of a rare vintage, with a pale face lined with countless fine wrinkles like a spreading network of cobwebs, and great blue eyes staring out from a pair of silver spectacles. In addition to his more exalted clients, the scholars from the British Museum all consulted him upon their wine cellars, for he'd an expert palate and fair prices, while I relied upon his expertise and good nature to supply my decanters with something more respectable than gin.

"On one such visit—as I said, less than a month prior to being introduced to the estimable fellow who would make my name known internationally—I arrived outside his shop to find Vamberry greatly upset, pacing the pavement before his window. It was obvious that a blow of some significance had befallen him. His usually papery complexion was painted with furious spots of color, his spindly limbs trembled, and as I approached, he suddenly leaned against the brick wall.

"'Mr. Vamberry, whatever is troubling you?' I inquired urgently.

"'I cannot credit it, I simply cannot!' he cried without greeting me. 'That I should be abused in such a way!'

"'But what has happened?'

"'I have been robbed, Mr. Holmes! Cruelly and shamelessly robbed!'

"As you can well guess, Watson, my ears pricked up considerably at this news. For Vamberry had often been kind to me, unsociable as I am, and here was a chance to attempt repaying him."

"And to involve yourself in a crime," I could not help but remark shrewdly.

Sighing, Holmes passed his fingers over the bridge of his nose. "I don't deny that motive, though I didn't invent the other."

"Of course not."

"But I don't begrudge your getting a bit of your own back."

I shook my head. "Detection is your passion, not merely your profession, and noting that is not a pejorative."

"Oh—I beg your pardon. I seem at odds with everything and everyone tonight."

"I know, and my apologies for interrupting. Pray continue."

"'Mr. Vamberry, when did you find your codex was missing?' I questioned. 'Surely that is what's been stolen, for you have never spoken so feelingly of even the rarest vintage, and the loss of a single day's till would hardly trouble you this much.'

"'I'm not meant to be here today at all!' he told me in a fierce whisper. 'I wanted something a bit unusual to share with old friends this evening, and I stopped by for a bottle, and—heavens, it was horrible, my first glimpse of the back room.'

"Obviously, Watson, my first thought was of Vamberry's two clerks, Evers and Manente—for Vamberry's hours were quite regular, and his shop was full of valuable wares and thus locked in the most secure manner by night. The place was a veritable fortress, with iron bars across both the ground- and the first-floor windows, a double locking mechanism on the front door, and a fenced back area with a very heavy padlock upon the rear entrance. It seemed that either one employee, or the two of them in concert, had taken advantage of a felicitous opportunity, and I hinted as much.

"'Yes, I've just now sent a lad to fetch a constable,' said he, wringing his badly palsied hands. 'My clerks are within, in my office. Both claim not to have set foot in that room today at all, having had no cause to do so. They are both clever, quick boys, just as you are, and I have been teaching them all I know of oenology—I cannot bear to think one of them has betrayed me.'

"'I may not be much experienced,' I told him eagerly, 'but I have often seen what is invisible to others, and I should be happy to lend you my eyes, with your permission, before the official police arrive. The sooner evidence is gathered, the better chance we have of recovering your property.'

"Vamberry readily agreed, and we made it our business first to check all the windows and locks, which showed no sign of having been tampered with. Then we hastened to the display room where the robbery had occurred, lined floor to ceiling with the palest golden brandies, cognacs, and liqueurs. The six empty frames sat neatly stacked upon the polished wooden floor, and the sight of them caused poor Vamberry to muffle a small sound of distress. Save for the missing codex, despite my best efforts, I could see nothing out of the ordinary whatsoever, not a bottle askew nor a scratch on the shelving, which again suggested to me that the culprit was neither rushed nor unfamiliar with his surroundings. Vamberry's establishment was always immaculately dusted, unfortunately, so I'd no help from that quarter either.

"But all my instincts informed me that the theft had been carefully planned. I began to fear in earnest that the codex was irretrievable, for if either clerk had removed the sheets and then made use of an accomplice posing as a customer in the other's absence, the confederate could simply have carried the papers away in a briefcase with no one the wiser.

"Bending to examine the floor, I grew still more discouraged, for the weather had been cold but clear and no impressions of muddied tracks were to be found. In fact, a single piece of data presented itself, and little enough to go on: it was a tiny scrap of loose cotton wool, barely more than a thread, and I pocketed this with every intention of showing it to the Yarders when they arrived.

"Swiftly, I also searched the front room, which was where the bottles of lesser value were displayed and the register sat proudly on a mahogany counter. When I rummaged through the contents of the dustbin beneath, imagine my surprise when I discovered considerably more cotton wool, masses of it, and damp to the touch. I hadn't the faintest notion what to make of this, but filed it away for after I had questioned my suspects."

I had at first been fighting twinges of lingering vexation, but was by now entirely engrossed in my companion's story. "As you say, this all looks very dark for one of the clerks."

"Granted, I was determined not to disregard other possibilities, but it is foolishness rather than broad-mindedness not to examine the most obvious suspects first."

"How did you approach them?"

Taking a demure sip of Tokay, his deep-set eyes regaining a hint of their natural mischievousness, Holmes answered, "I solicited their help, of course."

Smiling, I raised my glass. "Recruitment—the best interrogation technique known to the independent investigator."

"Exactly, Watson! I asked Vamberry if he could hold any arriving police at bay whilst I spoke to them briefly, each in private. He was agreeable and at once led me to the office. The senior clerk, a Mr. Aloysius Evers, had been with him for some five years, and sat quietly filling out orders for their European suppliers. Meanwhile Mr. Antonio Manente, the junior clerk of some two months' standing who manned the stockroom, paced along one wall like a wildcat trapped in a cage. The demeanors of the two men could not have been more diametrically opposed.

"'Oh, hello, Mr. Holmes,' Evers said, wiping a smudge of ink from his fingers with a kerchief as he emerged from behind the desk to greet us.

"Evers was a short, husky fellow with a round face, a milky blond complexion, and a habit of conducting conversations with his gaze riveted to his hands, which were constantly in motion. He would glance periodically at his listener, but more often he was scratching away in the ledger, brushing a cloth over the register and counter, dusting the stock, et cetera. Though he was friendly in a forgettable way and popular with the clientele, I had always enjoyed my conversations with Vamberry to the point where I had paid Evers scant attention. Now I read a residence near the wineshop in his boots, and 'Durham University' in his tiepin.

"'Mr. Vamberry has been filling you in, has he?' Mr. Evers shook my hand. 'Dreadful business, absolutely appalling, and without any sign whatsoever of a break-in. We don't know what to think, sir.'

"Mr. Antonio Manente abruptly ceased his pacing to listen to his colleague. Since he primarily kept the back stock organized and unloaded deliveries, I'd not often glimpsed him, and I was deeply struck by his appearance. You know, Watson, that I hardly ever look anyone in the eye at a level angle, and this chap was well over six feet. His hair was cut very close and yet curled into tenaciously thick tangles like the wool of a black lamb, and his dark brows were painted finely over keenly alert brown eyes. He had clasped his hands in a polite but unnatural manner behind his back, and when he turned to resume his anxious wanderings, I saw that they twitched worriedly.

"'But there must have been a break-in. Please say it is so,' he requested in the warm, avid timbre of the native Sicilian.

"'I fear not,' Mr. Vamberry replied, visibly woeful, 'though we have only Mr. Holmes's facility to go on so far. Perhaps the official police will see something he has missed.'

"This was a farcical suggestion, Watson, but I for decorum's sake held my tongue.

"'Is it not then possible that a customer has made off with them while we worked?' Mr. Manente exclaimed in shriller tones.

"'I hardly think so,' Mr. Evers put in ruefully, resuming his seat. 'That's what makes this all so dashed disconcerting. They'd have to have been bold as brass—the frames are still here, and it must have taken some little effort to remove the pages. But perhaps an expert lockpick came in the dead of night and took all the time he wanted over the heist, leaving few traces. We can only hope the police discover some clue as to the villain's identity.'

"'Police, ha—God, I wish there were no need for them, but perhaps you speak true.'

"'It's the suspense that has me rattled and nothing more, though of course I regret your loss very much, Mr. Vamberry. I say search us both top to toe and be done with it.'

"'Disgraceful!' the other exclaimed, eyes wide. 'Why should I be searched? I have done nothing, I tell you, nothing!'

"'Come, Manente, calm yourself. Surely you need not object to a search if you're guiltless.'

"'Oh, I couldn't search either one of you unless as a *very* last resort, lads,' Mr. Vamberry protested tremulously.

"'Very good of you too, sir,' said Evers, 'though if it becomes necessary, you must not hesitate simply to spare our feelings, eh, Manente?'

"Manente's lips pursed in agreement, but he remained silent, and I sensed tension between the two workers which had nothing to do with the uncomfortable situation in which they found themselves.

"'Gentlemen, I wonder if you would agree to assist me, as your testimony might well prove invaluable and Mr. Vamberry prizes your judgment and discretion so,' I appealed to them. 'He has agreed to let me pose you one or two queries, in an effort to avoid any unpleasantness in the police court, if possible, and to attempt to learn all we can before they arrive. Have you any objection? I should be very grateful for your aid, both of you—I am a student of the art of detection, and have solved some dozens of crimes without the aid of the Yard.'

"'By Jove, an amateur sleuth!' Evers exclaimed as he patted a stack of papers into order.

"'Consulting detective,' I could not help correcting him.

"'Eh? Well, whatever you call it, I am more than happy to assist. Manente?'

"'Question as you like.' He shrugged, but a twitch below his left eye betrayed his discomfiture. 'I've stolen nothing and wish only to see this quickly finished.'

"'Thank you. Your help will be most beneficial for everyone involved, I hope. If I might question Mr. Evers confidentially first, and then Mr. Manente.'

"The others promptly left us, and I sat down at the side of the desk opposite to Evers, crossing my legs and giving him a thorough study. He smiled at me briefly, then returned his attention to his pen, ink, and blotter, rearranging them.

"'It is a shame that one of your shipments of wine was discovered to be poorly corked this morning,' I began in a friendly fashion.

"Evers at once glanced up again. 'How on earth did you guess that?' he exclaimed. 'Do you know, you might really make something of this detective business, sir. Yes, a case of Chianti arrived and proved after inspection to be absolutely undrinkable. Some spoilage is inevitable, of course, but this was disappointing. How did you know?'

"'You've a faint scattering of minuscule red spots on your trouser leg, just where a fine spray of red wine would land if you were depositing an inferior product down the drainage grate. I can hardly think how else you could come by such a stain. Apart from that, you are presently requesting reimbursement from the vintner,' I added with a wry nod at his ledger. 'Cork taint is the only possible suspect when it comes to the disposal of unsold stock—so you see, there is no mystery in it.'

"'None at all.' He laughed. 'But how you baffled me. I'd thought you very clever indeed for a moment.'

"'I may not be clever, but I confess myself surprised. By reading upside-down I can see that it was a Nacarelli shipment you found lacking. You may have observed that I've purchased wine from that vineyard myself, and always found it quite palatable. Even Mr. Vamberry recommends it.'

" 'Winemaking is a delicate enough procedure that the best of houses can sometimes find themselves in the wrong. But you seem not to be questioning me upon the subject at hand, Mr. Holmes.'

" 'True enough. Frankly, I cannot credit you as the culprit.' I shrugged, affecting to brush a thread from my trouser leg with a bored expression. 'Had you wanted that codex, surely you would have made your move years ago. You have worked here for some time, have you not?'

" 'Five years, Mr. Holmes.'

" 'Quite so. I only wanted to know what you thought of Mr. Manente.'

" 'Ah.' Evers leaned back in his chair, looking regretful. 'You saw his demeanor earlier. He seems most . . . disturbed at the notion of a personal search. I don't know him at all well, I'm afraid, since we work at such disparate tasks here and he is not the most convivial of men. As for myself, I only wish Mr. Vamberry would empty our pockets and raid our briefcases, for I've nothing to hide in this sordid business.'

" 'Even if you are not confidential with Mr. Manente, can you tell me more about him? Do you know of any debts to his name, any stain upon his character?'

"Evers fiddled with the pen, bit his lower lip, and gave every indication that he disliked this line of questioning. 'I wish I could say no, Mr. Holmes. But I fear I cannot divulge what I've learned of his past to you either. I'm sorry, for I did promise to assist, but you understand that I don't want to see him judged unfairly, even though we are not close. After you've spoken with him, depending upon his candor . . . well, well, perhaps then I'll be forced to betray his confidence, but not before.'

"After this exchange, I sent Evers on his way and called in Mr. Manente. He was in a most pitiable state of nerves, Watson, with hands once again clasped behind him, and his rich complexion faded to ash. I reached out my own hand in greeting, and he took it readily enough, however, with a firmness of grip which suggested that his agitation was not due to any innate weakness of character.

" 'I hope not to keep you terribly long. Mr. Manente, how did you pass your day?' I began.

"'Unpacking crates, sorting stock, cleaning,' he said dully. Rather than take the chair Evers had vacated, he resumed pacing. 'I will not stand for this, I tell you. To be treated like a rat or a dog. I will *not* have my property searched, and that is all. My conscience is clear, whether Mr. Evers thinks so or not.'"

"Surely this attitude seemed very odd to you," I put in, moving to replenish our supply of Tokay. A little of the color had returned to my friend's bone-white complexion, a happy sign to say the least. "Why should an innocent man act so guiltily, if not because he had counted upon Mr. Vamberry's absence that day and then found himself in danger of discovery?"

"Why, indeed," Holmes agreed, holding out his glass. "Well, I am afraid that I required the answer to that identical question urgently. 'Mr. Manente,' said I, 'I know all about your criminal record, and I am prepared to overlook it after you've told me truthfully about the contents of your briefcase, whatsoever those contents may be.'"

My jaw dropped, and Holmes laughed. "Mr. Manente bore an expression not dissimilar to yours, my dear Watson, though his was tinged with considerably more fear. When he asked me how I knew of such a thing, his breath strained and his knees quivering, I told him readily enough. You see, I don't believe that Mr. Manente was hiding his hands from me deliberately—on the contrary, he was indulging a nervous tic. But I had determined that I should scrutinize them more closely, and when I had shaken his hand, I'd felt a series of callosities along the flesh of his upper palm. I'd also caught a glimpse of the skin at his collar, and that rather proved the point conclusively."

"Then I should be grateful to know what point, and how it was proved."

"With pleasure. He had been operating either a plow, a handcart, or a treadmill, and recently. Even so raw and untested as I was, I felt them at once—deep lateral hardenings of the pad directly below the fingers—but I might have taken him for a former farmer or stevedore if I'd not noted his skin coloration."

"Which was significant in what fashion?"

"His pigmentation was darker far than mine, but neither damaged by sun nor roughened by wind, and, I observed, very faintly paler when his head turned and his collar shifted. An old, faded summer's demarcation but a clear one. I cannot believe that any farmer would wear a paper collar in the field, nor can I picture one on the men pushing handcarts down at the quays. In the dock, when a man is put to hard labor, it is almost always indoors. He had always previously dressed as a gentleman, and roughened his hands while serving his time."

"Wonderful!" I exclaimed.

"Surely superficial to one such as yourself, who knows my methods," he said, but I caught the glint of pride in his steely eye. "And yet, marvelous enough that Manente all but collapsed into the chair at last.

"'Try to ruin me, then,' said he, fiercely. 'I can see that you and Evers are in it together. But I know my own character, even if—'

"'Softly, for heaven's sake!' I interrupted him. 'Now. Six months' hard labor is my guess, judging by the callosities on your hands, and I assure you that Evers has told me nothing as yet, though he strongly hinted he knew more than he said. What were you booked for?'

"'Manslaughter with a reduced sentence,' he answered hoarsely. 'I'd have served ten times that, by God—though if true justice had been done, I'd have been a free man after the trial. It was a pig died, not a human, and it broke its own neck without my aid.'

"Finally, Watson, my brain managed to slot two pieces of the puzzle together; I was not then quite so trained in my mental acuity as now, and the necessary data had been teasing at the edge of my mind in the most maddening fashion. But I have always devoured the London dailies with considerable appetite, and Manente's story flooded suddenly and completely into my mind.

"'Christina Manente,' I supplied. 'Your sister—she testified at trial to having been pursued for months by a drunken brute from the neighborhood. She was dogged relentlessly by the fiend and had become terrified to so much as set foot outdoors. On the last occasion you evicted him from her presence, he fell down the stairs in a drunken stupor, and his mother brought charges of murder against you, saying you pushed him deliberately. The press made something of a lurid romance of it. I take it you said nothing of your role in this drama to Mr. Vamberry?'

"'The last five establishments would not hire me when I was forthright. So I was silent. I have a wife, children. Must they starve because I love my sister also?'

"'I take it that something to do with your past presently resides in your briefcase?'

"'Court documents. I am due to meet the bailsman this evening to make a final payment, then all will be over and done with.' Learning forward exhaustedly, he rubbed at his temples. 'Do you suppose me a thief, Mr. Holmes?'

"'Not a bit of it. I suppose Mr. Evers an opportunist.'

"'Why so?' he asked. 'I do not like him—he flatters the customers and persuades them to buy wines they cannot afford. But never have I had reason to think him a criminal.'

"'Any clever man who planned to steal a work of art, knowing that he would be one of two prime suspects, would act only if he thought he could make the other appear guilty. I posit that Evers recognized you from the newspapers and hit on the lucky notion of framing a guiltless man. He seems to fear nothing from a search, so he must be absolutely sure of his hiding place.'

"'In any event, I am ruined. If Mr. Vamberry opens my briefcase—'

"'It won't come to that,' I said, a rush of confidence overwhelming me as I leapt to my feet. A sudden inspiration had struck. 'We shall circumvent a search altogether, with luck on our side. Follow me!'

"We hurried into the front room, where Vamberry and Evers stood with a most impatient-seeming officer of the Yard. Almost at once, I saw what I was looking for—a small crate of wine sat upon a handcart, ready for delivery. The bottles within were of a very dark green hue, which of course you recognize was of the utmost importance, Watson.

"'I don't know who the devil this Sherlock Holmes is, or thinks he is,' the policeman was declaring, 'but if you want my help—'

"'I see you've a delivery to make, Mr. Evers,' I interjected. 'Six bottles, and the glass of very heavy Italian manufacture. I don't wonder that you've elected to use a cart.'

"He went pale at this, though his posture remained unchanged. 'I don't see why it should interest you,' he muttered.

"'Only because of late I have been practicing feats of physical strength,' I returned casually. 'Let me provide you all with a demonstration of my progress.'

"With that, I lifted the crate and balanced the whole of it upon one palm."

I could not contain a peal of laughter at my companion's all too typical theatrics, and he grinned easily in return.

"Quite a commotion ensued, my dear chap, for Evers knew the game was up and made as if to run for it, and the policeman had a sprightly time of wrestling him into a pair of darbies. You see by now what had happened. The wine Evers discarded had been perfectly drinkable. He required the bottles for their opacity and, after washing them out, had dried them thoroughly with the cotton wool I'd discovered. What better way to spirit the codex out of a wine store than inside bottles of wine? When Vamberry opened them, he at once found his treasure, rolled up in six sheets of black paper within the glass."

"He must have been very grateful to you indeed."

"Oh, he was," Holmes owned, chuckling. "He gave me as a reward a case of excellent brandy, which you might possibly recollect from your earliest days at Baker Street."

"Good heavens, yes—that brandy was outstanding. It must have taken us three years to finish it all."

"Two years, eight months, I think. Anyhow, when his scheme fell to pieces, a desperate and vengeful Evers revealed Manente's secret past and claimed that his fellow clerk hid the codex in the bottles, but his groundless accusations came to nothing; I made sure of it. Evers was soon found to have lost a small fortune in wild speculation, and of course Vamberry was too good a chap to sack Manente for nothing, as

I'd supposed all along. Manente was most effusive in his gratitude, and soon thereafter had ended his dealings with the Yard and celebrated his freedom with a promotion from the estimable Vamberry to head clerk. A man guilty of nothing save protecting his loved ones freed, a cunning schemer exposed, a gentleman's property restored, and a pair of bachelors ensconced in new Westminster lodgings with a truly outstanding supply of spirits. A salubrious ending in every manner, eh?"

"Absolutely first-rate, my dear fellow," said I, angling my glass to him. "My cap is off to you."

"It was a very simple matter," he demurred. "But suitable for a leisurely tale on a cold winter's night."

I slipped into a reverie, as will inevitably happen at the closing of a year, and thought about my friend and his incredible talent, and about the incalculable number of Londoners who had at one time or another appealed to him for help when the darkness appeared to have closed in upon them irrevocably. It would be a travesty and a disgrace, I mused, if I—a medical professional and one in the singular position of calling myself his friend—could not wean him of the habits which would ultimately destroy his incomparable powers, no matter the frustrations and the setbacks that such a project would surely entail. If I would do as much to save a stranger from self-destruction, how much more would I do for Sherlock Holmes? Finishing my wine, as nightfall's ashen clouds gathered outside our window, I determined anew to stop at nothing in this worthy aim. With the sense of calm which follows such resolutions, I glanced up to find myself the subject of minute study by the most prescient observer of the age.

"What is it, Holmes?" I inquired.

"Not this year, I'm afraid, my dear fellow," my friend said softly, reading my train of thought as easily as he would read letters on a sign-post. His eyes fell back to his knee. "But perhaps one year. Though to be entirely honest, I have my doubts."

"And I have my hopes," said I. "We shall see who emerges victorious."

PART II

THE EARLY YEARS

The Adventure of
the Honest Wife

My earliest relations with Mr. Sherlock Holmes of Baker Street were rendered much the more intriguing because I spent an inordinate amount of time—or more than I believe to be usual with fellow lodgers, for I know of no other men who reside with independent consulting detectives—deciphering which aspects of his peculiar character were innate and which adopted owing to his singular choice of profession. As with every individual, some of his tastes must have been bred from the cradle, while others surely were cultivated to grant him greater chance of success in his field.

In no other arena did his attitude puzzle me so much as in his open aversion to the entire female gender, for in that particular respect Holmes is nothing less than a living contradiction. My friend is prepared to swear that no female is to be entirely trusted, and that the very finest examples of the sex are yet subject to flights of deception and caprice capable of driving any logician to distraction. He makes an abysmally poor misogynist, however. Holmes's easygoing gentility in the presence of actual women seemed to belie his disdain for hypothetical ones, and during no adventure did the dichotomy more greatly bemuse me than that of the Treadwell scandal of March, 1882.

I was at that time still suffering lingering symptoms from my Afghan service, which unfortunately had left me with an imperfectly mobile right shoulder and a mercurial nervous system. Peripheral noises, especially sudden ones, sent my heart racing, and I was the victim of myriad sharp aches and dull throbs which echoed the initial agony of the moment a bullet had pierced my flesh in that far-off country. Having passed a wretchedly poor night's sleep, wakened thrice by the cataclysmic volleys of thunder which herald the advent of springtime in London, I lay stretched upon the settee half-dressed at seven in the morning with a book in my hand and the hearth blazing like a small bonfire, supposing that abandoning the field of battle would improve my spirits and determined to attempt to conquer slumber again the next evening.

The scuff of a boot sole arrested my attention. I glanced up in some surprise when Sherlock Holmes entered the room neatly clad and fresh-faced, polishing a cuff link with his thumb. Seeing me, he paused, and then strode directly to his tobacco remnants of the day before, which he had recently commenced leaving out to dry upon the mantelpiece corner for some reason that I could not fathom and had hesitated to inquire over. He raised a genial black eyebrow in my direction.

"Whatever are you doing awake at this hour?" Holmes asked, pressing very unpalatable used shag into his pipe.

"Is that what you've saved the plugs for?" I reflected with a faint hint of distaste. "I know we are neither of us disposed to be spendthrifts at the moment, but I've some ship's on my desk just there. Help yourself, by all means."

He laughed merrily, shaking his head. "Thank you. However, it is not economy, but rather habit and inclination. I've a taste for intense flavor when it comes to smoking—the thicker the better. Does this bother you? Its concentration allows me to concentrate, if you follow me."

"I am not sure I do, but no, I don't mind in the slightest."

"Capital. And why are you up with the sun, then?"

"I am awake because I prefer to succeed at reading than to fail at resting. My shoulder doesn't care for this weather, and neither do my nerves, come to that."

"Hardly surprising—it was dreadful last night. I confess I am myself a light sleeper and passed much of the time over a medical treatise regarding the effects of alcohol on blood coagulation."

"You appear remarkably energetic."

"Sleep has never been so prized a commodity for me as for most men. Were it not a necessity, I should forgo it altogether—think of all the profitable uses the time could be put to! Humankind could have advanced a full millennium beyond its present state of modernity by now, if beds were but taken out of the picture."

"I wish I shared your sentiment, for it is eminently practical, but I confess I'd prefer to indulge in a restful night again."

He clucked sympathetically. "I can well imagine, Doctor. Nothing is so desirable as that which is denied us, after all."

Finding that I was dangerously close to complaining rather than simply remarking, which was not palatable to me in the slightest, I changed the subject. "Are you finished with your researches, then? Isn't this rather before your usual breakfast time as well?"

"Yes, I've an appointment with a client."

"Ah, I see. I'll clear off, then, and leave you to it."

"Stay if you like," Holmes said, sitting upon the arm of the sofa at my feet as he lit his eccentrically stuffed pipe. "Mr. Treadwell will be here within a quarter hour."

"But I should not wish to be in your way."

"Well, I shouldn't wish you to be either, but that eventuality seems rather far-fetched, doesn't it? And nothing lessens the effects of a bad night's sleep like setting straight to work, I have found," he added brightly.

Having quickly discovered that, while detesting the banalities of polite society, Sherlock Holmes was considerably more tolerant of an audience for his remarkable conjuring tricks, I rose to my feet with much more energy than I had imagined I possessed. Why he had seemingly selected me for the task must have had to do with simple expediency— I was present, and too ill to work, and thus an ideal spectator—but I heartily welcomed the assignment, for both his methods and the cases to which he applied them were already endlessly fascinating to me.

"I'll just be a moment," I said en route to my staircase.

"I'd never dream of starting without you," said he, with a faint trace of amusement.

After I had quickly shaved and donned more complete attire, I descended into the sitting room for the second time to discover Holmes already in the presence of his client. Mr. Treadwell was a formidable gentleman, not so tall as my friend but much broader in the torso, with an august tilt to his lip and a bullish brow below a sweep of blond hair which granted him a handsome, leonine appearance. While his abnormally dark eyes were intelligent, they also glittered with volatile annoyance. I did not think him a man it was safe to cross, idly wondering how many enemies he had left irreparably broken in his wake to have come by his fortune, for his attire was of the richest fabric and tailoring. He stood with his sandstone jaw cocked at an impatient angle above an emerald cravat, holding a heavy gold watch, which he snapped shut pointedly.

"Here we are. Mr. Lucien Treadwell, this is my friend and colleague Dr. John Watson," Holmes announced with an aloof smile, ignoring the answering scowl on the face of his would-be employer. "Our party is now complete. He helps me in these matters, and you may rely as I do upon his invaluable assistance."

This level of praise from my reserved new friend was as gratifying as it was unexpected. "I'm sure I'll do all I can to help, Mr. Treadwell."

"See that you do," he huffed. "I am here to hire Sherlock Holmes, not an entire committee."

"Well, well," said Holmes soothingly, "you may consider his presence a bonus. I suggest we all sit down, and that you tell us with as much detail as possible what seems to be the trouble."

Mr. Lucien Treadwell visibly attempted to swallow his choler as we seated ourselves. "I need a hired detective," he reported bluntly, "for a policeman would be less than useless in my situation. This matter is private, personal, and indeed has a direct effect upon my marriage. Therefore the fellow who gets to the bottom of it needs to be *my* man to the marrow. That's where you come in. I have heard that you are discreet, Mr. Holmes, and not overly expensive."

My friend disdained to react to this introductory speech, but I who was learning his habits could see the twitch of his jaw and the beginnings of a smile which could chill a room by twenty degrees.

"You see, gentlemen," Mr. Treadwell continued, his left hand worrying at the seam in his trouser leg, "I require evidence that my wife is having an affair."

"Good day to you, Mr. Treadwell," Holmes said pleasantly, rising.

"What sort of ludicrous game is this?" Mr. Treadwell bristled in shock.

"I have no desire to expend my valuable time learning the intricacies of your spouse's leisure pursuits," my friend returned acidly, gesturing at the door with his pipe. "While they doubtless are of interest to you, they are of the most profound uninterest to me, and no amount of money could cause me to see them in an attractive or intriguing light. Should you decide to persist in your course—and I have no means of dissuading you—I recommend you hire a detective."

"What the devil do you call yourself, then, Mr. Holmes, if not a detective?" Mr. Treadwell sneered as he too pushed to his feet. "A simple gossipmonger, perhaps?"

"As a matter of fact, Mr. Sherlock Holmes is an independent consulting detective, the final recourse for those who wish to solve the unsolvable," I put in. "If what you need is a paid spy, Mr. Treadwell, I would suggest you apply elsewhere."

Holmes cast me a look of stark surprise commingled with far more open appreciation than was typical for him. Then he crossed his long arms emphatically and returned his attention to his would-be client. Mr. Treadwell, meanwhile, was fuming and empurpling simultaneously.

"I've never heard such rank trash in all my days! A detective who can't be bothered to detect is worse than useless. Meanwhile, I've been driven nearly to distraction."

"I *detect*, as you put it, with tremendous frequency and skill," Holmes drawled, his pipe perched at the edge of his mouth. "But I do not *meddle*, and that is what you are proposing."

"Meddling, fiddlesticks. I require assistance, and you suppose you're too good for my money! Well, you aren't, Mr. Holmes."

"On the contrary. I suspect that I've been too good for better people's money, as a matter of fact."

"Of all the confounded nerve! It's preposterous—no, no, Mr. Holmes, I've been told by informed parties that you're the best in your field, and I'll have you yet, by God. I'm a man who gets what he wants."

Sherlock Holmes raised his brows in such an inimical fashion that most mortals would have quit the premises; but Mr. Treadwell stepped yet closer, the men's eyes locking combatively.

"What's the issue, then, if not money? Pride, eh? You suppose the task is beneath you? Well, there's your first mistake, Mr. Holmes. I'm presenting you with a *real* problem, I tell you, a genuine *case* to solve. There are clues. For instance, Alice has started keeping her letter box locked. What call could she have to do such a thing? I already check everything that comes through the post, so what can she have to hide?"

"I haven't the slightest idea," Holmes snapped, entirely exasperated. "If someone perused all of my correspondence, I should certainly take to locking it up myself. Meanwhile, one's merely providing oneself with some privacy is no reason to suppose her in an illicit liaison."

Mr. Treadwell, whom I heartily disliked by this time, took a turn before the hearth, scaring fiery tracks in our rug with his volcanic eyes. "Privacy has nothing to do with it! She's up to no good, I tell you, but she'll not make a fool of me. A man *knows* when his way of life is threatened, Mr. Holmes, and the smart man makes a stand to defend it. I'll have her yet. Locking her letters away, going out and coming back with the paltriest excuses—"

"Perhaps she finds the company at home less than congenial," I put in.

My friend emitted a quiet cough.

"Moping about all the godforsaken afternoon—"

"Mr. Treadwell, I seem to recall that I have already wished you good day," Holmes observed icily.

"Claiming the jewelry I've bestowed to try to repair the rift between us is poisoned . . ."

"I beg your pardon?"

"Alice's jewelry," Mr. Treadwell repeated, stopping before Holmes to grin in malicious triumph. "Ah, I see that's netted you at last! My wife grows thinner and paler by the week, refusing all my overtures, and when I try to get it out of her that she's pining away for love of another, she insists that my gifts to her have been somehow imbued with poison. Necklaces, earrings, bracelets, all of the finest quality, and she swears before high heaven I've laced them with something, which is obviously absurd. No, not absurd—downright impossible."

"It is at the very least . . . interesting," Holmes conceded reluctantly, setting his pipe down.

"And this when I've been nothing but generous over her ceaseless melancholic fits! She won't touch her baubles these last six months, even when we're attending society balls and dinner parties, and whenever I force her to wear anything, she's always visibly worse the next day. Sprawling about like an invalid, white as milk and mewling like a kitten. It's an excuse, I tell you, a wild fantasy concocted to throw me off the true scent."

"Dr. Watson, how common to your knowledge are simple metal aversions?"

"Do you mean the unexplained sort along the lines of hay fever, which cause scarlet rash, pulmonary distress, and the like?" I questioned.

"Just so."

"Common enough with cheap metals like nickel and so forth, but as for precious metals like gold or silver? I've never heard of a patient who reacted to either, nor come across such a case in any study."

Holmes's quicksilver eyes lost their focus as he stared past his would-be client, mechanically placing his hands in his pockets. This new information had produced a seismic shift in my friend's mood. Meanwhile, I could hardly contain myself for agitation—whatever ailment plagued Mrs. Alice Treadwell, bullying her into wearing finery she imagined was somehow harmful to her health was the act of a blackguard and a boor.

"Mr. Treadwell, was your wife fond of wearing her jewelry before she began locking her letter box?" This time, Holmes sounded genuinely intrigued.

"Why should I bother telling you if you're too kid-gloved to touch the case?" the extraordinarily contrary Mr. Treadwell shot back in a mocking tone.

Holmes, realizing that our caller was a more contumacious specimen than any we had previously encountered, shrugged his shoulders like a famous theatre critic being asked to sit through a penny concert. His disinterest was well thought of. I attempted likewise to affect an air of indifference, probably with poorer success, as I could imagine no finer pastime than that of thrashing Mr. Lucien Treadwell down our staircase.

"I haven't the time for this," the detective remonstrated. "Your case has no features of interest whatsoever save in the aspect of your wife's strange horror of her own jewelry, which frankly indicates to me that she *isn't* having an affair. What woman intent upon seducing a man would employ merely some of her visual charms and not all of them? But in any case, it doesn't matter—I'll have to speak with Mrs. Treadwell and look over the house if I am to be of any real use, and I've no intention of wasting my morning."

"Aha, so it is to be cash over principles after all! I thought as much. Would you call being paid twenty pounds for a trip to Hampstead a waste of your morning, Mr. Holmes? I am willing to pay so much in return for your services. Or have you really no skills in the detecting arena at all?"

My friend grumbled, and fished for his watch, and compared it with the time on the mantel clock as Mr. Treadwell glowered. I observed them, deeply discomfited.

"Well, I suppose I could cancel an appointment or two. But this is really very awkward," Holmes said with deliberate truculence, reaching for his hat. "Are you game for a visit to Hampstead, Watson?"

"It's most incommodious." My voice was equally dry. "But I'll join you all the same."

"Please procure a cab and await us below as we gather a few necessaries, Mr. Treadwell. We shan't be a moment."

When our highly disagreeable visitor had started down the stairs, I plucked at my friend's sleeve. "I am not enamored of Mr. Lucien Treadwell, Holmes."

He tamped out his pipe with uncharacteristic force and a lip quirked significantly, as if imagining the object standing in for his client. "*Fictio cedit veritati* so soon? The man is barely out the door."

"Surely you concur."

"I have vastly preferred the company of no fewer than three murderers who spring to mind, one of whom also dabbled in arson. He is vile."

"Then you've no wish to accept his offer?"

"God no, I should as soon shake hands with Mephistopheles."

"In that case, my dear Holmes, what interest could this wretched matter possibly hold for you other than the not insignificant sum of twenty pounds? I hope that you would never stoop to digging up sordid evidence of a lady's dalliances."

"Not for any sum, as I stated. No, Mrs. Treadwell may be in danger." The sleuth lowered his voice yet further. "I know her fears sound fantastical, but have you ever heard of aconitine poisoning?"

Aghast, I gaped at him. "Good heavens, Holmes. Monkshood?"

"Precisely. It is a very long shot, but that tincture can penetrate the skin, as you may be aware."

"Your idea is horrifying. But even supposing this bizarre fixation of hers is based in truth, why should the scheming husband consult you—indeed, *insist* upon your aid?"

"I never said her fixation was necessarily based in truth, but it could be, and that is enough cause for me to take interest. There may be forces at work here of which Mr. Treadwell is unaware, an enemy masked in silence and secrecy." Donning his gloves, Holmes cast about for his keys.

"Of course you are right. Though it is exceedingly unlikely that even the most potent preparation of monkshood could be made to adhere to metal in such a manner as to affect the wearer."

"I'm aware of the fact. Still, there are stranger things, et cetera."

I shook my head, slipping into my coat. "To think that you may accidentally have real need of me after all—Mrs. Treadwell could simply be the victim of some obscure nervous malady."

"Perhaps. In any event, abandoning her gems by no means indicates an affair. Mr. Treadwell suggested that transgression only because he is both dull and mean. No, lacking any legitimately damning clues, we must commence our investigation believing her blameless in that regard." My friend pressed his lips together and cocked his square chin at me, resembling a cat which has spied a dish of cream resting unguarded on a windowsill. "But her husband, despite his obnoxious manner, was telling us the truth, or at least the truth as he knew it; I should stake my reputation on that. Something foul is afoot."

"And yet you believe Mrs. Treadwell to be an honest woman?" I pressed as I followed Holmes's sharply angular form down our staircase.

"I don't believe any woman honest," he corrected me as we stepped into the clear early-spring light, turning to lock the door behind him. "They are all of them lying about *something*. The question is, what is this one lying about?"

"Holmes, that is absolutely disgraceful."

"Yes, a great many truths are disgraceful."

I already knew better than to challenge such outrageous aspersions on the comprehensive whole of the female character, for trying to prove to Sherlock Holmes that something is *not* the case is like trying to prevent water from pouring out of a sieve. Instead I stepped into the waiting cab, Holmes following after, and Mr. Treadwell called up to the driver an address on Prince of Wales Road. We set off, wheels echoing sharply against the paving stones in the swelling bustle of a mauve Westminster morning. Sparrows twittered on the dawn-illumined branches, and the sun gleamed in the vanishing puddles like the shards of a shattered decanter, but I could take no joy in these harbingers of finer weather—not when I pictured Mrs. Treadwell (a wisp-thin, ethereal creature in my imagination) donning an ornate diamond collar which bled poison into her cobalt veins, slowly destroying her.

Mr. Treadwell set the facts before us as we traveled, missing no opportunity to vex our spirits. He had been married for two years to Alice Treadwell, and their union apparently had once been a blissful match—he a wealthy and altogether ruthless banker, he boasted, and she the daintiest blossom upon the vine. However, six months previous, she had stopped leaving her letters lying about the house (the majority were from her sister, Rose, who resided alone in Brighton, and one or two other female companions) and taken to locking them in a carved teak box in her bedchamber. Mr. Treadwell was tempted to force the lock, but wished not to admit his grave suspicions in quite so obvious a manner, which notion Holmes applauded with seemingly perfect seriousness.

Alice Treadwell had, around the same period, ceased wearing a necklace of rubies and pearls which had previously been a staple item, claiming she felt sick to her stomach every time she handled it—and following up this assertion by spending a day in bed in a ghastly state after having been compelled to wear it to a charity dinner. A bezel-set porcelain brooch depicting the ruins of the Roman Forum had also been abandoned, as well as a bracelet of finest scarlet rose-cut Bohemian garnets, and an exquisite die-stamped hair ornament covered in seed pearls. Piece by piece, her entire collection—including new items Mr. Treadwell brought home in an effort to lift her spirits—were banished to a safe despite the protests of her husband and the coaxing of her servants. When asked why she would not wear them, Mrs. Treadwell insisted that they must have been treated with some noxious compound, hinting strongly that only Mr. Treadwell could have cause to detest her so.

"And do you?" Holmes interrupted blandly.

"Of course not." Mr. Treadwell's jaw jutted, and I thought I had been wrong to compare him to a lion—an alley tom would have been more accurate, all cocky swagger without gravitas. "She felt guilty, that was all. Guilt over her failure at running a household, guilt over comforting herself with another man, no doubt. God, the mere thought makes me ill, but I must steel myself to stay the course, since the pair of you are going to prove the latter conclusively."

"Failure at running a household?" I repeated when Holmes looked as if this assessment of the task at hand was causing him physical anguish. "Has that particular shortcoming to do with the melancholy to which you referred?"

"Indeed, yes. Alice is periodically quite useless." Mr. Treadwell made a dismissive clicking sound. "Many's the time I tried to explain to her what a privilege it is to want for nothing, to oversee bounty instead of penury, but to no avail. It's a good thing for Alice's sake that she's so comely and tractable, or she'd have nothing to recommend her at all—the flighty girl never attends to a word I say."

"What a shocking lapse," Holmes said without inflection, and for the remainder of the journey, all three of us wisely held our tongues.

We arrived at a costly townhouse of pure white stone, with cheerful white shutters and windows which sparkled like brilliants in the increasing glow of the ivory-hued easterly sun. Like its owner, it announced itself as rich without the need for gauche trappings, and I wondered whether in two years' time Alice Treadwell had managed to put any stamp of her own upon the dwelling. Having myself not long previous escaped a dismal life at a featureless hotel in the Strand, having nothing to do and no one with whom to do it, I could not help feeling sympathy for any fellow creature in a similar state of metaphorical homelessness. In contrast, while 221B Baker Street was already as suffused with Sherlock Holmes as its atmosphere was with shag tobacco—a phrenology skull wearing a jaunty fez in the corner, letters pinned to the mantel with a jackknife, several delicate chemistry pipettes carefully thrust into the soil of a potted plant for safekeeping—it was wholly mine as well, littered with my books and journals and cigar ends.

Holmes popped out of the cab as if propelled from a slingshot, and I followed suit as Mr. Treadwell paid the fare. The uneasiness which had plagued me only increased with proximity to our goal.

"Holmes," I whispered, "I understand that we must see her, but we cannot intend to walk inside and announce ourselves as—"

"Of course not," he replied stridently. "We are insurance assessors. Isn't that right, Mr. Treadwell?"

"Whatever you like, so long as you get some results," Mr. Treadwell barked.

When we entered the sitting room, we found a young and lovely woman reclined in an armchair, reading a volume of French poetry. My heart sank when I saw that I had been largely correct in my fanciful vision of Mrs. Alice Treadwell. Her hair was of a pale butter yellow, done up simply and shining in the golden lamplight, and her equally delicate face was quite bloodless save for the natural blush upon her lips. Upon further scrutiny, I wondered whether Holmes's grotesquely far-fetched suggestion of monkshood poisoning might not be correct after all, for this was not the natural pallor of a life spent listlessly indoors, that unfortunate affliction which plagues too many of our well-bred young society ladies, but rather the chalky whiteness of ill health. I thought additionally that he had been right to reject the calumny of infidelity, for there was such a spiritual air about her that I could not imagine a duplicitous nature behind the translucent skin. Alice Treadwell was in every apparent sense a woman of statuesque beauty and refined sensibilities, and when she looked up at us in startlement, I loathed our duplicitous errand no matter how intrigued Holmes was by her aversion to gemstones or how justified we were in wanting to ascertain she was safe.

"Who are these men, Lucien?" she inquired softly, rising and summoning a tired smile to her face.

"A Mr. Holmes and Mr. Watson, here to examine the house and make an offer on a new insurance policy," he explained gruffly. "I see that you've been reading the morning away again, eh, Alice?"

"It is not yet nine o'clock," she replied, but her tone was as docile as a shadow.

"You are quite right to think it unconscionably early, Mrs. Treadwell, and I do beg your pardon over the interruption to your day," Holmes apologized, extending his hand as if to a frightened forest creature. "We must have a brief look around your home in order to assess its size, study its moldings and finish work, and cast an eye over your furniture, but we wouldn't dream of disturbing you personally. Won't you excuse us so that we might leave you in peace all the more swiftly?"

"Be my guest," she agreed through her evident confusion.

"Mr. Treadwell, we shan't require you either, in fact rely upon your absence to make an impartial report!" Holmes added, grasping me by the shoulder and steering me precipitately out. "We'll just take some preliminary notes before rejoining you! This way, Watson; we passed the staircase as we came in."

Upon the instant we had regained the front hall and Holmes had smoothly shut the double doors in our wake, he pivoted to face me with a strange fire in his eyes that had not been present in the cab. For a moment, he looked almost angry, before his inscrutable features subsided into better-veiled agitation.

"It is not aconitine poisoning."

"No? But how can you be sure?"

"Two of the valuables she abandoned according to her husband, the brooch and the hair ornament, could not possibly have been in prolonged contact with her skin."

"Holmes, as a doctor, I must report that she appears very ill indeed—did you note her flesh's peculiar tone?"

"My eyesight is remarkably keen, thank you."

"Well, perhaps some credence must be given her ailment."

"Oh, she is not at all well; it is simply not the fault of aconitine poisoning."

"Good heavens, then what is the matter with her? And can it be related to her gems after all?"

"Her condition and her jewelry are certainly related if my hypothesis is correct. But in order to confirm my diagnosis, Doctor, we must needs search her dressing room. Quick march!"

I hastened in the wake of Holmes's feline tread up the richly carpeted staircase, my every instinct screaming that we were acting out of character for defenders of the fair sex. What sort of chivalry could possibly call for such skulking about? My friend, meanwhile, climbed with his head thrown back and his slim shoulders rippling with energy, hot on the trail of something entirely opaque to me. Finally, I could no longer keep silent.

"Holmes, please tell me you're not about to break into Mrs. Treadwell's private letter box."

Holmes stopped in mid-stride, pivoting on the banister rail. "Can you really suppose I would do such a thing?" he asked, sounding genuinely surprised.

"I'm sorry, but I don't know quite what to suppose. Nor what we are doing."

"I've a rather dark suspicion I need to clear up, Watson."

"Regarding?"

"A very private matter."

"To do with that lovely woman's faithfulness to her lout of a husband?" I demanded.

"Ah, there's your mistake, Doctor," he returned in a much cooler tone. "You suppose us to be investigating the wrong Treadwell."

I tried to question him over this bizarre pronouncement, but my friend silenced me with an emphatic wave of dismissal as we crossed into Mrs. Treadwell's private bedchamber. Without an instant's qualm he traversed the pretty room, artfully furnished and brightened with subtly rose-patterned wall hangings, examining all he saw at astonishing speed. The decorations provided a definitive answer to the query I had posed to myself outside—Mrs. Alice Treadwell had indeed carved out a space for herself, for here I glimpsed no trace of the curt braggart with whom we had just spent a long, weary hour. The thought comforted me briefly. I left off idle speculation, however, when Holmes dived for her vanity table, opening the various drawers, his pale fingers dextrously searching amongst hairpins and creams.

After a few moments of eager search I could not call fumbling, so focused was it, he pulled out a small bottle. As he held it up to the light, the acute planes of his entire aquiline face darkened. The stifled fury I had but glimpsed downstairs was revealed when his teeth flashed; an instant later, the expression had vanished.

"What is it, Holmes?"

"Theatrical concealer," he answered. "A brand I've used myself. Confound it all! Pinpointing a single hornet in a swarming hive is simpler than making deductions based upon female habits. . . . But there is no blush in this drawer, and I can find no kohl either. That must account for something. Yes, yes, I fear there is no other explanation possible."

"She wasn't wearing kohl, or blush, or lip rouge," I added, quite at sea. "Or not that I could tell. But we both thought her unnaturally waxen. Do you now hypothesize that this means of masking blemishes was to blame for her pallor, rather than disease?"

"Oh, undoubtedly. This specific variety produces a porcelain-smooth finish but, lacking the warming effects of stage lights, can impart a masklike quality. I employed it to portray a consumptive, but that is a tale for another occasion."

"So why then would a woman who is obviously not seeking to artificially enhance her beauty own a bottle of concealer in the first place?"

"Very good, Watson," he said approvingly, though his voice was grave. "Ah, there is the teak box in question, on the nightstand. Is that where she's hidden it all, I wonder?"

"Hidden *what*, Holmes?"

"Mr. Treadwell!" my friend exclaimed, whirling round. His sharper ears had caught what mine had not: the sound of our client's footsteps upon the sage green carpet at the threshold of the bedchamber door.

"Confound it, I require *immediate* satisfaction!" Mr. Treadwell hissed. "You are *my* hirelings, do you understand me, and to take such liberties within my home—"

"We were just about to fetch you," Sherlock Holmes replied, unperturbed. "I wonder if we might be allowed a glimpse of your wife's neglected jewelry collection?"

"It's here." Mollified somewhat, Mr. Treadwell drew back a velvet curtain which skirted the bottom of a side table; he revealed a small safe and began working the combination. "Are you going to get that infernal letter box open and earn your twenty pounds, Mr. Holmes?"

"That may not prove necessary after all," Holmes replied. Mr. Treadwell swung the thick door of the tiny safe open and my friend descended to one knee, lifting one or two radiant trinkets and holding them under a lamp. "And this is the entire inventory?"

"Quite a tidy fortune, eh? And for what, I ask you? A fat lot of good they do me when escorting a bare-necked girl who seems straight from the raw countryside whenever I attend a social event." Mr. Treadwell scowled, passing a palm over his tawny hair. My friend seemed to have only cursory interest in the stones and their settings, for he passed them back and our churlish host locked the safe once more. "Come, be frank with me, I'm fattening your coffers enough. Now you've seen them, do you think my wife a liar, or do you suppose these precious trinkets poisoned?"

"Poisonous in nature, perhaps, but certainly not *poisoned.*"

"What in the name of the devil is that supposed to mean?" Mr. Treadwell snarled as both men rose to their full height.

"It means that you're in luck, and I've seen nearly everything I require," Holmes trilled. "Might I prevail upon you to assist me in a small experiment which would prove my theory conclusively?"

"And just how am I meant to assist you?"

"Is there a good fire built up in the sunroom opposite the parlor?"

I confess I must have looked equally as confounded as our client when presented with this bizarre question. Fluidly, and with assurances that Mr. Treadwell must trust that my friend's actions were absolutely essential, Holmes delivered his instructions. He and I were to interview Mrs. Treadwell in the parlor. Mr. Treadwell, meanwhile, was to find a set of rags to protect his hands, enter the sunroom, close the door behind him, and pull the damper tight shut, thereby stoking the flames into a fury. He was then to open the door, allowing the acrid plumes of smoke to flood the ground level.

I had already seen perhaps a dozen people regard my friend Sherlock Holmes as if he was in dire necessity of a strait-waistcoat, but never with such conviction as Mr. Treadwell.

"Allow me to explain, Mr. Treadwell," Holmes expounded, tenting his fingers and tapping his thumbs against each other. "You asked whether I thought the jewels poisoned or your spouse a liar without entertaining a third possibility, and the one which I find the most likely by *far.* Based upon the evidence to hand, I believe your wife to be a good and faithful woman who has the misfortune to be suffering from a virulent form of hysteria."

"Good heavens!" he boomed. "Can it be?"

"I am nearly beyond doubt it is so. When you correctly identified her symptoms, you mistakenly feared for her virtue when really, her brain was at fault. The inefficiency over household management, the depression, the irrational aversion to your tokens of affection, the morbid hypotheses—all this and more can be laid at the door of impending insanity. We must take swift action to save your wife, Mr. Treadwell. There is not a moment to be lost. Dr. Watson here is in complete agreement with me that the affliction is so far advanced, she is suffering from delusions, paranoia, and generalized mental degeneration."

I opened my mouth, but when the sole of Holmes's boot pressed meaningfully into my shoe leather, I shut it again.

"No, no, it's too terrible!" Mr. Treadwell exclaimed. "Oh, I can hardly credit the magnitude of my mistake. What a blunder I could have made! Dr. Watson, what a fortunate thing you were present to confirm Mr. Holmes's diagnosis."

"Yes, aren't you grateful he's here?" Holmes insisted. "The good doctor has more than earned his keep this morning, if you want my opinion. He has proved invaluable."

"Quite so, and I'll add ten pounds to your fee for it, gladly."

"I hardly think—" My mouth closed a second time when a renewed assault was made upon my toe.

"But whatever can this fireplace scheme have to do with hysteria?" Mr. Treadwell questioned avidly.

In a sweeping motion, Holmes indicated the surrounding townhouse. "When a woman believes her residence is aflame, she always races to retrieve her most valuable possession; but it is my belief that Mrs. Treadwell's raving and disordered mind will instruct her to save something entirely worthless. This will prove hysteria beyond the shadow of a doubt. But you will see the concrete proof of my conjecture only if you agree to this experiment."

"By Jove, if you should confirm it before my very eyes!" Mr. Treadwell gasped. "Little Alice hysterical, and I never noticed. What a relief! You've restored me with hope, I don't mind telling you. It's a hundredfold better than being made a cuckold of, gentlemen—not that I wish her sick, you understand. I'll hire the best of specialists."

"No doubt," I said frigidly.

"Shall we, then?" Holmes suggested, gesturing toward the door.

When we had hurried downstairs and Mr. Treadwell had vanished into the sunroom, I rounded on Holmes for the third time that day, determined to go no further.

"Mrs. Treadwell," I pronounced softly but clearly, "is no more hysterical than I am. What on earth do you mean by all of this?"

"I mean possibly to save her life," my friend hissed, wrapping his fingers about my wrist, and my breath caught when the fierce glow returned to his languid gaze. "If she imagines that her letter box is a safe hiding place, then she has made a grievous error—trust me, Dr. Watson, and do exactly as I say, I beg of you. I cannot state the matter urgently enough. If Mrs. Treadwell saves that letter box, I intend to devise an excuse to take it away from her."

It was not an unconflicted decision, for following Holmes's imperious orders in the midst of a tempest was not yet second nature to me; but nevertheless I did trust him, and so—with mind awhirl—I accompanied him back into the parlor, where Mrs. Alice Treadwell had exchanged her book for her sewing box. She swept her queerly blanched face up to ours, smiling timidly.

"We've nearly finished, but I wonder, madam, if you would be so good as to list any minor inconveniences about the house," Holmes requested courteously. "Items such as leaks in the roof, a cracked kitchen flagstone—it would be an immense help to us."

"Oh . . . I can do my best. There have been repairs made twice to the kitchen stove, and Cook still isn't satisfied with it. The shed in the back area is in a terrible state. We've thought of building a new one, but it never seemed to be the right time."

For several minutes, Mrs. Treadwell quietly listed household annoyances whilst Holmes and I listened attentively. Finally, when my already restless nerves were keyed to a positively tremulous pitch, I glanced behind me to see billows of smoke ballooning outward from the sunroom door. Mrs. Treadwell's eyes followed mine.

"Sweet God in heaven!" she gasped, leaping to her feet and spilling all the needlework scraps from her lap. "Help, gentlemen! Oh, do call for help!"

Mrs. Treadwell flew like a loosed arrow up the stairs. At the same moment, her husband's burly outline emerged from the ashen atmosphere; he was holding a kerchief over his face. His queer black eyes watched her go.

"That's not the look of a hysterical woman," he growled, muffling a cough. "She seems devilishly determined."

"Determined to save something of no value whatever!" Holmes volleyed over his shoulder, bounding up the stairs as we rushed after him. "Mark my words!"

When we reached the landing, we were met with the sight of Mrs. Treadwell, her pale face white as cream and her hands clutching her skirts, wrapping a long hooded mantle of wine-colored velvet about herself as she dashed out of her bedroom. There was no letter box in her hands, I noted with a rush of relief, though why I should have been relieved I did not know.

"It's a false alarm, madam," Holmes reported, holding out his palms reassuringly. "A harmless mistake about the damper in the sunroom fireplace."

"Thank God for that," Mrs. Treadwell murmured, swaying upon her small feet.

Quick as thinking, Holmes had her as lightly by the elbow as if she were composed of glass and was directing her back into her bedroom. He was gone only ten or twenty seconds and then appeared again, pulling the door shut behind, his spare bones galvanized like lightning rods and his deep-set grey eyes glittering mirrors in his chiseled face.

"Can you imagine a better demonstration of a hysterical mind, Mr. Holmes?" cried Mr. Treadwell. "She runs to the very room where she might have saved her jewels, or even her confounded letter box, and she retrieves a cloak, of all things. A *cloak*, when her house is burning. I am in your debt, sirs. Here is your thirty pounds, and gladly too."

Sherlock Holmes plucked the notes from his client's hand. Without another word, leaving me to make a confused and hasty farewell, he walked directly down the stairs, out the front door, and into the road to stand in the brightening March light, waving down a passing hansom. I could do nothing, I had already learned in such predicaments, save follow him.

"Holmes," I said, when we were clattering in a fresh cab along Prince of Wales Road, "whatever just happened, I feel I have done you a disservice. Will you accept my apology? Though all was dark to me, I ought not to have doubted your motives, and you would never force open a lady's letter box."

Holmes had his index finger over his thin lips, his elbow propped against the cab's window ledge. "I might, actually," he granted with a smile confined solely to the left edge of his mouth, "but I should need a thousand times better a reason."

"What on earth did all that signify? I understand nothing."

"But you sense the majority of it, I would wager. The main point was in the bottle of concealer hidden in the vanity drawer of a woman who wears no frivolous cosmetics. You may not have observed the very peculiar shadow at the edge of her jaw, but I am trained to see such things, even when I've no desire to. Her face was badly bruised, quite recently—and I do not imagine it will take you much consideration, Doctor, to pinpoint the man responsible, nor to marvel over the steps she takes to hide the foul liberties he visits upon her person."

"The cowardly villain!" I cried, anger flooding my limbs. "When I think of that sweet, helpless young lady—why, I ought to horsewhip the scoundrel. Holmes, we cannot take his money and simply—"

"You have leapt to more than enough conclusions this morning, my dear fellow, though they were all of them justified," Holmes interrupted me amiably. "I took the thirty pounds because that execrable cad's wife isn't having an affair and he thinks I proved it to him. I earned the money, did I not? Here is your tenner—no, no, you did your part, and I insist; not another word out of you. As for Mrs. Treadwell, she will doubtless tell us all about it herself whenever she slips out of the house and arrives at Baker Street, for I palmed her my card when I escorted her back to her room. She is to waste not an instant in coming to see us."

More relieved than I could say, I nodded. Folding the bank note, I continued to hesitate, staring at it, until Holmes fairly snorted and recrossed his legs in annoyance, pin-striped trousers flapping. It was a situation in which losing was preferable to winning, I concluded, and smiled reluctantly at him when I slipped it into my wallet.

"So it seems that you were right from the start. She truly is an honest woman," I mused, settling back against the seat.

"Haven't you been listening? There is no such thing," Holmes retorted.

"But—"

"I wanted to know *why* she was lying because I strongly suspected that her husband—one of the less acute examples of the species yet produced, I think you'll agree—was not apt enough to discern a very good paste copy of an item of jewelry from the genuine article. Of course she wouldn't wear them in public any longer! The accusations of poison were simply an outrageous pretext, and a clever pretext at that, one she could supplement with careful applications of the concealer she already kept for use during her darkest domestic hours. Her husband had no idea what to make of any of it and wandered the halls of his own home frustrated and perplexed for half a year."

"She has been pawning her collection?" I exclaimed.

"For these six months, yes. Do keep up, Watson! It was one thing to fool her spouse, but quite another to fool a room of eagle-eyed socialites. I can probably tell you ninety percent of the story, but let us instead await the arrival of Mrs. Treadwell herself, and the literal truth. Or as close as she'll come to it, that is."

My mind was in such turmoil by this time that I was more than happy to allow a silence to fall between myself and my impossibly contradictory fellow lodger. We reached Baker Street in due time and climbed the stairs in companionable quiet, stoking the white-skinned coals in our sitting room and calling for tea. It had just arrived when there came a strident ringing, a hurried exchange of female voices, and a tripping patter upon the stairs. When the door burst open without a knock, Mrs. Alice Treadwell appeared, her breath coming in rapid gusts and an unnatural flush along her cheekbones. She wore the identical hooded mantle she had fled to rescue earlier that morning.

"Mrs. Treadwell, please sit down," my friend hastened to say, leaping up and taking her elbow. "Watson, pour her some brandy, there's a good fellow."

Mrs. Treadwell collapsed into the armchair which I had gradually been growing to think of as "mine" as I hurried to bring her a glass of spirits.

"Mr. Holmes," she gasped. "So you are a detective. My husband has found me out, hasn't he?"

"Mr. Treadwell has found out nothing, but I should be grateful to know the facts of the matter in order to satisfy my own curiosity." My friend seated himself in his own chair while I took the settee. "Please do not feel as if you must speak of his foul treatment of you. We know your husband to be an unrepentant brute and hereby vow to do no further business with him save that which might serve to benefit yourself, madam—but what, if you will pardon my inquiring, took place six months ago?"

"Six months ago my parents, George and Mary Darlington, were taken from us," Mrs. Treadwell replied weakly. "I mean to say, from my sister and me. I ought not to think of it as a blessing—it's heathenish, altogether despicable. But my unmarried elder sister, Rose Darlington, who has always been my most kindred spirit, became a woman of independent means overnight. Lucien is so well off that naturally I myself inherited nothing despite my . . . unique situation."

"A situation which I despise to witness, I assure you. The day this great nation grants women such as yourself the ready means to escape the clutches of monsters like Lucien Treadwell, I shall personally fund a parade through Piccadilly Circus." Holmes's voice was a light purr, but I could see that he meant every word.

Her blush deepened. "May we both live to see it, Mr. Holmes. In any case, despite my having nothing of my own to offer in return, Rose pressed me in ardent language to flee from Lucien and take refuge with her. At the time, I was too frightened, I am ashamed to say. I locked that letter away, though I ought to have burned it. When Lucien tried to open the box and found it fastened, he was too proud to force the latch, but he took other measures—no, I do not desire your pity.

"But neither did I desire my sister's," she continued, fiercely blinking away the tears, "and so I determined to have some money to present to her if we were to spend our lives together. I could not look myself in the glass otherwise. I . . . I stole out of the house and had my jewelry copied, selling each original as soon as the paste was finished, making up a ridiculous story about poison in the hopes my husband would think me too irrational to do battle with any longer. Every womanly means at my disposal I employed to avoid him in the meanwhile—headaches, fatigue, fainting spells, ennui. I meant to rebuild my life as Alice Darlington once more. No doubt you both think me contemptible."

"Actually," I interjected warmly, "I think myself a fool for having doubted your innate resourcefulness."

"And I think you as formidable an opponent as ever I have faced, madam, though I confess that I harbor hopes we may instead form an alliance," Holmes announced gallantly.

She attempted a smile which broke nearly as soon as it formed. "Dare I hope that you will not tell Lucien everything, then? What is it you want from me?"

"I only wish to know how much capital you've sewn into the lining of that cloak."

The lady's fingers darted to her lips as she gasped. "I cannot imagine how you know that I . . . In any case, a considerable windfall. Nearly fifteen hundred pounds in notes."

"Mrs. Treadwell—Darlington, rather; forgive me—you must depart immediately." Holmes pulled down our Bradshaw. "There is a train to Brighton at two fourteen from Charing Cross. Do not wait for your wardrobe or your books or to bid farewell to your friends. Take your very important cloak and go directly to the train station from Baker Street. Ask Peterson, the commissionaire below, to accompany you, and I shall make certain he is paid for the journey. Come, your protests are quite useless, for I *will* see that you are safely ensconced on that train. I wish you all the best of luck. And I do beg your pardon. Regarding the false fire, which was my doing, I was worried about the suspicions attached to your letter box and hoped there were no valuables within—but happily, you are still cannier than I had supposed."

"I cannot claim to understand you completely, but I am very grateful. Please, I *must* reimburse you for your pains," she whispered.

"Oh, no, I should not like to grow greedy," said he, contentedly. "You see, I have already been paid twenty pounds."

The Darlington Substitution Scandal, as it came to be known a fortnight later when the entire truth came out in the society papers, was the pet freak of the popular press for no less than a full month. Mr. Treadwell, to our surprise and considerable amusement, stuck firmly by Holmes's claim that his wife was hysterical; he further argued that no sane man stood a chance against the workings of feminine guile. When my friend, who could barely suffer to hear Mr. Treadwell's name without a disgusted curl of his lip, half-tilted his head judiciously at this quotation, I was left to ponder the inexplicable dualities of human nature, a topic with which I am not fully reconciled even to this day.

The Adventure of
the Beggar's Feast

It was my habit when I lived with my friend Sherlock Holmes in our suite of rooms in Baker Street, during the season of grey winds and charitable spirits, to volunteer a portion of my time working at hospital. Two afternoons in the week I would bundle myself warmly and take myself off to Barts, there to assist the surgeons and other medical personnel with whatever overflow of duties my training as a general practitioner and my brief military experience allowed. The staff grew accustomed to my presence as a locum there, and though my duties were difficult, they were never dull, for one session might find me setting all the broken limbs inflicted by a carriage accident, and the next tending to the victims of another unhappy bout of smallpox or influenza in one of the many slums cloistered in forgotten corners of our sprawling city.

On one such early evening late in December of the year 1887, I stood at the end of a ward devoted to accidental injuries hurriedly repacking my clean instruments in my leather medical bag, wondering just how put out Holmes would be if I arrived late for a string quartet recital at St. James's Hall. To my considerable surprise, the man himself appeared strolling in my direction seconds later, swinging his stick, his tall, thin form seeming even taller and thinner in the faint, slanting light from beyond the distant door.

"I'm just finishing. However did you find me in this maze?" I asked him. Holmes knew his own way around Barts, for he had conducted extensive chemical researches there, but that did not explain his discovering my whereabouts.

"Simplicity itself, my dear fellow: know thy best resources." He spun his cane against the polished floor and caught it up just as it began to topple. "It is a farcical blunder to act alone when assistance could halve the time required."

Laughing, I asked, "And who assisted you, then?"

"I'd made up my mind to consult the likeliest expert regarding the comings and goings within this anthill, and the third nurse I passed in the front hall sent me straight to you. It's an easy matter to tell which of the caretakers has her finger on the pulse of the establishment, so to speak—she is invariably both the weariest-seeming and paradoxically the neatest. This one obviously had not slept in over twenty hours, but there wasn't so much as a speck marring her nail beds. Such women have a marked tendency to know absolutely everything."

"Now you mention it, I could have told you as much myself."

"Yes, that's all well and good, Watson, but I mentioned it first," he admonished me severely, and I could not help chuckling again.

"All right, all right." I snapped my bag shut. "What's the time?"

"Four forty-seven by my watch. I've a cab outside, always provided you are through with philanthropy for the day and are ready for Haydn."

We were making for the door when a pair of orderlies with a nurse entered, wheeling another unfortunate victim of misadventure lying upon a stretcher. The slim, fashionably dressed young man had clearly suffered a severe head injury, for his brow was cocooned in considerable bandaging. While he seemed careworn—from excess of leisure or excess of woes I could not say—he was certainly under five and twenty years of age. My reaction upon glimpsing him was typical of both the seasoned medico and the veteran of the battlefield; while I wished him every chance at a swift recovery, a colleague of mine had clearly already done all he could, and so since the patient was resting quietly, by instinct I paid him no more mind than I would a hale soldier on patrol. I had already stepped around the gurney when Holmes stopped in his tracks.

"What's happened to this poor fellow?" he asked in his blandest, most ingratiating tone.

When the nurse—a charming and capable young woman by the name of Caric—saw that Holmes was with me, her stern face relaxed into her natural expression. "We hardly know, sir. Poor soul. He's been robbed, that much is certain, for there's nothing on his person to identify who he might be, and no money or valuables either. An ostler found him down by the river in Blackfriars, and called for a constable."

"And did the ostler arrive too late to see what had happened? Or had he glimpsed signs of a struggle and interfered in a more timely fashion?"

"It's all right, Nurse Caric," I assured her when her glinting brown eyes narrowed again, although I confess I was equally mystified by Holmes's keen interest. "This is my friend Mr. Sherlock Holmes, whose area of expertise is the detection of crime."

She seemed marginally mollified, but her hand remained protectively upon the sheet covering her charge. "I suppose it's all right, then, Doctor. The physician who treated him spoke with both the ostler and the constable when he was brought in, and I was with them. No fight was interrupted—the damage had already been done when he was discovered."

"Excuse me, but where was this precisely?" Holmes asked.

"In a narrow corridor off Pageantmaster Court, sir."

"Excellent. Do go on."

"I was saying that the fight was already finished," she continued with more visible impatience. "But it seems that when the ostler found him lying on the ground, he spied another man peering from the other end of the alleyway. That man was most revolting in appearance, he said—he'd long, matted hair of yellowish grey, his back was hunched, his face was coarse with a terribly crooked broken nose, and he was dressed in the foulest rags the ostler had ever seen. But when the ostler cried out to him, the man disappeared, and the ostler thought it best to stay with the injured gentleman and call for help rather than chase after a beggar who may have had nothing to do with the assault. The ostler was a most reliable, steady sort, if you want my opinion, and if you don't, the constable who left not half an hour ago shared it."

"Oh, I should a thousand times rather solicit your opinion than a constable's, Nurse Caric. The large number of hair follicles escaping your cap indicates that you have been on shift for over twelve hours, as is supported by the demarcations beneath your eyes, and yet despite the fact you have been hard at work—your hands, you see, are quite pink from repeated scrubbings—your apron is spotless, which indicates you must have changed it. Twice, I think, though I cannot be certain. Your opinion is invaluable, I assure you."

"Yes, I've changed my apron twice. But . . ." When Nurse Caric frowned, she wisely directed the expression at me rather than my companion.

"It was a compliment," I explained. "He . . . Never mind him. Can you tell us anything further?"

Smoothing down her fresh apron, she shook her head. "It's a common enough occurrence, Doctor. A man walks into an alley and doesn't walk out again. . . . If there truly were good angels watching over us, the least they could do would be to warn of such dangers. Leastaways, that's what I think, and I don't care who knows it. Pray God he awakens soon and knows himself when he does, for otherwise we've no chance of tracing anyone he loves to comfort him."

I nodded soberly. As Nurse Caric spoke, the orderlies wheeled the white-faced unconscious gentleman into a bare, curtained alcove. When the nurse departed in search of a clean hospital gown to replace his soiled finery, I followed after her for two paces before I realized that Holmes remained firmly in place, staring with eyes like his fencing foils at the anonymous assault victim.

"Holmes," I ventured, "the cab downstairs—"

"I wonder, Watson," my friend declared, putting his index finger over his lips and rocking back on his heels in thought.

"I can see that. What do you wonder about, I wonder?"

"I wonder why this person is not wearing his own clothing."

Stepping back to the gurney, I looked him over, thoroughly bemused; I could see no indications whatsoever pointing to borrowed attire, though I noted many signs he had suffered a thorough trouncing and been left in the filth of a dank passage. The young man wore the finest-quality woolen trousers. His waistcoat was done in rich, dark green velvet with polished mother-of-pearl buttons, his disheveled black silk cravat was of the most expensive cloth, and his superbly cut frock coat proved to be lined with navy satin when I pulled back the lapel.

"Why on earth do you say it isn't his clothing?"

"The cuffs of his shirtsleeve."

I peered down at them; they were greatly muddied, but they fitted the unlucky boy perfectly well.

"No, not the fit. The second hole. They've been threaded with cuff links more widely apart in the past, and now someone has pierced straight through the celluloid again. You don't mean to tell me that a man who can afford such togs has somehow lost two inches in circumference from his wrist and then not bothered to purchase himself new cuffs?"

Rubbing his slender hands together, Holmes rounded the makeshift bed, his eyes never leaving the hospital's latest unfortunate admission. I had seldom seen him so enamored of a puzzle. "I might add that the trousers fit, but the knee break is in the wrong place by a full two inches—always study the knees, my dear fellow; if I've told you once, I've told you a score of times. And a costly waistcoat with that strange pucker near the lowest rib would certainly have caused an argument between me and my tailor, were I in this lad's shoes—or rather, whoever's shoes these are. But in any case, he could never have afforded any of it, begging for a living on the streets as he does."

At my expression of frank shock, Holmes leaned down to loosen the patient's collar and gently finished removing his unpinned cravat. As he did so, I began to suspect that I too could glean conclusions from the evidence at hand, for something before me was not right—but just as was the case regarding the efficacy of nurses, it ultimately required Sherlock Holmes to articulate what I could only sense.

"You see what I see, but what do you conclude from it?"

"I cannot think."

"No, no, of course you can, you are simply unpracticed at taking mental leaps into the void. Shall I state the hypothesis as I view it, then?"

"Please do."

"The lad is a beggar, I said. I know it because these marks of grime are not the results of a street brawl—they continue underneath his clothing. He was this filthy before the tussle, not just afterward. And witness his hands."

My friend lifted one of them for my closer inspection. The appendage was callused in several places, but the most peculiar thing about it was its fingertips. They bore evidence of having been moderately frostbitten, the phalanges revealing several small healed-over vesicles and also older marks which seemed to me evidence of still worse hemorrhagic blistering. As a doctor, I knew well enough what I was looking at—and yet, I had never seen such queer successive evidence of having habitually frozen one's flesh before.

"This is a common affliction, but solely among a particular set. The only men and women I have ever encountered with hands like these are those who work the shallow," Holmes explained clinically, returning the unknown man's limb to the bedsheets.

"I beg your pardon?"

"Apologies, but the street language of thieves' cant invents appellations for practices that civilized English would prefer to ignore altogether, so on occasion my terminology cannot help but devolve into slang. 'Working the shallow' is a form of begging, not unlike a scaldrum dodge."

"Defining a term by means of another term I equally cannot parse seems an inefficient way of explaining it to me."

"What a logical remonstrance, my dear Watson!"

"Yes, it was."

My friend's lips quivered, settling into a self-depreciating smile. "In a scaldrum dodge, the mendicants self-administer injuries in order to appear more pitiful to potential benefactors. Cuts, bruises, abrasions, worse—when pleading for the odd charitable coin, a missing hand could mean the difference between starvation and sympathy."

"Holmes, do you mean to tell me that there are those who would prefer to lose a limb than—"

"Than a life?" He raised expressive brows, momentarily looking up from the supine figure.

Sighing, I pulled at a taut muscle in my shoulder. "Go on."

"Working the shallow, on the other hand, means begging in the dead of winter without proper clothing—as a deliberate strategy, mind—and the fewer garments they can get away with, the more money they are apt to take in. The amateurs attempt going without coats, while the most extreme practitioners bare themselves to the elements, pretending to have seconds previous pawned their last shirt and the like. So long as public decency is at least partially maintained, they will stop at nothing to appear penniless. We don't see such desperation in the vicinity of Baker Street, but I've witnessed it plentiful times in Whitechapel and St. Giles, to name but two neighborhoods, and likewise in far too many others to list."

"And I, in India. The poor wretches risk their health to do such a thing."

"The most daring of them risk everything." My friend had commenced searching extensively through the young man's garments, tucking his fingers into pockets and unbuttoning the extravagant waistcoat to search for hidden pouches. "If I'm right, and that is his trade, he wasn't robbed of his identification at all—he simply had nothing of value on his person to steal, apart from the tiepin. The clothes would have garnered a tidy profit in a pawn shop, but ripping a man's vestments from his body is not a crime to be enacted on a public street. Our hapless passersby are generally lured indoors if they're to be stripped entirely. No, our thief was impulsive, in the market for small treasures easily carried off. A watch, a wallet, a coin purse, a ring—save for the tiepin, our man was destined for disappointment, however."

"Holmes, *what* tiepin?"

"This cravat has a recent pinprick in it but no actual jewelry."

"The missing tiepin, then," I conceded, smiling even as I shook my head.

"Quite so. Ah, here we are."

Holmes pulled a thin scrap of paper from an inner waistcoat pocket and unfolded it, passing it to me after he had made a comprehensive inspection. It was a receipt from a furniture warehouse.

"The true owner of the waistcoat just bought himself a large curio case, whoever he is," I said, returning the small document to Holmes. "There is no name, though, and no delivery address—only information regarding the vendor. Small wonder the policeman overlooked it."

"Small wonder, and also every reason why he will fail to identify either the victim or the culprit," my friend snorted, replacing the evidence with due care.

"Holmes," I remarked, "we aren't going to a Haydn concert, are we?"

He gave me an innocent glance, an expression which on Sherlock Holmes looks like two parts surprise and one part mild injury. It was not an expression which, by the year 1887, fooled me in the smallest degree.

"The tickets are in my coat pocket, my dear fellow, and if music is your pleasure, we'll be rattling down the Strand toward Piccadilly within mere moments. Of course, this furniture warehouse *does* happen to be located in Blackfriars, on Gardner's Lane and High Timber Street, not far from where this unfortunate chap was attacked and left for dead."

I placed my hat on my head and picked up my bag. "Then we had better pay it a call, had we not?"

Holmes fairly grinned at me in agreement, tossed his stick and caught it again, and strode back in the direction of the Great Hall. We hastened down the staircase and out into the central courtyard, the garden a wash of sere winter tones, the grasses robbed of all moisture, and the fountain frosted over with ice. By some miracle, my friend's cab was still waiting for him, the driver muffled under a wealth of blankets and mist emerging from the impatient horse's nose.

When we alighted some ten minutes later in Blackfriars, the sun was swiftly quickening its descent into the great dun-colored river, plunging like a fallen phoenix. The apothecaries were pulling down the shades behind their polished glass windows, and the pubs, with their lambent yellow fires, were beginning to glow all the brighter for the gloom, like scattered lighthouses in a sea of bluish-grey. It was that almost mystical time that is neither day nor night, the earth tipping into dusk, and I confess that I thrilled at the chance to be pursuing an unexpected case rather than whiling away our evening being passively entertained. Holmes had walked half a block farther toward the river with his silk hat pulled low over his brow when his hand suddenly caught my elbow.

"Keep walking," he murmured. "But pull out your watch and glance discreetly across the street as if you're ascertaining how long it will take to arrive at your destination. Then look immediately back down at the time."

Settling my features into a blank, I did as he said and cast my gaze across the thoroughfare. One of the oddest creatures I have ever seen in all my travels approached us on the other side of the road, and my spine tingled when I recognized him by description. His stature was slight, his shoulders were rounded, his back was humped, and his gait was halfway between a lurch and a shuffle. He wore clothing of the filthiest repugnance, the sort of rotting and fetid garments draped over the skeletal limbs of the scavengers who drag the Thames for salable garbage or descend into the sewer system to dredge for lost coins—full of holes, hanging like so much tangled moss from his frame.

All of these foul characteristics were as nothing, however, compared with the unhappy man's face; his dirty grey hair hung in unevenly tangled knots around a visage which must initially have been loathsome, lumpen and coarse as it looked, but which was not assisted by a nose that had been badly broken many years previous, giving his vulture's countenance a smashed effect.

My friend's pace never varied, and it was not until we had rounded the corner that Holmes abruptly stopped and whirled about again, resting his fingers lightly against the brick edge of the building as he watched.

"This is the furniture warehouse in question," he informed me over his shoulder.

"But Holmes, surely we can postpone that visit—if Nurse Caric is to be believed, doubtless here is the very man who may have seen the well-dressed beggar attacked."

"She is absolutely to be believed." My friend paused. "Is that what you plan to call it when all is over and you convert fact to melodrama? 'The Adventure of the Well-Dressed Beggar' or some similar rubbish?"

"You need not presume to have already solved it," I returned, perhaps with rather more pique than was necessary.

Holmes only regarded me with an eyebrow cocked and his mouth quirked into an aloof smile. "Touché, Watson. Take off your coat and your scarf," he instructed me imperiously, unwrapping his muffler and pulling his arms out of his own greatcoat as he did so.

Reluctantly, I complied. When Holmes handed me his coat, I understood better what he intended and offered him my own. My tall friend's cape-backed topcoat of black wool hung far below my knees, giving me a disreputable air; Holmes, conversely, on the instant he had donned my brown tweed, I found to be inexplicably six inches shorter than he had been before, and I laughed in spite of myself.

"No longer John Watson and Sherlock Holmes, then," I surmised.

"No, I'm afraid those chaps wouldn't suit just now, as admirable as they are. Now, follow me and do exactly as I do."

When Holmes gained the opposite curb and joined the small stream of pedestrians, our subject had progressed a full block ahead of us. My friend selected a man who traveled at a brisk speed and fell into place directly behind him, his grey eyes locked blankly on our quarry over the stranger's shoulder, as if unseeing and lost in thought. Before long, I had fallen into step behind my own shield, copying as best I could Holmes's air of weary impatience to arrive at his destination.

Doubtless my excitement was more visible than his, however, for Holmes had somehow retreated entirely within himself, and the man who under normal circumstances garnered furtive stares from strangers thanks to his remarkable appearance was now no more noticed than a crack in the cobblestones. His disguise was not properly a disguise at all—merely my own coat and a bowed gait which rendered him the same size as mere mortals—and yet his alteration was entire, and I could only reflect, as indeed did many of our friends from the Yard, that had Holmes wished to travel the world with the hot metal aroma of footlights ever in his nostrils, he would have been loudly applauded across the continents. It is a peculiarity inherent to my friend's reserved nature, however, that while honest admiration from his sole companion and few esteemed colleagues can actually cause the man to blush, acclaim from the public falls upon wholly deaf ears, so perhaps after all Sherlock Holmes had chosen the profession which suited him best.

After traversing a few blocks, passing by greengrocers and newsstands and shipping offices, the remarkably ugly man descended a series of steps into a pub called The Blind Elephant, with gaslights held in iron brackets hanging from either side of its entrance. Without blinking an eye, my friend likewise marched down the steps and opened the door of the tavern, and a rush of warm, ale-scented air passed over us as we entered.

"At last!" the detective exclaimed eagerly. "The best house ale this side of London Bridge, my dear chap, or I am no judge—Perkins positively swears by the place, and by Jove, now I can see the reason."

All eyes went to Holmes, and then all eyes immediately slid off him again, just as he intended—for in a crowded metropolis, there is no way to skirt attention more effectively than by demanding it. Our surroundings were certainly cozy, for The Blind Elephant was equipped with secondhand club furnishings, so rather than the rough benches and rickety stools typical of such an establishment, Holmes and I sank into faded, scratched leather armchairs, each with a glass of passable porter in his hand.

The hideous figure we had been pursuing, meanwhile, returned to urgent conversation with the bartender just after our drinks had been poured. The proprietor was a short, swarthy, balding fellow with his scant dark hair slicked over his head. His attention to the beggarly man was complete—indeed, deeply sympathetic—and I marveled that such a low figure could command such seeming respect. Holmes was similarly puzzled, and while he appeared to focus on sipping his beer, his blank expression was enough to tell me that he was riveted to the exchange taking place.

"My men have been on it these two hours," the barman said soothingly. "Come now, Mr. Marwick. It's not right to see you take on so when you've done no 'arm to anyone. I've Scott Monty on the prowl, and Leatherfinger Jim as well. 'E's not likely to escape our clutches."

"But if he should get away entirely!" gasped the malformed creature, clutching a glass of brown spirits. His voice was as unappealing as the rest of him—a strange mixture of rasp and whine that scraped the ears. "Oh, Mr. Piccone, I would never recover from it. What use has my life been if this deed goes unpunished? I tell you that I would simply expire."

"Drink up, now, Mr. Marwick," Mr. Piccone suggested, again lending to the remark an air of deference which I could not begin to fathom.

Mr. Marwick took a sip of what looked like whiskey, but his palsied hand spilled half of it on the tabletop. Mr. Piccone clucked paternally, as only excellent barkeepers can, and wiped up the spill as if it had been his own fault. Then he replaced what had been lost and settled with his elbows upon the bar before his repugnant customer, awaiting further discourse.

"All of this is my accursed doing," groaned Mr. Marwick. "When I have my hands on him, I'll—"

"You'll nothing. Leave it to Monty and Leatherfinger—you know they won't take long once they've run him to ground. 'Ave a speck of patience, Mr. Marwick, only a speck, and all will come right. I promise. Take another sip, and then off 'ome with you, sir."

"I wouldn't be able to bear the sight of the place, I tell you—"

"None of that! No indeed. I'll 'ave none of it, and there's gospel in your ear. You've a dinner to oversee. Trust me. I know what's best to be done."

Mr. Marwick finished the drink by holding the tumbler with both his hands. Then, nodding gratefully to the bartender without paying him a cent, he picked up his cane and staggered off.

Holmes was dropping coins on the bar before I had got to my feet, and twenty more seconds saw us outside again, shivering at the wind. I ducked my head, and we ghosted along after the strangely riveting Mr. Marwick. While Holmes yet maintained the pretense of distraction, I could not compel my own eyes to shift from our remarkable quarry, and so gave it up after two blocks as a bad job. To my surprise, he seemed to be leading us directly back to our initial destination. Upon reaching the door of the furniture warehouse, Mr. Marwick scowled at a piece of trash and kicked it off the shallow single step, and then drew out a large key. Upon either side of the wide entrance there were iron railings, one of which he stopped to polish with his stained pocket handkerchief. Then he opened the door and went inside.

"By Jove, he owns the place," my friend exclaimed softly. "I have never seen anyone behave in a more custodial manner in my life."

"You noted, of course, that the barman gave him every courtesy."

"Obviously, yes—it perplexed me for a moment, but now that I have more data, the situation reveals itself without much work required on my part. He could not have been anyone *excepting* the warehouse's owner. I ought to have expected as much, when his walking stick was considered."

"His walking stick, Holmes?"

"Watson, I've some suspicion as to who this altogether odd chap is. Should you like your coat back? I confess that taking this many inches off my own height can be taxing when I haven't mentally prepared for it—one stretches extensively, then resigns oneself to temporary agony, and the like. In any case, I rather think that Sherlock Holmes and John Watson will fill the bill perfectly."

With that remark, Holmes appeared to consider concealment no longer of any use to us, and we quickly exchanged outer garments. My friend then promptly walked to the door Mr. Marwick had entered and pressed the bell.

A sliding panel whipped open, and a pair of rheumy, unlovely eyes glared out at us.

"We've closed shop for the night," grated Mr. Marwick's strident voice.

"We're particularly interested in purchasing a curio case, Mr. Marwick," my friend returned tranquilly.

After a blink, what we could see of the man's face contorted into a scowl. "I say that we're *closed*, confound it! Look elsewhere. Good day!"

"But we are particularly interested in *your* curio cases, you understand."

"The devil take you! What can the likes of you know of curio cases?"

"Mr. Marwick, I assure you that I intend the Amateur Mendicant Society no harm whatsoever. My sole interest is in assisting the patient of my medical friend here, and we know that—"

"You know nothing!" the little figure in the window panel screamed viciously. Two unsteady fists banged upon the inner doorframe and then ground into anguished eye sockets. "There is *no such thing* as the Amateur—"

"Perhaps if I were to introduce myself: I happen to be the employer of a group of street children known as the Baker Street Irregulars. My name is Sherlock Holmes."

The portal snapped shut. Off went the clumsy footsteps, and back they returned accompanied by the faint rattling of keys. When Mr. Marwick opened the door, he gestured at us to enter with an awkward flailing of his arm.

Even if Holmes knew by this point with whom we were dealing, I had not an inkling, and so took in my surroundings rather than ask potentially damaging queries. As a warehouse, the space was organized very poorly indeed: cobwebs and grime covered the major pieces of furniture, while smaller items sat huddled in unappealing clumps, many shrouded beneath cheap linens. An aroma of dust and mildew permeated the place, and the floor did not appear to have been swept at any point during the previous decade. The wide room conveyed the impression of complete dereliction, a graveyard for housewares rather than a display of them. I did not pity those forced to do business there, but I hereby confess I did not envy them either. Additionally, Mr. Marwick did not add any special felicity to the atmosphere, for the hideous fellow still seemed furious at our interruption—although now furious as well as inclined to discourse.

"What's this now? I've heard rumor of your boys. You're truly Sherlock Holmes?"

"The very same, and at your service," the detective assented. "This is my friend and colleague Dr. Watson, whose medical skills are often made use of by St. Bartholomew's Hospital."

"Is Jeremy all right?" Mr. Marwick demanded to know of me next, clutching at my coat sleeve.

"When I left him, nothing indicated to me that his condition had grown at all unstable," I answered. "He is resting, his injuries have been seen to, and while I did not tend to them myself, I'm confident my colleague did all he could."

"Well, that's something, then. It's not much, but it's something. Oh, what a wretched day. If you're Sherlock Holmes, I suppose you know all of it by now," he accused my friend scornfully.

"I can make a confident and educated surmise, nothing more. I presume the young man . . . Jeremy, did you say?"

"Jeremy Kitchen."

"Mr. Kitchen, then, was mistaken by street thugs for a rich gentleman and—"

"Wrong. That's the worst of it," our host snarled through a clenched jaw. "He wasn't mistaken for a rich man at all. But since you probably know everything else, I suppose I would do better to show than to tell you."

"You are hosting the annual dinner tonight, then?" Holmes inquired, a silvery thread of suppressed excitement in his tone.

Mr. Marwick nodded. "If you both will vow to reveal nothing of what you've seen here to any living soul, I'll show it to you, though I have never done such a thing in ten long years. If it were not for your

Irregulars, I should not even consider it, but their existence inspires me to trust you. Do I have your word that you will protect my secret?"

When Holmes had given his promise, I readily agreed despite my perplexity, and the three of us walked to the back of the warehouse, entering a smaller room within a great open space that must have once been an office, but now appeared simply a repository for crumbling yellowed papers. A sharply descending staircase was revealed at the back of this chamber, its metal steps and rails spiraling downward, and on the subterranean level, we found ourselves in a hallway lined with more unclaimed furnishings. Mr. Marwick reached behind a featureless bookshelf, and with the smallest click of a concealed lever, it swung to and revealed itself a doorway.

"My God," I breathed.

"I never imagined I'd see it in person," Holmes added softly. "Thank you for your confidence, Mr. Marwick. This is truly an unlooked-for pleasure."

The spacious room we entered, quite as long as the warehouse above us and filled with the happy sounds produced by flowing wine and rollicking cheer, was unmatched for opulence against any I have ever heard report of in England. It was walled in alternating dark carved rosewood and panels of mirror, while above our heads six enormous matched chandeliers blazed forth like small suns. I could spy no servants, but on every surface were heaped the most sumptuous presentations of food: mountains of cakes and jellies, piles of fine cheeses and cold meats, all the fruit it was possible to procure in the middle of winter, seemingly limitless crystal glasses of champagne.

And the people! Such elegance I had never before seen amassed in a single congregation, nor have I witnessed a gathering where the guests seemed to be enjoying themselves and each other more. Every attendee was bedecked in silk, velvet, and lace, and on every face a giddy smile shone forth. Then, with a comprehensive start of understanding, I noticed that a man a few yards distant from me had not shaved in months or perhaps even years, and that another neighbor was missing the farthest joints of three of his fingers, very probably owing to their having been severely frostbitten.

"We'll walk on through," muttered Mr. Marwick. "They know nothing of who I am, Mr. Holmes."

The opposite side of the sumptuous gallery featured a second door, and we exited through it, passing a guard who made a small bow to Mr. Marwick. Here the tunnel seemed to stretch far into the distance, lit all the way by wall sconces.

"There is one guard at the basement's inner door and one at the ground-floor outer," said Mr. Marwick. "The mendicants' entrance, you see, is through a service gate at the opposite end of the warehouse, the part which generally serves as a scrap yard. You, Mr. Holmes, have somehow managed to set eyes upon this year's ticket, and thereby discovered my address. I assume Jeremy had it on his person?"

"Exactly. The receipt for the curio case was in Mr. Kitchen's inner pocket."

Our host led us down the gently sloping corridor until we reached another door, this one quite plain. When we had all taken seats in comfortable armchairs in what appeared to be Mr. Marwick's actual office, the fire blazing, no one seemed willing to speak at first. Sherlock Holmes, as was usual, took the lead.

"The impoverished boys I pay to be my eyes and ears first told me of the beggars' feast several years ago," my friend informed us in a careful tone. "One was very proud when he discovered it was called the Annual Meeting of the Amateur Mendicant Society, for details surrounding the affair seemed a zealously kept secret."

"So they have been, until today," Mr. Marwick confirmed ruefully. "Those who had attended were encouraged to speak of it in the wildest terms, as a legend no more plausible than a pot of leprechaun gold."

"The tickets granting one entrance to the event—the curio case receipt, in this instance, with the warehouse's address plainly printed—were disseminated only to beggars. Beyond that, all my boys could agree upon was that it was a pauper's only chance to attend a banquet fit for a king and be dressed free of charge for the occasion, and also that none of them knew the identity of their annual host."

"Their host is one Mr. Cowderoy Marwick," the man who seemed the lowest of all beggars sniffed. "And they will never know it. Never. I have a single confidant, and that is Mr. Piccone, who owns a tavern down the street. The rest suppose I am merely a vendor of used furnishings, though to be frank with you, no one ever buys anything, as I've deliberately made the ground floor as inhospitable as possible. They also know me as a former tailor who is paid to perform their fittings for the soiree; I've amassed a large stock of attire in the dressing rooms below the warehouse. That occupation allows me to drop mysterious hints regarding the 'true' organizer of the feast, you understand, and so is ultimately quite useful as regards misdirection. Now, sir, tell me what you believe to have happened today."

Holmes cocked his dark head in thought. "You have already corrected me on that count—the reason Mr. Kitchen was attacked was not that he was presumed wealthy. But I believe I am right in saying he arrived at the warehouse, perhaps for a fitting, earlier this afternoon?"

Mr. Marwick flinched. "Yes."

"I presume you make it a hard-and-fast rule no one is ever to depart the premises while wearing the garments, for fear of assault? But Mr. Kitchen was . . . lured away somehow?"

"His equally impoverished lady love had come by a ticket, but thought it fanciful nonsense and had no intention of coming."

"Ah. Mr. Kitchen wanted to persuade her that the feast was real, lest she throw away a singular opportunity. What could convince her faster than to show her his attire? I fear you will have to enlighten me as to the rest."

"I have it on the best authority—that of a street Arab, and you know as well as I do, Mr. Holmes, that I mean nothing ironical in that statement—that Jeremy was attacked by the resident ruffian in this neighborhood, a homeless brute who resents the fact that despite his swagger and bluster, he has never been issued an invitation," Mr.

Marwick said in a tone of deepest grief. His voice had somehow become less abrasive than previously, or perhaps it simply grew more pleasant to the ear over time. "His name is Tom Scripps. We believe that when he saw Jeremy's clothing, he at once surmised that he would be a guest that night and took his revenge, stealing the diamond tiepin I had lent only as an afterthought. I pursued the foolish boy the moment I knew he was gone, but arrived too late. When I was discovered at the scene by the policeman, I admit that panic possessed me and I fled, although rage was not far behindhand. Thanks to my appearance, I am not always treated well by the constables making their rounds, you understand, and do my utmost to avoid them."

We were all silent for several moments. Then Holmes asked, "What actions have you taken, then, save for enlisting local aid to hunt for the guilty party?"

"I'll not ask how you knew that, for by all accounts, you know practically everything. Yes, Mr. Piccone has roused associates to run this villain down. It was the final straw, Mr. Holmes—Tom Scripps has bullied and bloodied quite enough of his fellow mendicants. He beats them for sport, steals their earnings. No act is too low for the blackguard. I cannot say what precisely Mr. Piccone's men intend, save that I gave explicit instructions Scripps should be ejected from the area and not harmed in any lasting fashion—but I could think of nothing else to do. Vigilantism is abhorrent to me, but bearing in mind a penniless child was the only witness, I fear formal charges would never hold up in court."

My friend sat forward in his chair, pressing his fingertips together before his aquiline nose. "Mr. Marwick, while I understand that we are acquainted solely by virtue of reputation, I wonder if you would consent to engage my services in this matter. Allow me to speak with Mr. Piccone, and I swear to you I shall watch this Tom Scripps so doggedly that an ironclad conviction—although perhaps for another crime, I grant—will be ours within the week. Surely it would be better for me to introduce the scoundrel to a stint at hard labor than for your associates to carry any sort of retaliatory violence upon their own consciences, and I assure you that for my part, nothing could be simpler."

Mr. Marwick's features gradually softened. "Why would you do such a thing?"

"It is a charitable season of the year," my friend pointed out with studied nonchalance. "And I would require in return that when you assemble your next feast's guest list, you allow me to make a few of my own small nominations. They may be a trifle younger than your usual attendees, but I can vouch without qualm for their characters, if not their cleanliness."

"How many are 'a few small nominations,' precisely?" Mr. Marwick asked shrewdly.

"Oh, heavens, certainly not more than a dozen Irregulars at the most," Holmes returned with aplomb. "Some of them *very* small indeed, though I readily admit you'd not know it by their appetites. Look to young Peaches particularly—he's not yet eight and could single-handedly dispatch Buckingham Palace's larder, I shouldn't wonder."

It required Mr. Marwick a few moments' thought before he reached a conclusion, and when he did, he simply rose and shook my friend by the hand.

"Capital!" the detective exclaimed. "The bargain is struck, Mr. Marwick. By week's end, you may expect to hear of Tom Scripps's relocation to the dock."

Holmes and I were turning to go when a question stopped us.

"But tell me, Mr. Holmes—how could you have known when you first knocked at my door that I, of all people, was the founder of the Amateur Mendicant Society? I have lived like this for so long, I thought myself beyond suspicion for a millionaire."

"You've St. Alexius's name inscribed upon your walking stick—which is a remarkably fine one, I might add," my friend replied readily. "Forgive me, Mr. Marwick, but might I ask why you would dispose of your fortune in such a strange fashion?"

"I'm the last Marwick, Mr. Holmes," the grotesquely compelling man responded. "I have no one left in this dark world to gift with an inheritance. In any event, the entire Marwick estate was built upon the very profitable alliance between rum and African slaves, and for that matter has never done me a single particle of good in all my life. I've given away a quarter of a million to various causes so far, Mr. Holmes, most of them quite conventional. But—before tonight's tragedy, of course—I've never seen anything I've done bring the impoverished as much joy as the Amateur Mendicant Society. The highest honor I can grant myself is that I managed to think of it in the first place."

"My dear Holmes," I said once we had regained the street, and the gas lamps had spread into pools of warmth brightening the winter's frosted air, "I have never been more gratified to have missed a Haydn concert. And that was very good of you."

He waved one hand companionably at me while searching out his cigarette case with the other.

"But please do tell me, who is St. Alexius, and how on earth do you know of him?"

"The Irregulars informed me that the dinner's final toast, or so they had heard, was lifted in honor of St. Alexius." My friend smiled. "I'd never heard of him either, but I did a little research and soon had my answer. St. Alexius was the only son of an extravagantly wealthy Roman senator, and he fled his privileged existence to live in the most austere poverty. I freely confess to you that I had supposed his kind had passed out of the world long ago. But on occasion, there is nothing more congenial than being proved entirely wrong. Let's you and I make a stop at Marcini's for a hot meal after we've spoken with Mr. Piccone, my dear fellow, for I believe the coming week will see me a very preoccupied individual."

Memoranda upon the Gaskell Blackmailing Dilemma

Excerpted passages from the personal diary of
Mr. Sherlock Holmes, consulting detective,
221B Baker Street, London W1:

Saturday, September 29th, 1888.

I have just seen Watson, Sir Henry Baskerville, and Dr. Mortimer off
at Charing Cross train station.

A knifelike autumn wind sliced along the platform as their carriage
pulled away. It no doubt accounted for the chill I felt, as I am hardly given
to fanciful imaginings—although I confess myself not entirely easy in my
mind regarding this case. When Watson and I followed the mysterious
bearded gentleman so shamelessly pursuing Sir Henry Baskerville, I
could have continued to look at myself in the shaving mirror of a morning
had I learnt anything useful. Instead, I had my own name thrown back in
my face, as it were, and could do nothing more useful than to consider
it a lesson in humility along the lines of "Norbury." (Watson, despite

being under standing orders to whisper this word when I am suffering
an attack of hubris, is too polite to carry out the assignment and shirks
dreadfully when I am making an ass of myself. I intend to take him to
task on this subject when I see him again.)

I now fear very much for Sir Henry and the enormous fortune he
stands to inherit—vast wealth has a tendency to make bodily threats
all the more material. Dr. Mortimer is right to fret over his friend Sir
Charles Baskerville's heir. These men, whoever they are, mean business.

Thus shall I speed to Baskerville Hall as soon as is possible, though
my instincts tell me not to reveal myself as a key player in this drama
prematurely. My appearance would only serve to put the guilty party
on guard. (This is largely Watson's fault—I'll admit that having an international reputation is good for business, but it is terrible for stealth.)
Perhaps a hidden lair would be preferable? Meanwhile, the good Watson
has been instructed to take every care, and doubtless he will apply himself
posthaste to providing me with grist for the mill via letter. I wish I had
one in hand already, but I suppose it is unreasonable to expect him to
write to me when he is still on a train.

Strictly speaking, I was guilty of a small prevarication with my
friend; I am indeed investigating a case of blackmail for one of the
highest families in the land whilst remaining behind, but I did not tell
him that the victim is a woman. It really wouldn't have done to give
Watson the impression I was charging to the rescue of another damsel
in distress, not three months after that exceedingly volatile Milverton
business. He was *adamant* over seeing that case through with me, and
ever since he fusses terribly when I take on cases of blackmail—as if
I wander the intricate suburbs and byways of our great metropolis on
the lookout for opportunities to become falsely engaged to housemaids
and to burgle safes. Ridiculous. One engagement was quite enough for
a lifetime, or so I dearly hope.

The doctor knows one thing: I *loathe* blackmailers.

What comparison can be made between an impetuous act of violence and the deliberate ruination of a human life for no reason save
personal profit—the slow siphoning of money, joy, and security all in a

single foul act? There is no honor in the deed—as honor can be found even in murder—no more mercy in its perpetrators than milk in a male tiger, as the Bard puts it. Despicable. I compared the late unlamented Milverton to a serpent, and I meant it with a passion. Snakes (as I have been careful to mention to no one) turn my stomach over, but not more so than do blackmailers.

Young Lady Violet Gaskell (daughter of the late Marquess of Cleveland) is a tendril of a most distinguished family tree. Ordinarily this would make no difference to me, but obviously the exalted have much more to fear from blackmailers than the plebeians. Her card revealed little. I will paste it here and continue the account after I've spoken with her anon.

Dear Mr. Holmes,

I am being threatened by the most vile scoundrel—I can say no more without incriminating myself, save to confess that it is a case of blackmail. You are my sole chance at redemption. Please agree to meet me at Chessington House, Surrey, at four in the afternoon on Saturday next, and I will make all clear. I beg of you, do not fail me.

In hope,
Violet Gaskell

Saturday, September 29th, 1888 (continued).

What a terrifically unpleasant afternoon.

There is something amiss about this Gaskell matter I cannot quite put my finger on. It is tapping at the back of my mind, but for the life of me I can't identify what it is. Having learned long ago to trust such instincts and wait to see what they reveal, I shall simply bide my time despite my native impatience. Meanwhile, my thoughts have been pulled on more than one occasion back to the Baskerville business. Watson must surely be at the hall by now, and whatever my sentiments on the subject of spectral canines from Hell (manifestly absurd), the physical footprints of an enormous hound are quite another thing (potentially perilous).

My brief journey to Surrey was an uneventful one. The weather was fine, and the foliage a veritable palette of fiery hues. Chessington House proved the sort of sprawling architectural study in opulence that tends to send Watson's accounts of my cases careening away from the pristine study of dispassionate logic to flounder in descriptions of trailing ivy and mullioned windows. He'd have loved the ramshackle pile of stones nestled within its blanket of red-orange leaves.

Chessington House was every bit as drenched in wealth on the inside as it was outside, as I discovered when the butler (name: Giles, originally from Newcastle, unmarried, asthmatic, parents obviously manufactory workers) showed me through to the parlor. I could have taken a world tour for the price of one of their fire irons, so I will say this for our blackmailer: he is after a considerable sum.

I waited four and a half minutes for Lady Violet, and when she did arrive, she slipped through an interior door from an adjacent darkened room rather than use the hall entrance. At once, I knew her to be truly distraught, for I detected a faint aroma of headache powder, and her delicate face was quite pale. Watson, had he been present and inclined to record the matter, would have altered this fact to allow her to enter from a backlit doorway, "tender lamplight spilling softly around the crescentic parabola of her womanly figure, as she stood with one hand resting against the sinuous folds of her violet day-dress, the sweet ellipse of her mouth parted in dismay," or some such drivel. I will *never* comprehend the man's obsession with silhouetted females. It is a source of peculiar bemusement to me. Time after time (eight times) he has written of women shaped like women (surely unsurprising) and lit them from behind (unnecessarily) with angelic nimbi, despite the fact that each time the lady in question was already seated when we arrived.

Some mysteries even I cannot solve.

But I digress. Lady Violet was twenty years of age, small of stature, a very dark brunette with blue eyes and the pale ivory skin of our pedigreed aristocracy, with the requisite stark cheekbones, and every bit as difficult to read as women generally are. Showing little in the way of strain, she pressed my hand most determinedly. She gave the impression of a strong, confident being who has been subjected to an unexpected extremity. I liked her from the first. The sole callus I was able to feel revealed nothing to me, as it was perched upon the extremity of her middle finger, and I already knew her favored womanly accomplishment to be the oil study. One does not simply walk into the richest family manse in Surrey without conducting due research—Lady Violet is a much-lauded talent in her rarefied artistic circles.

"How good of you to come, Mr. Holmes," she said lowly. "This business—you must pardon me for having been so terse in my letter, and so rudely insistent as well, but it comes as a cruel blow. Pray sit down."

"Your letter was to the point, Lady Violet, which I appreciated not in spite of its brevity but because of it."

We took seats on either side of a rich brocade settee. "I hardly knew what to write to you, I was so frightened," she admitted.

This confirmed my belief Lady Violet Gaskell owned considerable strength of character, for the penmanship upon the missive had been perfectly legible despite her apprehension. Nevertheless, I assumed what I have found to be a calming tone as I answered, "Scarcely any species of reptile incites greater disgust in me than the professional blackmailer, I assure you. Please tell me everything—and though doubtless it must pain you to speak of it, knowing the nature of the incident over which you are being threatened may prove helpful."

"It is the old story, Mr. Holmes. I fear that we must discuss a regrettable *affaire de coeur,* one which has led to a ghastly attempt to extort a small fortune." She pulled a sachet of lavender from a pocket within her magenta day-dress, smelling it gingerly. "Do excuse me. . . . I suffer from migraines on occasion and seem to be fending off an attack. The strain has been overwhelming."

"Well, we shall see what we can do to lessen it. When were you first approached?"

"Three days ago, Mr. Holmes. For the first two days, I hid my problem from everyone, but finally I was forced to confide in my aunt, the Dowager Lady Edith Cranley, my late father's sister. The shame of it was almost unbearable, but I had no choice in the matter."

"I take it you were in some fiscal difficulties?"

"Just so. You see, I've only very limited access to my own money, and she administers my trust. My allowance would not nearly have covered the sum he mentioned."

Sighing, she settled back against the cushions. "This could not have come at a more damaging time. I am engaged to be married, Mr. Holmes—to Sir Wellesley Lyttleton, in a fortnight. All the preparations are already in place. Of course, the blackguard must be counting upon this fact to ensure my silence."

"That is very plausible."

"As I'm admittedly a trifle unwell, I shall attempt to be concise, Mr. Holmes. Three days ago, then, I had a typewritten note requesting that I travel into the city and take a turn on foot through Hyde Park at one in the afternoon. You can scarcely comprehend the fear that such a vague yet threatening correspondence triggers."

"Perhaps not, but I have a peculiarly lucid imagination. May I see it?"

"It horrified me so, I burned it straightaway. I apologize—could a mere typewritten note have assisted you?"

"Smaller trifles than a note have done so in the past. If you receive anything further, please retain it."

"Of course. I am entirely in your hands, Mr. Holmes."

"What did the message say? Word for word, if you can recall."

"Do forgive me, but I cannot quote it exactly. I was to be alone when I entered the park, to tell no one I was coming, and should I comply, I would avoid a great scandal. My heart turned to granite in my chest when I saw the closing line—it said simply, 'A friend of Robert Winter.' "

"The gentleman who courted you in the past, I take it, and to whom you perhaps addressed correspondences of an amiable nature?"

"You're as clever as they say, Mr. Holmes." She smiled, dimpling, which was the merest datum for me but an unfortunate loss to the absent Watson. "Yes, four years ago during the season I met him at an officers' ball. Lieutenant Robert Winter was a recruit in the Corps of Royal Engineers, the Fifth Regiment, and I but a girl of sixteen. His career was rising, and he cut a truly dashing figure of a man—blond and broad-shouldered, with an easy grace about him. I was guilty of nothing more than fanciful letters, Mr. Holmes, just as you inferred, but even the hint of shame would be enough to put Wellesley off the match. He is most . . . fastidious in all his affairs."

"You mentioned—and forgive my candor—you've your own fortune but limited access to the same?"

Noticing unconscious gestures is of the utmost value to the investigator, and when Lady Violet brushed her fingers across her skirts irritably, I could see she was patently vexed by this topic. (As indeed should I have been if I were not allowed access to my own money.)

"I am not genteelly poor, Mr. Holmes, merely the victim of an unfortunately worded bequest," she elaborated. "Until such day as I am married, or twenty-five years old—"

"Supposing you were to manage to reach twenty-five years of age without attracting a suitor, we would face disgrace—but then, you never were a great follower of social norms," a voice like turned green apples groused. "This is the . . . the *hired detective*, I take it?"

When people refer to me as a detective rather than an independent consulting detective, they are being unspecific but technically accurate. When they refer to me as a "hired detective," on the other hand, they are being deliberately insulting.

"Yes, Aunt Edith," Lady Violet answered, coloring. "You mustn't be so—"

"Oh, what *must* I do or what *mustn't* I do this time?" the old woman snapped. She shuffled slowly to a pillowed armchair and settled into it as if a steel rod had been inserted through the crown of her head at birth.

The Dowager Viscountess Edith Cranley was not ugly; she was a distinguished elderly woman with her niece's porcelain complexion but with someone else's pugnacious jaw, and hair white as cigar ash. There was malice in her boot polish and rudeness to her personal maid in the pressed black lace of her sleeve cuffs. She was the sort of relic of the Empire who doubtless supposed that keeping hounds was a necessary tenet of respectable living, that the Irish starved en masse forty years ago owing to lack of foresight, and that illness indicates a want of moral willpower. The instant I encountered her, my aversion was established.

I am no revolutionary, but unchecked snobbery offends my sense of balance.

"The girl must marry, that's all there is to it," the crone announced. "Mr. Holmes, if that is who you are, there is no other outcome possible. You must ensure that this blackmailer is stopped, or else—"

"Or else what, Aunt?" Lady Violet asked, eyes wide.

"Or else I shall simply pay the wretch, and have done!" Lady Cranley cried, fluttering her fingers as if paying a blackmailer on a single occasion would forever solve her niece's problem. Knowing this belief untrue, I cleared my throat, annoyed. "The bequest Lady Violet mentioned . . ."

"She gets two hundred a month when she marries or turns twenty-five." Lady Cranley's tone clearly implied, *when she marries or is sentenced to hang at Tyburn*. "But she'll never hold up the family name if this foul scheme carries through, and she is already twenty-two—past time to be happily tied to a suitable spouse and having children of her own."

"I quite understand the situation," I said coolly. "Lady Violet, regarding the incident in Hyde Park—what transpired, exactly?"

"I was accosted by a stranger," she replied, voice strained. "As instructed, I was walking along, quite alone, when suddenly a fine trap approached. The man inside demanded I get in, and I didn't know how to refuse. I stepped up into the darkened carriage with my heart in my mouth. My persecutor smiled at me and quoted the very words I had written to this handsome engineer—harmless words, Mr. Holmes, but ones that Wellesley would find altogether scandalous. When I pleaded with the cad to return my letters, he said he wanted ten thousand pounds to remain silent."

"I should hardly call the loss of ten thousand pounds *harmless*," Lady Cranley sniffed.

I leaned forward, tenting my fingertips. "I hope it will not come to that. Describe the man."

"But I cannot," Lady Violet said bitterly. "Would that I were capable, but the carriage was dark and the man masked. Nothing stood out. I could barely distinguish a sleeve button in that gloom, let alone the color of an eye. . . . I am sincerely sorry, Mr. Holmes. My greatest fear is that there is nothing whatsoever you can do." And with that, she commenced weeping.

I have stared death itself in the face multiple times. But the only organisms which alarm me more than snakes and blackmailers are copiously weeping women—in part because I wish they were not in such distress, and in part because it is difficult to guess how best to stem the flow and return to the hard facts that will enable me to assist them tangibly. Thankfully my ability to soothe those who feel hope is lost is not inconsiderable, and I hastened to comfort her spirits.

"Lady Violet, despite your inability to identify your tormentor, I am ready and willing to act as your agent, and I do not exaggerate when I say that no one could possibly serve your interests better. I fear, however, that another case necessitates my leaving London as soon as possible. How were you told to communicate with the villain? If I can attempt to trace him, I may be able to put a stop to this without delay."

"Yes, do," Lady Cranley huffed. "It has taken me years to arrange a suitable match for my niece, and I will not watch an excellent marital opportunity dissolve at my feet."

Lady Violet pressed an embroidered kerchief into her still streaming eyes. "He said he would give me time to gather the funds. He is to write to me again tomorrow afternoon with instructions, which is the reason I so urgently wanted to see you today."

I pressed her arm. "Tomorrow afternoon, then, you must deliver the note to me and meticulously follow any instructions I might dictate." Passing her my card, I rose.

"I shall be at Baker Street on the instant I hear news," she assured me, also standing.

Just then the hall door banged open and a visibly fuming figure stepped over the threshold. A man of sixty years, with great bristling side-whiskers (gout sufferer, exceedingly wealthy, spent time in South

Africa, political conservative, breeder of spaniels), entered with a gnarled walking stick in his hand, waving its head vaguely at the ceiling. Lady Violet shrank back while Lady Cranley smiled in an abrupt show of greeting.

"I have been sitting in the courtyard for nearly ten minutes!" the old man snapped. "Were we or were we not meant to take a drive this afternoon?"

"But you sent no one to fetch—I was just coming, Wellesley," Lady Violet stammered.

My heart sank. Never were truer words written than that when sorrows come, they come not single spies, but in battalions.

"And who's this, then?" he growled, pointing at me. "Some sort of tradesman? What's he to do with? The wedding, no doubt?"

"Yes," Lady Violet said in a choked voice. "He's the florist. Mr. Holmes, allow me to introduce my fiancé, Sir Wellesley Lyttleton."

Saturday, September 29th, 1888 (continued).

I don't like this. I don't like it *at all*.

Little did Watson know it, but I had taken him to see Lady Violet's work at a Bond Street picture gallery upon the day Sir Henry Baskerville lost his second boot. The establishment was showing one of her portraits, an ethereal study of her friend the Lady Rosamund Grimsham. I made a pretense of examining some very fine Belgian landscapes, but it was Lady Violet's work I'd particularly wished to examine, knowing that I would soon be acting upon her behalf.

I suggested to Watson—and he most sturdily disagreed, the stout fellow, telling me that my ideas were crude at best—that art allows the close reasoner to deduce more about the painter than the subject. (I kept to myself the fact that the painting before us led me to gather Lady Violet was a highly perceptive, resolute woman.) It is confounding to me that Watson failed to take my point; when I play my own compositions on the violin, they sound like nothing imitative of the exterior world, but rather the inside of my mind. They are imaginary landscapes, as darkly fanciful as my musings, and serve when I am in the dumps to lessen despair by virtue of expressing it.

Watson is simply wrong—but then there is no art in his blood whatsoever. He has seen much evil in his life, but tragedy and hardship have quite failed to taint his mind with morose imaginings, for his nerves have now thoroughly recovered from the Battle of Maiwand. My friend is the best of men, a relentless optimist, and unfortunately he wouldn't know a Rembrandt from a harpsichord.

Why would a sensitive, comely young woman marry such a sullen old stick, meanwhile?

I am meant to defend this match from the ravages of blackmail and find myself longing for Lady Violet's exposure. As a florist—clever girl—I spent a mere three minutes in the company of Sir Wellesley Lyttleton and by the end of the interlude had pegged him for a slow-witted, petulant bully. A rich, slow-witted, petulant bully, I grant; but if one were to compile every separate fortune amassed by the East India Company, the wealth would be an insufficient recompense for marrying such a brute. Not when divorce is so nearly impossible. I would as soon permanently tether myself to a wardrobe as a female, but that doesn't mean I am unsympathetic to the plight of women who suffer cruelties for marriages of financial convenience.

And as I mentioned already, something disturbs me, something I still cannot yet quite identify. There is a crack in the lens I can barely make out. Infuriating. Lady Violet is my client and I must protect her interests—evidently, however, her interests lie in quite another direction from her request.

I wish the doctor were here. His advice would be invaluable—gallantry, thy name is Dr. John H. Watson. For all he was too thin and far too rootless and melancholy, he may as well have stepped down off a white charger that day at St. Bart's years ago. I had a telegram from him upon returning to Baker Street stating they'd arrived safely in Devonshire and were comfortably ensconced at the hall. While searching for the monograph on the contusions caused by garroting that I lent to him, I found that he had neglected to pack his woolen muffler, despite the fact it is nearly October. Is this the act of a prudent medical practitioner? Honestly, he can be very trying at times.

I gave it to Mrs. Hudson to send by the first post on the morrow. She keeps niggling me to eat, and packaging the scarf served to distract her, if only for twenty minutes.

So I have concluded my first day of investigations into the Gaskell case with distressingly little to show for it save the deepest concerns regarding Lady Violet's engagement. Pray God that tomorrow provides me with better opportunities to do my job, and to do it well.

Sunday, September 30th, 1888.

Three hours of restless slumber, inexplicably haunted by hounds with slavering jaws and hellfire burning in their pupils. My eyes are dry as newsprint and my neck stiff as a telegraph post. I never sleep much when working, but these night visions are equally as confounding as they are disturbing. It isn't as if I am worried about the doctor—he survived Afghanistan; he can face mythological dogs. Should Watson prove diligent in his efforts regarding the Baskerville affair (and diligence is one of his most pronounced characteristics, as mine is acumen), I shall reward him with picture postcards of backlit women.

I need to get to Dartmoor.

It strikes me that investigating the Corps of Royal Engineers, Fifth Regiment, with whom Robert Winter served and perhaps yet does serve, is the most logical place to seek out the so-called friend who made off with Lady Violet Gaskell's love letters. After consulting my commonplace book, I find that military men of an engineering bent frequent the Sackville Club. Lady Violet is not expected until the afternoon, and it would do well for me to escape the flat—Mrs. Hudson has tried to foist eggs upon me twice already this morning. This whole business has me so unnerved that I am off comestibles entirely.

Sunday, September 30th, 1888 (continued).

Damn, blast, and confound it all.

The Sackville Club is a comfortable brick establishment in Blooms-bury, so I hadn't far to travel, which was a lucky circumstance since today the skies have opened and the streets are foul little rivers. I presented myself to the proprietor, who was most helpful in pointing me toward a member of the Fifth Regiment. This gentleman was named Lieutenant Ernest Shattock (engaged to be married, boxing enthusiast, submarine expert, fiancée owns a bulldog). After I introduced myself as a former school chum of a fellow member of the Fifth, he was readily persuaded to partake of a brandy and soda and some leading conversation in the club's darkly paneled common room.

"I heard rumor the lads of the engineering ranks populated this place and thought I might take a chance upon finding my old friend," I mused, eyes passing idly over the men smoking cigars and playing billiards in the low light.

"It was well thought out, Mr. Holmes. What's your mate's name, then?" Lieutenant Shattock inquired affably, sipping at his drink.

"Lieutenant Robert Winter. Or at least, he was a lieutenant when last I heard tell of him."

Lieutenant Shattock frowned. "That's queer. I should have thought I'd know him, but the name isn't familiar. Joseph! Ever heard of a Robert Winter?"

The fellow named Joseph (gambler, dabbles in archery, originally from Glasgow), who was placidly reading the *Pall Mall* a few feet away, folded his paper down. "Winter . . . can't say as I have."

"Are you certain he wasn't a contracted civilian, Mr. Holmes?" Lieutenant Shattock asked. "Or posted to the Corps of Military Artificers?"

After I repeated that he was enlisted, the good gentlemen made a few other inquiries for me. All came to naught, however—Robert Winter, the man for whom Lady Violet had unwittingly risked her reputation, has apparently been erased from existence.

I quit the club none the wiser, with a brandy and soda disturbing my empty stomach.

This doesn't add up. I highly doubt the engineers were prevaricating. They were steady and thoughtful, as military men often are. Watson exemplifies the type. I hope his revolver is in his pocket. I told him never to be without it, and he generally follows my instructions, but a hound (whether supernatural or the common garden variety) can tear a man's throat out.

Thankfully, Watson is an excellent marksman. When I knew him less well and found myself strangely curious about him, I asked Mycroft to look into his brief military career: apparently he shot a sniper in Candahar at a farcically difficult distance before being posted to the Berkshires, which incident immediately recommended him to me as a potentially useful business partner. I mentioned the event to him once over breakfast. "Remarkable, Holmes!" he exclaimed, tanned face alight. "However could you possibly have deduced such a thing?" He was so pleased, I hadn't the heart to tell him I'd learned it in a letter from my brother, which flirted with invasion of his personal privacy; thus I merely smiled enigmatically and intoned something philosophical about logic.

I'll never understand the character of military men. Not Watson—his lust for adventure is keen enough that he grows as restless as I do when my career lags—but those who send other men into danger. My temperament wouldn't agree with command, masterful as I am. I should much prefer to take a risk upon myself in solitude than order comrades into harm's way. I'd make for an altogether wretched colonel.

Lady Violet is due to arrive at Baker Street at any moment. There, I think I heard the bell chime.

Sunday, September 30th, 1888 (continued).

Lady Violet has just now departed, and the note she delivered into my keeping with the blackmailer's instructions for delivering the ten thousand pounds makes everything clear. God, what a dunce I've been all this while. The case appeared so very simple that I allowed its lack of complexity to blind me utterly—that, and I have been somewhat distracted. I should have seen the truth plain as day when Lady Violet said she could tell me no details about her persecutor owing to the dimness inside the carriage. Instead I traipsed about in search of Robert Winter, of all people. Asinine. Watson will howl with laughter when I tell him about it. (And the anecdote will provide the perfect opportunity to implore that he mention Norbury with greater frequency.)

"Lady Violet, after copious reflection, I've determined that your only course of action is to throw yourself upon the mercy of your aunt's generosity," I told her. She nodded, clutching her gloves and looking faintly ill, pale blue semicircles beneath echoing the blue within her eyes. (Yes, it seems that my pen, like the good doctor's, veers into the overly descriptive when I am not vigilant.) "Lady Cranley must therefore wire the money to my bank without delay. The instructions to deliver the cash to a locker at Charing Cross train station tomorrow at noon exactly will then be carried out by me, as your intermediary, for the sake of safety and discretion. Is all this agreeable to you?"

"Nothing about it is remotely agreeable," she sighed. "But you have done everything you can, no doubt, and you mustn't think me ungrateful."

"Not at all. This time tomorrow, Lady Violet, the whole sordid business will be but an unpleasant memory."

"Thank you, Mr. Holmes." I took her petite hand, and she made me a small, elegant bow. "I'll not forget your kindness, nor your talents."

"As a sleuth or a florist?" I asked, smiling a little. "I must say, Lady Violet, your fiancé is a . . . memorable man."

The pain in her eyes was evident; the tendons of her throat were taut with regret. It was as I suspected, then. I know nothing whatever of love, granted, but any sane woman ought to be as enamored of Sir Wellesley Lyttleton as she would a particularly cantankerous badger.

"He is certainly a rich one, and my aunt owns traditional sensibilities. I can hardly blame her, for she was raised with them. Do you want to know what life I've always dreamed of, Mr. Holmes?"

"By all means."

"Living in a dear, shabby garret in Florence, painting. I should be quite alone, but I should have my canvases and oils and I should be happy as a lark. Does that sound foolish to you?"

"Not in the slightest. Your engagement is, I regret to say, an unfortunate impediment to such a life."

She offered me a weak smile. "That cannot be helped, I fear. But I have complained long enough, and you must have many demands upon your time. Good day, Mr. Holmes. I shall be forever grateful for your kindness during my hour of need."

When I shut the door upon her, I rubbed my hands together, marshaling my wild thoughts.

I've reached a decision of which I think Watson would approve. If I play at being a judge from time to time, he is indubitably a jury, and I believe on this occasion we would be in complete agreement as to our ruling.

What a pity I am forced to wait another day before departing. I must pack my things, send a telegram to Cartwright to determine if the boy is game to accompany me, and see that my post is forwarded to Devonshire with the greatest possible efficiency. Cartwright is a trusty lad, practically one of my Irregulars by this time, and I've my eye on a suitable cave dwelling. One mustn't reveal one's hand too quickly, after all, and I believe dark forces to be massing around Sir Henry. But supposing I mean to reside in a ditch temporarily, I should still prefer to have a clean collar of a morning. Hygiene will not be sacrificed if I can possibly help it. Also, if Watson is dedicated to writing me detailed reports, then by God I am going to read them. Backlit females notwithstanding, they promise to be most invigorating. I should hate to miss them, no matter how many picturesque ruins he describes.

I've reached the decision to inform Inspector Lestrade of my plans, that I might summon him at a moment's notice should I have need of a steady Yarder, which is not at all unlikely. Lestrade can no better employ his imagination than he can employ clairvoyance, but in this case that's all to the good. He is more trusting of me than the rest of the official force, and more tolerable to pass the time with, and it is a cunning game to see just how far I can advance his reputation by giving him credit for my own successes. I could distribute the wealth more evenly, but gifting all to a single individual is much more amusing—if Lestrade were ambitious, he could make chief of police for all the puffing I've provided. As he is not ambitious but simply wonderfully decent and rather dull, however, it's droll to ensure that he solves three times as many murders yearly as Bradstreet or Gregson (despite the fact they're both brighter than he and for no other reason than because I enjoy the faces he pulls when I twit him over lapses in his logic).

How does one approach Her Majesty's postal service about forwarding correspondence to the open moorland when one is in pursuit of a criminal mastermind? The formality rather escapes me. *"To Be Delivered to Mr. Sherlock Holmes, Devonshire, Third Crag from the Left, Grimpen"?*

Sunday, September 30th, 1888 (continued).

It fast approaches midnight. All is in readiness.

Mrs. Hudson has finally retired, after accusing me of "pining." I should have offered a rebuttal to this nonsensical assertion, but it did not merit a reply. Reclining in my armchair smoking shag tobacco for two hours straight is *pondering*, not *pining*, and it is my profession, for the love of God.

I hope this is not a sign of an early descent into dotage upon Mrs. Hudson's part. She is an admirable landlady, and hardly ever assesses damages when my chemical experiments go unexpectedly awry. This is probably because I already pay her triple what the rooms are worth, entirely apart from Watson's portion, but I am not inclined to quibble over domestic matters.

Watson posted a wire thanking me for the scarf, stating that a far more detailed letter would follow soon after, wishing me luck with the blackmail case, and advising I refrain from meandering into any accidental marital arrangements with under-cooks and kitchen slaveys, as I have done in the past. I will see that he pays for this when we are reunited—Watson's natural turn for verbal banter is beyond reproach, but when his gibes are calculated, he is, and I say this with great fondness, rather juvenile.

First things first, however: to assist Lady Violet Gaskell in teaching a lesson to the odious Sir Wellesley Lyttleton.

Monday, October 1st, 1888.

I sit opposite Cartwright in a private carriage hitched to *the slowest train in all of Christendom*. The railway will hear from me, and the tone of my letter will not be congenial to them.

My plan went off without a hitch. I visited my bank this morning, filled a small satchel with the ten thousand pounds Lady Cranley had transferred to me, and placed it in the designated locker at Charing Cross. Then it was child's play to blend into the milling crowds for long enough to watch Lady Violet retrieve it. I have never seen a woman look so delighted—as if she had been freed from a cruel cage. She will set herself up in Florence in a garret, just as she described, and no doubt do well there. Of course a woman as observant as Lady Violet ought to have been able to tell me *something* about her mysterious blackmailer, but since there never was any blackmailer or letters or Robert Winter in the first place, she declined to invent superfluous data lest I catch her in a lie. Elegant. My cap is off to her—I don't mind being bested on occasion, supposing my antagonist as patently brave and morally justified as is Lady Violet.

I considered suggesting that if she ever feels the need to extort her own money from Lady Cranley again, she must not use her own stationery, as it was this slipup that exposed her to me. A comparison of her plea for help with the "blackmailer's instructions" revealed the truth in an instant. She is such a deft and sensitive painter, however, that I don't imagine she will have need of any more funds from her family. When she does set up shop, I must remind myself to write to her, and purchase something to remember her by.

Good riddance to Sir Wellesley Lyttleton. The man is a boor. Watson will approve of this course of action, I feel certain.

Will this train *never reach Devonshire*?

The Lowther Park
Mystery

"Watson, I fear I must apologize: you are experiencing a dry spell sty-
listically speaking, but fully intend to return to your literary efforts in
half an hour or less, and I must prevent you," said Sherlock Holmes,
idly tapping the end of his violin bow against the carpet while shooting
me a despairing look. He lay draped over the entire length of our settee, the portrait of lassitude. "There's nothing for it, my dear fellow."

"I beg your pardon?"

"Not a single alternative remains to us. We must attend this afternoon's formal tea at Lowther Park."

I folded my newspaper in considerable shock. My fellow lodger,
whether owing to some quirk of his completely inscrutable upbringing
or else a natural disinclination all his own, was a man exceedingly loath to
pay calls of a social nature. This aversion to idle companionship appeared
to encompass the whole of humankind, save for his gentility where Mrs.
Hudson was concerned and his affable manner with the best Scotland Yard
had to offer. I once inquired whether the three letters he'd received by
the late afternoon post were all from potential clients, and he asked who
else I imagined they might be from, since his sole friend was seated twelve
feet away and thus need not correspond with him via the Royal Mail. His

reluctance to appear at garden parties, political dinners, fashionable soi-
rees, and especially congratulatory fetes honoring some nigh-impossible
task he himself had performed could not be overestimated. The same
man who could lie in wait like an arachnid in the midst of meticulously
strung filaments, tracing his prey with perfect calm despite darkness, cold,
and the tension wrought by nerves honed to their finest sharpness, would
flinch at the merest mention of a croquet match. And yet here he was,
wrapped in his faded blue dressing gown and soberly assuring me that
we were due at one of the grandest estates in Hampstead that very day.

"By George. Must we?" I questioned blankly.

"Regrettably, yes."

"How did you know that my writing felt uninspired this morning,
or for that matter that I intended to have a fresh go at it?"

"When you dropped your pen in annoyance an hour ago in favor
of perusing the papers, you neglected to clean the ink stain off your
right forefinger. You're a man of medical neatness but also considerable
practicality. Had you washed it, I would know that you've abandoned
the effort for the day, but since you anticipate getting ink on your hands
again all too shortly, I deduce that you mean to crack on."

"Wonderful! Correct in every particular."

"Hence my apology—I have need of you."

"At a garden party. You are expected, I take it?"

"I should hardly think of stirring were I not."

"And—presuming that I have also been invited to this affair, which
I take the liberty of doubting—why, might I ask?"

"Blood is thicker than water, Watson, although you'll admit that
asking me to shake the hands of dozens of aspiring Whitehall staffers is
very thick indeed." Holmes rolled smoothly to his feet and propped the
bow against his violin case. "My brother has requested that I observe
one of his government subordinates. Mycroft suspects that his loyalties
may be compromised."

"Good heavens! Your brother fears a traitor in his employ?" Dropping the folded paper to the carpet, I leaned forward in considerable
interest.

He cast his eyes at the ceiling, but there was no malice in the expression. "I ought to have anticipated that you would put it much more dramatically."

"You'd never have agreed to attend a social function were the situation not of the utmost gravity. This fellow will be in attendance at Lowther Park?"

"Tongues would wag were he absent, as he is hosting the event."

"Damien Kenworthy?" I exclaimed. "Do you mean the young cousin of the Right Honorable James Kenworthy?"

"And the family's star political son, or so I have heard."

"As have I. The Kenworthy family are connected at every level, are they not? Politics, textiles, Chinese imports, weapons foundries—the list is endless. Why should your brother think anything amiss with Damien Kenworthy's loyalties, and what is their relationship?"

"There exists hardly a diplomat of any name to whom Mycroft is *not* in some way related, as his fingers are present in so very many governmental pies," my friend reported glumly, "and he *will* insist upon my help occasionally. Never mind that I've as much interest in bureaucratic intrigue as I have in the seasonal weather patterns of the planet Saturn. The facts as I know them are—you'll come with me to Lowther Park, of course?"

"Of course. I'd sooner desert you at the height of a dangerous pursuit than leave you to fend for yourself at a high-ranking tea."

Holmes made a rueful face which conveyed better than words his awareness I was only half in jest, tugging his watch from his waistcoat. Had his air of tragedy not been so sincere, it would have been comical, but I managed to arrest the smile which threatened.

"This spring I spent five days in gin-soaked rags down Surrey Docks way, scouring Rotherhithe for word of that coiners' ring, do you recall it? I leave it to you to guess which reconnaissance I suppose the more palatable, though I confess the Thames at that particular turning something less than artistic. Go and change and I'll post you up in the cab."

Despite the nature of our mission, Holmes seemed reluctantly to brighten once we were clattering through London's sluggishly teeming arteries, both of us silk-hatted with white gloves neatly brushed, for the sky was dotted with fat clouds against the blue, and the summer air unusually clear and temperate. He lost no time in telling me of his sibling's dilemma.

"Mycroft was recently ordered to select a discreet gentleman to oversee a committee which will evaluate the efficacy of our national telegraphic system." Crossing his legs, Holmes linked slender fingers around his knee. "I need hardly tell you that such a study would encompass an array of practical uses, private ones no less than military, for the speed with which we can communicate is integral to modern interests of all kinds. Following his success as a high-level Cabinet secretary, Damien Kenworthy seemed an ideal fit. His colleagues praised him, reporting that in all matters he was shrewd, articulate, and diplomatic. My brother suggested his appointment, knowing Kenworthy's organizational mind deeply incisive. As Mycroft does not dispense advice without careful cogitation . . ."

"And as your brother's capacity for cogitation is unrivaled in the Western hemisphere, the appointment came to pass."

"Precisely." Holmes pulled a pair of cigarettes from his case and flicked a lucifer against the cab door, squinting out at the slate-colored traffic and the remnants of glinting straw ground into the cobblestones. Leaning forward to light mine, he pursed his lips in thought. "By all accounts, Mr. Kenworthy already excels at his new office, speeding every effort to assess England's internal system of communication."

"What went amiss?"

"Yesterday morning he placed a document on Mycroft's desk. It was an efficiency report similar in structure to the one Kenworthy has been tasked with producing nationwide—one ordered by the president of a large private electrical telegraph firm based in Barcelona, a rich businessman by the name of Francisco Murillo. Mr. Kenworthy suggested using the study of the Compañía Telegráfica de Murillo as a guideline. There was only one problem."

"Which was?"

"The Compañía Telegráfica de Murillo," Holmes trilled, "does not exist."

Seeing my bemused expression, my friend chuckled silently.

"Mycroft's particular value to the throne of England is to know everything, and thus he was slightly perplexed when a study of an imaginary telegraph company was given him by a trusted official. I confess that neither of us can think what to make of it yet, nor would it behoove us to spin theories in such a vacuum of facts. But Damien Kenworthy is privy to a great many sensitive documents because of this study, including reports detailing countless military communication protocols, and thus my brother supposed caution the watchword of the hour. Not," he added dourly, "that he went so far as to investigate it himself."

The fact that Mycroft Holmes was not personally reconnoitering, as the intellectual superior of the two unconventional siblings, did not at this point in our friendship surprise me. The elder (and far larger) Holmes brother was as likely to leave his orbit of the Diogenes Club, his government office, and his Pall Mall lodgings as he was to suddenly take flight.

"Thereby necessitating your emergence in polite society. My sincerest condolences."

"I detect traces of amusement in your tone, but I shall ignore them, as they are beneath you," Holmes said with the merest uptick of a smile. "I fear that even if Brother Mycroft wished to join us, which of course he does not, he cannot abandon his desk considering the present situation in St. Petersburg. You and I, Watson, constitute a stalwart vanguard of two."

Half an hour later as we pulled into the circular drive at Lowther Park, its grounds exquisitely manicured and its trees dark-leafed and velvety in the brilliant July sunlight, I noted the abundance of shining brass-fitted carriages depositing their artfully dressed passengers before the estate's pale stone entrance. Our cab looked quite humble by comparison.

"Dear me, I see that Lord Rallison has not tempered his affection for the gaming tables," Holmes murmured with a wink. "His thoroughbreds have always been matched before, and to see a liver chestnut mare with a white forelock harnessed beside a sorrel? Shocking, my dear fellow, and at such a public event, no less! Avert your eyes from this disgraceful sight, and let us discover what perils lurk indoors."

Inside, the manor was as quietly sumptuous as a museum, hung with pale gold draperies, each successive alcove housing a more idyllic Flemish oil landscape or a more delicately wrought portrait of a blushing heiress with pearls in her hair. While the opulence was dazzling to my eye, my friend coolly ignored it, just as he always disdained to note the obvious trappings of wealth. Meanwhile Holmes, assuming as if he were donning a coat that effortless courtesy which belied his wholesale aversion to the beau monde, passed his card to a manservant. A few moments later, we were in the presence of our host.

"The younger Mr. Holmes!" Damien Kenworthy exclaimed, extending his hand. "And Dr. Watson, I can only imagine, from the accounts I have seen in *The Strand.*"

"The same. Thank you for having us."

"You are both very welcome, I'm sure. Mr. Mycroft Holmes is a brilliant man, and one to whom I am much indebted for my present appointment."

The pictures I had seen in various newspapers had done a poor job of capturing the buoyant, boyish air of enthusiasm which seemed to infuse Damien Kenworthy's every cell. There are men possessing excessive energy who mask it under pretended indifference—indeed, I resided with one—but Mr. Kenworthy's eagerness appeared almost puppyish. He was a short, active man, with pale features and a flaxen moustache, but the pallor of his coloring was instantly offset by a pair of dark, glittering eyes. His gaze was perceptive, almost calculating. Holmes, his own remarkable keenness of vision veiled by the languor in his attitude, doubtless took in our host's rich swallowtails and active, blue-veined hands still more thoroughly than I did as he greeted the gentleman.

"My brother is rather a rare specimen, I admit," said he.

"Exceptionality appears to be a family trait," Kenworthy noted genially as he led us through the spacious house to the back veranda, where sober young gentlemen and chiffon-flounced young ladies with ivory-handled parasols in their slack fingers milled about. "Ah, just the thing! Mr. Holmes, Dr. Watson, may I present Mr. Francisco Murillo, the former president of the Compañía Telegráfica de Murillo of Catalonia, and a great help to me with our current project."

I exchanged introductions in considerable surprise. Before us stood a giant of a man, bearlike and swarthy with a broad, intellectual brow and a carefully trimmed black beard framing his full, almost obstinate mouth. He was dressed in a more ostentatious manner than an Englishman would have been, with gold piping lining his jacket and delicate shell buttons dotting his embroidered waistcoat. The sun gleamed from his slicked-back hair and shining boots. Murillo angled his heel and made a dignified bow to the pair of us, his attention fastening at once to my friend. Apparently, whether the Compañía Telegráfica de Murillo existed or no, it was possessed of a very live and formidable ex-president.

"Gentlemen, is it an honor to make your acquaintance."

"Surely the honor is ours," Holmes demurred. "The study will benefit considerably from your experience, or so I hear."

"Tut, I merely provided a template," he said in deep, rasping Spanish-accented tones. "I am in London on other business and when I met Mr. Kenworthy last week, at a function for foreign dignitaries, naturally I wired my former company in hopes that our work might be of some use."

"Very good of you, too. May I ask the nature of your new venture, Mr. Murillo, the one which brings you to our shores?" Holmes inquired with a barely visible spark in his cool grey eye.

"No firm venture as of yet, Mr. Holmes, though I hope to found a shipping line within the year. I own extensive holdings in England—property, securities—but I require capital. I completed the liquidation of my assets this morning and will return to Barcelona tonight. In fact, I must now begin to make my goodbyes."

"Can this be Mr. Sherlock Holmes?" crooned a lilting soprano from just behind my left elbow. "Miss Jacquelynn Bost, and *very* charmed to encounter you at last."

The voice belonged to a lovely maiden with a striking array of chestnut hair floating above her milky shoulders, who dangled her white hand out before my friend's cravat. He took it with, though only I could have noted the fact, something rather less than complete enthusiasm. As for myself, I was instantly captivated—Miss Bost's nose may have been snub, and her porcelain chin pointed, but when all was taken together with the merry curve of her lips and the eyes flitting from sight to sight like bluebirds, one could not help but think her a delightful addition to any gathering. She wore a vivid sapphire silk gown with a copper sash to set off her auburn tresses, and a bonnet emitting a spray of cobalt plumes, completing the image of a blithe and bonny spirit.

"Mr. Holmes, the moment you entered, I knew you could be no one else," she continued, lashes batting like butterfly wings. "That jaw, that stature—Mr. Paget's illustrations in 'The Red-Headed League' were as good as any photograph. I hope everything at Baker Street is quite topsy-turvy of late, and you've not had any recent tranquillity to plague your spirits. Oh, dear—forgive my presumptuousness, but I am an *avid* reader of *The Strand*, sir, and thus feel I know you quite intimately already."

"You have the doctor here to thank for that, Miss Bost," Holmes drawled. "As, in fact, do I."

"I feel so privileged to meet you, Dr. Watson. Do please say you're writing more adventures, that you're writing them in your head this very *minute* even as you speak. Swear to me that you are."

"I was writing this morning," I answered with a significant look at the detective. "But I was lured away."

"Well, I'd consider it a personal favor if you marched straight back to work, and speedily," she teased. "Your stories are that breathtaking, on my life they are. I always buy the new *Strand* twice when you're in it—one for reading and rereading, and a copy to keep on my shelf. Some of my friends think it mad, but other ladies understand me perfectly. One day I hope to have a great collection of them, but that's up to the pair of you, isn't it now? I'm always *ever* so grateful to hear more news of Mr. Holmes."

"The pleasure is entirely mine, Miss Bost," I replied, laughing.

"Speaking for my part," my friend breathed in a rapid murmur audible only to me, "that much is indisputable."

"Mr. Holmes, I have dreamt for *months* of encountering you personally this way. I would so like to know everything about the science of detection, though I believe it in your case an art, rather. Your life must be so *thrilling*, so—"

"I regret, Miss Bost, that Holmes and I must finish a previous conversation," I interrupted when my friend pinched my arm severely. He steered me back toward the house, to which our host and the mysterious Mr. Murillo had repaired. "Another time, perhaps!"

"For God's sake, we've been entrusted with a mission on behalf of the Crown," Holmes hissed at me. "A garden party is no place for small talk."

"No?"

"Not where we are concerned. And I hope you are well satisfied that I cannot appear in public without being chattered at like some grotesque hero from the lowest form of penny dreadful."

"My dear Holmes, *The Strand* is a literary magazine, and you haven't the slightest desire to appear in public anyhow."

"That has nothing to do with—"

"My briefcase!" The balmy air of the veranda was rent by a terrible cry. "God in heaven, what has happened? Thieves! *Thieves!*"

Dozens of pristinely coiffed heads swiveled in shock. The commotion centered on Mr. Francisco Murillo, who stood in the doorway leading to the stone veranda, clutching an open briefcase with two hands. Swaying in the extremity of his distress, he waved the empty receptacle as a wild flush spread across his ursine features.

"I left this case in Mr. Kenworthy's private study," he snarled. "It contained securities, deeds, over two thousand pounds in valuables.

Who in the name of the devil can have done this, and to an innocent stranger? I have been made the victim of an unconscionable crime!"

"But—but that's impossible," Kenworthy stammered, pale face growing still paler. He had appeared within seconds of the dreadful shout. "I locked the door to the study myself. I've the only key!"

While the assembly glanced about them, scandalized heads bobbing aimlessly like the beaks of so many sparrows, Sherlock Holmes stilled in concentration. It is ever the case that crises hone him, render his already caustic presence as sharp as a knife's edge, and in such circumstances, he positively gleams with the confidence of being entirely in his element. Though I have witnessed it some scores of times, I have not tired of it; as for our new acquaintance, Miss Bost was lit up like a Chinese firework.

"Might I strongly suggest, Mr. Kenworthy, that the entire party be prevailed upon to stay on the premises until we can make a bit more sense of this situation?" the sleuth suggested.

"By all means, yes—yes, of course. Ladies and gentlemen!" Mr. Kenworthy called out. "With my most abject apologies, I charge you all to remain until we have made a preliminary investigation. Pray God this is all some ghastly joke, and we find Mr. Murillo's property directly!"

"A robbery *and* a detainment! Oh, I can't believe my luck, I simply *can't*. And to think that Mr. Sherlock Holmes is here, at the very scene of the crime!" Miss Bost exulted as the guests were ushered back into the house.

I half-expected another dour remark from Holmes, but criminal chaos had enormously improved his humor; instead he made the tiniest of bows to the lady as she passed us by, aglow with feminine enthusiasm.

"By Jove, I don't know what to think—nor what to say, of course, Mr. Murillo." Kenworthy mopped a kerchief over his brow. We hurried inside once the servants had courteously cleared the veranda of guests and led them to the dining hall, where more refreshments were being laid out. "The study is this way, Mr. Holmes. I had placed the briefcase at his request on my own desk, knowing the room quite secure. Dear God, if someone here has—"

My friend had already pounced with catlike swiftness before the study door, tracing the outline of the lock with his fingertips. He went fully to his knees with a frown. Pulling his lens from the inner pocket of his morning coat, Holmes leant farther in to study the gleaming metal, which—even without magnification—was visibly gouged with shallow but deliberate scratches. The mechanism had recently done battle with a foe, so much was clear. After he had completed his examination the detective glanced up at me, grinning inexplicably.

"See anything of interest regarding this lock, Watson?"

"Well, of course. It appears to have been rudely tampered with."

"Ah. I was much more intrigued by the design," he said with a shrug. "American innovation originated at mid-century by Alfred Charles Hobbs, a classic patented Protector lock. No matter, however. Shall we go in?"

I followed, wondering how the lock's make could possibly bear upon the case. Once we were inside the study, our host and his outraged acquaintance Murillo close upon our heels, Holmes lost no time in commencing his exploration. A fine bulky desk of polished oak presided over the small, windowless chamber, and two plush armchairs sat in the front corners. It seemed an efficient, masculine workplace, well lived in, with a collection of decanters on a mirrored cart at the corner of the room and a ready box of cigars upon the side table. I could see nothing disarranged, but that was hardly surprising—if the thief had wanted to plunder Murillo's briefcase specifically, he or she need not have touched aught else.

"You left the briefcase here?" Holmes inquired without looking at Kenworthy, dragging his fingers over the desktop.

"Yes. I then returned to the festivities after securing the door. The lock has been tampered with, you said?" the diplomat finished nervously.

"I did not. However, that is the studied opinion of Dr. Watson here, and I have never known him to be far astray."

Both Kenworthy and Murillo released muffled sounds of distress at this assertion, whilst I quirked my eyebrows at Holmes as he finished a quick perusal of the fireplace. I could not help noticing that he was by no means giving the scene of the theft his most thorough attention.

His gaze slid to and fro, lighting on nothing particular in a way which seemed extremely unlike the man, and twice he made an entire slow circle without seeming to view his surroundings at all. Holmes the investigator operates on two levels: that of gathering data, and that of ruminating over it. It was bizarre to me to see him introspective in the midst of the former stage rather than the latter. He glanced at the carpet cursorily, wandered from window to door and back again with his thumbs brushing idly round each other, fiddled with Murillo's emptied briefcase where the Spaniard had replaced it on the desk, and soon made me so uneasy that it was all I could do not to demand he reveal what the deuce the matter was.

Kenworthy and Murillo likewise watched him in increasing disquiet; everyone present save for my friend attended to each tick of the standing clock in the corner, picturing the burglar striding away from the property with his pockets full of bank notes and a whistle on his lips.

At length, Holmes spun away from the plundered leather case to face us, clasping his hands, mingled embarrassment and sorrow writ clear upon his visage. "Well, really! It's no use prevaricating—unfortunately, I admit to you that I'm at a complete loss. The like has hardly ever happened to me before now, but Mr. Murillo, I believe this theft to have been the work of a master criminal who has left not a single tangible clue save for some clumsy scratches when he meddled with the door. I've failed to glean anything from the room, and was no more successful with your briefcase."

"My dear Holmes," I could only marvel, "however is that possible?"

"I hardly know myself, confound it—I only know that I have been thoroughly bested. Now no doubt you'll think your trust in me misplaced." Never have I seen his face so shadowed in gloom. "I cannot blame you."

"On the contrary!" I exclaimed, aghast.

"Come, come, your disappointment is only logical! I'm sorry, everyone, but even I can see nothing when there is nothing to *see*. The obvious forced entrance is our sole indication. We are dealing with a very cool hand indeed. Only the most expert of cracksmen could pick that lock—I myself could not do it in under ten minutes' time. Perhaps I could not manage it at all, and I am no raw amateur."

"Surely there are steps to be taken!" Murillo remonstrated.

Taking his lower lip between his teeth, Holmes shrugged. "My only remaining avenue of inquiry is to question our fellow guests with the most exacting precision, and pray that one of them gives something away. What hope lies in that corner, however, I cannot tell you, as the thief may well have made an escape by now. Undoubtedly, this marks a low point in what has previously been a largely successful career."

Murillo collapsed into the nearest armchair, devastated at his misfortune. Kenworthy, looking no less bleak, gripped his associate's arm and offered him port from the sideboard. My first thought was to provide some words of encouragement for my poor friend, who was as shaken as I had ever seen him. When he swept out of the room with a defeated growl in his throat, I made terse excuses and pursued, hoping that in the thick of his black humor he would consent to speak to me at all.

"Holmes? Holmes! I hope you know that I would never—"

My friend abruptly stopped at the end of the passageway and turned to face me, suddenly looking as delighted as I have ever seen him appear at a society function. His narrow ribs shook with suppressed mirth, his thin face was flushed, and his eyes were bright as coins. We had been duped, I realized. My relief was so profound that it did not at first occur to me to be irritable over the deception.

"What do you make of it?" Holmes whispered. "Isn't it gorgeous?"

"I make nothing whatsoever of the real leader of an imaginary telegraph company, whose briefcase has been emptied from within a study with an unpickable lock," I retorted, though his joy was infectious.

"Well, never mind. I make something of it, so you needn't concern yourself."

"You are acting entirely out of character."

"How so?"

"That was the least comprehensive study of a crime scene I have ever witnessed you enact."

"Watson, you wound me."

"No I don't. And that show of defeat—what were you playing at?"

"But it wasn't a show at all! No, no, no. Solving that crime is quite impossible, Doctor, as I already mentioned perfectly seriously. There were no threads to grasp. I shall take what solace I can in solving another one entirely."

The sleuth strode off again, this time in the direction of the dining hall, where the guests must have been anxiously awaiting us. I began to ask whether he meant to question them, but Holmes waved for my silence. He stopped before a carved sliding door, listening to the murmur of voices just beyond by pressing his ear firmly to the wood. Satisfied, Holmes put his hands in his pockets and leant back against the wall.

"You have no intention of questioning the suspects," I surmised, all at sea.

Holmes's head dipped subtly. "That would be an egregious waste of my time."

"Why?"

"Because they know approximately as much about this as you do, my dear fellow."

The sliding door cracked open, revealing the russet head and excitable features belonging to Miss Jacquelynn Bost.

"There you both are!" She drank in the sight of Holmes leaning next to the panel, I standing beside him with my arms folded, wearing an exasperated expression. "My own conscience is clear, so I confess myself *terribly* well pleased at the turn of events. Isn't it all *marvelous*?"

"Absolutely," Holmes agreed with genuine enthusiasm. "I really couldn't ask for better, Miss Bost."

Glowing, Miss Bost withdrew and the door slid silently shut once more.

"Holmes, what the devil is going on?"

My friend crossed his lips with his index and middle fingers. "Quieter. Several things are going on, Watson. First and foremost, my attendance was not expected by our adversaries. You haven't your gun, have you?"

"No," I answered, startled.

"Pity, that."

"For heaven's sake, Holmes—"

I came to an abrupt halt when his hand caught my elbow. Measured footsteps approached from the direction of the hallway. Steeling myself for whatever danger might befall us, I backed up to the wall as Holmes had done and waited, my breathing quiet and my posture braced against attack.

Mr. Francisco Murillo emerged from the corridor looking extraordinarily well recovered. At the sight of us, he stopped short, but then continued on his path with confidence. Mr. Damien Kenworthy appeared seconds later, running a barely trembling hand through his flaxen hair.

"Have you finished questioning the others so soon?" Murillo demanded.

"Finished? I've not yet begun."

The Spaniard's teeth clenched above his sable beard. "No?"

"Oh, no, it sounded so dreadfully tedious. I'll start as soon as we've bidden you bon voyage properly. To tell the truth, I've been thinking over the data, and have only just come to terms with their meaning. As it would take me a matter of some two hours to interrogate everyone in the house, I thought it better to say farewell first, and to apologize again for my lack of progress," Holmes demurred unflappably. He yawned. "We can't have you spreading rumor of my incompetence across the Continent, not when making amends could ensure a better report of my talents. Reputation is everything to a consultant, you understand. You'll say nothing, I hope?"

Kenworthy's neck began to redden as he peered from Holmes to Murillo and back again. "I say, Mr. Holmes, we sympathize that so far your investigation has proved a failure, but you needn't sound so glib. It's Mr. Murillo who has suffered by it, after all."

"This is outrageous—a shocking scandal—but I cannot possibly waste any more time," Murillo dismissed them in a harsh grate. "As Kenworthy says, I have lost my capital, and if I do not depart, I will lose my ship as well."

"What a pity." Holmes smiled as if there were ice resting on his tongue.

"Your appalling lack of manners has been noted, Mr. Holmes," Murillo snapped, and I instinctually edged closer to my friend. "Nevertheless I wish you luck, since you seem to be in dire need of it. Mr. Kenworthy here will surely inform me if the sum is recovered."

"And it will be!" Kenworthy cried. "On my honor, sir—Mr. Holmes here is the best criminal investigator in London. A single setback does not guarantee permanent defeat. He will do right by us eventually, and then I shall see that the money is placed back in your hands with all speed."

"It is enough to severely test a man, but it cannot be helped," Murillo growled. "Very well. I must take my leave of this godforsaken place."

"Not before I cast an eye over that briefcase," my friend objected.

Murillo froze in mid-step. "It is empty. What use could it possibly be now—to me, to anyone?"

"That is precisely what I want to find out." Holmes's voice had turned as inflexible as his posture, which now radiated antagonism.

"Come now, Mr. Holmes." Kenworthy's ashen skin was beaded with moisture. "I have been humiliated enough tonight, have I not, what with a robbery taking place in my own locked study? I admire your exactitude, but I cannot suffer a wronged man to be detained against his will. Mr. Murillo will lose his ship if he dallies."

"Then Mr. Murillo," Sherlock Holmes declared, "will lose his ship."

The next few minutes unfolded in a dramatic fashion which will never leave my mind no matter how elderly and doddering I may become. As if fire had touched his heels, Murillo was running, sprinting with speed that belied his great bulk down the central passageway, Holmes racing after him with a shout. My own legs sprang into action an instant later, sending me veering past artworks and vases and potted ferns, and led me hurtling into the sunlight beyond the front door.

I reached the carriage-choked drive seconds after Holmes and Murillo, little aware that I was about to witness a terrible sight. My swifter friend had caught the pursued with one long arm about his neck, but the Spaniard did not yet consider himself to be bested. Crashing backward with all his weight, determined to knock the wind from his captor, he sent Holmes's elbow through a coach window that shattered into scores of glinting dagger points before my eyes.

Though I shouted, I cannot recall what exclamation of dismay escaped my lips. Holmes kept his grip with a pained grimace, but I could see as I rushed toward them the stain of blood upon glass, a scarlet trickle dripping down a shard like a dragon's tooth, and I knew that one splinter at least had done potentially serious damage.

Outrage battled with fear for supremacy in my heart—but these dark feelings only served to speed my actions, and Francisco Murillo proved no match for the pair of us. A harsh uppercut from me sent him staggering, and Holmes, with acrobatic dexterity, caught his own wrist with his opposite hand, pressing with all the force of his wiry forearm against the brute's larynx. Within ten more seconds, Murillo was on the ground, robbed of both his consciousness and his briefcase, as my bleeding friend eagerly flicked open the clasps and revealed the contents. The leather valise was brimful with papers.

"My dear fellow, wait—" I attempted, less worried at the moment about documents than about my friend's health.

"Internal military communications reports," Holmes gasped, still struggling for breath after his collision with the carriage. He coughed violently, but did not cease his rummaging.

"Stop, I tell you! Let me—"

"Highly sensitive government files, telegram protocols . . . Oh, just imagine the look on my brother's face when I hand this over!"

"Yes, yes, you're very clever. And in a moment, if you don't let me examine you, I'm going to procure physical restraints."

"By Jove, they would have got away with it, too, if not—look to Kenworthy!"

Following Holmes's upraised eye, I swung about to face the manor's front doorway. But Damien Kenworthy only collapsed to the stone steps, his head buried in his arms, the picture of a fallen man with no hope of recourse.

With the aid of several stalwart Whitehall aspirers and two retired generals, we managed to secure Kenworthy and Murillo within, sending word both to the Yard and to Mycroft Holmes that the proper authorities were required in Hampstead immediately. I, meanwhile, convinced Holmes that bleeding all over the house would hardly be appropriate, as there were ladies present, and whisked him off to the kitchen to patch him back together, dismissing the frightened staff after they had provided me with a medical kit.

Once I had him sat upon the table, after having twice lost my temper far enough to bark at the impossible creature, the manic man of action quieted into a more docile version of Sherlock Holmes, and he allowed his coat to be peeled off and his shirtsleeves sliced farther open. The gash ran from his elbow up the back of his arm for six inches, but was gratifyingly shallow save for one deep gouge, and could be stanched with cloth and plasters until I was able to stitch it up at Baker Street. I breathed a sigh of relief and set to work with the iodine.

"Your argument regarding the delicacy of the fair sex is not entirely sound," Holmes noted with a twinkle in his eye, folding his ruined jacket and pushing it aside as I cut a length of bandaging. "Miss Bost is a lady, and doubtless would much prefer to witness firsthand blood which was shed in the cause of justice. I say, you look slightly dazed, Doctor," he added, concerned.

"You could have been severely injured," I muttered. "In fact, for all you know, you *are* severely injured, but you are the most stubborn patient I've ever been unlucky enough to treat. Now, be still while I prevent this from becoming infected."

"Watson, I did not mean to alarm you."

"Perhaps not, but setting intentions aside, you did alarm me."

"Don't look like that, my dear fellow—it's only a scratch."

Sighing, I shook my head. "I know that. Still, it was all a bit excessive, Holmes. I have been used to aiding you in perilous situations, and very occasionally aiding you at tea parties, but never simultaneously."

"Very true." Holmes observed me with mock gravity. "It was a double-fronted war, to be sure, and one you fought most valiantly."

"You flatter me. By way of reward, rather than keeping me in the dark until your public denouement, you shall at once tell me what in the name of the devil just happened."

My friend, happily, was so delighted to have wrestled a villain to the grass at a garden soiree as to be amenable to this request.

"It was the Protector lock." His eyes tensed at their edges as I cleaned the cut, but otherwise he failed to react at all. "We both knew Murillo's former company to be fanciful, but the lock was the second lie. That variety of lock can be picked only with the greatest skill, and using a very fine tool. A half-diamond pick or even a snake rake, as it's called, would fail utterly, and my own preference is to employ a leather needle when cracking such a subtle device. Nothing and no one capable of causing those clumsy gouges in the metal could pick that lock. Therefore?"

"Kenworthy desired us to suppose the lock had been picked when it had not."

"Exactly so."

"But what was their scheme, Holmes? Where did the Compañía Telegráfica de Murillo enter into it?"

"Doubtless Damien Kenworthy will fill us in on the exact details, but here is what I surmise. Kenworthy, as befalls so many of our young aristocrats for one reason and another, found himself in need of money. Selling household treasures and family heirlooms is the surest way to expose that sordid secret, and so he determined to steal himself a valuable commodity instead—the most sensitive of the military papers to which he had access. He engaged Murillo as an accomplice.

"Now, the creation of a plausible scapegoat is a very touch-and-go business. But Kenworthy's plan was subtler than most. He set Murillo up as the ex-president of a telegraph firm and gave Mycroft a study claiming the same. The mistake, he thought, would not be noticed at once. Instead, Murillo would attend Kenworthy's event as a benign acquaintance, bearing an empty briefcase, and lock it within Kenworthy's study. Kenworthy would then deface his own lock, suggesting an intruder had penetrated the house, or even casting suspicions on one of his guests. Following the robbery outcry, but *after* the study had been examined, he would leave Murillo—overwhelmed and distraught—with free access to the supposed crime scene. The safe containing the true valuables, the military documents, would be left open, or else in a quiet moment Kenworthy would open it himself and turn the papers over. After a failed investigation into his lost capital, Murillo would then exit Lowther Park with state secrets hidden in a supposedly empty briefcase. Do you follow me so far?"

"Very clearly. But why—"

"The trick to stealing from Parliament is in laying the blame at another's doorstep. Tomorrow, or the next day perhaps, once Murillo's whereabouts were well and truly untraceable, Kenworthy would have appeared with his hat in his hand and a look of horrified contrition before my brother. He would confess the papers were missing, call the mysterious unsolved robbery at his home a clever hoax, accuse Murillo of the theft, and then point out—proving once and for all that Francisco Murillo could not be trusted—that the Compañía Telegráfica de Murillo *does not even exist.* Kenworthy would have been demoted, I imagine, but not arrested. Mycroft, however, knew the truth about the company at once, of course. And so here we are."

"If you are right," I said, tying the knot on the bandage, "it was a low and despicable scheme."

"That may be true," Holmes reflected, "but it made for a highly meritorious garden party. The best I have ever attended."

Holmes was not the only guest who thought so. It proved that Miss Jacquelynn Bost, whose slightly rabid regard for my friend's work could not fail to endear her to me, was the society columnist for a well-known London women's magazine, and very apt to recount personal anecdotes for the delight of matrons and housewives. She lost no time whatsoever in declaring the Kenworthy tea "the nonpareil event of the fashionable season" thanks to the "stunning drama of having firsthand witnessed Mr. Sherlock Holmes prevent a crime of national moment." It was Mrs. Hudson who brought this document to my attention, and when I showed it to Holmes, his remark was one in which I took a certain degree of modest pleasure.

"You have made your point, Watson," he acknowledged with an ironic twist to his brow, putting his cherrywood pipe between his lips decisively. "*The Strand* is, if only by comparison, a *highly* literary magazine."

PART III

THE RETURN

An Empty House

**Excerpt from the diary of Dr. John Watson,
March 17th, 1894:**

I did not suppose this afternoon would be easy or even tolerable. No
devoted husband could have imagined it thus. It shames me to say,
therefore, that I found events so strangely . . . unrelated to myself, as
if John H. Watson were a spectre existing on a thin grey plane and the
day had simply ground along without him.

It seems that if one is connected to a tragedy intimately enough,
perversely, one may as well not be there at all.

The earth of the cemetery beneath my boots was dry sand before
the gates, grating stone along the paths, dead leaves edging the margins,
and finally shivering grasses surrounding the tombstones. Birds called to
one another and in the distance oblivious church bells chimed, stopping
for no one. Above us, the sky fretted with impending thunder while the
gusting winds likewise warned of cataclysms. March is a wicked month
in London, I have always felt. Its weather hints at remorseful improvements and then rains glad cruelties upon the heads of all and sundry.

Stop.

All this petty vacillation might appear to be what Holmes used to
call "color and life," but in reality is much worse than those harmless

turns of phrase he so disdained in my fiction-tinged accounts. This is prevarication, delay in stating the inevitable: that I shed no tears, that no one leapt into the pit of clay, that even a dog would have whined, and I did nothing. How much better a man I should think myself if I could have truly *felt* any of it! Granted, I had supposed I was prepared for the eventuality of her death, for her illness was unmercifully protracted. Picturing her face two days ago—that sweet countenance with its wasted lips and hollowed eyes at peace finally and forevermore—gladdens me whenever I fail to succumb to unreasoning selfishness.

Yet here I sit, my head and my throat aching, able to write only of the weather.

I buried my wife today.

Mary would never have demanded this exercise of me, I am sure of it. But there. My own requirements of myself will be met, by heaven. Honesty will be had, if not sensibility.

I buried my wife today, and can scarcely set it down, and now will try no further. Had I a heart left to mourn anyone, I should think it fit to wail like a savage at present, rage at the mad moon with my fists raised.

The fellow who would have done so being absent, I shall retire and hope some spirit returns to me in my slumber.

Excerpt from the diary of Dr. John Watson,
March 18th, 1894:

Reading back over my previous entry, I am thoroughly sick at my own weakness and apathy in the face of fresh bereavement. When others fail to meet my expectations, base complaining is never my response—why then should I carp at the page when I fail to meet my own? There is no course to choose but onward, after all, and I fear no place lower for me to sink.

Resolved: to take courage, to honor the departed, to ever seek comfort by means of occupations at which I can be proud in the execution if not happy in the act. Many men and women are allowed no more than this. And can I truly think myself unlucky, when I have loved and been esteemed in return by such valorous spirits as I have encountered in my life?

No indeed. I've been blessed beyond imagining—to have spent a placid, insipid eternity in lesser company would not be preferable, and I would not choose it. I must remind myself of this. Daily, it seems.

In my lowness yesterday, I neglected to record salient details. Mary has been long without kith or kin, and my family is likewise quite dissolved—parents in the ground, a brother lost to me years before he destroyed himself. Therefore I expected a modest turnout, for all that my wife was a beacon to those in need, and am glad to say I was mistaken. Mr. and Mrs. Isa Whitney were present, Mrs. Cecil Forrester, several of my own regular patients, the entire Anstruther clan, and a gratifying number of neighbors who wept most touchingly during interludes in which I found myself numb as a fence post. It was to my own considerable surprise, therefore, that I felt so roused by a reedy and familiar voice just after the ceremony had ended.

"Doctor Watson! I'll not say I'm glad to see you, for I'm nothing but sorry under the circumstances. But by George, it's good to find myself in your company."

Turning, I encountered none other than Inspector Lestrade. His close-set eyes shone bright as polished marbles, hard and canny as usual—yet beneath the shrewdness, there lay considerable sympathy which in no way resembled pity. I've always liked Lestrade heartily in such moments of candor, when he isn't fuming with pique or preening like a lapdog, and I gripped his hand harder than I'd meant to. When I am not in Lestrade's company, I don't think often of him. When I am, I wonder at this lapse, as he is equally as compassionate as he is forgettable, and I simply like the fellow, and it isn't as if I possess any remarkable characteristics myself that would justify my putting on airs. The remarkable one left us years ago.

We exchanged unbearably polite remarks regarding Mary's final weeks and what luck the rain had forestalled. Finally, I cut the chap off in mid-platitude. I'd begun to sense a despairing roar lodged in my lungs, writhing to escape, and thought best to prevent its release.

"Lestrade, thank you for coming. Though as to how you knew to be here—the obituaries yesterday, I presume?"

Lestrade smiled his terrier's smile and swung his hands behind his back, clasping them. The familiar gesture pleased me. He looked well, despite his habitual wearied brow and twitching chin.

"Aye," he owned. "Though for all that some folk never held my brains in much esteem, I'd have known something was amiss anyhow. You'd used to stop by so often to compare our case notes, twice a week at the least, and lately . . ." Trailing off, he shrugged slender shoulders.

Lestrade was right, of course, and must have missed me. It seems that I have been neglectful of my few remaining friends. Thanks to twenty-four ardently penned chronicles of my friend's cases published between July of 1891, just after I had lost him, and December of 1893, when I understood I was to lose Mary as well, I'd become something of a fixture at the Yard.

"I ought to have wired you," I said with regret. "Don't take offense, please, but there were pressing matters on my mind."

"Not another word! You've been needed elsewhere. Obituaries, ha—a good guess, that. You'll make a detective yet someday, Doctor."

The cast of my face must have shifted from unwell to ashen, for he likewise paled and, pressing my arm, said, "My apologies—I'd no wish to rattle you."

"You haven't," I sighed. "I'm merely fatigued, I expect."

"God save us, 'fatigued' can't begin to describe it. You're the last man in Christendom I'd have wished these past three years on, Dr. Watson, and if I've broached a subject which offended—"

I shook my head; for he had brought up an old wound, a close and familiar hurt that reassured me rather than rent. Or so I always tell myself it ought to do. Some pains blanket us, it seems, dulling the senses, and others we clutch to us like daggers sunk hilt-deep. In my mind's eye, a very thin man rubbed his hands together, grey eyes aglow, whilst he angled his head at the inspector as an alert sparrow studies a likely worm.

"No, no," I replied, shifting. "Not at all. And now you mention it, I am indeed at work upon another tale. You recall that dreadful business over the Abernetty family?"

Narrowing his eyes, Lestrade attempted another cautious smile. It was to cheer me, not to ingratiate himself, and I liked him all the better for it. "Well, of course I do. What a ghastly case that was, to be sure! I can hardly think of it without my skin crawling. You're really writing it up?"

"I am."

"Horrid affair." He shuddered. "Why, that case happened very soon before . . ."

"Before Switzerland, yes. I've been writing of him constantly these three years—you needn't avoid Sherlock Holmes's name so. Please dine with me." I gestured at the exit of the churchyard, where well-meaning folk averted their eyes from my face in respectful silence, kerchiefs pressed to the salt on their cheeks. "If I stay here an instant longer, I'll go mad, and anyhow I've not eaten in . . . Do you know, Lestrade, I can't think how long. I really am forming detective-like qualities. Sleepless nights, and now eschewing meals? It won't do at all. Come along and remind me of the exact details of the parsley clue."

Lestrade shook his head as he preceded me away from the obscenely fresh grave. "I'll never forgive Mr. Holmes, you realize, for that one—I couldn't make head nor tail of it before the blasted butter gave all away. Made a complete ass of myself."

"We both did."

"Oh, pish, you know as well as I do you weren't the one who tried to convince England's highest-strung logician that there's such a thing as murderous ghosts."

Half-smiling, I admitted, "I didn't suppose he'd approve that theory, no. That doesn't mean I wasn't frightened."

"Well, you didn't show it. What a spineless little rabbit he must have thought me!"

"He didn't, not at all. He even said as much."

"Oh, come, there's no need to rag me over it," Lestrade scoffed.

"No, it's true—he once mentioned you after you were frightened of the hound, that horrible night out on the moors at Baskerville Hall. Holmes said had you not been scared for your skin, he'd have thought you far dimmer than he'd supposed, but that it was sheer bull-headed nerve got you up again. He admired that. He didn't phrase it very kindly, but then he never did, did he?"

Spots of color appeared on Lestrade's cheeks and he cleared his throat loudly into his gloved fist. "No. From Sherlock Holmes, that's practically a medal of honor. Thank you for telling me. Sometimes I'm curious whether the man himself was ever afraid in his life—is it any wonder his standards were so high? *Was* he made of clockwork, Doctor, or did you ever see the worst ones affect him?"

I thought of Holmes striding into my consulting room with an unhealthy translucence to his skin—not even greeting me, though he looked me over with as much care as he would any client—and then flinging all my shutters closed as if they had personally offended him.

"You are afraid of something?"

"Well, I am."

"Of what?"

"Of air-guns."

"Yes, the worst ones affected him," said I. "Quickly now, there's a decent chophouse just this way, and the rain is starting."

We arrived without incident at a pub with tarnished mirrors and a charred atmosphere. Chestnut husks crunched beneath my boot soles. Some sort of food I cannot recall passed my lips as the inspector talked on briskly of the Abernetty case, his cadences as familiar as the ticking of my pocket watch.

It was a tremendous kindness. I never told him that I recalled every detail as if it were yesterday, and—though he knew as much—he never reminded me of the fact.

Excerpt from the unpublished manuscript "The Adventure of the Abernetty Family":

"I know you've never believed in evil spirits, Mr. Holmes," Lestrade said, jerkily tugging at his cuffs. I had seen the inspector irritable countless times, but never had I seen him so unnerved. "I didn't either—I don't, I mean, that is to say. But you can see all that I can see, still more I've no doubt, and

God help us, if ever a man did watch a curse ravage a household, it would look exactly like this."

Sherlock Holmes, his ~~expressive mouth~~ thin brows drawn together ~~in a taut line~~, shook his head emphatically. The sun seeping through the half-pulled curtains of the ill-fated Abernetty house was now well past its meridian, and my friend had taken on the air of a tethered greyhound straining against the implacable grip of its leash. The sinews beneath the quiet tailoring of his coat were tense with anticipation. Now that the three bodies found in various attitudes of grisly agony in the allegedly haunted abode had been examined and taken away, and the most minute search for traces of a poisoning agent come to nothing, the passion beneath Holmes's phlegmatic exterior had grown more visible by steady degrees.

"I just mean," Lestrade again attempted, his lean face likewise tight with worriment, "that supposing the Devil had a hand in the affairs of—"

"It won't wash!" Holmes exclaimed, striking an impatient fist against his palm. Waving his hand as if in ~~regret~~ dismissal ~~at~~ of his outburst, he leaned against the windowsill. "These circumstances may have all the trappings of a lurid ghost story, but only children are untutored enough to actually be frightened of spectres. Let us sum up, so as to clarify our thoughts: five members of a family said to be accursed owing to their bloodthirsty dealings in the South American coffee trade are dead—the ruthless patriarch at his offices, the complicit mother at an art benefit, the innocent sisters over cards here in their parlor. Time of death for all five was practically simultaneous despite the three separate murder scenes. Now. I grant you that the Devil may have inspired such events, but he never executed them."

"Then who did?"

"I am not yet certain. I need more data, not fanciful embellishments of facts which are already before us."

"But it is impossible, I tell you, that they should all have been struck down at once despite being miles apart."

"Of course it isn't impossible!" Holmes flung his arms wide. "What heights of rarefied nonsense are you subjecting me to today, Lestrade? Are you through with them, or should I fear further inanities? It happened, ad oculos, therefore it is possible. The Abernetty family was poisoned."

"How?" Lestrade pleaded. "We've found nothing at any of the crime scenes to indicate such. And the servants might be foreigners, right enough, but the individual accounts they give corroborate each other—nothing save the usual midnight shrieks and freakish alteration of clock hands and such has been afoot. Are you telling me that invisible assassins drove needles simultaneously into—"

"Lestrade, you flatter ~~my mind's expansiveness~~ me, but even I have not such a fanciful imagination as that," my friend groaned. "Simplicity is much more elegant. They all died within five minutes of each other. Therefore, they were commonly poisoned and the effect was inexplicably delayed."

"I cannot think of any poison to match such terribly grotesque symptoms," I put in, greatly troubled. Just contemplating what the three sisters' final moments must have been like sent hoarfrost down my spine. Their corpses would live in my nightmares, I was already certain of it. "They all suffered acute respiratory distress, fluid on the lungs, and seizures before finally suffocating before one another's very eyes. I've never seen anything like it before in all my days—it's as if they drowned on dry land."

"Precisely so!" Lestrade cried. "What horrible drug could have achieved such an effect?"

"I know of none. What causes drowning in the midst of a clear blue day? It isn't arsenic, cyanide, belladonna, any of the common—"

"Watson," Holmes demanded with exquisite asperity, "were this crime of the common herd, would I be here?"

Excerpt from the diary of Dr. John Watson, March 23rd, 1894:

I had expected by this time a return of appetite if not relish, and comfort in writing of Holmes despite the fact that the exercise often feels like pressing upon my old injury. Neither has resulted so far.

I begin to wonder what, if anything, I can do to pull myself from this mire of stupefaction.

My twice-yearly rendezvous with Mrs. Hudson took place as usual, at the tea shop on the corner of Baker Street and Melcombe Street, despite the fact she had written me to say that I need not come if I was unable. I could think of no plausible excuse, however, not even for myself, and so assured her that I was quite well enough and met her over thin sandwiches and an excellent pot of Ceylon.

"Oh, you poor dear," she said, embracing me when I reached the low chintz-covered table. "My most heartfelt condolences, Dr. Watson. If there's anything, anything at all—"

"I'm fine, Mrs. Hudson." I hung my hat on a peg. "You look very well."

She looked precisely the same—Mrs. Hudson has a crown of snowy hair and a perfectly oval face, bright blue eyes, and amiable, even features which must have gladdened the late Mr. Hudson's heart whenever he saw them, the lucky chap. I thought she must have been pretty and knew she must have been slyly clever as well as shy. While she had always treated Holmes as if she had a tame dragon for a lodger—deferential, admiring, cautious—she also held considerable affection for him, and for me by extension.

"Well, I'm sorry to tell you that I can't return the compliment. You look almost as thin as when you took rooms in Baker Street, and you've dreadful dark circles under your eyes," she fretted, pouring the tea. "I do wish you would come to two-twenty-one, Doctor, and let me cook you a hearty meal for the sake of old times."

Though I smiled, I said nothing—for Mrs. Hudson knows why I will not visit her there, and our talk turned to other matters.

Our former rooms have been kept as a strange monument to my lost friend by his brother, Mycroft Holmes, a man of most narrow and concentrated habits. More accurately, Mycroft is an acolyte at the temple of fixed daily patterns. I could not help but conclude that even the practice of having a brother had become so ingrained in the poor soul that he simply refused to act as if he didn't have one any longer. This was the only sensible explanation I could conjure, for Mycroft was seven years Sherlock's elder, and must have been a great influence on him. Surely the loss of a gifted younger sibling he had protected in youth would be enough to tilt even a great mind—perhaps especially a great mind—a few degrees off kilter. Thus the sitting room, my old room, even Holmes's bedchamber were regularly dusted, paid for monthly by the elder Mr. Holmes, and madly, miserably empty.

As tragic as this was, it would be perjury to suggest I found his behavior shocking. Though the peculiar siblings utterly forswore demonstrative sentiment, they were in their own silent fashion devoted to each other, and the immaculate preservation of 221B proves as much. Mrs. Hudson probably feels like the caretaker of a highly specialized museum, and in a way she is.

If the mummification of our lodgings makes Mycroft Holmes feel that his brother is alive, well and good. I write short stories. The measures are not dissimilar. But I cannot be in those rooms again. Not unchanged, not after all he suffered, not as if Sherlock Holmes had not begged me to leave him behind for my own safety for half an hour in the Strasbourg *salle à manger*, not as if he had never looked at me with an unidentifiable shadow over his brow, half-obscured by an attempted smile, and remarked, *"I think I may go so far as to say, Watson, that I have not lived wholly in vain."*

"After your last publication came out, I worried for you," Mrs. Hudson was saying. Plucking myself from my reverie, I poured her more tea. "It was Christmas and all, and that choice of topic . . . It didn't sound like you, Doctor."

"'The Final Problem'?" I picked up an egg sandwich, took a bite, and set it down again. "I thought it sounded rather like me—at least, it sold very well."

The kindly old woman bit her lip, nodding, and I mentally chided myself for my incivility.

"Please forgive me. It was high time, Mrs. Hudson." Taking her hand, I smiled as best I could. "I am still writing of our exploits, do not doubt it. However, when Mary's ever-worsening condition was considered . . . well, I had begun to sense that I must look life square in the face, in all matters, and that is what I did. What I will continue to do, without undue morbidity or self-pity. I promise you."

She pressed my hand and returned my warm expression. "You've eased my mind, then, and I thank you for that. And I'll trouble you no more over what can't be remedied anyhow. I've one more question, though—why on earth did you write that you had never heard of Professor Moriarty?"

"Tricks of the trade, Mrs. Hudson," I returned affably, making a manful effort at the remaining sandwich fragment. "Explain too much at the start and the reader revolts."

"Ah, I see. It was better for the story that you didn't know."

The memory of a Swiss boy—out of breath, cherry-cheeked, eager—caused my vision momentarily to lose focus. Three years ago, Holmes thumped his Alpine-stock against the grass and gave me a resigned shrug.

"No, no, go on back to Meiringen, my dear fellow. This lad will keep me from straying off of any cliffsides, and you shall catch me up at Rosenlaui. We've seen the Falls, and anyway I must not be selfish. Surely if the unfortunate woman wants her last memory to be that of a kindly English doctor easing her path into the undiscovered country, you cannot deny either her excellent tastes or her wishes in the matter, can you?"

I pressed my thumb so hard into my wrist that I could feel the bruise forming, took a breath, and sipped my tea.

"You have it exactly, Mrs. Hudson." Edging the plate toward her, I watched her take another cress sandwich. "It was better for the story that I didn't know."

Walking toward the Underground after I left her, I thought well of my vow to my former landlady. It was the best I could make and no better, but I believe it an efficacious one nonetheless. Once finished with this journal entry, I shall put myself to a more useful occupation and continue work on the Abernetty matter. It is not as if—my mind having been so thoroughly consumed with my wife for these six months and more—I've any patients to distract me.

Excerpt from the unpublished manuscript
"The Adventure of the Abernetty Family":

"But nothing!" Inspector Lestrade growled in the front hall, arms burrowing into his coat sleeves. "There is no evidence here to find, I tell you—you cannot contradict me."

"*I think you'll find that I can,*" *Holmes snapped.*

"*Then you would be wrong for the first time, and what of that! It's use-less. And either all the servants are telling the truth, and spiteful phantoms meddled with timekeeping and lost books and unravelled hems and put salt in the sugar bowl for years, or else all the servants are lying. In either case, best of luck. I'm for the morgue, where pray God they've made some progress with the bodies. Anyway, it'll be a sight more cheerful than this wretched place.*"

My friend gnawed at his cheek for a moment, but soon gave up the matter as lost. "*Go on, then. Wire me the instant you have news. I shall remain here and find what is missing.*"

"*What could possibly be missing, Mr. Holmes?*"

"*The answer, for the love of heaven!*" *the detective cried.*

Shaking his head, Inspector Lestrade departed, slamming the front door behind him.

"*Come, Watson.*" *Holmes sighed, fingers pressing winglike at the bridge of his arched nose. He walked down the hall and I followed, deeply discouraged.* "*Back to work.*"

Holmes ~~seemed to fall~~ fell into an uncharacteristic reverie upon re-entering the parlor where the three young Misses Abernetty had been discov-ered. ~~The air in this room was thick with the intangible atmosphere of recent death—not an aroma, but a feeling like an echo of stopped watches, of missed trains, of misdirected love letters, of all that will now never come to pass.~~ He shook his sable head, jaw tense with chagrin.

"*You and I may not credit curses,*" *I mused, my eyes likewise upon the arrangement of spent hands of whist and scattered tea things,* "*but despite the fact the strange events in this household smack of chicanery and harassment rather than demonic influence, there is certainly a depressing air about rooms where young people have died untimely.*"

"~~*Quite so,*~~*" ~~Holmes agreed, squinting somberly at the table. "For a man who drove Amazonian tribes to slaughter one another wholesale, all to swell his already fat coffers, to be struck down—the universe approves of balanced sowing and reaping. I cannot help but think it fitting that a greedy sensualist who made it his practice to incite evil in others should himself be felled by an evil~~*

~~deed. But the daughters were blameless. That they should have died so, having committed no sin worthy of such a punishment, is offensive to the rational soul.~~"

My friend froze over the tabletop, his lips parted on a stifled gasp and his slender hands floating with palms down before him. He could have been Moses readying himself to divide the waters, or a magician casting his final hex over a bubbling potion.

"Whatever's the matter?"

"Watson, look!" he cried. "The parsley has sunk into the butter!"

"But what of that?"

"Watson," he hissed, gripping my wrist convulsively, "it is scientifically impossible for parsley to sink into butter."

Excerpt from the diary of Dr. John Watson, March 25th, 1894:

If I continue no better, at least I continue no worse. But God, how weary, stale, flat, unprofitable, etc. . . .

My poor friend always claimed that finding the line of least resistance was the starting point of every problem; he insisted that once the astute reasoner discerned a path by identifying an anomaly, blazing a trail through the bracken would prove simple thereafter. It is this very belief that has begun to chill me of late. I see no gentle byways, no sinuous and subtle markings in the landscape whereby traversing them the weary wanderer might glimpse a friendly spark of light through a many-paned cottage window.

But I stray from the point. Hearing Holmes's voice commanding, as he had used to do, "Refrain from poetry, Watson, it hardly suits at the moment," I shall make a better effort to explain myself, if only to myself.

I have been considered a bold campaigner. Every man finds himself at times without a map to guide him, however. Returning from the Second Afghan War, I felt aimless—until I quite by chance met a crusader fully as solitary as I and discovered that, while his greatness of character far exceeded my own, our temperaments were so wildly antithetical as to be perfectly matched, and thus I felt enormous pride at being recruited to serve upon the singular missions of Mr. Sherlock Holmes. At the loss of this latter commander, I felt similarly direction-less, and I mourned him with all my heart, though I could not actually bury him. I had a wife then, however, one as warm as the sun around which more minor bodies orbit, and thus retained a certain grounded-ness in spite of my grief.

One sees patients, one runs his household, one kisses his beautiful spouse when he finds her lost in one of his seafaring novels, caresses her hair where it gleams like the tufts of midsummer meadow grasses, blesses the fact she was ever born in the first place, and one remains tied to the gritty ache of life on earth and heartily glad to be so.

Having now lost Mary, I cannot but feel as if the very laws of gravity have deserted me. I may as well be Holmes, and have erased the principle from the garret of my mind.

Confound it, I appear to have resorted to poetry after all.

Excerpt from the diary of Dr. John Watson, March 30th, 1894:

Enough.

Seeing a patient out the door this morning with a tonic, a prescrip-tion, and a false smile, I returned to lock up my small private stores and found my eyes lingering on the cocaine bottle.

Reprehensible. And this after all my hard urgings on poor Holmes, whose lambent mind was capable of inventing torments I could no bet-ter comprehend than I could prevent.

I find I cannot even write of him with pleasure at present, and that is the hardest blow of all. At the time of the Abernetty business, he was in the thick of preparing to topple James Moriarty's empire, and dreams of waterfalls and Alpine-stocks grow more unbearable nightly.

I can continue like this no longer, I have concluded, and have thus set certain plans in motion. Let me say no more at present, but I harbor hopes for recovery.

Excerpt from the diary of Dr. John Watson, April 3rd, 1894:

A note arrived from Lestrade day before yesterday suggesting that I could earn a few extra quid per year assisting the Yard in a medical capacity. He knows my practice has suffered heavy blows following my wife's decline. It was well thought of, and for that reason have I turned him down in person.

I appeared in his familiar office with hat in hand and was quickly waved into a chair. Lestrade, prim lips pursed in concentration, was penning a telegram. He finished the task with that air of officiousness, which always used to amuse me and to chafe my late friend, one I was happy to see again, and then clapped his hands with an expectant expression.

"Unpleasantries must be seen to first: I fear that I cannot take you up on your generous offer," I told him. "I have been to the maritime offices today and there answered several advertisements for ships' surgeons. My prospects are very good indeed. As I'm better than qualified, I've every expectation of gaining a berth."

Lestrade, poor fellow, was most dismayed and attempted to dissuade me. But my mind was made up. He argued and spluttered and harangued for a quarter of an hour, and this when I had never before consulted him over so much as a train timetable. It is a lesson I shall take to heart not to misplace my friends once I have made them, for I cannot think of anyone else in London who would have so powerfully attempted to keep me here. When I had finally steered him round to my view of the matter, he rose and clasped my hand over his desk, frowning darkly.

"You'll stop by for a pint before you make any final arrangements?" he pressed me.

I assured him that I would and stepped out into the thin light of Whitehall Place easier in my mind despite the disproportionate heaviness of my heart. It is the right choice—the only true choice. Now all that remains is to see it through.

My restless soul cannot wait to be packing a trunk, gaining a certificate of my own health from Anstruther, and leasing my practice until I decide whether or not I will ever want it back again. Holmes's spirit inhabits these ancient cobbles as deeply as he inhabits my memory, and Mary's gentle presence brushes her small fingers along every corridor of my house and practice. The isle is full of noises, sounds and sweet airs that hurt as much as they delight. Once or twice, I had thought fleetingly of returning to California or even India, but such measures appear distastefully nostalgic.

What I seek cannot be found by traveling backward.

Soon I will be at sea. My skills are apt to the life, I think, at least temporarily. If they are not, I shall be tested, that is all, and this is what my circumstances demand: a place and a purpose.

I am a man who must be put to some *use*.

This morning I remembered a particular occasion in 1886 when Holmes had been in the dumps for four weary days, scraping his fiddle and ignoring my pained looks every time his morocco case made its sinister appearance. After an interminable interlude which would have tried the patience of a saint, let alone myself, he sat down at the breakfast table and—miracle of miracles—took an egg. I may have drily remarked as much, and his keen eyes feathered at their edges in that manner he had which meant that if only Sherlock Holmes had ever learnt to apologize, he might have done so.

Instead he coughed and snatched up the nearest paper.

"You look a trifle unwell, my dear Watson," said he, nose-deep in the agony columns. "Never fear, I shall find us some occupation. You only want a little exercise—men of your sort can't abide kenneling. Just pass the salt, there's a good fellow."

Holmes was not always right, though he would like to have been. But he was right on that occasion.

Before my departure in May or thereabouts, I've resolved that I shall pay a call to Baker Street and to Mrs. Hudson. I must see both again, ere I go. For the final time, I'll look at the dining table, the lone cigar I know absolutely must still reside in the coal scuttle, the pair of armchairs before the fire. There is a botanical reference volume I left behind there in which I used to press occasional flowers during my engagement to Mary, all of them plucked by her during walks through London's parks and byways and placed in my buttonhole; these dried artifacts I will gather, and lay at her gravestone.

Then, having let my own residence and said my goodbyes to the place, I shall have honored ghosts in every way I could, and leave such places behind me for a new life among strangers.

I feel much revived. The city's harsh air is the sweeter to me now that a change is imminent, and one of which I am certain Sherlock Holmes would heartily approve. This strange business of Ronald Adair's inexplicable murder piques my interest, for instance, and I may make some small effort at unravelling the matter as a final tribute to the wisest and most singular man of my entire acquaintance. Thereafter I shall quit the safety of dry land and tilt at windmills on the open sea. Come, tempests, come storms, come whatever Fate wills save sad indolence!

The time for great alterations is upon me. I can think of no sharper nor more constant reminder of my sorrow than my residence and that of Baker Street, the continual bitter quiet of an empty house.

Excerpt from the unpublished manuscript "The Adventure of the Abernetty Family":

Holmes, ever the masterful showman, held the kernel high in the air before the cook, whose healthy South American complexion blanched even as she bared her teeth in defiance.

"It is the deadliest substance in all the Amazon," my friend declaimed, eyes riveted to the small brown shell as if it were a costly jewel. "Related to the castor bean, only a thousand times more potent. After careful processing, the native tribes can render it edible. But when raw, it is used as a lethal poison akin to ricin."

"Of course!" I gasped. "Dear God, if only I had recognized the symptoms when greatly exacerbated. The fluid in the lungs combined with convulsions—"

"*Precisely.*" *Holmes's implacable gaze swept to the unrepentant face of the poisoner.* "*You extracted the oils and combined them with fresh butter, rendering the mixture softer than the usual. Today was hot enough for me to observe so, for the parsley had sunk into it, an impossible occurrence in dealing with pure butter. You fed the lethal concoction to every last one of the Abernettys, and following their metabolizing the stuff, they died in agonies. It was a monstrous vengeance.*"

"*I'd do it a hundred times over* ~~despite the fact you've found me out,~~" *the cook growled in heavily accented English.* "*A family for a family. Ignatius Abernetty's for my entire tribe, lost these fifteen years. What could be more fair? I saw to it they lived in fear of devils, but they never noticed the one beneath their noses!*"

"*There is no loss keen enough to justify your actions,*" *Holmes said with the sternness he acquires when confronted by unspeakable tragedy.*

Her eyes burned as bright as the sun over the equator. "*Yes, there is. You speak out of ignorance and not understanding. Have you ever been stripped of everything you love, Mr. Holmes?*"

~~My friend, a shadow crossing his aquiline features, hesitated for longer than I have ever seen him do, as if trapped within the universe of his own morbid visions.~~

~~"No, I have not," he said at last, speaking as if the weight of the world entire rested upon his shoulders.~~

~~"If not, can you imagine it?"~~

~~"I think I can, madam," he answered gravely.~~

~~"If you can't, then you don't know what you'd do, to what lengths you'd go," the cook whispered, "to feel whole again."~~

Excerpt from the diary of Dr. John Watson, April 5th, 1894:

The most strange, the most glorious, the most glad and inconceivable miracle of my life has just happened.

I must confess myself quite shaken; my hand leaps in sudden fits and starts across the page as I write this. My balking brain can make no logical sense of what took place, and I find myself often pausing simply to sit at my desk and allow my mind's eye to erase the wall of this familiar study and instead to show me events as they just unfolded. I find myself watching them as an admirer of a particular play—or a singular performer—would return to the theatre time and again, gladly bearing money in hand to repeat the identical experience.

This was no farce, however, for all that a disguise in the form of an elderly bookseller played a part. The dramatic scene in my consulting room, the journey to the empty house, the changes in the wax dummy's familiar profile—they were real. They must have been. My shoulder aches from when Colonel Moran tried despite the blow to his cranium to wrench himself away from my fierce grasp, and the high shriek of my friend's summons on the police whistle remains in my ears even still.

My friend—I can hardly credit it.

Sherlock Holmes is alive, and what is more, now I am aware of the fact, and for the very gladdest of reasons.

Sherlock Holmes has returned to Baker Street.

The Adventure of
the Memento Mori

It will come as no very stirring surprise to the followers of these accounts
that the spring of the year 1894 was a period of extreme adjustment for
me in the deepest personal sense. I yet spent my days in sharp remembrance of the dear soul whose life had so brightened my own and, while
black coats had eventually been put aside for quiet grey suits with sable
armbands and jackets cut rather slimmer than of old, I still was forced
to push away dark reflections. Feeling the loss of someone precious, I
have found, never occurs when one expects it—when the attention snags
upon a petite blonde passing in the street, or the ears catch strains of a
dearly loved song. Mary lived in such disparate sights as scraps of em-
broidery thread and the hairline crack in our front doorstep that always
used to vex her so, and rather than avoid her memory, I hoarded these
reminders like the newly widowed glutton I was.

No less alarming, though a circumstance so impossibly joyful it
often threatened to overwhelm my powers of basic comprehension, was
the fact that Mr. Sherlock Holmes was now alive and relatively well and
residing in Baker Street—and not, as I had weeks previously supposed,
lost to me forever at the bottom of a merciless cauldron in Switzerland.

As my goal has ever been to polish my friend's good name rather than tarnish it, and since Holmes's soft-spoken and sincere account of his falsified death led me to conclude that both he and I had been in mortal danger prior to his . . . disappearance, I shall call it . . . I long endeavored to keep these records free from the suggestion that his return was both a cure and a wound, a burn and its balm. Sherlock Holmes had taken it upon himself to rid London of the vilest criminal network ever created, and apparently my part had been to mourn the fallen hero publicly. That aforementioned hero was still very much alive, however—one might even say spry now that he had eaten a meal or two and slept in a bed—and continually materializing upon the doorstep of my medical practice.

"Watson," Sherlock Holmes announced after bursting into my consulting room and stopping half-poised upon his toes, "there's work to be done!"

"Yes," I sighed. "If I am to save this practice, a great deal of work is to be done."

Holmes regarded me with the intensity a sable-headed magpie might devote to a glittering trinket obscured in a mound of rubbish. I sat at my desk, elbows resting upon paperwork which I did not wish to contemplate then or ever; Mary's illness in its final stages had caused me to all but abandon my post as medico save where she herself was concerned, for there was something unspeakably painful about tending to mild attacks of gout and croup while my wife was dying. I could not bring myself to part from her, and whenever I attempted to maintain at least a semblance of a career, I found my attention too scattered to practice medicine responsibly in any event.

At first this negligence of mine was not at issue, for I had money saved. Now, having been on the verge of abandoning London entirely prior to my friend's dramatic return, I was forced to contemplate the grim reality of my situation. This endeavor proved greatly hampered by my being dragged away at all hours of the day and night to investigate crimes. Why Holmes had determined following the affair I called "The

Adventure of the Empty House" that he should invade my office with such regularity remained a mystery, but one I was determined to let lie. I am not, after all, the world-renowned sleuth.

My friend deposited a small object upon the accounting ledger before me. It was addressed to *Sherlock Holmes*, and he had presumably sliced the wrapping meticulously with a letter opener. Pulling back the brown paper, I discovered a used cigar box, and within it a small silver brooch nestled in crumpled newsprint. Though of no great value, it was a pretty trinket. A lock of raven hair, artfully curled, rested in the center of the ornament under polished glass. When I turned it over, I found it had been inscribed with the words *"Omnes vulnerant, postuma necat."*

"'All hours wound, the final one kills,'" I translated. "This is a remembrance of someone."

"A memento mori, yes—at once a reminder of the particular departed and a philosophical meditation that every life is fleeting."

I pushed it away. Holmes whisked his hat from his head and flung it deftly upon one of my two armchairs, followed by his overcoat, which was liberally speckled with raindrops. It had been a cold April, rain lashing down in frigid shards to shatter upon the cobbles, and the skies appeared not to have registered that it was now May. My friend leaned forward over my desk, pale eyes gleaming, with the faint dash of color along his cheeks that meant my morning was about to take a turn for the unconventional.

"I've accounts to settle," I said pointedly. "You look much better daily, I am happy to note."

"What?"

"When you first popped up like a jack-in-the-box, you were half-starved and as pallid as a corpse. This is a decided improvement."

"Yes, well, Mrs. Hudson has been relentlessly forcing her heartiest Scotch stews upon me. It is a singular anomaly of human nature," Holmes mused, continuing to scrutinize his mail with avidity, "that we as a species seem so compelled to mystify what is after all a natural cycle."

"Not so very singular. I'm engaged at the moment, Holmes."

"You are familiar with the Stoics? Of course you are. I've always been drawn to the notion that the mind of man is capable of distinguishing truth from fallacy through dispassionate reason, but back when we were all translating Seneca in our form books, I couldn't help being struck by his preoccupation with mortality. Medieval philosophers built on that foundation to an almost obsessive regard for *transi* tombs, architectural renderings of angels snuffing out lights, and skeletons in fantastical states of disrepair."

"Holmes."

"While these artifacts are artistic enough in some cases, I always thought paying such extravagant attention to decay rather useless, since it isn't as if we can stop the march of time simply by marking it. And of course, the practice of wearing physical tokens taken from the bodies of the dead dates back to ancient—"

"Eleven times."

He blinked. "I beg your pardon?"

"Eleven times during the past fortnight, you have appeared here and have whisked me off to solve whatever conundrums the Yard has failed to clear up in your absence, and my practice was hardly flourishing *before* your arrival."

My friend's hand dived into the inner pocket of his frock coat, emerging with a folded note. "This accompanied the brooch."

I took it. The missive went in this way:

I have read much of your exploits. Save me please, Mr. Holmes, for it is not too late. Single red and white tower rising, faint roar of the train, sun sets to the left, lightning-scarred elm, smell of death. Help me if you are able, for I can tell you nothing more, save that I know I cannot survive here.

Sherlock Holmes took several tense steps to the right of my desk, and then to the left, drawing his fingertips along the thin line of his lips. For myself, I admit that my pulse thrilled at the obscure but remarkably imperative plea. There can be no comparison between my interest in banking ledgers and my interest in mysterious appeals for aid.

"It came through the second post," Holmes said in his usual clipped, precise manner. "As you can see, no return address is indicated. Peculiar."

"That is unfortunate, for her message is most cryptic."

"Yes, it is a woman's writing." Holmes's eyes fell shut as he continued to pace. "Tell me what else you can deduce."

"But I—"

"My dear fellow, I swear to you that your mind, with its altogether unpredictable limitations, is of the utmost value to my thought processes."

My having been unintentionally slighted by Holmes for years and all too recently believing that I would hear such backward compliments no more, this remark failed to distress me. I lowered my gaze and did as he asked.

"The jewelry itself is unremarkable—as you said, memento mori are common enough." Frowning, I lifted the receptacle. "The wrapping is ordinary brown paper, and the box constructed of inexpensive pine. I can draw no conclusions from either. Doubtless you've already identified the newspaper yourself?"

"The *Evening News*, first printing, day before yesterday."

"Well, there you are, then. The accompanying note is hastily written and appears to be penned by an educated woman. Have I missed anything?"

"Of course you have." Holmes made yet another abrupt about-face, tucking his tented fingers under his determined chin. "Though I fear that the physical evidence cannot lead us to a deduction regarding the exact whereabouts of this person. Other than the facts that the note was written in the dead of night, in a cramped, presumably secret space, and that the author has as little idea where she is as I presently do, and has more than likely been in some grim form of captivity for over five months, I can tell you nothing."

"However can you have discovered all that?" I exclaimed.

He waved a hand in the air. "There are no fewer than three small drippings of tallow upon the surface of the box and one on the note itself. No great leap of judgment, therefore, to discern that she had both limited light and space in which to accomplish her designs—and since the matter is manifestly a pressing one, this roundabout way of describing her residence can only mean she doesn't know herself. Otherwise, she certainly would have given me a specific locale."

"But Holmes, you claim she has been kept a prisoner for five months or more. How can you have reached so exact a figure?"

"Surely we can assume that she has consulted me thanks to the popularity of *The Strand Magazine*, since she reports here that she has read of my exploits, and I make it my habit to avoid the attention of the popular press. In addition, she knows our—my address," he corrected himself without inflection, "but not my postal code, which is left blank. Her knowledge comes from your tales, not a directory. She has not seen the latest issue, however, which circulated five months ago. Or she would not have consulted me at all."

This inference, like the others, was delivered in that distantly clinical tone Holmes ever adopts when exerting his extraordinary faculty. I expected no less, and no more for that matter, but a hot charge of anger shot through me in spite of myself. For he was right; not only had my last story in *The Strand* garnered an enormous readership, but the newspapers had seen fit to offer their own editorials upon the article's contents. Surely there was not a free man or woman in London who had failed to notice that Sherlock Holmes was dead—had been dead for three years—and that I had been writing adventure stories about him all the while.

"Watson?" My silence, where of habit further questioning would have followed, prompted my friend to step toward the desk.

"It's nothing."

Frowning, Holmes tilted his head at me. "It isn't nothing."

"Leave it, please, I am too far extended of late."

"But—"

"I said never mind. What of the written clues she has provided?"

Holmes settled into the chair not occupied by his hat and coat, a worried line firmly fixed between his brows. "They trouble me. Under ordinary circumstances they would not, but as they seem to be the only way to find her and I am just returned from abroad . . ."

I comprehended him at once, and the realization was unsettling. "You are less familiar with London's topography than you were."

The detective gazed into the middle distance, which in him always indicates concentration rather than distraction. "One must stringently categorize the value of each detail in such a case as this."

"How so?"

"To take the data in order of importance, the fact that the house is within earshot of a train will be of use to us only when its locale is more exactly determined, and likewise the sun setting to her left will become relevant *after* the building itself is identified, not before. A lightning-scarred tree implies a rise of some kind, an element of height in the landscape, though that is merest probability. It is upon the first and last phrases we must rely, and yet I cannot place them as I normally could."

"'Single red and white tower rising . . . smell of death,'" I read aloud. "The latter is most ominous."

"Perhaps." He rubbed at his jawline in frustration. "Perhaps not. The sheer length of her incarceration makes it likelier far that she is in an isolated location rather than a populated area, which to me indicates a country suburb of London. And in order for the smell of death to be a valid guidepost, it must be a constant element of the landscape rather than an occasional one. If the reek of decaying corpses were to blame, suspicions from even the occasional passerby would be alerted and a general alarm would go up. I think it far more probable that the house is downwind of a tannery."

"Wonderful!" Perhaps it was my natural affection for intrigue—or perhaps yet again I had simply missed these moments—but I could not help delighting at such casual displays of brilliance. "A tannery likewise suggests the countryside rather than London proper. It's remarkably well reasoned."

"It's insufficient!" My friend's fists clenched briefly, but harder than was usual for such a reserved man. "At any other time, Watson, at *any* other time—it's maddening. Within a few weeks, I should have memorized the new buildings in the outer towns. It's ghastly to be shackled this way, this wretched feeling of *blank* spaces in my mind—"

"We can find a way to manage," I promised him, alarmed.

"How?" he demanded. "My talents may be undiminished, but my information is outdated. Since the tower is 'rising' in the active sense, it is under construction. Yes? Red and white indicate brick and stone combined in a decorative manner, so the project is clearly well funded. I suspect we are dealing with a municipal building of some sort, as 'spire' is a much better word for a church tower and the turret of a grand estate would likely not be singular. The best fit is a clock tower, for my money. But that fails to pinpoint—"

"Croydon!" I gasped. "My God, Holmes. They're building just such a clock tower in Croydon—they began it the year after you died."

"After I—" Holmes began, and then most uncharacteristically ceased speaking.

When once I had heard myself, I could hardly blame the man. With a blank look, he rose from his chair. The casual observer might have thought him absorbed only in the conundrum at hand, but I knew that I had rattled him. It is such a difficult matter to disconcert Sherlock Holmes by design that doing so unintentionally was enough to throw me off my own guard entirely. He did speak soon enough, however, and of the case, as I had expected.

"Watson, are you certain this structure is to be found in Croydon?"

"Unquestionably."

"It would not be the first occasion that we were summoned to Croydon by a grotesque package." My friend's brows grew stormier by the second.

"No," I agreed, remembering Miss Susan Cushing and her ghastly receipt of salt-packed severed ears some six years previous, during what were for me far happier times.

My friend dived across the room for his hat and coat, his spare frame galvanized as if by electricity. Whirling, he found me lost in reflection. A spasm of uncertainty creased the edges of his hooded eyes. The silence that stretched on as he carefully selected his next words proved far too loud for my frayed nerves.

"Oh, for heaven's sake." Standing, I tucked the note back into the cigar box with its somber pin and passed the package to Holmes. "Is your cab still outside? I'll just look up the trains."

A grim smile flashed to life upon Holmes's narrow features as he darted out the door, and I reflected whilst flipping through my Bradshaw upon his curious propensity for sudden disappearances. As a precaution, one I had more than once proved grateful for in times of direst need, I slid my service revolver into my pocket. Its weight, even if the weapon was never called upon, would provide a certain degree of familiar reassurance.

The train ride to Croydon was a brooding one, for I think both Holmes and I were too well aware that my having observed a nascent clock tower by no means guaranteed that we were heading in the right direction. Rain continued to pelt the drab row houses and the rubble-dotted yards of outer London, and as we left behind us the great stone heart of the Empire, I fretted over whether my memory would in fact do us service. My information was sound, but were it to fail us, I knew that I would grow despondent over what more I could do. It is not in my nature to shirk responsibility. As for Holmes, I was accustomed to the almost feral energy which coursed through him when he was on the hunt, but on that morning his spirited drive seemed less focused than usual. He would alternately scowl out the window at the drenched trees and cast odd looks at my reflection in the glass.

"Why do you think she sent the brooch?" I inquired when a copy of the morning paper had proved an utterly ineffectual distraction and Holmes had for the third time heaved a quick sigh through his prominent nose.

"I haven't the smallest notion." Holmes pulled out his watch, glared at it, and then snapped it closed. "Watson, I once was consulted by a woman who ran a pub in Lambeth. She suspected embezzlement by her eldest son and I proved her correct, but that was the least of her troubles—the property was falling down about their ears, the landlord was a rascal, and hardly a day passed without a riotous brawl during which the patrons cracked each other's pates open."

"Ah," said I, entirely bemused.

The train clacked onward, and the sun rose higher, and Holmes hissed through his teeth a tiny breath that he was not himself aware of, I am certain. At length, studying an expression on my face which may or may not have been incredulity, he continued.

"Her establishment caused her more distress than was tenable. After turning the light-fingered son out on his ear, she took digs with her sister in Newham. The quality of her life improved tenfold."

"I congratulate her," I offered stiffly.

"Even after the issue of embezzlement was resolved, being the mistress of such an establishment could bring her no pleasure. She was not admitting failure, on the contrary, but rather steering the ship of her life on another trajectory."

"Admirable."

"So you see my point, of course."

"I fear I must disenchant you on that count."

I waited for an explanation with my brows mildly raised. But Holmes only fell to chewing at his thumbnail before muttering something about the time the train was making and lapsing into a brown study. Not a word could I get out of him in that state even when I was in my own prime, so I took my notebook from my jacket pocket and attempted to calculate which of my regular patients might be induced—with gentlest persuasion—to settle their outstanding bills, the next measure being continuing to wear a hat that had already begun to split at the brim.

Our boots sank into thick, mineral-scented mud as we quit the platform of the train station in Croydon. The skies had cleared somewhat, but charcoal-edged clouds still glowered heavily above, and the wind flailed the delicate May leaves with a punishing force. My heart sank when I did not at once set eyes upon the structure I had recommended, but soon I oriented myself aright and angled toward it, pulse quickening.

"There," said I, pointing. "It fits the description, does it not?"

Before us rose a half-completed clock tower, the bricks stained a dull maroon by the storm and the white stone shining with moisture. It was a perfectly ordinary building save for the two facts that Sherlock Holmes stood beside me and a fellow creature wanted our help, and so it meant much more; it meant that I was a part of something again, that I could be of some assistance. Labor had ceased during the inclement weather, but a workman with a green cap pulled low over a bullish, good-natured face was wheeling a barrow full of trowels and other equipment out from under a slicked tarp awning nearby.

"By Jove, if you are right, my dear fellow, and this is the place—I say, sir!" Holmes called out.

The builder dropped the handles of his barrow and wiped his palms on plaster-stained corduroy trousers. His chin came up as he gave us a querying half-smile, revealing merrily disorganized teeth. "Aye?"

Holmes offered his hand in the open, genial manner he always assumes with strangers who might be possessed of valuable information. "A very good day to you! My friend and I are merchants from the city—we've a partnership in a luggage shop and business of late has been gratifyingly steady, you understand? In an effort to absorb all the intricacies of our enterprise, we've decided to approach a few tanneries and learn more about the process in the interests of quality control."

"Have y'now?"

"We wish to take a scientific approach."

"Pretty foul afternoon you lot are in for," the laborer answered doubtfully.

"We are men of strong stomachs with a professional stake in the matter. Though I thank you for your concern. There are tanning facilities hereabouts, we understand?"

"Not so very many, but aye." The affable chap rubbed at his bristling chin. "Just over that rise yonder is a road that passes two tanneries a mile or so off. Then again, to the west of us by the post road there's a few more. Head in either direction and offer a little something for their trouble, and you should get what you're after."

"Thank you very much indeed for your help."

"Just follow your nose." He lifted the handles of his barrow, grinning with a backward glance.

My comrade strode off with a purpose, and I hastened to keep pace with him. Though we had been given two choices of compass direction, he directed our steps with vigor toward the north, and we soon began to climb the gentle slope of a hill dotted with darkly whispering oaks. I had begun to feel the French sensation that I was repeating an experience before I understood that I was only recalling the facts of the case, as indeed Holmes was.

"You are thinking of the lightning-scarred tree," I surmised.

"Excellent, Watson. While that landmark could prove to be anywhere, it hints at elevation, and even a hint in this instance is better than nothing."

Not long after we had quit the town proper, the houses grew widely scattered. My friend has no great affection for the countryside, and while I cannot agree with him that secret depravities lurk within every isolated homestead, I admit that on this occasion the emptiness of the place—dark branches glistening with rain, sharp-edged grasses gleaming knifelike along the road's edges—oppressed my spirits. The thin keening of the wind was the only sound save for our own brisk footsteps.

We had walked for nearly a mile, passing fewer and fewer residences, when a whiff of something rancid met my nose. My friend, no doubt, had already identified the aroma.

"We're quite close, I think. Holmes, what's the matter?"

The detective stopped, his posture as alert as that of a thoroughbred at the starting gate. To our left were fields; to our right was a walled estate with a gravel drive and a tall, decorative iron fence discouraging any visitors by means of a large padlock. Approaching the gate, Holmes reached out and drew his fingers lightly down one of the bars.

"This house is all wrong," said he.

He was correct, although I did not yet know why. Something about the structure was unnerving, like hearing a stealthy footstep when one had imagined oneself alone. I joined him, staring through the gaps in the ornate metal fence. What was visible seemed a pleasant enough dwelling constructed of stately stone in a modern style, with drenched ivy clambering up the walls and the shutters of the many windows pulled tight against the rain.

Then, with a start, I spied an elderly plane tree; a raw wound as if marking a blow from a fiery ax marred its mottled trunk, the unlucky branch long since carted away.

"Holmes, surely this is the place!" I hissed. "But what do you mean when you say that it's wrong?"

"I mean that nothing about it makes sense. Why build a new house on the outskirts of town, in an atmosphere ruined by tanneries? Apart from that, the precautionary spikes atop this fencing are most disturbing."

"Are they?"

"Yes. They face inward. What does that suggest to you?"

"My God. That they are designed for keeping residents in rather than intruders out?"

"I can see no other logical explanation."

I spied a few feet away from us a plaque in the stone wall next to the iron gate. The engraved letters read *Dr. Henry Staunton's Private Rest Home for Ladies.*

"This is an institution for the mentally ill," I breathed.

"Which is in appearance entirely respectable, but constructed on property that in every way discourages casual visitation."

The look of disquiet that shot between us sent my pulse charging through my veins. An instant later, Holmes had stepped onto one of the crossbars of the locked gate. Using his wiry grip to pull himself upward, he stepped carefully onto my shoulder where I had braced myself against the stone. Once seated upon the wall's apex, he steadied himself with one hand gripping the nearest macabre iron spike, and managed with his fist closed around my forearm and one or two toeholds in the eroding stone to pull me up after him. We landed on the opposite side, breathing hard and brushing the grit from our fingers.

"Tradesmen's entrances are never locked during daylight," Holmes declared. "Quickly!"

As we sprinted across the grounds, I saw my friend making note of the relative position of the sun in the sky and the lightning-ravaged tree and knew that he was mapping the interior of the house in his mind, the spatial relations that would help us to find our mysterious correspondent before the alarm could be raised. Though Holmes was correct about the door in the rear being open, as we passed through the kitchens a surly-seeming creature with tangled blond hair and a stained apron cried out at us to stop.

"What on earth do ye mean by this?" the crone shrieked. "Who are ye to barge in and—"

Neither of us heeded her. A wide, shadow-shrouded staircase flew past us, then a murky passage, then another, like the twists and turns of a maze, and despite the fact we had never set foot in the place, my friend never wavered in his course.

"You know where we're going?"

"The second floor," he replied, "for at this distance the incomplete tower would not otherwise be visible."

Finally we reached a long hallway papered in a twining beige leaf pattern that had faded and peeled so badly it looked as if winter itself had ravaged the flora. Holmes strode to the end of the corridor and set his long fingers on a doorknob. Finding the door locked, he dropped to one knee and produced his pocketknife, opening a slender blade. Within seconds, he had picked the lock and we had pushed our way into the room.

An emaciated lady, deathly still, lay upon a bed beneath a shuttered window which sent cool bars of grey light across her wasted countenance. Though I could see but poorly in the gloom, I noted at once that her hair was black as onyx, the color identical to the lock trapped within the memento mori in Holmes's coat pocket.

I know my role at such times and hastened to her bedside. She had once been a lovely woman, with very slender lips and a high, thoughtful brow—but her cheeks seemed flushed with fever and the edges of her mouth were cracked and peeling. When her eyes flicked open at my touch on her heated skin, I found them a startling shade of pale green. Her hand clutched at mine and I gently disengaged it, instead pressing my fingers to her wrist. Her pulse was as frantic and fluttering as the wing of a moth.

"It isn't helping," she moaned in a paper-thin voice. "Please don't make me stay here. I can't bear it any longer. I'll swear upon a Bible it isn't helping."

"What isn't helping, miss?"

"The treatment," she gasped, shuddering. "The doctor won't *listen*."

"There, there. It's all right now—my name is Dr. John Watson, and I vow that we won't let anyone harm you further. Tell me what he has given you, if you are able."

"I don't know. Some sort of potion. It looked like drops of silver."

Holmes's piercing voice came from behind my shoulder. "Mercury poisoning, would you not agree, Doctor?"

"Almost certainly."

"Will she be all right?"

"I can't yet—"

"What the *devil* is going on here?" a masterful voice thundered.

The afflicted woman in the bed shied away in fright as I instinctually flung an arm between her body and the intruder. Filling the doorway was a stoop-shouldered gentleman of about fifty years, with a boldly rectangular face and a sneer of outrage on his lips. Though his tailored clothing and neatly brushed brown beard were the height of respectability, there was a look of almost reptilian cold-bloodedness in his flashing eyes.

"Dr. Henry Staunton, I presume." Holmes confronted him. "Your churlishness is misplaced—we were summoned. This woman is a client of mine."

"A client?" Dr. Staunton scoffed. "Impossible! You will both cease alarming my charge and remove yourself from my property or I shall summon the police forthwith."

"By all means," said I, carefully producing my revolver and turning so that the quivering lady should not see it. "Please summon the police."

"God in heaven! What sort of housebreakers are you, to barrel in at gunpoint and bully my patients?"

"I am Mr. Sherlock Holmes, and he is not bullying her." Holmes revealed a gun of his own. "I would venture to say he may in fact be saving her life. Now, Watson, I can think of no finer course of action than to follow Dr. Staunton's admirable advice, and to send for some stout local constabulary."

"Preposterous!" Dr. Staunton bellowed. "This is a private institution. I'll set the dogs on you first!"

Our client screamed, shrinking farther against the wall in terror. I was on my feet by this time. "You'll do no such thing. Holmes, where are we to put him?"

"Worry not, Watson. I've every intention of locking both him and his staff in their cellar," Holmes said frigidly. "With tremendous pleasure."

Little remains to tell of what I would recall as one of the most macabre cases Holmes and I were ever prevailed upon to solve—and the second of a grim pair taking place in the quiet town of Croydon. We lost no time in imprisoning the doctor and his four nurses, which would have been a daunting task save for the fact that bullets are very effective arguments. While I tended to the lady and looked into the state of the other inmates, Holmes himself ran for the stables, saddled a mount, and had soon fetched a set of burly policemen.

It was what happened next that I hate to think upon. Alongside the officers, we discovered overwhelming evidence of the most grotesque experimentation upon Dr. Henry Staunton's subjects. Ice baths, electricity, starvation, isolation, various hysteria remedies too foul to name—apparently, no atrocity was considered too outlandish to attempt in the name of progress. Never shall I forget the sight of his "treatment room," a chamber of horrors better resembling a feudal dungeon than a haven of healing, and one which the official force quit in revulsion after less than five minutes' perusal. My friend and I remained, shaken beyond our worst expectations.

"The depths to which human depravity can sink will never cease to confound me." Holmes's face was rigid with disgust as we gazed at a wall of instruments I did not even attempt to identify. "What are we to make of the species in light of this room? Where is progress, where is logic, where is reason itself, when a savage smashing his comrade's skull with a rock would be kinder treatment of the race? I ask you, what is the limit to our perversion?"

"It doesn't bear thinking on," I agreed, overwhelmed by the evil surrounding us.

"Hell is empty," Holmes concluded under his breath, "and all the devils are here."

Stricken, I pressed his still too-thin arm in reassurance. "Some of the angels are too, my dear fellow."

He dropped a set of forceps back upon a tabletop, his jaw set stonily. "Not enough of them."

"No, there I will not contradict you."

"What is the solution, then?"

"I have no answer. I don't know that anyone does, Holmes."

When my friend's eyes snagged upon the sort of sewing needle which ought to have been found at the nearby tannery and instead was set in a case alongside others like it, he froze with such a look of valiantly restrained anguish that I instantly steered him straight out of the room. My never having seen the expression before, it startled me deeply. The mere fact that he allowed me the liberty of propelling him away, when ordinarily I am ever the one who follows his lead, told me with what graphic colors his imagination was painting possibilities from the data at hand.

Planting his back against the wall in the corridor, I admonished him, "All right, that's enough, don't you agree?"

My friend's shoulders could have been carved from granite, but his face was now slack and neutral enough to cause the gravest alarm. That his time abroad had been more nightmare than holiday I had already deduced from the obvious physical signs, but to see the ruthless mastery of his mind so adversely affected confirmed my worst fears. I wondered with a sharp ache in my chest—and always shall wonder, I believe—what terrors I missed when I could have been of service, even if only to the smallest degree.

"Holmes," I insisted, giving him a shake, "you're conducting a fruitless and damaging exercise, and I won't have it. Are you listening to me? Holmes, *stop*."

When I raised my voice, he came back to himself with a tiny shudder. I let him go, studying him carefully. Raising his hands to his brow and brushing his closed eyelids with his thumbs, he breathed several times before saying, "That was—for a moment, I . . ."

"No, take your time. Slowly. There, that's right."

"My sincerest apologies for that appalling display."

"Don't be ridiculous."

He laughed silently, though I could detect no mirth in the expression. Patiently I waited as horror ebbed and calm settled into its void. Less than ten seconds later, he had pushed himself upright and was distantly ironical again.

"Well, if anyone is going to watch me being ridiculous, then thank God it's you. I know I was vexing you earlier, but I appreciate your accompanying me this afternoon," he added crisply. "I suspect that it should not have been very tolerable otherwise."

"My dear chap, no matter how much pressure I am presently under, you must know that nothing better pleases me than watching you bring light where all is darkness."

"Nonsense. I should never have found the place at all if not for you."

"Well, you have said before that a trusty companion is sometimes of use."

"Always," he corrected me with an unreadable look. "You misquote me dreadfully. Always of use."

"And I am doubly glad to have been so on this occasion. You had better question Miss Rorden before the police monopolize her."

"Dear me, is that my client's name? I am clearly quite incapable without you," he joked, quirking a somber smile.

"Yes, Miss Emilia Rorden. And you were preoccupied with herding a pack of villains into a root cellar."

"I confess that even given the shameful treatment she has suffered, I am eager to speak with her. Despite her weakened condition, she is obviously a highly resourceful young lady. Come to that, is she strong enough?"

"Go gently with her, but I believe so. I've given her a mild sedative, and yarrow tea with a cold water bottle for the fever. None of the other women here are at all healthy, but they aren't presently in any severe danger either, and we've summoned an ambulance. Lead the way, Holmes."

When we had regained Miss Rorden's sickroom, I saw that my immediate measures had taken some effect, though whether her constitution could ever fully recover from mercury poisoning was beyond my control. Holmes pulled a chair up to her bedside, saying, "You have been much tried already, Miss Rorden, but I beg leave to speak with you for a few minutes before we take you away from this terrible place."

Miss Rorden's hair gushed over the pillow in a tangled black cascade like a spill of creosote; her chiseled features were still both wan and fevered above the rubber bag I had filled with ice and placed beneath her pillow. But her green eyes were clear as tinted glass now and she nodded, weakly taking the hand my friend proffered her.

"Do you know how you came to be here?" he asked.

"I suffer from epilepsy, Mr. Holmes," she whispered as strongly as she could. "The fits are not severe, but they are frequent. They were a burden to my family, not to mention a public disgrace on more than one occasion. Eventually my parents despaired of curing me by conventional means and sent me to the only specialist they could afford. In my feverish state when I wrote to you, I had forgotten his name, recalling only certain tokens by which you might know my whereabouts."

"Henry Staunton. He will trouble you no further, I promise that, Miss Rorden. Go on."

"I fear we have all been the victims of the vilest quackery imaginable. The lengths he went to, the torments he devised—"

"We know of them already and you need not burden yourself with that part of the account today," Holmes interrupted gently.

"Thank God. I am one of the lucky ones, I know it, to be merely subjected to slow poisoning. Thinking about what some of the others went through . . . oh, it's unbearable. In any case, I fear that our mortality rate here has reflected the care Dr. Staunton takes with his patients, which soon revealed a bizarre quirk of his nature to us."

"And this was?"

"Whenever one of us seemed likely to expire from the ill-use, he would ask which of our loved ones we cared for the most and bring a memento mori to the deathbed, requesting a lock of hair. There was always a gleam in his eye when he did so—not of sympathy, or even apathy, but of pleasure. It was . . . monstrously cruel, Mr. Holmes, to treat the expiring as if they were some sort of prize. He must have collected a dozen such remembrances, always carefully addressing the package in his own hand and assuring whoever stood at death's door that, though she was likely to have passed away by the time it arrived at its destination, nevertheless her kin would always treasure this final gift from her."

"Trophies," my friend mused in quiet revulsion. "Possibly he also kept locks for himself postmortem; possibly the ceremony was enough to satisfy him. You say that he would actually send these tokens to your parents? Your husbands?"

"Whomever we most urgently wished to bid farewell to, yes. But it was obvious that the true joy he derived was from the added mental torment of our realizing the end had come—of tearing us away from our last shred of hope. No one escaped this ritual. He would snip a lock, we would indicate a recipient, and we knew we were done for. After a very short interim, his latest victim would be in the ground."

"Dear God, he's entirely mad," I breathed.

"Very probably madness, at the least virulent sadism, or a combination of the two." Holmes spoke in a mellow tone so as not to further upset the lady, but I needed nothing more than his ramrod posture to know that Dr. Staunton's days on earth were numbered.

"Three of the four nurses here are as vile as the doctor, but one is merely plodding and stupid," Miss Rorden continued. "After I was subjected to the ceremony of consigning a lock of my hair to its case, and he had prepared it for posting, I remembered your name from *The Strand*, Mr. Holmes, and where you reside. I had a vague recollection of the impossible feats you were said to accomplish, had hazy visions of you finding and saving me. My only chance at survival seemed to be smuggling you a message, however slender the chance it would arrive safely. When next I saw the nurse who is more witless than cruel, I convinced her in great desperation that my remembrance to my family had been misaddressed, that I had made an error in telling the doctor where it ought to be delivered, and that she *must* bring me pen and paper. When I think of what Dr. Staunton would have done had he found out my ploy! We spirited all away under a staircase where I wrote to you by candlelight, Mr. Holmes—it must have been delirious, barely legible."

"It was brilliantly thought of and courageously executed."

"There was no way for me to know that it would go out with the morning post, but it must have, oh it must have, for you are here," she concluded on a sob, and he tightened his grip on her hand. "He would have killed me within a day or two. Dear God, to think of it! He has killed so many of us."

Seeing that the interview could go no further, we soothed her spirits and I administered another round of compresses, which further reduced her temperature and soon found her drifting in a troubled but genuine sleep. Thus were all Holmes's deductions confirmed, and I am flattered to say that while my never very humble friend could have taken the credit, he ever afterward would admit only to having "helped to hang" the infamous Henry Staunton, as I myself had identified the crucial clock tower.

Sitting across from each other in the train returning to London upon the late evening in question, the women Staunton had abused so shamefully having been rushed to the nearest hospital, we both regained our energies and spirits somewhat. Holmes, however—though revived—seemed distinctly ill at ease. During one stretch of countryside, in fact, he appeared for some twenty minutes to be upon the verge of speech. My friend was never one to mince words, so I waited in baffled silence as he fidgeted.

When at last Holmes did give way to utterance, he announced imperiously, "You ought to sell it."

Having never seen Holmes look so aloof and so apprehensive simultaneously, I took a long moment to study him. "And what am I selling?"

"Your practice, of course."

At times, friendship with Sherlock Holmes is an easy matter of shared concerts, quiet suppers, and the ever-present chance of witnessing his remarkable intellect blazing to life over a conundrum worthy of his artistry. At others, such as the moment to which I refer, his assumed authority can be just a trifle vexing even to men who habitually charge themselves to keep their tempers.

"Indeed. How do you propose I live, then?"

"Howsoever you please, so long as it's at Baker Street. It is most inconvenient for me to travel so far every time I am in need of your assistance."

When my mouth opened upon a truly tart reply, he held up a hand in a far more placating manner. "No, please hear me out."

"I really don't see why I ought to, Holmes."

"A profession is only as valuable as it makes a man feel, my dear fellow."

"So you propose that I discard mine?"

"You're a writer."

Such a wealth of conflicting feeling assaulted me that I could only retort icily, "You mean *biographer*."

Silence flooded the train car, a silence in which I took a certain harsh satisfaction.

"And what if I do?" he asked, looking for an instant almost frightened.

"A poor one, as you have said repeatedly."

"As I regret. When I came back, and required aid in besting Colonel Moran, I could turn to no one else, nor did I desire to do so. I needed you, and you said, 'where you like and when you like.'" Holmes paused, passing a knuckle over his lips briefly. "I had not expected that. Only hoped it. I owe you more than a set of rooms."

My face turned to the window. The tree line blurred as I thought of my combined home and practice and all that had taken place within its walls. Of the laughter, and the shared silences, and of the memento mori of my late wife's flaxen hair hidden in my bedside table, and of the note I yet retained that ended, *"Believe me to be, my dear fellow, very sincerely yours, Sherlock Holmes."*

"You said in my consulting room dressed as the old bookseller that several times during the last three years, you have taken up your pen to write to me," I remarked when I could speak normally.

"Yes." Holmes's voice was faintly strained, and though I have never once desired to hurt him, I was perversely glad of it.

"What did you wish to say?"

"I don't follow you, Doctor."

"When you took up your pen, what would you have written? Now I am here, you see, and you aren't dead after all, so you can simply tell me. Would it have been merely terse notice that you continued breathing, or would you have included commentary upon the weather in Tibet? Updates regarding your success in researching coal-tar derivatives, perhaps? A colorful portrait of the Khalifa would have proved a most welcome diversion."

"Watson, please don't."

"Fine, as you wish—I should never dream of forcing your confidence. How many times?"

"My dear fellow—"

"How many times is *several*, Holmes?"

"I was guilty of some slight prevarication on that subject. It was not several."

"You never thought of writing me at all, then?"

"It was *dozens*," he said fiercely. "Forty-seven that I can recall specifically, when I actually went so far as to lift a writing implement and set it down again for caution's sake, and every day for three years in the more general sense. I am machinelike, yes, and I am unfeeling, demonstrably, but I am not stupid; I am something of an expert where John Watson is concerned, and I have never in my life gained any pleasure by inflicting pain on the undeserving. What do you take me for, a foul creature along the lines of Dr. Staunton? If so, why should you have suffered my company for this long? No one else on earth has the slightest desire to, after all."

Sighing, I pressed the heels of my hands into my eyes. "I do not *suffer* your company, Holmes. And I ought not to have asked about the letters when I knew it would distress you. That was very unworthy of me."

"No it wasn't. It was a perfectly fair question."

"Nevertheless."

"So to continue on the topic of the day I returned, as that seems to be what you desire to discuss, I told you that I had wished to write to you, and could not. I also told you that I found myself in my old armchair in my old room, and wishing only that I could have seen my old friend in the other chair. Unsurprisingly, I seem to wish the identical thing whenever you are not present, and so I'll ask you plainly: come back to Baker Street." He paused, eyes determinedly fixed upon his knee. "Implying it would be for your sake was not untrue, but it was partial. You would do better to leave your house and practice, and I would do better to see your chair occupied in a more permanent fashion. I said that I owed you a thousand apologies—allow this to be my first. Please. Say *yes* at any moment and I give you my word I'll stop talking."

Chuckling helplessly, I dropped my head back against the seat cushion. As was so often the case, seconds before I had been furious with my friend, and now I could think of him only as the most marvelously strange fellow it had ever been my good fortune to meet. Returning to Baker Street, I thought, would be financially prudent, mentally stimulating, and occasionally maddening. It would be sublime.

"I'll think about it," I told him.

"But we—"

"*Holmes.*"

My friend wisely subsided, and pulled out a pair of cigarettes, and we spent the remainder of the journey quietly smoking. I did think about it, as I had promised him. And before the month was out, the furniture van pulled up to my door.

Notes Regarding
the Disappearance of
Mr. James Phillimore

Beginning this tale is impossible without confessing that penning it is academic in nature; it will never see the light of publication. Sherlock Holmes and I are in complete agreement that the matter cannot possibly be made widely know despite the fact it featured an extraordinary client—one unlike any we had ever encountered previously—and excellent examples of my renowned friend's powers.

Even so, I find myself writing the narrative, and for an eccentric yet definite purpose. Not for *The Strand*—I should never set down in what Holmes rather waspishly terms the "promiscuous" popular accounts of his exploits anything which might harm the innocent or even unjustly malign the guilty—but for my own reasons. I will be certain to elucidate them carefully at the close of this exercise, that I might explain to Sherlock Holmes why I bothered to scribble a story no one on earth is destined to read save for the one man who wishes I would not write about him quite so assiduously. The irony is not lost upon me. But in any event, I find I cannot resist recording the opening act of the drama, representing as it does a textbook example of those qualities which serve to make my friend one of the worst fellow lodgers in

London—and no less, as I shall later demonstrate paradoxically, one of the best simultaneously.

Following his dramatic return from abroad, Sherlock Holmes prevailed upon me to reinstate myself at our familiar rooms in Baker Street. The man is possessed of unearthly powers of persuasion when once he sets his unparalleled mind to a project, and since I have always shared his taste for adventure and intrigue, there seemed no option more agreeable than to throw in my lot with my comrade of old. Within a night or two of sleeping in my familiar bedchamber, the leaves of the plane tree in our back area rustling a friendly homecoming welcome just beyond my window, I felt as lucky a fellow as was possible under the circumstances. My profound happiness over these incredible developments did not mean, however, that Sherlock Holmes has ever been an easy man with whom to reside. On the contrary.

"Good heavens!" was all I managed to ejaculate upon my descent into our sitting room on the morning of May 26th, 1894.

Sherlock Holmes stood in the middle of the comfortable parlor wearing his dressing gown and slippers, feet wide and lean arms akimbo, aiming a medium-sized bow fitted with a steel-tipped hunter's arrow at my writing desk several yards distant. This furnishing he had cleared of all my papers, several of which were freshly organized bills incurred in the process of moving house. They lay scattered upon the floor as if he had simply swept an arm across the surface and sent all flying helter-skelter. The documents, along with several notebooks, a fountain pen and holder, my blotting paper, and a surprisingly ample check for my recently sold home and practice, had been replaced by a haunch of cured ham which already evinced the excellent marksmanship my friend boasts in the realm of archery, with several arrows protruding from its center. Holmes is not the world's foremost shot with a revolver, but for reasons which he has characteristically never disclosed, his skill with a bow is admirable.

"Do not tell me," said I, holding both hands up as I ventured between the detective and the unfortunate piece of meat. "Allow me the dubious pleasure of guessing. You have been engaged over a case which hinges on close-range arrow shots, most probably a murder—"

"Dear me, mistaken already. I haven't been engaged," Holmes interrupted, his always brusque tenor rendered stinging in his exasperation at my interference. "Lady Deborah Garry, the aunt of the notorious rake Alfred St. Edward Garry, died in an unfortunate hunting accident while I was in Montpellier. I read of it in *Le Monde*. Her demise was *not* an accident, however, but rather a killing of the most ruthless variety, which I am about to prove if you would only—"

Crossing my arms, I continued, "After seeing that the surface of the dining table is currently occupied with our breakfast settings, and that your own worktable is still covered in the chemical study you were engaged upon yesterday, you saw fit to clear my desk of objects in the most expedient manner possible—"

"Your grasp of the profoundly self-evident is in rare form this morning, my dear fellow."

"And now, probably because you haven't had a case since last week, you are conducting an experiment which effectively renders *every* surface of our flat unusable."

"That is definitively untrue, as it is being used at present."

"Not by me, however."

"I do not dispute the fact. Watson, you're terribly in the way."

Holmes owns, I have remarked many times, a masterful presence. His great height would likely render this true even in the absence of his casually forceful nature, but I have never been accused of unmanly meekness, and my friend had already been trying my patience for days. My shoulders must have bristled, for his lip curled combatively.

"Extend me the small courtesy of assuring me that my desk will return to its previous state, *sans* any trace of ham, within the next ten minutes, and I shall happily move."

"Impossible," he scoffed, gaunt features twisting in impatience. "Detailed measurements must be taken."

"Steps toward restoring my belongings must be taken."

"Watson, I have never before witnessed you obstructing the cause of justice," he averred snappishly.

"Clearly my character has continued to develop quirks over time, as doubtless has your own. It is a natural phenomenon associated with aging. Pick up my things or the results of yesterday's studies of potassium iodide are going out that window," said I, pointing.

"You wouldn't," he said in unfeigned horror.

"Try me," I shot back.

The door of our sitting room opened after a discreet knock and Mrs. Hudson poked her head within. "There's a gentleman to see you, Mr. Holmes. He hasn't any card, but he says his name is Mr. Edward Phillimore, and it's a most urgent matter, . . . Oh, heavens!"

It is a testament to the marvelously phlegmatic nature of our landlady that the sight of Holmes aiming an arrow more or less in my direction earned merely a mild exclamation and an uplifted eyebrow on her part. Fiddling with the lace at her neck, she shyly ventured farther into the room.

"My dear lady, I am presently occupied upon an experiment which has presented grievous unforeseen difficulties," Holmes answered without turning away from me.

"Can I be of any help? Only I wonder whether it's quite safe and all, Mr. Holmes, erm . . . well, *wielding* such a thing indoors."

"I can assure you that I am a trained expert as regards the wielding, but *distractions* at a juncture this critical I admit are very vexing indeed. Now, off with you."

"But the poor gentleman's brother is missing, and he claims that only you can help him." Mrs. Hudson persisted. "He is most upset."

"Forgive us for startling you, Mrs. Hudson. Please send him straight up," I requested, draping the haunch with a napkin from the table. Smiling gratefully, she turned to go, shutting the door behind her.

"What the devil are you playing at? You are not the manager of my career!" Holmes exclaimed, at last setting the weapon on the sideboard.

"And this is not the only set of liveable rooms in London!" I cried in my profound annoyance.

Holmes appeared very satisfyingly shocked, grey eyes wide and mouth open upon a scathing retort I was never destined to learn. Mr. Edward Phillimore entered a few seconds later, and, after making all necessary introductions, I settled myself in my armchair to hear him out.

Mr. Edward Phillimore was indeed, as Mrs. Hudson had indicated, upset. He was a slight man, quietly dressed in a black suit with a grey waistcoat and a rounded hard felt hat with a modest charcoal band, a slender silver watch chain and a temperance pin his only ornaments, and I did not need my friend's powers of observation to note that he had been badly shaken by the disappearance of his sibling. His hands were noticeably palsied, his general air of agitation was pronounced, and his eyes were glistening at their edges, lashes wet with distress. The poor fellow's clothing hung a bit loose upon his frame, as if his appetite could not be roused in the absence of his missing kin and tragedy had shrunk him. He reminded me of nothing so much as a dull-coated mouse, all nerves and flat eyes and twitching, directionless energy.

Rather than greeting our guest, Sherlock Holmes proceeded abruptly to snatch my papers up from the floor and arrange them into a neat pile on his own chair, a development which was as gratifying as it was unexpected and which I watched with satisfaction. He spared a mere glance at Mr. Phillimore, but his hawklike gaze sliced across his client with the cutting precision that informed me he had already reached several conclusions.

"You find us somewhat disorganized this morning, Mr. Phillimore. Apologies. I am presently engaged upon a matter of some importance and thus can spare you but limited time for consultation. Therefore, consult. Aside from the evident facts that you are a bachelor, an importer of Kashmiri silks, a teetotaler, and an identical twin, I know very little of the matter you are here to discuss."

For a moment, I thought Mr. Phillimore looked so surprised as to be physically ill. His brow glowed with sweat following this remark, and his lips gaped in fishlike wonderment, which caused my less than tactful friend to snort mildly.

"Come, come. Your marital status and your aversion to strong spirits I know from the ring finger of your left hand and your lapel pin." Holmes commenced retrieving my notebooks as I stared, mesmerized at the sight of him actually tidying—a miraculous enough development apart from the fact he was doing so in front of a client. "The rest of my deductions about your case are frankly meretricious, as I learned them in the *Daily Telegraph* this morning. Your thriving importation business—Phillimore, Saxon, and Greer Textiles, I think it was—has recently been helmed by your partners while you conduct a widespread search for your missing twin, Mr. James Phillimore, and that estimable publication provided me with no further details as to your conundrum."

A pause followed this address. "Pray continue from there, if you would be so kind," I urged as my friend wandered the carpet gathering scattered pens. "You have our full attention."

Our guest swallowed with difficulty, pressing his hands together hard enough to mask the shaking. "You must help me, Mr. Holmes. I am at the end of my wits. My brother James and I reside together—and, as you say, we are identical in nearly every fashion. Our establishment is a bachelor one, but happy and peaceful for all that, for I am of retiring habits and find myself entirely contented with the simple comforts of work and family. Three days ago, James departed our residence in Enfield Town, Middlesex. Upon realizing at once that the fineness of the morning would likely not last through the afternoon, he prudently returned for his umbrella. Since that time, no one has seen him."

My friend had moved on to restoring my ink pot and blotting papers to their rightful home, so I continued in my self-appointed role as interlocutor.

"Remarkable," I said sympathetically. "You are obviously close—it is small wonder that his unexplained absence has so affected you."

"The anxiety over him, the dreadful uncertainty . . . Mr. Holmes, I can bear it no longer!" Mr. Phillimore cried in a blatant bid for a scrap of the detective's consideration. "The maid, a most reliable and careful girl, is prepared to swear that she witnessed him leaving as she watched through the parlor window where she was clearing away the breakfast things. She offered him his umbrella on his immediate return, left him in the foyer consulting his Bradshaw, and did not hear the outer door close again. Indeed, she shut and locked it herself after feeling a queer draft some quarter of an hour later. My brother has vanished utterly, Mr. Holmes, and I find myself a lost man." He drew a deep breath, eyes shutting despairingly.

"Where were you at the time?" my friend questioned, casually hoisting what appeared to be a gigantic napkin-draped pincushion, transferring his ham from my desk to a space he had cleared upon the dining table. Had Mr. Phillimore's circumstances been less distressing, I am sure I would have struggled not to laugh.

"At my importation firm in Stepney. Mr. Holmes, please say that you will take my case," the unfortunate man begged. "My brother is . . . he is not altogether well. I fear that some of his habits have led to dissolution in the past, and at present, it pains me grievously to think that he quit the house in some undiscovered manner and met with misadventure. The thought quite horrifies me. It is *most* unlike him to keep me in the dark in this fashion. I have always been the steady one, and James has had reason to bless my generosity previously. But we have ever reconciled despite our differences, have never flagged in our devotion to each other, and I cannot stand to imagine that one of his former associates caused him physical harm." Choking, Mr. Edward Phillimore pulled out his handkerchief.

To my severely stifled amusement, Holmes had by this time actually polished the surface of my desk with his own kerchief and had swiveled to sit upon it, lighting his pipe. The effect of his new client's heartfelt devastation was sobering to say the least, however, for both of us, and he fixed his eyes on our visitor with focus regained.

"Habits, you say," my friend commented delicately, in that engaging manner he could switch to with such readiness when once a client had gained his goodwill. "I fear I must ask you to elaborate on your twin's foibles, Mr. Phillimore, if you believe they could prove of any ultimate use to me in finding him."

The poor man winced gamely. "I would do anything to locate him, even if it means ruining his already soiled reputation. Where to begin? James gambles and loses to dangerous parties. Perhaps that is the most perilous aspect. He drinks to excess. I have known him to experiment with opiates in the past. His taste in women is both unwise and indiscreet. For a time, he kept a mistress who worked in a low music hall. Please do not think ill of him for his past trespasses, but given the situation at hand, I hardly know what to think, sir."

"You are very right to explore all avenues. Was he in the midst of a crisis when he vanished?"

"Not of which I was aware. James has been far steadier of late before this altogether unprecedented disappearance. I had thought him quite recovered from his previous licentiousness. Or at least . . . he gave me cause for hope."

"But as you've admitted, you could easily be mistaken. Are you in contact with any of his companions in infamy?" Holmes persisted, studying the ceiling.

"Yes, I've made efforts in that direction, fearing the worst. They are hardly to be trusted at the best of times, but they have revealed nothing these three days—not to me, nor to the Yard. I feel as if I am suffocating in this complete darkness, Mr. Holmes. I can neither sleep nor eat nor conduct my business with any mindfulness. My brother imagined it might rain and he evaporated into the clear blue," Mr. Phillimore said with a bone-racking shudder.

"It's really rather piquant, isn't it?" Holmes directed at me with the sinister air of enjoyment he is so seldom capable of hiding.

"Sudden disappearances are not generally characterized as 'piquant,'" I reminded him.

To anyone else, Holmes might have appeared unmoved, but I could see a hint of chagrin tighten his stark features. "Quite. Why haven't you calling cards, Mr. Phillimore?"

"Calling cards? Why, my fresh order is at the printer's and in my distress, I have not yet secured it." The afflicted man's eyes teared once more. "Please will you agree to help me, Mr. Holmes?"

"Indeed, I will. You may rely upon my full energies being devoted to your cause. After breakfast."

Had Holmes sprouted wings and taken flight, he could not have stunned me any more than he did with this implication that he thought an intriguing case of secondary importance to a meal being consumed, and I believe my eyebrows expressed this sentiment.

"Give me your address," Holmes ordered, writing it upon his shirt-cuff with one of the pens he had just retrieved from the floor. "Very well. We shall see you in Middlesex in a few hours, Mr. Phillimore, and during that time, I should like for you to cudgel your brains over any relevant details you may have accidentally omitted. Good morning."

With that, the quivering supplicant departed, and I regarded Sherlock Holmes with a silent yet determined gaze I calculated would bear more fruit than direct interrogation. It did so, and more quickly than I had dared to hope.

"It doesn't quite wash, you see." Holmes tore two pillows from his armchair and collapsed full length upon the bearskin, threading his slim fingers behind his head as he continued to smoke languidly. "Supposing we had accompanied him, I shouldn't have had time to work out why and could have botched matters spectacularly, despite your habit of painting me with an unduly flattering brush. Anyhow, it will give you time to consume an egg or two. If you'd do me the favor of not speaking for the interim . . ."

"Gladly," I responded, going to the table after casting a satisfied glance over my restored writing desk.

I was not destined to assist Sherlock Holmes by keeping my peace on this occasion, however. The thunderous steps preceding the equally stormy arrival of an unannounced visitor caused me—as a man whose alertness had not faltered since my friend's near-strangulation at Colonel Sebastian Moran's hands—to freeze upon a pin's head, directing my frame at the opening door. The face which confronted us when it flew open was an unforgettable one. His eyes were slit with serpentine cunning, his form fat and yet wan with unhealthy pallor—altogether, an unpleasant walking threat of a man wearing loudly checked brown trousers with a florid scarlet necktie and a devious smirk that canted unevenly across his visage. He reminded me of a bloated species of maggot, and my posture reflected this association.

"All right, then, Mr. Sherlock Holmes," he declared upon arrival, staring down with bald-faced contempt at my friend's unlikely position on the carpet. "My name is Atlantus B. Conger, and I've a meaty bone to pick with you."

"How unfortunate," my friend drawled, tilting his head as he studied the intruder. "On both counts."

For the second time that morning, I found myself edging between Sherlock Holmes and an object of distaste. "State your business, sir, without hesitation, as we are better accustomed to our visitors making prearranged appointments."

Thrusting a poorly manicured finger at Holmes, Atlantus B. Conger announced, "You've been engaged to find James Phillimore. That sniveling worm of a brother consulted you. Well, I want to know what you've been told and I want to know if you'll play straight with me when you do learn more, you savvy?"

"I do," Holmes assured him, closing his eyes as if too overwhelmed by tedium to remain awake. He flitted a lazy hand toward the stairs. "Mr. Conger, I invite you to rekindle your acquaintance with the door."

"Oh, is that how it is?" the brute snarled, clenching a thick fist which—though doughlike—had doubtless seen its share of violent activity, for it was scarred and scabrous. "I'll have you know that James Phillimore has recently frequented my establishment, proved himself a bit heavy-handed at cards, and presently owes me three hundred and twenty-nine pounds."

"What a tremendous pity." Holmes took a delicate sip from his pipe. "Your establishment, you say? I take it to be the variety of establishment where guests are invited to part with all their earnings, since I frankly cannot imagine any of the honest private clubs or gambling halls being owned by a former bare-knuckle boxer wearing quite that shade of cravat. The pugilism might pass, granted, but as for the choice in neckwear . . ." He angled a brow. "Unthinkable."

"My little den is as honest as it needs to be and I'll thank you to watch that mouth of yours," Conger snarled.

"Yes, yes, the proprietors of all the finest betting enclaves charge unannounced into unrelated gentlemen's homes during the breakfast hour." Holmes rolled his eyes, a movement which in his supine position directed them at the fireplace.

"Put on all the airs you like, you arrogant toff, that don't change the fact of his owing me—"

"Three hundred and twenty-nine pounds, yes. You mentioned it."

"You can bet your last tanner I did! Add to that figure some ten quid for all the poppy of mine he's smoked and I'm out three hundred and thirty-nine pounds through no fault saving my own generous nature."

A bright smile briefly illuminated Holmes's sober features. "Dear me! Someone has taught it arithmetic."

"By Christ, that's enough of your lip. Are you actually this keen to have your head stove in, or just too thick to know when you've met your match? I've broken better men than you," the card sharp's oddly asymmetrical mouth spat.

"I don't believe you have," I demurred, planting my feet.

Holmes, pipe frozen between the empty teacup he had appropriated as its resting place and his mouth, leveled a look at me which might almost have been mistaken for fondness in men who indulge in such sentiments.

"Mr. Conger, allow me to sum up," he murmured, yawning in a manner that caused the villain's chaotic array of teeth to grind. "You have hosted Mr. James Phillimore at your doubtless highly refined and tasteful gaming parlor, plied him with opiates, and his debts are now onerous to you. You disavow to me hereby that you had anything whatsoever to do with his disappearance, am I correct? I suppose you rather slower than many other thugs of your stripe, but not so dense that you would consult me over a murder you actually *committed*. Very well—should I locate Mr. James Phillimore, and find him in a condition to settle his outstanding obligations, I shall encourage him to do the decent, provided you pledge in return your full cooperation as regards my investigation. Please bear in mind that, should you fail to be truthful with me, I will enjoy crushing you—that is, supposing my friend Dr. Watson here doesn't get to you first. If your claims are honorable, I can at least assure you that I will not keep my own findings a secret. Now, quit the premises."

The entire affair could have gone very ill at that moment. However, seething, the scoundrel growled a curse and did as he was asked, slamming the door behind him and causing my newly reinstated portrait of General Gordon to rattle in its frame. Where he had before looked thoughtful, now Sherlock Holmes appeared so introspective I might almost have called him anxious, tapping his pipe stem against his lip before carefully returning it to the porcelain.

"It appears that Mr. James Phillimore had reason to disappear after all. Are we likely to have any trouble?" I asked as I sat down, drawing an egg holder closer along with a spoon.

"No," Holmes answered, frowning. "But I don't care for it, I confess to you. This is a darker matter than merely vanishing in such an extraordinary fashion."

I did not understand him, and thus a brief silence followed. When Holmes rolled his head in my direction and viewed me calmly slicing a thin piece of cured ham from his former target to accompany my egg, he laughed so heartily in his uniquely noiseless manner that camaraderie at once overtopped every other petty consideration, and I found myself chuckling helplessly at my as-yet-untouched plate.

"And to think that everyone assumes I am the mad one," he reflected, making a rueful clucking sound.

"As the cat said to Alice, we are all mad here."

"Watson, our regrettably obnoxious visitor has cleared my mind somewhat." Holmes sprang to his feet, smoothing his dark hair back into orderliness. "Hurry and eat. I must dress. We must go."

"I'll just look up the trains to Middlesex," I agreed.

"To Stepney," he corrected me as he flew through the door of his bedroom.

"Describe Mr. Phillimore?" Mr. Timothy Greer, partner at the small and plain but seemingly bustling firm of Phillimore, Saxon, and Greer Textiles, repeated following my friend's request.

Holmes had taken us with seemingly undue haste to Stepney, apparently to interview our client's closest colleague, Mr. Greer. He was a spherical gentleman with the sort of open, generous bearing and healthy complexion which makes some lucky fellows seem far younger than their years, and well dressed, with the single rather theatrical addition of a maroon velvet waistcoat. Of course, surrounded in the warehouse by brilliant imported silks draped over dressers' models and folded into the semblance of curtains on broad cutters' tables, a single colorful vest was less likely to provide any visual impact. Mr. Greer appeared eager to please despite the ongoing need for his supervision around his hectic workplace, waving us over to a more private alcove equipped with a set of armchairs as my friend explained himself.

"One never knows when seeking a second opinion may prove invaluable, you see," Holmes expounded. "Multiple interviews allow the investigator to gain a clearer perception of the world which gave birth to the point of crisis, like an archaeologist sifting through shards. I may not know what each fragment means until I have slotted them into their rightful places, but when all is reassembled, the picture of Rome's fall grows far more complete."

"Your imagery is most disturbing, sir. You think this a true emergency, then—that some tragedy has befallen James?"

"I did not say so, but cases of sudden disappearance demand we leave no stone unturned. And siblings are all too often rather blinded by intimate proximity. There may be aspects of his brother's life that my client would have balked at relating in any salient detail. If you would be so kind, start from the beginning and tell me everything you can about Mr. Phillimore."

"Of course." The room was close despite its size, and Mr. Greer swiped his brow with an elegant flick of his kerchief as we all seated ourselves. "Anything I can do for the cause. I confess myself gratified to learn that you were called in, Mr. Holmes. The missing man—"

"Ah, but—I beg your pardon—I was not referring to Mr. James Phillimore," Holmes objected, to my surprise, holding up a single finger. "If you would be so kind as to describe Mr. Edward Phillimore, however, your partner in the silk trade, I should be much obliged to you."

"My business partner?" Mr. Greer again repeated, seeming as puzzled as I was. "The man who consulted you this morning?"

"Yes, quite so. Your partner Mr. Edward Phillimore seemed most distressed, and if the severity of his agitation could possibly have any bearing upon the case, it would behoove me to know of it."

"Surely you don't doubt his honest concern?" Mr. Greer exclaimed.

"On the contrary, his anxiety appeared entirely justified. But imagine that you are speaking to an expert in evaluating works of fine art. If I am to identify a painting as a hitherto undiscovered Andrea del Sarto, I must examine every brushstroke, every nuanced choice of pigmentation. I promise you that describing Mr. Edward Phillimore can only assist me in locating Mr. James Phillimore."

"Because they are twins, and therefore so much in tune?" Mr. Greer wondered, his face clearing.

"Perhaps," Holmes agreed cordially.

"Certainly I will do all I'm able, and you are right in thinking them exceedingly alike. Well, then . . . Mr. Edward Phillimore is a very steady, hardworking sort, but with a delicate constitution and a general air of extreme anxiety. It does not go unnoticed by strangers, and therefore it falls to me to fulfill many of the firm's more social obligations. This affliction has haunted him since his youth, I regret to say—he was bullied dreadfully at school, or so I have gathered from melancholy hints, and his personality never regained that boisterous confidence so particular to free-spirited youth. In many ways, despite his good nature and his competence, Edward is a haunted man."

"Apart from shyness, did his work suffer by this tendency toward fretfulness?"

"Never—as a matter of fact, on the contrary, Mr. Holmes. Edward is remarkably conscientious, and I should point out that this exactitude leads to the most gratifying care over his own affairs while failing to enter the realm of hardness toward others' shortcomings. The man is no callous moralist. He is most devoted to his missing twin, for instance, and Mr. James Phillimore . . . I hesitate to say it, sir, but I am not entirely surprised at his uncanny absence. In his younger years, he was a dissolute character indeed, and Edward has multiple times been the saving of him during his direst lapses. Opium, drink, reckless wagers—his history is an extremely colorful one."

"So we were given to believe." Holmes tapped the arm of his chair with spindly fingers. "Might I venture to surmise that Edward's devotion to the temperance cause stems from these cautionary experiences?"

"Without question. He is most passionate on the subject and wears the emblem of the organization daily."

"Yes, I noted as much when he called upon me. Do you know of any particular incidents which might have left James open to blackmail attempts? Vices which fell upon the wrong side of the law?"

"Oh, I couldn't say, Mr. Holmes." Mr. Greer frowned as if regretful he could think of nothing more sordid to relate. "But Edward was always worrying over him, so I'd not rule out the possibility. It hurts me not to give his sibling a better character, but then again, neither could Edward were he sitting here in my stead."

"Despite the inevitable strain caused by James's destructive tendencies, was Mr. Edward Phillimore right to characterize their relationship as a close one?"

"They are loyal to one another entirely, sir, even when the missing sibling is at his lowest ebb. I hate to picture Edward's state if anything has truly happened to James—it is as if each were only half-formed before birth, the reckless and vice-ridden one existing to be the other half of his esteemed counterpart. Have you ever read *Dr. Jekyll and Mr. Hyde*, Mr. Holmes?"

"No, but surely you don't mean to imply that there was but one Phillimore brother?"

"No indeed, but that was the way they acted—mirroring one another. I know it sounds fanciful, but there is often such intimacy between twins, though I have never before witnessed such dichotomy."

Holmes pressed his finger along the edge of his arched brow, an innocuous gesture which I knew signaled grave concern. "Was either of the brothers inclined to fits of violent temper? You have mentioned that Edward struggled with despondency and nagging worriment. If his brother were ever threatened, does he seem the sort who might take matters into his own hands?"

"Heavens, Mr. Holmes, I cannot imagine such a thing. I'm sure he has always acted according to his conscience in all the many years we've been acquainted. And yet . . ." Mr. Greer paused. "Were James in danger, I can think of no lengths to which Edward would not go to protect his only kin."

"Naturally not. One final question. When Mr. Edward Phillimore took his leave in order to seek out his missing brother three days ago, did he call round in person to tell you the news?"

"Why . . . well, come to think of it, no. He sent a wire. You are sure there is no further detail on which I can satisfy you?"

"I rather think that will be all. You have illuminated much, Mr. Greer."

Holmes thanked the affable Mr. Greer efficiently and we quit the silk warehouse for the briny air of London's busiest maritime district, surrounded by unadorned manufactories and glum tenements housing the families which scraped out a living from the frenzied commercial hive engulfing them. My friend, to my bemusement, seemed grimly satisfied by the previous conversation. He turned to me with a statement on his lips, hesitated, shook his head, and set off in search of a cab.

"My dear Holmes, what is the matter? Mr. Greer just confirmed what we already know in every particular," I pointed out as he whistled at an approaching driver. "He may as well have painted us an exact portrait of Edward Phillimore as he appeared in our sitting room this morning."

"I know," admitted Holmes. "Which profoundly worries me."

Enfield is justly credited for its meadows, its lush greenery, its sixteenth-century palace, and the charm of its local markets, but since the arrival of the railway's branch line, it has become a haven for all the plentiful folk who wish to find useful employment in London and are willing to submit themselves to a daily journey. Having just quit the filthy cacophony of Stepney, I could see the immediate advantage in sacrificing time for a suitable living space. The air was sweeter, the houses were neat and cleanly, and the very daylight seemed the more wholesome in the absence of London's grim atmospheric shroud.

After knocking, we were shown into a nicely arranged sitting room which eccentrically boasted a wide array of brilliant Kashmiri silks everywhere draped over furnishings and employed as wall hangings. The effect was, if a bit exuberant, decidedly cheerful, and further buoyed by a variety of sleek-leafed potted plants. A marmalade cat curled in a beam of sunshine at the edge of the settee, and despite the bachelor nature of the establishment, friendly domesticity suffused the chamber. Yet something in the air was amiss, the absent twin's presence seeming to hover just out of sight in the reflections of portrait glass and the shadows of imperfectly closed doorways.

Mr. Edward Phillimore sat at a claw-footed writing desk, studying accounts. He glanced up when we approached, the gleam of renewed hope momentarily brightening his features. When Holmes removed his silk hat with all the sobriety of a physician making a tragic house call, the glad spark was replaced by a grimace.

"Mr. Phillimore, I have only one question to put to you, but I must beg you to answer it truthfully," my friend said in the peculiarly gentle tone he reserves for those who are much affected by neuroses but with whom he sympathizes.

"Yes?" Mr. Phillimore replied, lips quivering.

"How did your brother, Mr. Edward Phillimore, die?"

I was shocked, my eyes flying first to my friend and then to his piteous client. The effect this blunt but kindly delivered query had upon our new acquaintance was most alarming. His already writhing features collapsed, and he half-fell forward onto the desk with a piteous sob. I averted my gaze in pained silence, but Holmes continued staring with the same intense focus he devotes to all unique specimens, be they human or otherwise. After a few seconds, however, he approached his client and gripped him firmly by the shoulder.

"Come," said he, as commanding as ever. "I cannot blame you for expressing your sorrow, but I can assure you that I've no desire to add to your woes."

"God, I am the last man on earth to deserve your mercy, sir, but I daresay no one has greater need of it." Mr. James Phillimore dropped his forearms and sat shakily staring at damp palms. "Oh, what you must think of me!"

"My friend Watson here will tell you that I've my own peculiar definitions when it comes to wrongdoing. If there has been but a single crime committed—that of perjury, which is what I suspect occurred— then after you have made your case to us, I will act as my conscience dictates rather than by the letter of the law, which in my experience can include a bit too much of the alphabet. Now, then! Bear up, man, I cannot be of any assistance otherwise. Oh, very well, shall I tell it to you myself? Your clothing, while nearly fitting your thinner form, instead belonged to your late brother, a man who by all accounts was a most upstanding gentleman. And Edward Phillimore was reportedly plagued by an anxious character, but you are instead suffering from opium withdrawal."

My amazement at Sherlock Holmes's revelation was echoed upon the face of the unmasked James Phillimore, who straightened his shoulders and managed a definite nod. My friend rounded the desk and sat in the chair before it, crossing his legs and adopting an air of blank neutrality.

"I take it you have seen the signs before," Mr. James Phillimore murmured, eyes downcast in shame.

"Yes—agitation, spasms, palsy, abundant tearing, et cetera—all of which you displayed at Baker Street; and a stronger hint was given me in Stepney." Holmes directed an abstracted gaze at the Turkey carpet as he reflected, perhaps in a belated effort to spare his client further distress. "Stop me if I go astray, but I believe I've all the threads in my hand. You had reformed your scandalous habits for a time, but continued secretly to nurse an opium addiction which you could not seem to shake off; stronger men than yourself have succumbed to the poppy habit. Three days ago, you relapsed still further into old errors, falling into the debt of Mr. Atlantus B. Conger—a regrettable sort of person in every particular."

"How can you know that?" Mr. Phillimore demanded, raising his head.

"I earn my bread and cheese by knowing what most do not know. I cannot do more than surmise as to what passed between you and your brother Edward when you arrived home after your spree, however, so you must assist us on that count."

Shivering, Mr. James Phillimore answered Holmes in a wracked whisper. "I was barely aware when I arrived home—for days I had been using myself wretchedly, drinking and playing at cards only to reach for the pipe and fall into soft dreams when I could no longer see straight, staggering between the tables and the cots Conger keeps for revelers on a binge. My brother, God rest him, went through my pockets after finding me in a state of helpless stupor upon the settee. The only item he discovered out of the usual was a note indicating I owed this scoundrel Conger well over three hundred pounds. My twin . . . Oh, heaven save me," he gasped, attempting to wrench himself back into control.

"He was shocked, doubtless." Holmes said slowly. "He took the news as a blow to the pair of you."

"Edward was always delicate of constitution. He had nursed a weak heart for many years. And the sum mentioned . . . We are not rich bachelors, Mr. Holmes, though we live well enough between his importation firm and my own work as a solicitor's clerk. We cannot afford to reside in London, as you see. We have debts. The house is in need of repairs. You can imagine the picture I am painting—setting these concerns atop his heartbreak over my complete relapse, the amount quite broke him. When I awoke in the small hours, my sibling was dead of nervous prostration, and it was at my hands and mine alone."

When Mr. Phillimore again collapsed into weeping, Holmes said quietly, "Which leads us to the crime. It was the middle of the night, with no servants afoot to distract you from your mad idea or to hamper you in its execution. You have met unsavory types in your wild spells. You contacted some of them and requested that they arrange to bury your brother in secret. I have no doubt that you paid a pretty penny for these denizens of the underworld, whoever they were, to whisk your brother's remains away from this house with no one the wiser, as it is the only possible explanation for events as they later unfolded. So—you called for help, and they took Edward away to his final resting place before dawn. Did you deliver him into the hands of anatomical scavengers? Or was the ceremony a legitimate one?"

"I would never have dishonored Edward's remains!" the stricken man cried. "Not on my own life, Mr. Holmes! It was in the wrong parish with the wrong name, but . . . yes, all else was aboveboard, though it cost me dearly."

"Then no crime which need concern me has been in fact committed . . . yet," Holmes concluded with a sharp look at Mr. James Phillimore. "After your twin's stealthy burial, you dressed as yourself and left the house, immediately returning for your umbrella and being very careful that the maid should see and remember your doing so. You then went upstairs and simply donned your twin's attire, and the switch was complete. Thereafter, it must have been an easy matter to escape your residence undetected, and you reappeared as Edward when you returned. My hat is off to you for a truly ingenious and remarkable ploy, though similar substitutions have taken place in Plymouth and Limoges. After the initial deception succeeded, you wired Phillimore, Saxon, and Greer to say that you were searching for James and could not return to work until he was found. Your only true mistake was to forget to carry his calling cards, an oversight no conscientious man of business would make. My sole remaining question is . . . what do you plan to do with the rest of your life, Mr. Phillimore?"

Our client dashed a cloth over his eyes, nodding.

"I have borrowed heavily at a usurious rate, but plan to repay Mr. Conger this afternoon," he replied in a rasping voice. "My purpose in delaying my arrival at the textile concern was to thoroughly learn the accounts and pore over my brother's records. Edward was a better man than I will ever . . . the best man I . . ."

Finding he could not continue on this topic, James Phillimore struck his fist violently against the desk. "James Phillimore is dead, Mr. Holmes, and I set you an impossible task that you might prove so to the authorities should they ever question me. Who could doubt I had done all I could to find him when I took the trouble of calling in the renowned Sherlock Holmes? I am sorry to have deceived you, but my anguish was real. I will repay my debts, I will mend my ways, and I mean to honor his name by being the best Edward Phillimore of which I am capable. That is my plan, Mr. Holmes—for the good son to live on, and for the prodigal who was forgiven in vain so many times to die in obscurity."

My friend considered this for several dragging seconds, faint lines of worriment etched along his high brow. Then he nodded, stood, and returned his black hat to his head. "Come, Watson," said he, and we departed the brilliantly jewel-toned house of grief.

Once we were outside, my friend turned to me, catching me by the arm.

"You disapprove?" he asked, brows plunging together.

"Not in the least," said I, as certain of that fact as I have ever been of anything.

Pursing his lips, Holmes added, "Not everyone is given the opportunity to return from the dead, and to grow better than he was before to boot. You mentioned earlier . . ."

He stopped, giving a small, distressed cough, looking as exasperated as I have ever seen my aloof comrade. Holmes's square chin was tense with frustration, and his entire thin form uncharacteristically rigid. Understanding, I smiled, and steered us in the direction of the railway station.

"Baker Street is not the only set of liveable rooms in London, but it is certainly the most desirable to me personally," I assured him. "And if you read about yourself in *The Strand*, then you must already know that I never imagined you any better than you were in the first place."

Sherlock Holmes, ignoring me in favor of checking his pocket watch and muttering something about trains, thankfully seemed to believe what I had told him, for he dropped the topic. And on the next occasion this often extremely trying gentleman forgets the salient fact that my admiration for him is not affected by his myriad eccentricities, I shall hand over this unpublishable manuscript, since he apparently from time to time ignores evidence which is every bit as clear as a printed magazine page.

The Adventure of
the Willow Basket

"An artisan of considerable artistic skill," Sherlock Holmes answered in reply to my latest challenge, producing a thin cigarette. "A glass-blower to be specific, although I nearly fell into the rash error of supposing him a professional musician. Shocking, the way the mind slips into such appalling laxity after a full meal—I'll be forced to fast entirely tomorrow in case my wits should happen to be called upon."

Staring, I marveled at the man before me, who scowled at his nearly exhausted supply.

"Dear me, I shall have to stop for tobacco on our—"

"No, I won't have it!" I lightly slapped the white linen tablecloth between us, causing our whiskeys to shiver with a sympathetic happy thrill. "Eight in a row is quite too many, Holmes! Even you cannot pretend to clairvoyance."

"You wound me, my good fellow." He lit the cigarette to suppress an impish expression. "I have never pretended to clairvoyance in my life, though I have placed eleven such repellent creatures in the dock for swindling the credible out of their hard-earned savings. One, a Mr. Erasmus Drake, defrauded over a dozen widows using only a mirror, a pennywhistle, and a cunning preparation of colored Chinese gunpowder.

He won't be free to roam the streets for another three years, come to think of it."

"Well, well, never mind clairvoyance then, but you have just identified the professions of eight individuals at a single glance! I shall have to commence approaching complete strangers and demanding they give us a full report of their lives and habits in order to corroborate your claims."

"Watson, surely you know by now that you needn't trouble yourself."

"All right—how do you know he is a glass-blower?"

The detective's eyes glinted as brightly as the silver case which he returned to his inner coat pocket. We sat at our preferred table in the front of Simpson's, before the ground-glass windows where we so often watched the passersby. But despite the glow bestowed upon London minutes before by her army of gas-lighters, the illumination beyond the wavering panes no longer sufficed for even my friend's keen gaze to pick out those details by which he had built his reputation, and thus we had shifted in our seats to examine the restaurant patrons instead.

Holmes's turbot and my leg of mutton had long since been whisked away following our early repast, and we sat in a small pool of quiet amidst the throng of hungry journalists and eager young chess players, their sights fixed upon sliced beef in the dining room or cigars and checkered boards up the familiar staircase. There seemed not a man among them my friend could not pin with the exactitude of a lepidopterist with a butterfly; and, while his remarkable faculty always gives me as much pleasure as it does him, on that evening we reposed with the more luxurious complacency of two intimate companions who had nothing more pressing to do than to order another set of whiskeys.

"I know he is a professional glass-blower because he is not a professional trumpet player," Holmes stated in a teacherly manner, gesturing with flicks of his index finger. "His clothing is of excellent quality, only a bit less so than yours or mine, suggesting he is neither an aristocrat nor a mean laborer, but rather a respectable chap with a vocation. His cheeks are sunken, but the musculature of his jaw is strongly developed, overly so, and there are slight indications of varicose veins surrounding his lips. His lungs are powerful—I don't know if you heard him cough ten minutes ago, but I feared for the crystal. He has been expelling air from them, with great strength and frequency. At first I nearly fell into the callow error of supposing him an aficionado with some brass instrument, possibly playing for an orchestra or one of the better music halls, for which failing I blame the exquisite quality of the Simpson's seafood preparations."

"But then?"

"When I glimpsed his hands, I instantly corrected my mistake—his finger-ends display no sign of flattening from depressing the valves, but they do evince a number of slight burn scars. Ergo, he is a glass-blower, one I would wager ten quid owns a private shop attached to his studio if the cost of his watch chain does not mislead me, and you need not disturb his repast, Watson."

I was already softly applauding, shaking with laughter. "My abject apologies. I was a fool to doubt you."

"Skepticism is widely considered healthy," Holmes demurred, but the immediate lift of his narrow lips betrayed his pleasure at the compliment. My friend is nothing if not gratified by honest appreciation of his prodigious talents.

For some forty minutes and another set of whiskeys longer, we lingered, speaking or not speaking as best suited our pleasure, and I admit that I relished the time. My friend was in a rare mood—for, while he is tensely frenetic with work to energize him, he is often brooding and silent without it. The extremities of his nature can be taxing for a fellow lodger and worrying for a friend, though I suspect not more so than they are burdensome for Holmes himself. It was a pleasure to see the great criminologist at his ease for once, neither in motion nor plastered to the settee in silent protest against the dullness of the world around him.

I was just about to suggest that we walk back to Baker Street when we wearied of Simpson's rather than flag a hansom, for it was mid-June and the spring air yet hung blessedly warm and weightless before the advent of summer's stifling fug, when my friend's face changed. The languid half-lidded eyes were honed to needle points, and the slack draft he had been taking from his last cigarette tightened into a harder purse.

"What is it?" I asked, already half-turning.

"Trouble, my dear Watson. Let us hope it is the stimulating and not the unpleasant variety."

It was then I spied our friend Inspector Lestrade casting his gaze around the dining room, turning his neatly brushed bowler anxiously in his hands. His sharp features betrayed no hint of their usual smugness, and his frame, already small, seemed to have shrunk still farther within his light duster. When I raised a hand, he darted toward our table with his head down like a terrier on the scent.

"By Jove, there's been a murder done!" Holmes exclaimed, as usual failing to sound entirely displeased by this development. "Lestrade, pull up a chair. There's coffee if you like, and—"

"No time for coffee," Lestrade huffed as he seated himself.

Holmes blinked in urbane surprise, and I could not blame him. I too suspected that beneath the inspector's obvious anxiety lurked another irritant—while Lestrade is often officious, he is never curt, and he had not bothered to greet either one of us.

Musing, I took in the regular Yarder's stiff spine and brittle countenance. My examinations drew a blank save for the obvious conclusion that his nerves had been somehow jangled. I could not imagine what the matter might be, for the year was 1894 and I had not seen the inspector since April and the arrest of Colonel Sebastian Moran. Surely following Holmes's return from his supposed death in the grim plunge at Reichenbach Falls, if Lestrade had cause to consult the great detective, he ought to have been reassured rather than dismayed at the chance, since we had worked so often and so well together before.

"Tell me about the murder," Holmes requested, "since you decline to be distracted by coffee."

"Beg pardon?" Lestrade growled, for he had fallen into a reverie, with his fingertips pressing his temples.

"Report to me the facts of the homicide, since you refuse the stimulating effects of the roasted coffee berry."

"I do speak English, Mr. Holmes." Lestrade coughed in fastidious annoyance, recovering himself. "It's a bad business, gentlemen, a very bad business indeed, or I should not have troubled you. I applied at Baker Street and Mrs. Hudson said you were dining here."

"That much I have deduced by your—"

"Shall we skip the parlor tricks, Mr. Holmes?" Lestrade proposed with unusual asperity.

Holmes's black brows rose to lofty heights indeed, but he appeared more curious than offended. As I had not observed the pair interact other than during a terse welcome back to London from Lestrade at Camden House in April, followed by some professional discussion of the charges Colonel Moran would face, I sat back against the horsehair-stuffed chair in bemusement which verged upon discomfort.

"It is a murder," Lestrade admitted, clearing his throat. "Mr. John Wiltshire was discovered in his bedroom in Battersea this late morning, stone dead, without a trace of any known poison in his corpse nor a single wound upon his body to suggest that harm had been done to him."

"Remarkable, in that case, that you claim a murder has been committed."

"He was drained of blood, Mr. Holmes. His body was nearly free of it." Lestrade suppressed a shudder. "It had disappeared."

A chill passed down my spine. As it has been elsewhere mentioned in these chaotic memoirs that Holmes rather more admires than abhors the macabre, I shall not elaborate upon this quirk of his nature—I must mention, however, that Holmes's entire frame snapped into rapt attention, while Lestrade's bristled in what I can only describe as animosity.

"There's some who would think that horrible, but you're not to be named among them, I suppose." The inspector leveled a challenging stare at Sherlock Holmes.

"I readily admit to thinking it varying degrees of horrible based upon the character of the deceased." Holmes yawned, reverting to his typical supercilious character. "The facts, if you would be so kind."

"The facts as I have them in hand are these: Mr. John Wiltshire dined with his wife and an old friend on the night of his death, and later

Mrs. Helen Wiltshire called for a bath to be drawn for her husband. The housekeeper asserts that the ring occurred, the water was heated, and nothing else of note took place. The upper housemaids all confirm that Mrs. Wiltshire slept in her own room that night, afraid to upset her husband's apparent need for quiet and solitude. Other than the fact a man has apparently been bled to death by magic, you'd not find me disturbing your supper."

"You know very well that we would hasten to come whenever you have need of Holmes," I asserted.

A glass of whiskey appeared before the inspector. Nodding subtle thanks to the jacketed waiter, Holmes ordered, "Do have a sip—it seems as though the circumstances merit it."

Lestrade's countenance dissolved into what might—save for his own restraint—have been a sneer even as he tasted the drink. "Another deduction?"

"You have clearly been much taxed," said Holmes, as dismissive as ever. "Pray, what would you have us do? I require an invitation or a client, and presently I have neither. Shall I look up 'vampires' in my commonplace book and wire you upon the subject, or test your patience so far as to accompany you to the crime scene? Has the body been moved?"

"No. I came straight to you," Lestrade retorted, taking another swallow, "whether I liked it or not."

My mouth fell open, and Holmes's deep-set eyes widened fractionally. I fully expected a blistering retort to follow close upon this subtle hint of dismay. To my great surprise, he merely rose, however, nodding at the quaint tobacconist's shop nestled inside the restaurant, and said coldly, "I am at your disposal, Lestrade, after buying more cigarettes. You are giving me the distinct impression I shall have need of them. Watson, settle the bill if you would be so good."

Never will I forget that crime scene, for it occurred after what had been so casually glad a day for me, and the shift into horror was as swift as our cab ride. John Wiltshire lay dead in his tastefully appointed bedchamber, its heavy emerald draperies thrown wide to let in the sunlight and now open to the cloud-shrouded gaze of invisible stars. He reclined in a bath over which a muslin cloth had been draped, the atmosphere in the room stale with police traffic and tense with revulsion, and a still-damp rubber tarp on the rug nearby informed me he had been examined by the coroner and then returned to his original attitude.

Mr. Wiltshire's head and upper torso were visible; his mouth was slack and his lips were white as chalk. The setting and its centrepiece were utterly jarring, stately furnishings surrounding a body that appeared horribly—nay, obscenely—withered. Should I have reached out and touched the late Mr. Wiltshire's skin, I could picture it crumbling to dust like paper left to desiccate for centuries. He had in life been a slender man, with deep pouches beneath his eyes and a wide, downturned mouth.

The coroner was finishing his notes wearing a grim expression and, after a gesture from Lestrade, he stepped aside to allow Holmes and myself to view the deceased. My friend whistled appreciatively, garnering a dark look from the Yarder.

"Skin white as that cloth and utterly parched, vessels drained, form shrunken, as if he had shriveled into a husk," I summarized. "But are we *certain* there were no epidermal wounds inflicted which could have caused this? He was examined on this tarp, I take it."

"Indeed, Doctor. A minute examination was made in this room, but Inspector Lestrade insisted the deceased be replaced lest his original positioning or the water itself provide a clue for Mr. Holmes here," the coroner answered, nodding politely.

"By the Lord," Holmes said coolly, "and here I supposed the circumstances of the killing itself the only miracle which took place today. Admirable, Lestrade."

My friend appeared to be getting a bit of his own back at last, and the official detective ground his teeth as Holmes dipped his torso toward the bath. Avid as the most passionate connoisseur, he lifted the dead man's dripping hand from the water and examined the ivory cuticles, checked the underside of the limb draped over the lip, made a close study of his dark hair and his unmarked scalp, even lifted the wizened eyelids to reveal his unseeing pupils. I watched, eager to help if I could, but all I beheld seemed the stuff of nightmare and not medicine. Holmes next drew his delicate fingertips along the copper rim of the tub, going so far as to touch the now-tepid water and bring it to his nose.

"For heaven's sake," Lestrade muttered in my ear—but at me there was directed no pique, merely the easy camaraderie of old.

I half-drew a hand over my moustache to hide a smile, but added under my breath, "If Holmes weren't the most thorough investigator the world has ever known, I doubt he would be here."

"More's the pity," Lestrade sighed as my companion pushed upright again.

"I have exceptionally acute hearing, you realize," Holmes mentioned tartly. "Fascinating. As I happen to trust in your thoroughness, coroner—Adams, isn't it? Yes, Mr. Adams, I suppose you correct in stating that the body lacks superficial wounds. They should have caused the body to bleed into the water if he was killed here, in any event, and this liquid is far too pure to indicate a man's entire life-force could have possibly been drained into it. I can see no trace of blood at all. Testing it for minute amounts may prove necessary, and I have that ability, but, supposing we can keep this evidence intact, more urgent matters demand our attention."

"Certainly, sir. I have a sample retained already."

"Very good. I detect no more sign of poison than you do, but anyhow poisoning is a medically impossible means of sapping a fellow's blood, unless we are dealing with a substance altogether unknown to science. So here we have a man whose blood was somehow siphoned, and the water is clear. Supposing the corpse had been moved, that would have proved nothing whatsoever, but . . ."

"But the corpse was not moved," Mr. Adams obliged when Holmes paused expectantly, "because the deep depressions upon the back of his neck and the other on his forearm—there, where it was resting—indicate he was robbed of his blood here somehow, and left to die."

"Capital!" Holmes exclaimed.

"Yes, we worked that one out on our own, Mr. Holmes," Lestrade groused.

Sherlock Holmes did not deign to reply, instead turning his attention to the crime scene as Mr. Adams excused himself, intending to help the constables make arrangements to remove the remains. Holmes expended every effort, as he always does, diving into corners and walking with his slender hands hovering before him, seeking any aberration which might bring light where all was dark. After some fifteen minutes of studying carpeting, framed photographs, a mahogany bedstead, and every crevice of every object in the room, however, he tapped his fist against his mouth and turned back to Lestrade.

"Will you be so good as to deliver me this unfortunate fellow's biography?"

"Readily, Mr. Holmes. Mr. Wiltshire is employed at a banking firm in the city and has been for some six years since. We've scarce had enough time to question anyone, but this afternoon his direct superior sent me a good report of him. The servants seem to think him a somber man, but altogether a satisfactory employer. He has no outstanding debts and no known enemies—he lives in a quiet fashion with his wife, Mrs. Helen—"

Holmes snapped his fingers. "I hadn't forgot the detail, but was admittedly distracted by so very dramatic a corpse. They entertained an old friend last night—the wife, take me to the wife," he commanded, and quit the room.

Lestrade followed, and I matched my stride to the shorter man's. "I cannot help but sense that our presence on this occasion distresses you, Inspector."

He glanced backward in surprise. "Oh, I could never be distressed by your help, Doctor. It's always a pleasure to see you. It's merely that Mr. Holmes—well, never mind, Mr. Holmes has never cared a fig what I think, and I don't see why he should start now, so I'll say no more. He's right to want interviews at this stage. There *was* a visitor, and it was the wife who rang for the bath to be drawn. I've not been able to question Mrs. Wiltshire yet—she fainted dead away at the sight of her husband

and only recovered whilst I was fetching you. Never mind Mr. Holmes's quirks when there's a murderer to run to ground, I always tell myself."

Still mystified for multiple reasons, I could do nothing save accompany him downstairs. We waited in a pretty parlor with all the lamps blazing, a room full of light and colorful decorative china, its walls masked by potted greenery. Something about its coziness unnerved me, and the chamber seemed all the more garishly cheerful when my imagination flashed upon the ghastly events doubtless taking place upstairs, as the shrunken rind which had once been a man was taken out the back through the servants' entrance and at last to the morgue.

When Mrs. Helen Wiltshire entered, she naturally appeared greatly disturbed. Her comely complexion was sickly with dismay, her full lips were atremble, her green eyes were red at the edges, and her pale blond hair was disarrayed from her clutching it in the extremity of her emotion. She was of an age with her late husband, midway between thirty and forty, and was a lovely woman despite her distress. My friend was up in an instant and led her to the settee, where she perched as if about to take flight.

Holmes smiled gently as he regained his own chair, displaying the almost mesmeric softness he expends solely upon the fair sex, and only when he desires information from them; but then, I am not being quite just when I say so. My friend may not seek the company of women, but he genuinely abhors seeing them harmed.

"Are you quite comfortable, madam? Should you like a little refreshment to strengthen you? My friend here is a doctor, and he will be happy to locate something fortifying."

"I . . . I don't think that would be . . ." Mrs. Wiltshire shifted, attempting with scant success to smile. She was silent for so long that Sherlock Holmes continued, face alive with encouragement.

"You are of Scottish origins, I observe. In the vicinity of Paisley, Renfrewshire, unless my ears deceive me."

A wash of color infused Mrs. Wiltshire's dulled cheeks. "Aye, Mr. Holmes, though I've lost a good deal of that manner of speaking."

"Yes, it's extremely subtle. You went on a long stroll this morning, Mrs. Wiltshire? It must be pleasant, living so close to Battersea

Park and its walkways, especially at this time of the year—though I discern from your boots that you wandered alongside the Thames on this occasion."

She glanced up, twisting her fingers in her coral skirts. "Why, yes, Mr. Holmes. I was out walking. That is the reason I learned only at around noon that—oh, I can't, I can't," she said upon a small sob. "I very often take long constitutionals. I've never regretted the habit so much as I did this afternoon, when I arrived home and discovered the house was in an uproar and the police had already been summoned over . . . over . . ."

"Quite."

"I was most unwell afterward. I've only just found a tiny store of strength—I hope you will forgive my weakness, but . . ."

Again she trailed off, and again Holmes continued. "Will you please tell me about your caller of last night?"

Helen Wiltshire nodded, more tears forming. "His name is Horatio Swann, an explorer of some note."

"Indeed!" Holmes exclaimed. "Yes, I have heard of him. He has made quite the name for himself in scholarly monographs."

"Yes, that is the man," she agreed with another weak twitch of her lips. "My husband and he were acquainted years ago, but Mr. Swann has been traveling in Siam, studying indigenous wildlife. We passed a most pleasant meal, and afterward John seemed fatigued at having spent so much time over vigorous conversation and plentiful claret. I ordered him a bath and left him to himself. He could grow . . . melancholy at times, Mr. Holmes. But for such a fate to befall him . . ."

To our universal dismay, Mrs. Wiltshire at this point dissolved entirely and ran from the room.

Lestrade exchanged a glance with Holmes, all pique forgotten in the peculiarity of the moment. He leant forward with his elbows on his knees. "She must have been quite devoted to him."

"It would seem so," Holmes replied without inflection.

"The poor woman must be wrought to her highest pitch of nerves over such a ghastly shock. We must seek out this Horatio Swann," I conjectured, "and ascertain whether he has anything to do with the affair."

"As usual, Watson, you have hit upon the obvious with uncanny accuracy," said Holmes drily. "But I wonder . . . Well, there may be nothing in it after all."

"Nothing in what, Mr. Holmes?" Lestrade questioned, a furrow forming above his narrow nose.

"It's only a whim of mine, perhaps a trivial one at that. But why should one walk along the Thames, noisome as it is, when one could walk through Battersea Park?" Holmes mused, rising and ringing the bell.

A maid appeared within seconds. "Show in the housekeeper, please—what is her name?" Holmes inquired.

"Mrs. Stubbs, sir."

"Mrs. Stubbs, then. Thank you."

Lestrade nodded absently, stretching his legs out before him as if in agreement over Holmes's choice of witness, and I dared to hope that whatever mood had plagued him had been a fluke, and that all would henceforth be well again. Mrs. Stubbs proved a broad woman with neatly arranged curls, the flinty spark of extreme practicality in her eyes, and a direct manner. She stood upon the carpet with her hands clasped placidly before her, the slump of her shoulders the only indication she had been sorely tried that day.

"Yes, gentlemen?"

"Mrs. Stubbs." Holmes remained standing, making small perambulations as he questioned her. "My name is Sherlock Holmes, this is my friend and colleague Dr. John Watson, and this is Inspector Lestrade of Scotland Yard. We wonder whether you might help us in clearing this matter up. You have been the housekeeper for how long?"

"Six years, sir. As long as the Wiltshires have lived in Battersea."

"You find the position agreeable?"

"I do."

"Would you describe for me the nature of your late employer?"

"John Wiltshire was a good provider, and I hadn't much cause to speak with him. At times, he seemed a bit wistful perhaps, but he never lashed out or gave me the impression such spells were anything more serious than fatigue."

"Then you would say Mr. and Mrs. Wiltshire were happy together?" Holmes pressed.

Mrs. Stubbs sniffed, seeming more impatient than offended. "As happy as anyone, I hope. They never quarreled, and when banking cost him long hours away, she never begrudged him the time."

"Did she not? That was understanding of her. They seem to have had an unusual affinity. Have you any theory as to what happened last night?"

This at last seemed to move her, but she maintained a neutral expression, swallowing. "That'll be for you gentlemen to decide, I'm sure."

"Was there sign of any intruders this morning?" Lestrade put in.

"No, sir. Well, not precisely."

Both Holmes and Lestrade paused at this, tensing.

"What do you mean by 'not precisely,' Mrs. Stubbs?" Lestrade urged.

"It's a silly thing, but the new scullery maid has misplaced the marketing basket." Mrs. Stubbs shrugged. "She's more than a bit simple, and everything is so tospy-turvy today—I'm sure it will turn up. Last week she managed to put the cheese wheel in the bread box after clearing the servants' supper."

Lestrade sagged, disappointed.

"Would you describe this basket, Mrs. Stubbs?" Holmes requested, abruptly resuming his pacing.

Our eyes flashed to the detective in disbelief.

"It's a plain split willow basket, about a foot and a half long though not so wide, with a handle for the shoulder, lined with a blue cotton kitchen towel," Mrs. Stubbs answered readily, though her tone was skeptical.

"Thank you," said Holmes, speeding as he strode in tight loops before the fireplace. "One question more, I beg. What was Mr. Wiltshire's mood like after Mr. Horatio Swann had departed?"

"Morose, sir," the housekeeper replied flatly.

Sherlock Holmes stopped, quirking an agile brow. "The usual affliction?"

"Worse, sir. Perhaps he'd a premonition." Mrs. Stubbs set her lips grimly. "To die in such a way . . . God knows he deserved warning of it. Do call for me if you need aught else, but I've plentiful extra tasks to see to and would fain take my leave."

When she had departed, Lestrade slapped his knees and hopped to his feet, his unexplained ire fully returned. "This is a serious investigation, Mr. Holmes!"

Holmes twisted to face the inspector, his brow furrowed beneath his high hairline, for the first time visibly vexed at the criticism. "I assure you I am treating it as such."

"Oh, yes, I'm certain the *exact* description of this misplaced potato basket is going to greatly assist us in tracking down the killer! Why don't *you* solve that mystery—question the scullery maid, that'll be a good start—and *I'll* catch a murderer. I need to see whether my men have finished," Lestrade growled, storming out.

"What on earth can be the matter with him?" I wondered, regarding Holmes in amazement.

My friend lightly framed his face with his fingertips as if in an extremity of exasperation, shaking his dark head. "I had six theories at the beginning of the evening. I've eliminated five of them," he confessed, striding in the direction of the outer hallway.

"Then what is wrong?" I repeated as we donned hats and gloves.

"A conundrum even I cannot solve."

I opened my lips to protest but found Sherlock Holmes's face as stony as I had ever seen it; he pivoted away from me, thrusting his hands into his pockets as we made to quit the ill-fated Wiltshire residence.

"But the murder, Holmes! Hadn't you better question more of the ser—"

"That conundrum I *can* solve," Holmes interrupted me. "As a matter of fact, I just did solve it, about five minutes ago. There was never any difficulty in the matter. Come, Watson. We must see what Mr. Horatio Swann has to say."

* * *

As circumstances had it, we could not call upon Mr. Horatio Swann until the next morning, as Lestrade had not found us at Simpson's until well past seven after traveling from Battersea and stopping at Baker Street, and Mr. Swann lived some miles distant, in a grand house near to Walthamstow. Lestrade supplied us with a four-wheeler and a pair of constables lest matters take a dark turn, and the journey would have been pleasant enough, passing through the small brick towns with their peacefully crumbling churches and snowlike dusting of white petals from the blooming hawthorn bushes, had the inspector not been sullen and Holmes resolutely silent. I, meanwhile, was abuzz with anticipation, desperately eager to discover what my friend had made of the dreadful affair.

When we three at last stood before the stately structure in question—walled round with charming grey stone, a winding lane leading up to a curved set of steps, mullioned windows all sparkling as they reflected the dancing shadows of the white willow branches—Holmes hesitated upon the gravel. Lestrade and I by habit likewise slowed to see whether he would deign to share any of his thoughts.

Then Holmes froze entirely, his spine quivering. We waited, with bated breath, for him to speak—or at least I did.

"Well, what the deuce is the matter?" Lestrade queried, every bit as waspishly annoyed at my friend as previously.

Holmes chuckled, rubbing his hands together. "It's all too perfect. I told you I had heard of Mr. Horatio Swann yesterday, did I not? I have followed a few of his monographs upon the subject of certain freshwater wildlife with particular care."

"And what of it?" Lestrade demanded.

"Rather an outlandish residence for a scientist, wouldn't you say? Call for the constables. We'll want them."

Brown eyes widening in astonishment, Lestrade did as he was bidden, returning a few yards up the lane and gesturing for the bobbies to follow. By the time they had done so, Holmes had cheerily knocked upon the door and been admitted, I at his heels.

The taciturn butler led us—and, after some persuasion, the Yarders—into Mr. Swann's study. From the instant I entered it, my eyes knew not where to light: the place was a splendidly outfitted gentleman's laboratory, replete with chemical apparatus and walls of gilt-stamped leather books and specimen jars. Of these last, there were dozens upon dozens, lining the shelves like so many petrified soldiers at attention. When my friend saw them, he smiled still wider.

Mr. Swann, surprised, emerged from behind his desk. He was a strongly built man with a shock of ruddy hair and a ruggedly hand-some visage. Our host still wore a dressing gown and house slippers, as we had begun our journey as early as possible. He appeared merely intrigued at the sight of Holmes and myself—but when he glimpsed the uniformed constables behind Lestrade, his expression shifted to a rictus of pure rage.

My friend made an expansive gesture. "Gentlemen, allow me to introduce Mr. Charles Cutmore, the mastermind behind the infamous Drummonds Bank robbery which so confounded the Scottish authori-ties, the renowned author of no fewer than twenty scientific articles of note, and likewise the cunning orchestrator of the murder of Mr. John Wiltshire—whose name was actually Michael Crosby, by the by, and who some seven years ago aided this man in making off with six thousand pounds sterling. The pair of them had a female accomplice, to whom you have been introduced under the alias of Mrs. Helen Wiltshire. A pretty bow to top this strange affair, would you not say so, Lestrade?" Holmes rejoiced.

The inspector stood there stunned for an instant; but a howl of fury and a charge for the door on the part of Mr. Charles Cutmore ceased all rumination. The set of brawny constables hurtled headlong into action, and the pair wrestled their frenzied captive into a set of handcuffs.

"You've no right!" Charles Cutmore spat at us. "After all o' this time, by God, how d'ye think ye've the *right*?"

"I've a question of a similar nature, Mr. Cutmore," said Holmes. "After all of this time, safe in Siam with your plunder, why return?"

A steely shutter closed over the bank robber's face even as he renewed his violent efforts to break free. He was dragged, spitting curses at the lot of us, into the adjoining parlor as the men awaited instructions.

"What the devil was that?" Lestrade cried. "A clearer confession I've never heard, but that doesn't explain—"

"No, but this does," Holmes said almost reverently, turning as he lifted one of the glass jars from its shelf.

A minuscule red creature swam within, suspended in murky green-tinged water. It was no bigger than my thumbnail, and the shape of a repulsive maggotlike larva. I felt my skin tingle with disgust when I saw that, though eyeless, one end of the tiny worm was equipped with a gaping suckerlike mouth.

"Behold the Siamese red leech," Holmes declaimed grandly, presenting it to us. "Not our murder weapon, Lestrade, but one of its kindred. Some of my own studies regarding blood led to a side interest in leeches, and this is one of the only deadly specimens in the known world. It possesses biochemical enzymes in its mouth which render its victims numb and dazed when attacked—and, after it has bloated itself upon its unsuspecting meal, expanding to hundreds of times its normal size, the same chemicals shrink the wound until it is practically invisible."

"How can that be possible?" I marveled, nearly as fascinated as I was repelled. "The human body contains over ten pounds of blood. Surely such a small creature could never absorb it all."

"Incisive and to the point as ever, my dear Doctor. The metabolism of this leech harks back to primordial horrors humankind has not witnessed for some thousands of years of evolution. It essentially becomes a sponge, vessels growing and swelling and stretching to accommodate its meals—meals which might, I remind you, in the remote swamp prove to be few and far between. When it has recently eaten, it better resembles an organism along the lines of a misshapen jellyfish and can live off a single feeding for months, the way a python can digest its hapless prey at long leisure."

"My God, how hideous!" the inspector breathed, echoing my own thoughts. "But how did you learn of all this?"

"Charles Cutmore and Michael Crosby were known to be the culprits in the Drummonds affair, but they went deep underground," my friend explained, setting down the deadly specimen. "Crosby had never been photographed, though his description was circulated—he was the faceless banker who enabled the inside job to take place at all—but Cutmore was already making advances in his studies of marine animals, marsh grasses, freshwater habitats, and the like when the theft was discovered, and his photograph was published by the Scottish authorities, which is how I came to know of him. The pair were at school together in Edinburgh. Much more was known about Cutmore than Crosby and, at the time of the robbery seven years ago, Cutmore was affianced to one Helen Ainsley, with whom we spoke. I never dreamed that Charles Cutmore and Horatio Swann were the same biologist until yesterday."

"It still isn't clear to me," I interjected. "You yourself asked him why he returned. Whyever should Cutmore murder Crosby, and after all this time?"

"There we enter the realm of conjecture," Holmes admitted, "and shall know all only when Cutmore is questioned. But here is what I propose: after the robbery, Cutmore made off with considerably more than his share of the profits—note comparatively the residences of the conspirators, after all. So. Cutmore fled to Siam, publishing under an alias and waiting until such time as he could return to the British Isles without his features being so recognizable. Crosby, meanwhile, disappeared into the great cesspool of London and took Helen Ainsley with him, marrying her in Cutmore's absence and continuing to practice banking, from time to time mourning his lost fortune. They may well have believed that the man who betrayed them would never return. But suppose that Cutmore still harbored affections for Helen Ainsley and regretted his callous abandonment of her? Or imagine that she refused to fly with him to so distant and foreign a land? The reunion last night may have purported to be a friendly one, and Cutmore may even have vowed to restore what he owed them—we have seen the results, however."

"You think this was a crime of passion?" Lestrade drew nearer, glowering.

"Of a sort. Of a very premeditated sort. You have met Charles Cutmore," Holmes reminded him, half-sitting on the desk. "He and Mrs. Wiltmore were once engaged. He does not seem to me the type to remain in hiding forever supposing he desires to return to someplace, or someone for that matter."

"But what of her husband?"

"Surely you can see that her marriage to the man calling himself John Wiltmore was a matter of expediency—they knew one another's worst secrets and were very much thrown together. I do not claim to have any practical knowledge of the matter, but whoever heard of a married couple who *never* fought, as Mrs. Stubbs claimed? If they seldom fought, I should merely have suspected a happy union, and the same goes for an unhappy one if they fought often. But never? It wasn't a union at all. In fact, I should lose no time arresting her."

"On what charge?" Lestrade demanded.

"That of ordering a bath for her freshly unsettled husband and placing a Siamese red leech in it," Holmes replied, his piercing tenor grown grave. "You don't suppose that Charles Cutmore marched up the stairs and dropped it in unnoticed? When I asked him why he returned, he refused to answer, though he had already given himself away—he was trying to shield his former fiancée. The urge was an honorable one, though she shan't escape the law. I haven't evidence enough lacking her confession to prove my findings in the mystery of the missing willow basket, but judging by her behavior at the house, she'll crack on her own once Cutmore is charged. The pair of them have been in contact for far longer than a day, I believe, probably since shortly after his return to England and his purchase of this estate."

"The missing willow basket? Make some sense, by George!"

"Where is the leech now, Lestrade?" Holmes spread his hands in a dramatic show of long-suffering.

"Good heavens," I gasped. "Holmes, you're right—you must be. They planned it together. You said she had been walking by the Thames and not in the park. She took the leech, wrapped it in the cloth, and made off with it in the marketing basket. It must be in the river now."

"Managing to make the most distasteful body of water in the history of mankind still more objectionable." Holmes chuckled, clapping once. "Well done, my dear fellow."

"To think that he left Helen Ainsley behind and then never forgot her, only to lose her again," I reflected. "It's a terrible story."

"And you claim," Lestrade hissed, advancing farther on my friend, "that you knew all this *yesterday*?"

Holmes glared down his hawklike nose at the inspector. "Can you be serious? Are you suggesting you would have believed me if I told you last night that John Wiltmore was killed by a Siamese leech?"

"I might have believed you."

"You might have laughed in my face. This relentless persecution grows tedious, Lestrade."

"Persecution? I'm persecuting *you*? Oh, that's rich, Mr. Holmes. Very funny."

"Oddly, I don't find it the slightest bit amusing."

"Gentlemen—" I began.

"Let's have it out in the open then, shall we? Man to man?" Lestrade's shoulders hunched above his clenched hands as if he longed to express his emotions with pugilism.

"By Jove, yes, let's," my friend hissed, standing to his full height.

"Perhaps I had better give you some privacy." Fearing nothing for my friend's safety but feeling dreadfully awkward, I took a step backward, only to find that Lestrade was pointing at me furiously.

"That man," Lestrade snapped, "would—no, don't leave, Dr. Watson, you'd best hear my mind on the subject. That man there, Mr. Holmes, would have taken a bullet for you, I'd stake my own life on it."

Holmes said nothing as I gaped at them.

"And what do you do?" Lestrade was turning crimson with fury. "Instead of seeing it through together, you leave the doctor out entirely, and then you make him think you were *dead*. You stood up there at the altar with him on his *wedding day*, for the love of all that's decent, and do you suppose he enjoyed being written out of the picture? For that matter, how do you suppose *I* felt when I learnt about your demise from a common news hawker? Or when I discovered down at the Yard that Inspector *Patterson* was dashing about rounding up the scoundrels you had apparently been trying to capture for three long months? I should have thought we deserved better from you, Mr. Holmes, and you ought to know it."

Sherlock Holmes, always remarkably pale-complexioned, had turned absolutely pallid during this speech, though his face betrayed no expression whatsoever otherwise. Meanwhile, my heart was in my throat. I had hardly begun to speak when Holmes held up a perfectly steady hand demanding my silence and said frostily, "You want to know why I left the papers needed to destroy the Moriarty network with Patterson and not with you?"

"I'd find the subject of interest, yes," the small inspector seethed.

Holmes towered over him with that air of aristocratic mastery only he can assume. "I selected Patterson for the task because he was *not* you."

"Of all the . . ." Lestrade spluttered in outrage.

My friend commenced idly examining his fingernails. "Professor Moriarty was proved to be directly or indirectly responsible for the murder of no fewer than forty persons, though I suspect the true death count to be fifty-two. I chose Patterson in part because he's above the common herd—for a Yarder anyhow—but also because he's a *member* of the herd: I hardly knew the man, having previously worked with him only twice. Whereas you and I, Inspector," he continued, pretending to struggle for the exact accounting, "have worked together on . . . Let me think. Dear me—thirty-eight cases, today marking the thirty-ninth. Now, I realize that so many figures in a row must be difficult for a man of your acumen to grapple with, but I shall add one more and have done. Ask me how many times I was shot at during the course of this very interesting little problem we are discussing."

"How many?" Lestrade inquired faintly.

"Nineteen," my friend reported, though this time fire underlay the ice of his tone. "And if you think I am not aware of the fact that 'that man,' as you referred to him, would take a bullet for me, then you are still denser than I had previously supposed."

So saying, Holmes swept out of the room.

We were silent for a moment.

"Oh, good Lord," Lestrade groaned, rubbing his hand over his prim features. "I'm the biggest fool in Christendom. That was . . . God help me."

"I'm going to . . ." said I, gesturing helplessly.

"Yes, yes, go!" the inspector urged, pushing my shoulder. "I'll just confer with the constables while I reflect on the fact that Mr. Holmes is right to call me dense. Go on, quick march."

Hastily, I gave chase. Not imagining my highly reserved friend had any wish to remain in a house where such a scene had just been enacted, as his levels of detachment border upon the eerie, I dived for the entryway and the faintly blue atmosphere of the mild spring morning beyond.

I found Sherlock Holmes some thirty yards distant, leaning against the ivy-draped stone wall. He seemingly awaited my arrival, although he confined his eyes to the smoke drifting skyward from his cigarette. When I had reached him, I halted the words which threatened to leap from my tongue, knowing this situation required more careful handling. Several tacks were considered before I settled on the one likeliest to succeed without causing further harm, and immediately, I breathed easier.

"Well, my dear fellow?" Holmes prompted in a tight voice when I said nothing. Crossing his sinewy limbs, he lifted a single eyebrow although he still failed to look at me. "Have you any salient remarks to add to this topic? Come, come, I am eager for all relevant opinions upon—"

"Holmes," said I, gripping him warmly by the forearm. "Everything I have to say has already crossed your mind."

He did peer at me then, searching my face with the sort of razor focus he ordinarily devotes to outlandishly complex and inexplicable crime scenes. After what seemed an age of this scrutiny, a sorrowful smile crept over the edges of his mouth.

"Then possibly my answer has crossed yours," he continued to quote in an undertone. "You stand fast?"

"Absolutely," I vowed.

A flinch no one save I would ever have caught twitched across his aquiline features; he then clapped my hand, which still grasped his arm, and broke away to stub his cigarette out against the wall.

"The inspector is sorry over his outburst."

"He needn't be. As Charles Cutmore seems to have learnt to his detriment, the returning can be harder than the leaving."

"Holmes—"

"Do you know, as many features of interest as this case held, I find I tire of it dreadfully, my dear Watson," he announced, wholly returned to his proud and practical self. "A ride back to London with our friend Lestrade and his men and our quarry I think is in order, then a pot of tea at Baker Street and a complete perusal of the morning editions on my part whilst you work upon whatever grotesquely embellished account of our exploits you plan to inflict on the world next, followed by a change of collar and an oyster supper before Massenet's *Manon* at eight."

So it came about that the good Inspector Lestrade, whose opinion of Holmes's dramatic demise had been such a low one, came to look upon the matter in another light. Whether he ever again spoke to my friend of that impassioned conversation neither man was confiding enough to inform me; I highly doubt they broached the topic afterward. To this very day, however, when Holmes requires a stout colleague or Lestrade has need of England's foremost criminal scientist, they call upon one another without hesitation. The horrible death of Crosby the banker was determined by the assizes to be murder and will be tried as such. Thus, though the fates of Charles Cutmore and Helen Ainsley have not yet been determined, they belong to that felonious fraternity who have such ample cause to bemoan the existence of my fast friend, the incomparable Mr. Sherlock Holmes.

PART IV

THE LATER YEARS

The Adventure of
the Lightless Maiden

"You needn't fret over spending the money on stocking up, my dear fellow." Sherlock Holmes's steely eyes darted momentarily to mine before he resumed his minute perusal of *The Echo*. "Elliot's Fine Tobacco and Cigar Emporium is giving every indication of closing, I grant, but I have it on best authority that they merely mean to move to a more convenient shopfront round the corner on Broadstone Place."

"How the devil did you know I meant to lay in a supply of their cigarettes?" I exclaimed.

Mrs. Hudson had just cleared away the egg cups and the curry dish from our simple breakfast and my friend sat across from me, peering down at his agony columns. It is possible only for one who has seen him at his worst, who has learnt the uncaring lassitude associated with narcotics and depression, to imagine the satisfaction which I glean from a Sherlock Holmes who not only has ample work at his nervous fingertips, but consents to eat and sleep when the work is through. He had not yet dressed, though his black hair was slicked back neatly, and, thanks to the influence of a hot cup of tea, he boasted very nearly the complexion of a normal human.

"There was nothing noteworthy about the observation, I assure you. I smoke every incarnation of tobacco at a rate some have found altogether alarming, but you are more moderate in this as in all things and generally prefer a pipe or a cigar—when you buy tobacco, it used to be from Bradley's in Oxford Street, a Virginia Arcadia mixture, and naturally they also supplied your cigarettes, which you needed to purchase only once a fortnight or so. Remarkable restraint, I found that figure—my cap was off to you."

I made a seated bow, and he huffed appreciatively before continuing.

"When I began frequenting Elliot's owing to its proximity to Baker Street and its high-quality products, however, you discovered that Elliot's offered a most enjoyable cigarette composed of a medium-bodied Turkish and Virginia blend. You tried it, and found it agreeable. Your cigarette consumption has increased by at least twenty-two percent since then, and ever since Elliot's began posting ominous notices and discounted prices, you have peered at your case with more obvious alarm—as you did just now; twice, in fact—where it resides upon your desk. I hereby relieve you of your apprehensions: Elliot's is not closing, merely relocating, and your filthy habits are quite safe."

"Well, both I and my filthy habits thank you, in that case. But how did you know about the relocation?"

"Ah, that took me to rarefied realms of abstract conjecture."

"Might you explain them to the layman?"

"I asked the clerk at the register," he drawled, and when our mirth over this answer had subsided, I poured us more tea and we settled back into convivial quiet.

Elsewhere in my continuing efforts to chronicle the unique life-work of Mr. Sherlock Holmes, I have remarked that the year 1895 was one in which the fullest breadth and scope of his remarkable powers were required of him owing to the volume—and likewise the complexity—of cases supplicants placed in his capable hands. Thanks to this near-continual exercise of his faculties, and lacking the significant gaps between exploits which I ever grimly regarded as the fetid pools wherein bred my noble companion's darkest inclinations, Holmes was for the majority of that twelvemonth the very image of his own best self. Our final case of that year, which I here recount, reflected this change for the better—and though the logician in Holmes was taxed rather less than he would have wished, it nevertheless possessed many of the fantastical elements so dear to his dispassionate heart.

My mind soon began to drift again after I finished my tea, though this time not to cigarettes. I had so far abused my newspaper as to allow its outer edge to sag against the still-exposed butter dish whilst my eyes lazily traced the patterns Jack Frost had wrought upon our sitting room windows the night previous, when my friend interrupted my reverie with a light cough.

"You'll want to finish dressing, Watson," said he, this time without looking up.

"Will I?"

"If my surmise that we two shall soon be entertaining a client proves correct, then yes."

"What indications led you to surmise that, then?"

"She made an appointment." Winking at me, Holmes rose and pulled a sliver of stationery from the pocket of his dressing gown, passing it to me as he headed for his bedroom. "Just read that over, my dear fellow, and tell me we're not in for a bit of merriment if nothing better."

I carried the letter with me upstairs, and as I did so, I attempted to make use of my friend's methods in examining it; however, I could deduce only that the sender was a woman who used very cheap paper and resigned myself to the actual contents. These were bizarre enough to give me considerable pause.

Dear Mr. Holmes,

Though Harold has said it's no use and you won't come, I paid him no mind, for I've read so very much about you and I know that a lofty imagination like yours must love nothing better than to marvel at scientific advances. Were you not the inventor of an infallible blood test, as Dr. Watson writes about in A Study in Scarlet? *What an immense achievement! My instinct tells me*

that we might well be kindred spirits in this love of experimental
progress, though I admit I am only a participant and not the cre-
ative genius behind the study.

Still I rejoice at feeling a part of something greater than
myself, and cannot but hope that the world's most celebrated crimi-
nologist may share my tremendous enthusiasm! Therefore I pray
that you'll do us the honor of witnessing the first spiritualist ever to
contact the dead by means of photochemical processes at the Winter
Solstice 21st December. Harold claims a note won't sway you but if
you'll consent to see us in person on the 18th, I'll make all clear and
you'll be sure to agree to witness a miracle of modern innovation.

Your servant, expectantly,
Miss Constance Cooke
Bournemouth
Hampshire

To say that this missive baffled me would be to do it scant justice. For, while my friend was himself a chemist of no paltry skill, his interest in the shadowlands where ghosts and shades abide was slightly less keen than his interest in the intricacies of the international stock market. In other words, always supposing such matters had no direct bearing upon a case of murder most foul, it vacillated between negligible and nonexistent. I have seen significant checks made out to *Mr. S. Holmes* languish upon the sideboard in imminent danger of sopping up cold roast beef drippings rather than being invested, and my friend has just as readily faced down phosphorescent hellhounds as he has less spectral monsters.

Thus it was that I wore a puzzled expression when I rejoined Holmes downstairs. He had donned a black frock coat and subdued grey check trousers and was lighting his pipe with the only dish warmer our landlady had failed to remove. A moment later Mrs. Hudson appeared and, pouncing, retrieved it with a muttered injunction that further con-flagrations would be met with ill grace, and to think of her age, and of the Christmas season. Holmes bade her an unperturbed farewell as she disappeared once more.

"Why on earth have you agreed to see a pair of charlatan mediums?" I queried, waving the letter. "I am frankly shocked you haven't already incinerated this appeal."

He shrugged, sending an ivory puff of smoke to mingle with the aroma of our crackling fireplace. "Where's the harm? If they are honest—"

"You don't believe that they're honest."

"Conversely, if they are dishonest—"

"You don't care a fig about the armies of tea leaf readers and mesmerists and animal magnetism proponents littering our cities and coastal towns. Investigating a crime of that sort would be akin to your proving that objects fall toward the earth when under the influence of gravity—you would reproduce laughably predictable effects and surprise no one. Something concrete made you agree to this meeting. What was it?"

Holmes's grey eyes shone with suppressed laughter. "Good heavens, are you deducing me, Doctor?"

"I don't need to—I know you."

The laugh escaped, but was stilled quickly. "The ink doesn't match the paper."

"Beg pardon?" I glanced down again at the note. Footsteps, one set heavier and one barely audible in its wake, sounded from the staircase; the performers were entering our small stage.

"The script is written with a high-quality fountain pen, a Waterman turnup nib unless I deceive myself, but the paper is of the lowest quality," Holmes said at a quieter volume. "It may prove irrelevant, but—Come in!"

The man who pushed the door wide produced a premonition of vague distaste in me. Doubtless Holmes already knew his life history, but my lesser senses could report only that I would never have approached him at my club for a friendly game of billiards, even supposing the place deserted. He'd dark, meticulously oiled hair which curled gently about his collar, a vivid green waistcoat paired with fawn trousers, and a violet necktie stuck with a small jade stone. Above his smooth chin hovered a hearty and expressive moustache, a scholarly complexion, and a pair of calculating blue eyes which narrowed at the sight of us. All of this ought to have conveyed nothing to me save neutral interest—and yet there was a hint of a roll at his self-satisfied jaw, and a paunch at his affectedly sucked-in waist, that made me suppose him less than forthright about the image he had cultivated.

"Mr. Harold Slaymaker," he announced himself, diving forward to shake Holmes's hand. "I could hardly credit the honor conferred when my fiancée here informed me you'd agreed to meet. A pleasure, Mr. Holmes, and a thrill, if I may say so without embarrassing either of us."

"This is my friend, Dr. Watson," Holmes replied in a neutral tone, though I could see that his half-lidded eyes were absorbing every detail of the stranger's manner and dress. "We may suppose him equally as thrilled as I am to meet you. My name is Sherlock Holmes, as you say, and I was happy to grant the lady's request."

"I am Miss Constance Cooke," the young woman said in a voice like a songbird's earnest warbling, "and so gratified to meet you both, Mr. Holmes . . . Dr. Watson."

As our guests seated themselves following a brief nod from Holmes, I studied Miss Cooke, for her appearance was such as to arrest the most disinterested observer. Her features were delicate, nearly elfin, all save for enormous wide-set eyes of darkest ocean blue which glistened even in the humble winter lamplight of Baker Street. Her figure was modeled on a similarly petite scale, dressed in an ivory wool traveling costume which lacked trimmings and verged upon the threadbare, but her hair—never have I seen such an ethereal nebula of pale gold, nearly white curls. Though pinned beneath a small straw hat, it swept out in a delirious arc at the edges, giving Miss Cooke an air that was a remarkable blend of the angelic and the puckish. When I met her lustrous eyes, I found their expression charming and frank, but could see little beyond that despite the depth of their color. I would not go so far as to call Miss Cooke vapid, but I had no difficulty in matching her demeanor with the breezy tone of her note.

"Congratulations are in order, I gather, Miss Cooke," Holmes said, surprising me by bending over her hand in a gesture which might have appeared courtly had I not been certain he was examining the ring which adorned that appendage. He then settled into his armchair with his long legs crossed before him.

"Oh!" she exclaimed, smiling. "Thank you, sir. You are too kind. The wedding was to be a quiet affair some three months ago, only a few family present at the courthouse and then a nice, friendly celebration at our new home. My sister readily agreed to help with the cooking, and my aunt with the flowers, but these ceremonies incur so *very* many unseen costs, you understand. Harold thought it best if we wait until his financial situation is more stable, following the publication of his remarkable discovery."

Her speech was delivered in an innocent, rambling fashion which entirely belied my earlier assumption that she was scheming to deceive us. Miss Cooke, I suspected, could not have deceived us if her life depended upon the quest.

"You mentioned a photochemical process?" I queried.

"She did—Constance is always bolstering my spirits, but through no trial has she ever been more supportive. Our very presence here proves her dedication! This is indeed a great breakthrough, following years of labor," put in Harold Slaymaker. "But just listen to me, talking quite unlike a scientist—I suppose I had better tell it to you from the beginning."

"The beginning is often an admirable place to start." Holmes sighed, his eyes falling shut as he took a contemplative draft of shag.

"Yes, and my own starting point must of needs be ancestral. I come from a family highly sensitive to the spirit world," Mr. Slaymaker explained with an air of rueful gravity, as of a man thrust into an avocation by fate, "though the pedestrian methodology my kinfolk employ would likely not appeal to you, Mr. Holmes. Some might call their techniques crude, and others . . . Well, I hesitate to repeat what others have called them."

"Harold's aunt is a *very* well-known communicator with the inhabitants of the afterlife. She reads tarot in Poole to universal acclaim," the young lady put in enthusiastically, "and people come from great distances to hear her and see her paranormal collection. She has photographs of spirits that must be seen to be credited, lamps possessing *quite* unusual characteristics, and a seemingly ordinary sewing needle which can unfailingly divine whether or not a party is telling the truth. And then, Harold's sister is celebrated the world over for her scrying ball, and his cousin George—"

"Constance, Mr. Holmes needn't be bothered with my *entire* family history. They are enthusiasts, if you will, but hardly scientists," Slaymaker added regretfully to the pair of us. "They possess a certain talent for detecting emanations, granted. But the dazzling effects they attempt to achieve—all too successfully—class them with the sort of quack prognosticators who give the rest of us a bad name. My own work is a far more meticulous business."

"And that is?" Holmes inquired pointedly.

"The conjuring of *spectres*," Miss Cooke breathed. "Or, rather, *the* spectre. Eva Rayment, the Lightless Maiden of Bournemouth."

Mr. Harold Slaymaker proceeded to tell us an extravagant tale I expected at every moment to be challenged by an irate Sherlock Holmes, but the sleuth sat placidly in his chair all the while. Whether my friend's toleration of the ghost story or the ghost story itself was more incredible, I could not begin to guess.

In the seventeenth century, or so local legend had it, the first Rayments came to reside in Bournemouth, and they built a sprawling turreted estate in the densely wooded forest half a mile from the restless seaside. They were recalled as a noble but unhappy strain, much beset by tragedy. Since then, the Rayment clan had all but dried up in those parts, and poor investments made by the modern namesake had caused what was once a fine English manor house to fall into rude dereliction. It was nevertheless known far and wide along the coastline for the wild beauty of its decay, and for the extreme likelihood that spirits occupied its every attic and pantry. Its residents had long since scattered to various country homes and metropolitan lodgings, but anyone might make a tour appointment via the estate agent, for the Rayments in London hoped to sell the place before it was reduced to so much romantic rubble.

A century ago, when the family seat was still rich with stained glass and gilt-spined tomes and stately tapestries, a hapless but lovely child had been born to the dwindling family. The mysterious little girl was named Eva Rayment, and from her birth she gained a reputation in the surrounding countryside for extreme eccentricity and seclusion. I attempted to mask a pleasant chilling of the blood as I listened—for whatever else Mr. Slaymaker and Miss Cooke were, they made an admirable pair of storytellers, and my fingers soon itched for a pen. The only glimpses caught of Miss Eva were in the murk of twilight, when she would from time to time practice chasing a hoop across the yard after the sun had slipped silently away, or paint the last of the clouds before they melted darkly into so much night sky. She was seldom if ever viewed in daylight, so said the villagers—and if she did appear riding with her governess, she was always swathed from head to toe in gloves and a thick black veil, no matter what the weather.

"When I first heard of Miss Eva, I thought her biography the fancy of some marvelous antique raconteur, but you see, all this had a perfectly *logical* explanation," Miss Cooke impressed upon us.

"She was cursed with a violent aversion to sunlight," Mr. Slaymaker explained. "From the moment her parents discovered the illness, they put every possible precaution in place to ensure her safety, essentially imprisoning her—to no avail in the end, I fear. It's a tragic account. Eva Rayment died a maid of twenty after having suffered a fall from her horse during a very early morning ride. By the time help reached her after the day had broken, the burns were so severe that nothing could be done."

"Sun poisoning," said I, when a skeptical sliver of Holmes's gaze flicked in my direction. "A rare enough allergy, and a deadly enough affliction in the severest cases, though most outbreaks of accidental exposure can be ameliorated through application of Saint-John's-wort poultice or lemon oil to reduce swelling. Extraordinary. I know of its existence, but I've never encountered a patient suffering from the syndrome. All are highly reclusive, and the most sensitive often die from some similar misadventure at a young age."

"But you *will* meet one, Dr. Watson!" exclaimed Miss Cooke. "You will when you accompany us to Bournemouth for the summoning, for she haunts her former home, and I am like her twin come back from the grave, Harold showed me, and when the photochemical process is—"

"A little slower," Holmes said with a palm raised, "and with better sense."

Swallowing, she nodded, fair curls all aquiver as Mr. Slaymaker cast her an indulgent glance. "A painting of Eva Rayment hangs in the hall of one of the only habitable wings of the estate. You have no cause to credit me until you've seen it for yourselves, but it's like looking into a mirror with my face staring back! Harold took me to make a comparative study, and *oh*. The likeness—"

"How long had you been acquainted with Mr. Slaymaker at that time, Miss Cooke?"

"How long? I believe it must have been about a fortnight."

Holmes did not bother to hide a frown. "Indeed. Rather a grotesque outing, but between Mr. Slaymaker's scientific exploits and the active interests of his immediate family, you must have heard plentiful tales of the supernatural by that time."

"Oh, I've never met Harold's family, Mr. Holmes."

"No?" my friend said, his languid yet powerful focus aimed square at Mr. Slaymaker.

"Estrangement is always painful, but they are carnival barkers and shell game enthusiasts," the fellow answered, spreading his hands wide. "I am a scientist. We are divided upon the subject, I fear. Resentment upon their side, disapproval upon mine."

Holmes turned his attention back to the lady. "You say that you resemble the late Miss Eva?"

"Uncannily," she returned with pride. "She walks along the edges of the forests and the seashore often, lamenting that she died without ever having loved. Many of the locals have seen her."

"And have you?" Holmes inquired blandly.

"I have sometimes thought so, when the moon was full. Harold, though, always says that I must trust only in *reproducible* effects, and I always become so flustered when I fancy I really have glimpsed her that I can never swear so to his professional satisfaction. It is a failing I'm attempting to remedy." She blushed.

"You did not grow up in Bournemouth, Miss Cooke." My friend failed to phrase this as a question.

"Why do you say that?"

"Because if the likeness is truly so uncanny, and the legend so widespread, someone would have compared you to Eva Rayment long before Mr. Slaymaker here."

"Oh, I see! To think I already *know* how clever you are, and still questioned you. Forgive me. Yes, my kin live to the west, in Wareham, but I relocated to Bournemouth after being engaged as a typist for Mr. Tiberius Clark, who runs a local law office there. He didn't want a London girl, and I needed the position badly, Mr. Holmes, in order to help support my immediate family. My parents are not well. . . . My aunt assists with the housekeeping, and my mother's condition is poorly enough that my sister may as well be a full-time nurse. I was so lonesome there at first, away from them, but very soon after my arrival I encountered Harold down on the promenade." She beamed at him. "After that glad occasion, I never felt solitary and neglected again. We have been very happy together."

"She does me tremendous honor to say so," Mr. Slaymaker returned, kissing her hand.

"Conversely you, Mr. Slaymaker, are a native," Holmes surmised. "Though your accents are very similar, as I said, so strong a resemblance to a famous local legend could not have eluded Miss Cooke had she been raised there, whereas you revealed the likeness to her within two weeks' acquaintance."

"You are perfectly correct, Mr. Holmes, and I must make a confession to you: the tale has long held a strange fascination for me."

"Ah. What is its connection to your chemical researches, then?"

"There we hit upon the crux of the matter! I have been devising a method by which ghosts that exist on a plane invisible to us might be compelled to manifest themselves. Countless scholars have postulated that spirits linger in the astral realm owing to lack of completion—be it a regret, an act of vengeance unfinished, a lost love, or in Miss Eva's case, a sad dearth of true fulfillment in the world while living. Leaving all of that aside, however, I am after much harder data. Granted, there is an emotional variable to my work, a psychic energy if you will, but my studies mainly revolve around particular spectrums of light."

"Harold is a genius," Miss Cooke averred.

"Constance, pray don't unduly flatter me, or they shall think us all bluster and no substance," Mr. Slaymaker admonished her somewhat tersely.

I already found myself recoiling from the praise this tender creature was heaping upon a man whose theories seemed to me so much chaff in the wind, but I positively dreaded the moment when Holmes would disabuse their treasured illusions and throw them both out on their ears. However, I had again misjudged him, for he leaned forward with a welcoming eye and his elbows resting upon his knees.

"Describe for me, Miss Cooke, the methods Mr. Slaymaker employs," Holmes requested.

Rising slowly, she advanced to the fireplace and then turned to face the room.

"I dress in a costume of the last century, a pale chemise lined with silver with a white sleeveless robe—every detail perfect, every thread *exact*." She glanced from one to the other of us, scarce able to contain her excitement. "It is always the full moon when we attempt contact, for the light is best then for Harold's methods, and in any case, it is such a *spiritual* time, don't you agree? I walk the paths along the edges of the forest," and here she stepped gracefully forward; "and when I reach a clearing, I cease moving and simply *bathe* myself in light."

Miss Cooke stopped, eyes closed as if in rapture, and held her palms open at her sides in the middle of our sitting room. Mr. Slaymaker looked rapt, I disbelieving, while Holmes's brows dived toward his superior nose as if he were growing unaccountably angry. I could not fathom why he had allowed the charade to continue for so long—he certainly expected no otherworldly revelation, and surely he had determined very quickly that Miss Cooke believed every nonsensical word she was telling us. My friend and I both have threadbare patience where villains are concerned; but whimsical fools are another matter entirely.

"I remain motionless for long periods, hoping that Eva Rayment will see me—will see *herself* as she could have been, flooded in illumination which cannot harm her," Miss Cooke whispered with her eyes peacefully shut. "Oh, it is *so* difficult to remain calm at such moments, but Harold has told me that spirits see our world only poorly, and that we must be still. In the meanwhile, he produces light from the dim of the woods, light of a spectrum to appeal to her, and often I sense a . . . a presence lingering at the edges of my closed lids. I can practically feel the glow of her, as I have mentioned, though thus far she has never spoken to us. But she will!" the young lady cried, opening her eyes and clasping her small hands together. "The full moon may be insufficiently powerful, but when it coincides with Winter Solstice, as it will on the twenty-first, Mr. Holmes—oh, *won't* you come?"

And here, I again supposed, all would come crashing to a spectacular halt, for traveling from London to Bournemouth to witness a ludicrous scientific charade would prove distasteful enough to my methodical-minded friend as to cause physical pain. Meanwhile Sherlock Holmes rose, walked to his desk, and drew out his appointment book.

"December the twenty-first it is," he announced with a dazzling smile. "We shall be very pleased to meet you at Bournemouth. By the way, Miss Cooke, did Mr. Slaymaker here assist you in any way with your original letter?"

"Oh! You know so much, Mr. Holmes, quite as much as Harold here, and I must cease being so surprised at it. Why, he was paying a call on me when I wrote to you, and I asked to borrow his pen, for it works so nicely, but the sentiments were entirely my own, I assure you," she replied.

"I have not the slightest doubt of it. And now, as we've other pressing matters to attend to, I will wish you both an agreeable afternoon. You may expect us in Bournemouth on the twenty-first without fail."

When our guests had departed, I turned to Holmes in open astonishment.

"There are more things in heaven and earth, Horatio," he said before I had managed to form a question.

"But not by their summoning!" I exclaimed.

"No indeed," he concurred, gliding into his bedroom and emphatically shutting the door behind him.

Bournemouth railway station and the entrance to its sloping, well-maintained pier must have been a merry sight in the summertime, what with the clock tower's many delicate spires, the low red bathhouses, the buggies for daily rental, and the sun skimming the salt froth that bubbled tenderly against the pale sand of the beach beyond. Had it been July, I've no doubt whatsoever I should have been charmed. It was nightfall in December, however, and no matter how cold London may grow, it does not plummet in temperature as does the wind sweeping off the cutting waves of the ocean. My jaw was set against its onslaught, and Sherlock Holmes shot me a significant look as we bypassed unpaved lanes lined with sea grass to rendezvous with our questionably sane clients.

"You think me frivolous," he observed, though there was no pique in his tone.

"My dear Holmes, I have never known you to be so, and do not intend to start now."

"Then you think me credulous, which is worse."

"Not at all. I may perhaps think you secretive, and close-mouthed, but then I have always thought so; therefore doubtless you are well used to the sensation."

"My researches in the past few days have proved most fruitful," said he insistently. "A final link finishes my chain. Of course I will reveal all to you when the time is right—"

"Of course," I agreed drily.

"—But I have no wish to perjure myself when the possibility remains that I could be mistaken."

I knew better than to push him further, and so we walked with a purpose to a rise just above the shoreline, and a yellow-painted pub with a dull grey awning. While a barren enough place during the off season, it did command an enchanting view of the stark winter tides and the slow-spiraling silhouettes of gulls in the desolate distance. Smells of fried fish and spilled ale assaulted my nostrils as we entered the creaky building.

"Mr. Holmes!" Harold Slaymaker called, jumping up from a low wooden table. Beside him rested a large carpetbag, presumably containing his apparatus. His clever face reflected both gratitude and apprehension, and his sweeping moustache leaped with excitement. "We hardly dared hope that you would really come. Welcome, welcome! Constance, is this not a dream come true?"

Miss Cooke sat beside her fiancé, wrapped in a long wool cloak beginning to fray at its edges, and her whimsical sprite's face glowed at the sight of us. "Oh, how splendid! I *told* you they would keep their word—I could feel it. Now it will be worth it, Harold, you shall see."

My opinion regarding whether or not the expedition would prove worthwhile must have been briefly evident upon my features, for Holmes delivered me a meaningful kick below the table just after we seated ourselves. Our clients had finished their modest pints, and Holmes made no overture to arrest the attention of the barman.

"Miss Cooke, Mr. Slaymaker, the weather is hardly congenial to this sort of trial," he announced. "Had you not best postpone—"

"But weather during the Winter Solstice will never be 'congenial,' Mr. Holmes," Miss Cooke chided him sweetly. "Let us brave the elements in the cause of science—after all, I bear the brunt of the work during the event itself, and I am eager to start. You can see for yourself! Oh, *do* let's be off."

"If you are set on this course, I cannot dissuade you," Holmes replied. "But you will answer for it."

To my pronounced disquiet, he addressed Slaymaker, and in a warning tone which threatened grave consequences. But Slaymaker either did not hear or did not heed, for thirty seconds later we were outdoors, tramping through lip-numbing winter gusts toward a nearby copse, the charming ring of distant trees blasted by the cold and the saline mists of December. In the dimming half-light, they appeared cursed objects rather than merely natural wildlife, though in truth bowed by the elements, not by a centuries-old hex.

"Holmes, if there is something you are not telling me that could have a direct bearing upon Miss Cooke's well-being, now is the time to bare your soul, regardless of your flair for the dramatic," I whispered.

"Never fear, Watson," he replied in clipped tones. "She is in no immediate danger." This reassured me, but I could shake neither my agitation nor the cold which had sunk its talons into my bones.

When we had reached a narrow path with a good view of the gentle, sandy slope which divided the mournful forest and the beach, Miss Cooke turned to me.

"Will you be so good as to hold my cloak, sir?" she inquired. "Harold will have his hands quite full producing the necessary light."

Reluctantly, I acquiesced. A small garland of flowers adorned her crown, and she wore the archaic clothing she had described to us at Baker Street, pale wrists gleaming brittle as ice shards in the gloom. I could have thought her a portrait study from a sentimental artist's brush, all fey glimmers and ethereal coiffure. Miss Cooke wasted not a moment, but walked slowly toward the copse, adopting the same reverent posture she had used when enacting the scene at Baker Street.

"What a vision she is," Slaymaker exclaimed softly. "If this doesn't summon the Lightless Maiden, my researches must be reevaluated comprehensively. No man of my devotion to pure logic can possibly wish for luck at such a time, and yet I find I can't help myself. Excuse me, gentlemen, but I will be only a dozen yards or so off—the powder I employ to reveal any spirits present is extremely delicate."

I shall never forget it. There stood Holmes and myself, arms folded into our breasts and necks tucked into thick scarves, watching the lady slowly advance upon the trees. To our right hovered Harold Slaymaker, readying what looked to me like a flat pan and a simple flash charge. The moon by now shone in earnest, painting the crests of the waves as white as Miss Cooke's chemise, as white as the curve of her shoulder where the robe had slipped, and it shone full upon her when she suddenly reached up and began to unfasten the locks of her hair.

Ivory curls billowing, Constance Cooke neared the tree line. Slowly, almost mesmerically, she pivoted, turning her palms upward as if she were an Egyptian queen worshipping the sun thousands of years in the past. Several chemical flashes went off in our periphery and we perceived that Harold Slaymaker was illuminating the scene in brilliant punctuations. I sensed my friend stiffen beside me, and indeed I knew not what to make of such a seemingly fruitless tableau. I knew only that Constance Cooke's tiny features and her wide cobalt eyes, grey now in the moonlight, were beautiful, and that she must have been suffering terribly from the cold.

"Enough of this travesty," Holmes snapped, turning upon his heel.

Hastening after him, entirely confounded, I paused when I heard Slaymaker's shout from behind us. I glanced back to see Miss Cooke—no longer an apparition, merely a disappointed girl—now standing on the sand path, marking our departure with dismay. My friend never hesitated, however, abandoning the scene as if fleeing blindly might prevent his transformation into a pillar of salt.

"Holmes, please," I urged him. Gaining no reply, I gripped his elbow. "Is that poor young woman at risk? If there is a crime in contemplation—"

"No crime in the smallest," he snarled, "save for the crime of being an utterly callous creature humanity at large would be well rid of."

"Wait, but," I stammered, "you cannot mean that Miss Cooke—"

"Harold Slaymaker is a disgrace to the species." Holmes cast a minute glance at my bad leg and then continued at a much more measured speed toward the train station. "I can tell you without fear of hyperbole,

Watson, I *dearly* wish that were a punishable crime. As it happens, however, all we gain is confirmation of what I suspected from the first—that I can do less than I would like to. I will do *something*, though. You may take me at my word that he will pay. Apologies for dragging you out on such a night, but I had to be certain of my facts. Shall I find a serviceable inn, or are you hale enough for us to cart ourselves back to London?"

"Well, certainly—I'm no more frozen than you are and considerably less so than Miss Cooke. But Holmes, what are we to do?"

"We are to return to our fireplace, my dear fellow, and hot toddies, and stimulating conversation, and every good thing two gentlemen require when their daily toil is at an end. And tomorrow," he added on a growl, "I shall do several other things. They will give me, I can say with complete confidence, enormous pleasure in the execution."

If Holmes indeed contemplated his future activities with pleasure, his face did not reflect as much on the train ride home—he alternately scowled and fidgeted, and it was not until Baker Street and the welcome refreshments he had mentioned that I was able to get another word out of him at all.

I heard nothing more of the Slaymaker case for two days, though in my worry I pressed Holmes multiple times upon the subject and he curtly informed me that the lady would come to no harm. In fact, Christmas had been and gone before Holmes one sleet-plagued afternoon approached me at my writing desk with an envelope in his slim hand. It was postmarked from Poole, addressed to my friend, and unopened.

"Go on," he said, delivering it to my grasp. "I know the contents already, so you might as well do the honors."

Thinking here at last was the key to the mystifying Lightless Maiden affair, I slit through the seal. I could hardly contain a gasp when a confusion of cheaply printed photographs spilled onto my desk.

A mass of pictures, the sort of penny postcards one finds so often at the seashore, lay scattered across a manuscript I had hesitantly titled "The Lone Cyclist." They showed a ghostly figure bordered by tree line and by tidal break, in several similar poses, the very image of Miss Cooke as we had seen her on the night of the Winter Solstice. It was as if the ghost of Eva Rayment had indeed been captured—no doubt providing a ready profit in the tourist trade. My face swiveled up to Holmes in astonishment.

"Oh, come Watson, *really*," he pleaded, leaning against my desk. "You wound me. This is altogether too much. I shall give you thirty seconds to think, and then I despair of you entirely."

As it happened, I did not require thirty seconds. I required only ten.

"That brute Slaymaker was photographing her," I cried, slamming my hand down upon the penny postcards. "She was a stranger to Bournemouth, and the legend inspired him to make use of her for profit! He costumed her, he wished the moon to be full when they experimented, he created flash effects to enhance the light, he enjoined her to be still—all the while, he must have had an accomplice hidden in the brush with a camera."

"Certainly not on the night we visited, for I should have heard any other party in the bracken. But on the previous occasions—yes."

"Oh, the cad, to use her for his own devices so! It's positively deplorable, Holmes. Where did you get these?"

"From his kith and kin in the shell game industry, with whom he claims to brook no commerce. They do a brisk mail-order business as well as a promenade trade. Finding these was child's play."

"How did you know at first?" I asked eagerly, turning my chair to face him. "Here, at Baker Street. Why did you agree to visit Bournemouth?"

"I have never lost my heart to a woman, Watson," Holmes answered with only a hint of irony, "but had I done so, and that woman lived practically in rags, buying ha'penny foolscap for letters to her parents and sending all her income home to tend to them, I should not postpone our nuptials pending the outcome of an imaginary scientific experiment. I should wed her, and thereby improve her lot in life. And despite my marked lack of sentiment, neither would I buy her an engagement ring made of *brass*, when I possessed such expensive taste in writing implements."

A bitter silence fell. Staring down at the postcards, I shook my head.

"I already wrote to Miss Cooke, and enclosed one of these pictures as proof." Holmes rose, clapping me on the shoulder as he made for his armchair.

"You did?" I repeated incredulously.

Holmes seated himself and made a long arm for his Stradivarius bow.

"I always rather regretted that Mary Sutherland business," he confessed softly. "She was my client, after all, and I never told her that she had been courted by her own stepfather. I can't think what I feared at the time—a scene, a scandal, an inconvenient hour? That she would prefer to disbelieve such a sordid charge than to trust me? That she would be hurt by it? Appalling cowardice, my dear fellow. I may have put the fear of God into Mr. Windibank, but I went no further, whether owing to pure negligence or apprehension over Miss Sutherland's reaction I honestly can't say. But whether she would have fainted or wept or railed or called me a liar doesn't signify. What would any of those eventualities have mattered when set against her life, and dreams of bettering it? I hope, in vain perhaps, that I am a stouter fellow today. Miss Cooke and Miss Sutherland may be intellectual equals, but that does not mean they deserve to be duped."

"It does not," I agreed, smiling.

Holmes was balancing the end of the bow on one fingertip, making tiny adjustments but sparing an instant to glance at me. "I cannot fathom what you are thinking just now."

"Truly?"

"I assure you."

"It has been a very good year, my dear fellow. That is all. A most excellent, wonderful year."

Holmes was just then distracted by a complex matter of coordination and dexterity. But he flashed a grin at me, and I knew that he had understood me entirely.

The Adventure of
the Thames Tunnel

September of the year 1900 will be forever associated in my mind with the Iron Hand, simultaneously the name of a vicious criminal network which had been terrorizing the St. Katharine Docks and of its anonymous leader, a ruthless dictator whose identity was so fiercely guarded that his orders were carried out solely by lieutenants bearing tattoos of sinister claws on their forearms. Had the band been a typical collection of crude miscreants, they should never have come to the attention of Sherlock Holmes, in the same sense that master sculptors are not hired to lay brick. But as their violence increased in audacity, so did the legends surrounding their commander, and Holmes began to note odd discrepancies which had eluded the attention of the regular force. Some two weeks, eight previously unsolved murders, and countless other offenses later, it will be recalled that the Iron Hand himself proved nothing but a myth created by the syndicate—although the popular press had no notion that it was Holmes who finally, and at tremendous personal risk, brought the gang to its knees.

On the night of this triumph (involving a complex trap devised by my friend which was far too convoluted for me to do it any justice in these memoirs), Holmes and I arrived back at Baker Street rain-drenched, muddied, bruised, exhausted, but fortunately unharmed. It had fallen to us to assist the Yard with rounding up the leaders of the Iron Hand in an effort perhaps exceeded only by my friend's annihilation of Professor Moriarty's network, and it was now close on three in the morning.

Holmes's elegant movements were dulled with the fatigue born of too many sleepless nights as we trudged indoors. Meanwhile, only residual nerves caused by my having stopped my friend's skull from being crushed with a brass-headed club enabled me to keep my eyes open. The sleuth poured a pair of neat scotches, promptly eliminated his, and all but melted into his armchair.

I began by sipping my drink, then saw the wisdom of his approach and finished it. "Holmes, you're soaking the furniture."

"I have earned every liberty I take with it," he intoned happily. "Was there ever such a repulsive band of villains as the ones just packed off in a fleet of Black Marias?"

"I should hope not indeed."

"God, but the energy I've spent over the last fortnight! Do you ever wonder, Watson, whether fires have primitive memories of sorts, and the embers of a coal engine after dragging a train up the Alps retain the echo of their exertions?"

Eyeing him shrewdly, I decided that this was nothing worse than his typical rambling when he was past the point of mere depletion, and I allowed it to pass. He looked as if he were considering rising and then turned his coat collar up and settled into it like a feline creating a makeshift nest. It was a testament to his profound enervation that he seemed to have no intention of so much as washing.

"Oh, for heaven's sake, at least try to make it as far as your bed."

"Impossible," he murmured. "Quite entirely impossible."

"My dear Holmes, you haven't even removed your boots."

He cracked a friendly eye at me, which drifted instantly shut after he had snugged an afghan around his shoulders, seeming content never to move again. "Good night, old fellow."

Shaking my head fondly, I performed my own ablutions with rapidity, and I think fell asleep before my cheek so much as touched the pillow. After what seemed only an instant, I started awake again to find Holmes's wiry fingers gripping my upper arm and candlelight glinting off his dark hair.

"What on earth is the time?" I rasped, not without a hint of asperity.

"Seven in the morning." Holmes's eyes shone hectically, and his exertions of late had imparted nigh-gaunt planes to his angular face.

"Are you all right?"

"Do you mean after last night's scuffle with the weighted club and the twenty-stone thug wielding it? Perfectly. Thanks to your good self, my brains remain quite intact. I should have missed them."

"We both should have, I imagine. Well, what's wrong, then?"

"Watson, you can be the most dedicated pessimist. Supposing something wonderful has happened, and I'm here to share the glad news?"

Fighting a groan, I rolled onto my back, scrubbed a hand through my hair, and told myself sternly that the only course was military stoicism. "Impart to me this glad news."

"The prospect of inaction is never a happy one for me, my dear Doctor, but especially not after so trying a matter as this Iron Hand affair. Swinging so far back and forth like a pendulum between vigor and sloth wreaks severest havoc on my mental processes. But we are in superb luck!"

"Are we indeed," I managed with a notable lack of enthusiasm.

"Inspector Hopkins is downstairs and it's certainly a murder— Hopkins's hands are the first thing to give him away when he's agitated, and he hasn't stopped fiddling with his cuffs these five minutes. I shall give you a quarter of an hour to refresh yourself and dress and then we must discover what's the matter with the poor fellow. In the meanwhile, I'll ring for tea."

With this announcement, he was off again like a hare. Dragging myself out of bed and shaving with the speed born of expertise at being rousted from slumber, I admonished myself that adequate sleep is never guaranteed to a man of medicine, and also that Stanley Hopkins so revered Sherlock Holmes that at least the problem could not be a trifling one.

I found the pair of them smoking, Holmes carefully coiffed with his slippers tucked into his armchair and Hopkins on the settee with his spine as straight as if he were still wearing the blue coat and polished buttons of the roundsman. Our friend Hopkins, despite his own ingenuity, has never lost his veneration of the great detective's methods—even had he not been rubbing his thumb over his opposite cuff as Holmes reported, his bright, almost zealous expression would have betrayed his excitement. He is a well-built, forgettably handsome fellow with a small divot in his chin, and would be quite unremarkable in appearance save for a pair of truly soulful and perceptive brown eyes.

"My apologies for the earliness of the hour, gentlemen." Hopkins's lips tightened in sympathy. "I know well enough that you've both been clearing the streets of the Iron Hand, and everyone is bragging of last night's triumph. You must be regularly done, but I know better than to delay over asking for help when the matter is as mystifying as this one."

"No, no, you did quite right, Inspector." Holmes contemplatively flexed his left hand, where a bruise was beginning to show from its having dented a ruffian's jaw. "We are always happy to help, are we not, Watson?"

"Delighted."

"Dear me! Have some tea, Doctor—Mrs. Hudson has just been and gone, and you'll soon feel quite human again."

I doubted this severely but followed his instructions, finding them sound. Pouring for Hopkins, I remarked, "Holmes says ten to one it's a murder. Nothing too disturbing before breakfast, I hope?"

"No, Doctor, but the circumstances are enough to beat me. I'd have you both in a cab already, but the trains could hardly be stopped, and the tarp is insufficient considering the pedestrian traffic—we've been forced to move the body, but there are two constables guarding the scene."

"Hopkins, if you want to make any more of a topsy-turvy mess of this tale, supposing you hang upside-down like a bat as you tell it?" suggested Holmes with an angelic smile.

"Quite right, sir." Hopkins coughed abashedly. "Well, the first thing you'll want to learn is that we've had no trouble identifying the dead man. The victim is one Mr. Forrester Hyde."

"Good Lord!" Holmes exclaimed. "Not the expert cracksman I landed in Wandsworth Prison over six years ago?"

"The very same, though it was a month before my promotion to detective."

"Watson, we've our own account, I trust?"

Already feeling energized, I got to my feet as Holmes waved in the direction of my journals and his commonplace book. "Yes, I can lay my hands on it soon enough. Eighteen-ninety-four. You say Hyde has met his end, Inspector?"

"And a terribly strange end it was, to be sure, Dr. Watson."

"You're certain it was a murder?"

"He had a fatal encounter with a bullet, and nothing indicates he could have done such a thing himself." Inspector Hopkins smiled wryly.

Holmes's eyes narrowed. "And he was shot at a railway station, I take it, since you had to consider the sensibilities of a crowded area in the early hours of the morning and mentioned the impossibility of stopping the trains. A well-frequented line with a high concentration of the weekday laboring force who are the true heroes of the city, then. Which?"

Hopkins chuckled appreciatively. "Wapping Station, the East London Railway."

"Watson, before we hear the inspector out, might you just refresh our recollections as to Hyde's history?"

"Yes, I have it here." Running my finger down the relevant page of Holmes's index, I seated myself. "Ah, I remember. Forrester Hyde was a hardy, dashing sort, very well liked by the audacious types he ran with, especially the ladies—there's a woodcut here from the day he was captured. Strong jaw, arrogant chin, dapper waxed moustache. For a cracksman, he certainly preferred not to keep his head down. He claimed to come from a coffee plantation fortune and patronize all manner of arts, not to mention specific artists of the fair sex. He wrote for several columns and was at one time a well-known theatrical critic who lived like a gentleman of leisure."

"He gave that impression," Holmes corrected with his pipe dangling from his fingers, "but he was a vile scoundrel who wormed his way into feminine confidences and thence into their safes. Once he had their trust, he would be allowed inside their lodgings under the pretext of false appointments, et cetera, and steal what he could find—judiciously, I might add, and never within the same immediate circle of acquaintants. In reality, he came from a none too respectable clan in the Leathermarket Gardens area, evinced the strongest talent for acting and mimicry I've ever seen, and used hotels when he wanted to give the impression of lavish spending. For the rest of the year, he rented a cheap flat on Lamb Walk."

"Just so! You caught him out over a detail in his clothing after being consulted by a ballerina of some renown, did you not?"

Holmes shrugged demurely. "One might own a few sets of expensive togs, even tie an array of cravat knots and keep one's boots perfectly blacked, but if a chap lacks servants and a valet, I can discern it easily."

"How so?" Hopkins inquired, as athirst as ever for tutelage.

"Well, this rogue obviously saw to his own entire toilette every morning. It doesn't matter whether your waistcoat is expensive supposing it hasn't been brushed properly after washing, nor your shirtsleeves and trousers aired, for that matter. The roughness of the nap on all three items practically shrieked he was an impostor."

"Excellent!" Hopkins exclaimed.

"Facile, surely. The ballerina, who shall remain nameless, already suspected him. Once I'd glimpsed him, I knew she was right. He'd have been caught long before then had he been greedier and the word spread—as it was, he needed only to keep up with the theatrical papers, submit his articles via mail, flatter the struggling with promise of good notices, and woo them in the language of flowers. The rest of the time he worked as a desultory construction engineer."

"You followed him to his real home in Lamb Walk with Inspector Gregson and a warrant, but though you did find the ballerina's sapphires hidden in the false bottom of a valise, you found nothing else," I continued.

"By George, that was wretchedly vexing!" Rousing, Holmes slapped his knee. "I blamed him for several more larcenous acts, but could tie him to no particular stonecutter or pawn shop, and so admitted defeat on those counts after a lengthy search. He likely sold a piece at a time and lived off the proceeds, never hoarding enough to incriminate himself, faked forced window latches and the like in other dwellings—anything so as not to arouse alarm."

"But the dancer's property was more than enough for a conviction on robbery charges, and . . . well, it seems that Hyde could have been released anytime during the past year," I finished.

"It was Wednesday, gentlemen, and he was dead two days later," Hopkins supplied.

"Ah, here we come to the meat of the matter." Holmes's torso gave an almost imperceptible twist of excitement in his armchair. "What happened between Wednesday and this morning, Inspector?"

"Forrester Hyde—who it appears kept to form and made every effort to charm his fellow prisoners—was released without much fuss back into the city, since as you say he was convicted on only a single count of theft. His whereabouts after he departed are unknown, but sometime during those two days, he attempted to return to his respectable profession of engineering. After a search, the body revealed a notebook containing information about contacting three foremen, though we all know how difficult it is to regain employment following incarceration. The other items on the deceased were quite immaterial—an inexpensive cigarette case, a key that presumably matched his new lodgings, and an initialed watch with a brass chain. His clothing is good quality, but secondhand. I found a jerry shop ticket in the pocket of the jacket."

"Very good thus far, friend Hopkins. And what befell him?"

"He was shot through the heart at close range with a small-caliber revolver that would have been easily concealed. There were powder burns on his coat. Hyde was able to crawl for a scant few feet, but we think he died in under a minute at most, and according to the blood that pooled, the body was not moved. This would have been sometime between midnight and two a.m., according to the coroner."

"You claim he was killed at Wapping Station?" Holmes asked incredulously. "Surely not. No, no, it is too outlandish, even so late at night! We are expected to believe that a man was shot on the platform with no one the wiser?"

"By no means, sir!" Leaning forward, Hopkins clasped his hands together. "I expect you to believe that a man was shot beside the tracks in the *middle of the Thames Tunnel*, and without a single witness."

"Ha!" Holmes crowed. The brightness of his eyes was crystalline with slightly manic sleep-deprivation, but gratifyingly clear, and avid with interest. "Pray continue your account, my good man."

Hopkins reported that on the previous evening, the 12:14 train experienced a brief stop in mid-tunnel due to someone's having triggered the emergency brake. The conductors at once endeavored to ascertain whether there was a safety issue, but their search for the perpetrator was inconclusive, and—after every precaution had been taken—the train continued on its way again.

"Surely the method if not the motive is obvious, then," Holmes argued. "As to what Hyde was doing precisely, we must yet determine, but a fatal altercation must have taken place during the time the train was stopped, and the body was thrown from between two cars to the edge of the tracks. All is coal smoke and foulness as the engine passes under the Thames, and where decades ago it was packed with fashionable promenaders and fancy goods markets, now you can hardly see your hand before your face while still under the archway. Even a careful conductor could easily have missed spotting Hyde where he lay."

"Agreed. Well, in part. No blood was found in or between any of the cars afterward, however. And the marks in the mud are most uncanny. Foot impressions begin about five feet from where we found the body and end in a pool of his blood, but there are no deeper gouges or splatters to indicate he fell from the train. In fact, signs appear to suggest that he materialized within the tunnel."

"Hopkins," Holmes said in a tone of such exquisite patience that his irritation could not have been clearer, "we have more than once conducted this discussion, and I remain more inclined to believe that *you* cannot read visible footprints than that criminals can fly."

"But you shall see for yourself that the dirt and soot are clear as day, Mr. Holmes! And anyhow, there was no train ticket on the body."

"Now you sound like one of Watson's lurid *Strand* fabrications."

Smiling, I said judiciously, "If the evidence at hand seems too daunting, Holmes, another few hours' sleep would not go amiss."

Holmes waved away this suggestion as if it were preposterous. "No, no, I shall have a look, of course. There is an explanation for everything under the sun."

"The body is at the morgue en route to Wapping." Hopkins set down his teacup. "We'll stop there, with your permission, and then continue on to Wapping Station. I've good men standing watch, and we need not fear they'll displace anything."

Holmes and I went for our coats and boots, which thankfully had dried somewhat. "In that case, I am in your hands, Inspector Hopkins," Holmes announced.

"Just wait until you see the remains, sir. I quite shrink from thinking of them."

"Of a bullet wound?" Holmes asked in visible bafflement.

"No, of the other signs, which I shan't report lest I bias your judgment," Hopkins said with a shiver. "There's something worse afoot here than a simple murder, that I can promise you."

Deadhouses, no matter how well maintained, always excrete an aroma of inevitability, that commingled scent of metal and decay that reminds you how long some elements can outlive others, and how short a time it may be before your own tenuous thread is snapped. This smell festers much more strongly in the summer months, but was present nevertheless as we walked into the stone morgue, approaching a table where a body lay under a sheet. When Hopkins pulled back the covering, Holmes's high forehead knit in consternation, and I admit I was myself taken aback. While I recognized an older, gaunter version of Forrester Hyde—his squarely masculine head and even features, now of course minus the ostentatious facial hair—my eyes were by no means drawn to his face.

"Whatever can have caused these abrasions?" the detective murmured.

"That's what plagues me too, Mr. Holmes," Hopkins assented. "Dr. Watson, you'd better have a look."

I leaned down over the source of the fuss as Holmes cast his eyes over the rest of the body. The bullet wound was straightforward in the extreme—a neat, puckered hole now wiped clean of gore. Much more disconcerting were the victim's hands: his fingertips were bruised and scraped, his nails raggedly torn away, even the edges of his thumbs having bled their share before he was killed. Had he dipped his hands within a sausage grinder and yanked them out again, he could hardly have done more damage.

"Any conclusions?" Holmes inquired, his attention still fixed on the body's shins and ankles.

"I've one comparison, but I'm afraid it confuses rather than illuminates matters," I admitted.

"Why so?"

"Well, the only time I've ever seen anything like this, there was a fire that had broken out in a derelict building, and very shortly thereafter the doorway was heaped with rubble. Men and women clawing for an egress made such marks upon their hands universally. The ones who survived, anyhow, and before the firemen tore the grating from a window."

Nodding, Holmes lifted the left hand as if cradling exquisitely delicate porcelain. "I would have said the same, Doctor. It is very unlikely these are anything but self-inflicted. There is no torture I can think of that batters phalanges in this haphazard manner. And had he been trying to climb something, his knees would be equally damaged. No—he was trying to escape from somewhere."

"Just as I feared, then," Inspector Hopkins lamented. "As Dr. Watson says, this only adds to the confusion."

Holmes replaced the appendage with extraordinary care. I noted that his movements, though steady, were still more languid than usual, and determined that I had better force some food into the man before he dropped in the street.

"On the contrary," said he. "It is an uncommon fact; therefore it is a helpful one. One uncommon fact can potentially be worth twenty of your boot prints, bullet shells, or cigar stubs. So Hyde was likely captured—or at least *trapped*—shortly after having been released from prison. Anyone could have discovered the date of his parole, but he would have lost his lodgings years beforehand. His destination must have been unknown to any save close confederates. Therefore he was either followed after leaving Wandsworth, or betrayed by one of those trusted individuals, as the odds are astronomically against these injuries being coincidental."

"But what can we do?"

"Might you wire the warden for me and find out whether he received any regular correspondence there?"

"By Jove, that's the ticket! In a trice, Mr. Holmes. I'll just write it out, and then we'll be en route to Wapping Station." Hopkins turned on his heel, clattered up the stairs, and left Holmes and me standing with puzzled brows on either side of a most peculiar corpse.

"Did you find anything else?" I inquired.

"Nothing to signify. He had a bad knee and favored it, likely due to an old insult he sustained as a convict. Or else, it is not outside the realm of possibility that it was a tennis injury. Who can say? We are through here."

Duly, I replaced the sheet. "We are going to stop for a sandwich, Holmes. At the very least, toasted cheese."

"Do you know, Watson, I never liked Forrester Hyde," he reflected with a gaze lost in the mists of time. "Granted, he never made much of himself as a criminal genius, which already disposes me against him, but I recall he had a mean, vengeful streak, and a still thicker stripe of unchecked rage. Such men all too often prey upon the opposite gender and, rather than retaining any scrap of chivalry by simply going in for robbery or embezzlement at a faceless business, exploit women because they fear no revenge from such victims whose positions are already tenuous. He was no exception. When we appeared in court and he spied the ballerina who was his downfall, he spat at her despite the fact she was a galaxy away, up in the gallery. You remember her, I suppose, despite the passage of years?"

"Miss Elizabeth Gayle," I readily answered. "Though I know her to have been very low at the time—and who would not have been, betrayed as she was—despite her melancholy she could not seem to repress sudden flashes of humor. Her wardrobe entirely lacked the ostentation favored by so many of her profession; she preferred cleanly draped lines and dark fabrics, though nothing she wore was morbid or plain in the slightest. As pale and slender as a birch tree, a shimmering configuration of light brown hair, large and luminous eyes, and a serenely sad countenance livened by a small, delightfully puckish mouth. She was quite riveting. Yes, of course I recall her."

My friend, pressing his fingers to the bridge of his nose in satirical despair, made to follow Hopkins.

"I say, Holmes, I was not in jest when I remarked we must consume a little sustenance."

"Come along, my dear Watson. We must have all our wits about us, or at least *I* must. Your own are rather more dispensable."

In vain did I remonstrate and in vain reason with the man until finally, abandoning hope, I consumed the two apples I'd purchased from a street urchin, and we rejoined Hopkins to survey the scene of the crime.

It is difficult not to envy those who were able to enjoy the Thames Tunnel at the apex of its beauty: the sheer marvel of its craftsmanship; the otherworldly pathway beneath the river itself; the polished marble steps leading under the turgid waters; the blue and white mosaic floor; the brilliant glow of the gas lamps; the opulently dressed pleasure-seekers stopping to have their fortunes told and to listen to the melody of the great echoing organ. The sight must surely have been a wonder in its time, but those days are long past. Now, just as my friend had mentioned, the Thames Tunnel is a soot-encrusted chute connecting Wapping with the South London Line, transporting cargo and weary-eyed passengers back and forth with none of the attendant awe associated with speeding through a corridor surrounded by a titanic volume of water. For what, after all, is there to see save fellow laborers with faces like crumpled newsprint? Or if one chooses the window as a vista, all-enveloping darkness until one reaches the opposite station?

The air was foul and thick with grit as we stepped onto the platform from the stairway. Four uniformed constables guarded Wapping Station, and we had been promised by Hopkins that the same configuration was repeated on the other end of the tunnel—one set of two patrolmen on each side of the platform—for a total of eight officers. No one, he vowed with such fervor that Holmes hid a laugh in an abrupt cough, could possibly have disturbed the integrity of the footmarks. In a dignified yet still transparent glow of pride, Hopkins ordered yet another set of four policemen to make certain that the trains had been stopped, and to light their brightest bulls-eye lanterns for the examination of the evidence.

"Thank God you're here, Doctor," said Holmes under his breath.

"I am always glad to help, but what can you mean?"

"If friend Hopkins grows any more stimulated, I fear for his heart despite his relative youth and vigor. Just think of the strain."

Smothering a smile as Hopkins informed us that all was in readiness was an arduous task, but I managed it. We followed after the constables, descended a set of iron steps for the railway workmen down to the tracks, and then stopped as Holmes whisked himself into place before the group.

"Everyone take the utmost care to step only on the railroad ties, on the gauge side and not the field side, if you please!" he called out, his ringing voice weirdly diminished in the foulness of the atmosphere. "Granted, our quarry may have done the same, but it takes a bold fellow indeed to walk in mid-track when the trains have not been stopped.

A quarter hour of your time, and we shall return triumphant having escaped the underworld!"

Holmes—who could be very popular with the roundsmen when he wanted something from them—received applause and cries of "Hear, hear!" for this exhortation from the Yarders, while I shook my head in undisguised worriment. His behavior was not at all out of character, but his eyes gleamed quicksilver-bright and his gestures grew more expansive by the minute. My iron-willed friend has more than once driven himself directly into loss of consciousness due to lack of the most basic human maintenance; this was a spectacle I desired specifically to avoid.

As we walked along the ties, the light grew dimmer and the air thicker until the lanterns were of scant use. Still, it was no worse than an ordinary London Particular, and one by one we began tying our scarves round our faces to keep out the hovering charcoal.

"Here we are, Mr. Holmes!" Hopkins, who walked alongside my friend in the lead, whistled grandly to signal the halt of the party. "Everyone with a lantern, do as Mr. Holmes and I bid you, and this will go at first-rate speed. Mr. Holmes, allow me to present to you the murder site!"

We could barely see one another, but I could not miss the humorous flash of my friend's eyes as he glanced at me, and even in the gloom I was forced to bend and—ostensibly—clear the foul atmosphere from my lungs.

"The footmarks begin here." I could hear Hopkins's familiar voice but could see nothing from my position, so I planted my hands in my pockets and followed the line of the light as it hazily illuminated the inspector's back and Holmes's profile as it paid Hopkins's account the most minute attention. "And here they are the most concentrated. Much is explained if, as you said, he traveled via the ties and then leapt over to the margin, as indeed much is explained if he descended on foot—still alive, though mortally injured—from the stopped train. Both hypotheses present serious difficulties. But as you can see, he has faced in a number of directions just here, where the ground is all but churned, and then we shift to the signs of a man crawling on hand and knee, blood dripping from his waistcoat. Can you see them?"

"Yes, they are unmistakable," said Holmes.

A jolt coursed through me at his tone. Sherlock Holmes had noticed something already, had transformed from a distant, ironical man into a sleek panther crouched in a cover of spreading foliage, a predator alert, as it stalks its natural prey, to the merest quiver of a leaf.

"Hyde crawls for about as far as you might expect from the severity of the wound," Hopkins continued, "and the wider puddle here is where he expired."

"Indeed, I gathered as much. And you are right to say that nothing indicates he landed here after having been expelled from between cars. However, do you not, Hopkins, find the details of this jumble of initial marks rather indicative?"

"In what way?"

"Well, I admit that I may be very fanciful, but the weight balance of some of these prints seems to me unusual. Note that just there he seems to be moving forward—you'll perceive a slightly deeper depression between one foot and the other, which confirms a superfluous observation I made in the morgue regarding a knee injury—but in any case, those indentations are quite different from these, for example, when he staggers back. Do they suggest anything to your ample acumen?"

"Yes!" the young inspector exclaimed. "Good heavens, you're right, Mr. Holmes, you must be! My cap is off to you already, sir."

The detective paused. "What am I right about, if I may beg the extreme honor of knowing my own mind?"

"He was reeling to and fro, Mr. Holmes, from the shock and the pain of it—first on his toes and then on his heels, and from the very beginning! Therefore we can eliminate the notion that he entered via either of the stations. The murderer stopped the train, shot Hyde before the squeal of the brakes and the clatter of the tracks would cease to cover the noise, and then pushed the still-living Hyde from between the cars, thereby making a masterful getaway. Then the killer mopped up any traces of blood onboard before we were alerted. Have I got the right end?"

"Well, I grant that you are at least partially correct, though I admit I was thinking of something rather more outlandish regarding one aspect of that theory. Tut-tut, never mind—my trifling whims get the better of me from time to time, you understand."

"You might share your idea anyhow, sir. I am all attention."

"I certainly will, if it comes to anything. You may assist in that regard, as a matter of fact."

"At your service, Mr. Holmes."

"Constable! Shine your lantern so that I can make a note on my cuff, will you? Many thanks. Now, Hopkins, give me the names of the engineers Hyde wrote down and presumably contacted in search of employment, please. I shall be indebted."

A few polite murmurs broke out as we shifted our feet and waited for the pair to complete this transaction. When they had finished, my friend thanked the mystified inspector and turned back to the group.

"Quick march, lads!" he cried. "This is no atmosphere in which to linger. I've had drafts of shag that were cleaner—onward and upward, and Hopkins, feel free to disband the guards. Oh, but just arrange for a photograph to be taken of the footmarks first! Would that inconvenience you?"

"I—not at all," our friend managed. "You heard Mr. Holmes, gentlemen! Back to the station and I'll assign a pair of you to photograph the scene."

Upon regaining the platform, Holmes made our swift goodbyes and strode for the stairs, vaulting up them as if the devil were in pursuit. When we reached the near-blinding daylight aboveground, I registered with chagrin that Holmes's zealous gaze had turned positively feverish.

"It's the nearest restaurant possible for us, and there you shall tell me about your findings," I announced.

"There isn't time, Watson." Already casting about for a cab, he spied one and gestured with his stick to the driver. "By all means, refresh yourself. I can suggest nothing better, for I've a tedious hour or two ahead you needn't assist me over, and so I shall meet you back at

Baker Street. Enjoy your meal, my good man. I'll have a cup of coffee at my destination."

"Which is?" I demanded helplessly.

"Scotland Yard."

"But why?"

"To follow a hunch."

"Holmes, you are a person, not an automaton, and therefore you require sufficient nourishment to remain alive in order to follow hunches."

"Watson, your intentions are doubtless as pure as the shores of Eden, but I am so tired that should I so much as ingest a biscuit, I would be unable to lift a finger for forty-eight hours. Wish me luck!"

"Best of luck, but Holmes, what did you see on the tracks?"

He turned back as he stepped upon the rail, every vein aquiver with the intoxication of the chase. "Hopkins has always been dismal with footprints—you recall the business of Black Peter, and that matter over the Russian woman's pince-nez was even worse. I do not blame him for being blind to the only possible conclusion in this case, however, for it is rather incredible."

"And it comprises?" I managed to keep the frustration from my tone only with severest effort.

"I have seen a great many queer tracks in my time," Holmes said, leaning out the hansom's window at a jaunty angle after he had slammed it shut. "But even I have never before seen a set that clearly indicated the party had emerged from a solid brick wall. Great Scotland Yard, driver! And quickly!"

Needless to say, I returned home and partook of lunch provided by Mrs. Hudson with a gnawing anxiety in my belly. Surely Holmes could not be serious in his suggestion that Hyde had essentially materialized in a tunnel only to be shot to death, and my fellow lodger's relentless energy was beginning to verge upon a frenzy I had seen more than once prior and grown to dread. After a bowl of lamb stew had been eradicated, though, I began to feel more optimism. Never had I heard that tone of giddy secrecy in Holmes's voice save when he was convinced beyond a doubt. So I took occupation of the settee, with a pillow under my head and a novel propped upon my chest, intending to await his return.

When the sitting room door flew open with a bang, the shadows had made significant advances, the expiring sun having commenced a tactical retreat. My eyes flew open as Holmes swept into the room, muttering of notions too soft to catch and too abstruse to comprehend anyhow, more than likely.

"Apologies, Holmes, I must have drifted off while waiting for you. What did you discover?"

"It has to be right, it *has* to be right," he hissed, striking his palm with his fist. "Oh, the odds are a thousand to one in my favor, but as to proving it, I cannot work *miracles*!"

"Good heavens! Sit down and explain, if you are willing."

Holmes did sit, the bags under his eyes beginning to be lightly etched with lavender. "Watson, do you know how valuable you are to me as a sounding board?"

"Whatever I can do, including nothing at all, I shall gladly attempt." Pouring a small pair of whiskeys, I passed one to him and took my accustomed chair.

"You are the best of confidants, my friend. You neither know the point I am about to make nor rush me in arriving there. It's transcendentally clarifying."

"You flatter me unnecessarily."

"No, no, you are like the transparent glass which nevertheless focuses the beams emanating from the lighthouse, you are—"

"Let us leave the compliments out of it, since you have urgent news."

Holmes, sitting with his elbow propped upon the chair arm, blew a breath through his teeth. "We must go back a step or two. I've already reminded you that I never liked Forrester Hyde, but you will also remember how chafed I was to pin him on only one instance of theft, since we could prove no other possession of stolen property. That was singular. I had thought him frugal, and wise to make few waves—what a dunce I was! You really ought to have mentioned that I was not paying the problem its full attention, my dear Watson."

"I fail to grasp your meaning, for it is obscure in the extreme."

He surged forward in his chair, fanning long fingers. "When a man finds a stirring vocation at which he excels, Watson, what does he do? Does he hide his talent and return to the gutter? Does he commit himself to it piecemeal, neglect it for weeks at a time in favor of physical drudgery?"

"No." I drew the word out, seeing his point. "No, he practices it, and with a will."

"Yes, he does!" Holmes cried. He thrust three sheets of foolscap at me, and I took them. "Hyde contacted this trio the instant he was released from prison—Richard Black, Davy Burntree, and Stephen McKay. Take a look at my notes from the Yard's files this afternoon, and from the city's bureau of records, and see what you make of it."

My friend's handwriting was generally clear though steeply sloping, but his physical enervation had rendered it almost illegible. Thus it took me nearly a minute's perusal of the three scribbled biographies before the pattern blazed to life before my eyes.

"Do you mean to tell me that *all three* of these men worked as engineers on the Thames Tunnel when it was converted from a pedestrian pleasure walk into an operative railway line, and alongside Forrester Hyde, and ten years before we ever encountered him?" I exclaimed. "Holmes, this—I cannot think what this means. Obviously, it changes everything, but in what manner? Were you serious when you said—"

"Oh, every ounce of my being was serious, Doctor. Forrester Hyde walked out of that brick wall with an eager—not to say panicked, though I think it a fair assessment based on the depth of the mud indentation—gait, and then met his end. On the surface, this seems impossible, so we must reexamine our facts and see if we have recorded any amiss, which errors might be tripping up our thought processes. We know that he died very soon after his release, implying if not presupposing that unfinished business plagued him. We know that he robbed other women besides Miss Elizabeth Gayle, and that I identified neither fences nor stonecutters with whom he worked. We know that he worked as a construction engineer when he was not fleecing female artists out of their tangible valuables in exchange for soon-to-be-useless reviews. Taking into account that I never found his hoard, and that I know for a fact he emerged from a solid wall—"

"Holmes!" I cried. "Yes, yes, I see your thoughts."

"I had no doubt that you would, eventually."

"Somehow he must have stashed his ill-gotten gains in a secret chamber within the tunnel. Just a moment, though—you said that it seemed as if he emerged from the wall itself, but you found no tracks leading there. Even supposing he did build a hidden room, that's impossible."

"By no means. A clever pack rat would surely create multiple entrances, particularly bearing in mind that the one we know about is so inherently perilous owing to the active trains. The balance is strongly in favor of another's existence."

"Very well, that explains the footprints. But the rest is confused and haphazard, at least so far as I can make out."

"I do not find it so very esoteric." Holmes's voice had slowed to a logician's drone. (I surmised this was due to the fact that he was finally seated, and at home, and therefore inclined to collapse.) "Step by step, it plays out in this manner: suppose that Forrester Hyde, after discovering his native oeuvre, sought local allies to assist him in building an impenetrable vault—impenetrable because no one save his associates knew it was there at all, lodged between the decorative interior wall and the much more formidable supporting structure. He could not have accomplished this without confidants. I surmise that he paid them handsomely for assisting him, but told them that the secret room had another purpose entirely, else he would have been forced to share the bounty for the remainder of his larcenous career. An eccentric's study, a place for his most vile illicit assignations . . . Forrester Hyde could convince people of practically anything, and when enough money enters into the equation, securing the silence of others isn't so very difficult."

"Yes, that follows. London is full of whimsical Bohemians. Your own brother founded the Diogenes Club, for no purpose other than to avoid friendly communication."

"The example is apt."

"Why should he have sought these men out upon his release, then?"

"Ah, that is a more subtle point, but I am near certain of it. Once I had arrested him, if his erstwhile colleagues happened to catch wind of his incarceration, they might easily have concluded his lair had been intended for other purposes and raided it accordingly. But supposing they were still employed as foremen, it would be highly unlikely that they had made off with a fortune, and his cache could be assumed intact. Is that reasoning clear?"

"It seems sound enough to me."

"Very good. Now allow me to suggest a purely hypothetical scenario to you—and you realize that I would do so before no one else with so few clues to work with: Forrester Hyde has no train ticket on his person because he needs none. He accesses the entrance to the vault within the Thames Tunnel—from where originally we cannot say, but I posit from a hidden door on one of the passenger platforms—with every intention of collecting his bounty and escaping by retracing his steps. Something happens in the interim, however, an unforeseen threat, which forces him to flee onto the tracks. To no avail, of course, since his mortal foe proved to be whichever man pulled the brakes on the Wapping-bound train. It smacks of conspiracy on the part of Black, Burntree, and McKay, does it not?"

"Yes, but enacted by which of them? And for the purpose of robbery, or the still more sinister intent of ending his life?"

"I confess it freely, Watson: I haven't the slightest idea." Holmes appeared almost comically frustrated by this confession, draping himself over his chair as if he were as boneless as an ulster carelessly tossed there. "We know where he was killed, and therefore that he was forced to exit via the tunnel for reasons which are still obscure to us. But he found that the passage of time had been his enemy. He was fully capable of unlocking the alternative egress, presumably, but what is an unlocked door in a brick wall when ravaged by urban decay? And what would happen next, if he refused to go out the way he came in?"

"His fingers!" Shaking my head, I pictured it all too easily. "Holmes, you know already that you are a genius, but I hereby affirm it for the thousandth time. He had not accounted for natural processes and cracks plugged tight with grit and ash. Fighting the weight of the door, he found himself captured by a mere room, doubtless with some peril at his heels. Desperate to escape, he eventually clawed his way out—which caused the unexplained injuries we saw at the morgue."

"So you are of a mind with me, then," Holmes said softly, staring at the carpet as if all of life's mysteries could be solved there. "When he reached the exit onto the field side of the tracks, he stumbled out in his eagerness. Shifting, he saw the light of an oncoming train. It is what happened afterward that we must determine, and that task seems to me nigh-impossible."

"Why?"

"Well, consider our options. Any unknown crony of Hyde's could conceivably have pursued him from Wapping. More likely, considering the fact he had recently corresponded with them, any combination of his three former coworkers could have committed this deed, and secured alibis, and lied about their doings thereafter. How can I build a case destined to fall apart at the seams? I have a body, known associates, and one hopes a photograph of some very strange footprints. We can investigate the hiding place from the tunnel side as well, knowing whence he emerged. Otherwise, the culprit is virtually untraceable."

Holmes looked so dejected that I hardly knew how to answer him. However, within the next ten minutes of my puttering about refreshing tea and uselessly staring out the window, a telegram arrived. I recall with fondness the pale silvered tint of the overcast light in our sitting room, the quick breath my friend took through his nose as he read the missive.

"Is it bad news?" I ventured.

"On the contrary." Holmes's eyes flashed up to mine. "My suggestion to Hopkins has borne fruit: Forrester Hyde did have one steady correspondent when he was in prison. I cannot help thinking that same person might shed some light on this matter."

"But who was it, then?"

"Elizabeth Gayle."

"My God." Absorbing this signal development, I quickly recovered. "Are we to pay her a visit?"

"I can suggest nothing better to do."

"Where does she live, then?"

"Hay's Mews, Mayfair."

"That's only a hansom ride away. Holmes, why should a woman who had been so wronged by Forrester Hyde write to him in jail? She seemed a highly sensitive soul, as an artist, but hardly an impractical one, and she sought us out in the first place, after all."

"There exist many reasons for such erratic behavior, ranging from complete delusion to the birth of a secret child fathered by Hyde." He darted his thin arms into his jacket and adopted a contemplative look. "Or some other motive as yet unknown. I have given up attempting to plumb the depths of the female psyche, Watson. It is not unlike contemplating infinity—a worthy, even a spiritual meditation, destined from the beginning to fail entirely."

I have already described Elizabeth Gayle, and therefore I will not repeat myself regarding her willow-thin poise or her regretful smile except to say that the years had treated her with kindness. Her dark honey-colored hair was done up in Bohemian braids, and she wore a tasseled maroon shawl over a charcoal traveling costume with draped bell sleeves. We discovered her in the act of hurriedly packing a small case, and my heart seized at the sight, because it meant that my friend Sherlock Holmes was right—surely, she knew a great deal about this dire business to move with such agitation, for her limbs as I remembered them had been svelte and graceful. She was escaping a spare, clean room papered with an ivy pattern, and her eyes when she met ours were red-veined and weary.

"Miss Gayle, please forgive the intrusion and grant me the courtesy of speaking with you," Holmes attempted, removing his hat deferentially.

"Mr. Holmes! Why, it is you, and after all this time! What are you doing here?"

"That remains to be determined. Do sit down, for I fear that you are under some strain."

Miss Gayle sank into an armchair, limbs quivering. "That is all too true, I fear. Mr. Holmes, before you begin to question me—for I see that question me you must, and I recall your tenacity of will with great admiration—please allow me to make my own statement, for it would save us precious minutes and as you can see, I am in a terrible rush. I vow to tell you all—in fact, I firmly believe I owe it to you, and I always pay my debts in full—but I beg of you to let me speak my own story rather than submit to an interrogation, however genteel. There is much that you do not know. And as it will be painful to report, I should prefer to begin at once."

"A fair request, and one I do not begrudge you in the slightest," Holmes allowed. "In your own time, then."

Seating ourselves after she gestured to a rather threadbare sofa, we watched her take a few agitated breaths. Miss Gayle adjusted the shawl draped over her shoulders, finally shaking her head as if in tragic amusement before beginning her account.

"First, you are under a misapprehension as to my name. Professionally, it is Elizabeth Gayle, but legally, that is not the case."

"What in fact is your name, if you please to tell us?"

"Mrs. Forrester Hyde," she whispered.

At our shocked expressions, she actually smiled. "From the beginning, then?"

"Please," Holmes assented, rapt.

"You have met the man, so I will not embark upon the subject of his charm, but it was mesmerizing. When he introduced himself to me, it was as he did to so many others: as an urbane man of the world—confident, casually radiating luck. Forrester seemed somehow more *alive* than anyone around him, as if the streets were filled with inked illustrations of other men and he was the only person present in the actual flesh. We were wedded in secret, which he claimed would serve both our careers, because I would be free to socialize with artists and freethinkers and his praise of my skills could not be accused of bias. What a ripe fool I was then! His hotel was often our home, and sometimes my digs—modest, but nevertheless much grander than what you see now—were where we made our partial life together. He claimed to travel a great deal, and I never dreamed he had another set of London lodgings until, long suspecting him guilty of affairs, I followed him there and discovered what manner of man my husband truly was.

"Forrester actively hated women, Mr. Holmes, with a venom that went far beyond some men's typically callous treatment. Instead of being ashamed that I had learned about his double life, he boasted to me—of his conquests, his sneak-thievery, his cleverness in building the hidden chamber in the Thames Tunnel, the impossibility of my divorcing him, and the power he had over me as a critic. He seemed to gorge himself on my sorrow. It may sound asinine to you gentlemen, but after my marriage exploded before my eyes, my own idiocy in having been duped by a persuasive blackguard was such a source of embarrassment that I came to think of dancing as the only love I had left in my bleak life—and my spirits could not bear the idea of losing my art as well over a vengeful review. Thus, initially I chose to do nothing. Claiming I could love only him, I continued to play the part of a wronged wife—and my husband was so cruel and self-obsessed, it saved my career."

"You ought never to have been forced to make such a choice," I could not help declaring.

"Granted—but I was, nevertheless. That being said, I knew of his crimes against others like me, and could not rest until this execrable man's capacity for harm was nullified. The sapphires you found in the hidden compartment in Forrester's bag did indeed belong to me, Mr Holmes. But you never suspected that I had planted them there."

"You framed a robber and a cad with evidence of thievery?" Holmes confirmed with what could only be called admiration. "His behavior toward you at the trial was extraordinarily vicious, but now his rage is much more explicable."

"The betrayal of a dishonest brute involves more courage than cowardice, Miss Gayle," I added with a will.

"Yes, I cannot presume to censure you for that action, which temporarily rid London of a blight, but frankly the matter I came to see you about is a far more urgent one, and one you have not yet touched upon," Holmes continued. "How came you to be corresponding with your estranged spouse, and how came he to be shot by an assassin aboard a stopped Wapping-bound train? You cannot deny, in light of what seems a hasty departure from these lodgings, that you have been somehow involved."

Miss Gayle paled, but pressed on. "No, I cannot, and you shall have the whole truth out of me, Mr. Holmes. I resumed my relationship with Forrester for my own purposes owing to the fact that his last spiteful action before the bars shut upon him was to pen a scathing review of my performance in a new production of *The Talisman*."

"Knowing that ballet was your passion as well as your livelihood, a cruel vengeance indeed," Holmes replied gravely.

"It was." She tilted her head a little, wincing as she recalled it. "I needed money; as you can see, I still do. Having convinced him before that I was obsessed with him, I thought that I might convince him I was desperately sorry, and that way retain some semblance of respectable living. It worked, to a point. Forrester readily believed me pathetic enough to adore him utterly, and so the practice of writing letters proved no obstacle—but as to the subject discussed? Not one penny did he send me, gentlemen. He thought of nothing from prison save retrieving his hoard. He was obsessed as much with the secret chamber as the treasure within, I think, a weeping dragon forcibly separated from its mountain of gold. When he was released, he even wrote to the engineers who had helped him build it, terrified he should discover one of them had abandoned London for the South of France, suddenly wealthy. None had, of course. They were callow, biddable creatures, and they lacked the key to its elaborate lock. As did I."

A creeping sensation brushed icy fingers along my shoulders just as Holmes's expression shifted, the fines lines around his eyes deepening suddenly in concentration.

Miss Elizabeth Gayle—for so I will always think of her—smiled her melancholy smile once more, but this time it possessed teeth that could rend.

"Forrester was likewise a callow, biddable creature. Oh, yes, I did it, Mr. Holmes," she said in a muted but matter-of-fact voice. "It was not enough anymore—the light jail sentence, the imminent release—not when he vented all his impotent rage in that stone-walled hell by continuing to torment me. Forrester was wise enough to tell me nothing of where the key was concealed, but he told me everything else I needed to know—about his paranoia; about Black, Burntree, and McKay."

"What on earth have you done, Miss Gayle?" I breathed when Holmes sat, silent as a statue.

"She wrote to the engineers herself," my friend replied mechanically, breaking from his reverie. "She told them to trail her husband upon his release—very carefully, so as to gain entrance to the room in the Thames Tunnel after Hyde led them there, carrying the only key. But she knew another entrance existed. And so she took precautions, and bought a ticket for a commuter train to Wapping."

"Very good, Mr. Holmes," she said approvingly. "Any outcome would have satisfied me—had the engineers stolen the bounty, I should simply have stolen it back from them. As it was, Forrester managed to lock the upper door on his confederates and was forced to flee via the tracks. The damage done to the tunnel exit nearly undid me, but he escaped at the last possible moment, hands bloodied, bag in hand. This I snatched from him as he attempted to board, and I rid England of an ugly presence. So much was happening—the shouts of the conductors, the bangs and clanks of the steam engine as the train idled—that no one noticed a tiny gunshot from a weapon wrapped in thick wool. The jewelry is no longer in my possession, Mr. Holmes—a series of packages has been delivered, and the valuables have been returned to their rightful owners, so far as I could determine them at this late date. I have kept nothing for myself except this."

Standing, she removed a small revolver from a pocket hidden within the folds of her skirts.

I started, and Holmes raised a palm in undisguised alarm.

"I know better than to imagine you will not make use of that weapon if you feel the need, madam," he attempted, "but I promise you there are many preferable alternatives."

"But there aren't, are there? Only force remains, at the end. You cannot condone a premeditated murder, and I cannot ask you to betray your consciences," she whispered with a harrowed half-smile. "I can incapacitate the pair of you as easily as I can kill you, but you have been of invaluable service to me in the past—my heart is light when I think of Forrester's death, on behalf of many others as well as myself, but hurting either of you would grieve me. Now, I am lifting this valise and going to the train station. If you try to stop me, it will go painfully for you both, though I should not dream of faulting you for setting the police on my trail afterward. Au revoir, Mr. Holmes, Dr. Watson. To say 'Thank you' seems inadequate—and still, I humbly thank you both for the part you have paid in freeing us all."

She departed with her usual floating step, a black cloak over her arm, gently shutting the door. We had sat there dumbstruck for some few seconds before Holmes mentioned, "I suppose we ought to pursue her."

"Yes, I suppose so."

Neither of us stood, Holmes matching his hands together in prayerful-looking contemplation.

"Watson, since Mrs. Hyde was my original client when I was introduced to this sordid affair years ago—albeit under false pretenses, granted—and now Hopkins has engaged me, do you think I am facing a conflict of interest?"

Judiciously, I considered. "That is possible, but when your original client embarks upon vigilante justice which ends in bloodshed, as a sworn defender of the law you must reconsider your position."

"Oh, of course." He shrugged, eyes half-lidded and bloodshot, the reaction already overtaking him now the mystery had been solved. "But on the other hand, do you admit that as an independent contractor, I've the right accorded any private citizen not to be shot at in the course of my workday?"

"Why, naturally. You are employed neither by the Yard nor in any military or guardsman capacity. You are merely a consultant."

"And while you are former military, one could make the argument you are here in the service of literature, not crime-solving. I should not like to see you wounded over an art form."

"That is very kind of you."

Perhaps a minute later, after checking his watch, Holmes rose rather lurchingly to his feet. "Don't dawdle so dreadfully, my dear Watson, not when there's a murderess to run to ground. We must seek out friend Hopkins and enlighten him as to this case's most signal features of interest."

While Sherlock Holmes did not shirk in his clear duty to inform Inspector Hopkins of all that had taken place, neither did he appear to make any great haste over doing so, for following this desultory exchange, we took our time in finding a cab. Whether this laxity was due to his natural inclination to sympathize with the killer rather than the deceased or to his being on the verge of physical collapse, I could not say. But by the time we found the hidden entrance to the Thames Tunnel, masked behind a staircase on one of the platforms, my friend was swaying to the point that he had need of my elbow for support, and Mrs. Hyde, née Gayle, had vanished entirely. No doubt Hopkins fulfilled all his obligations to the letter, and her ingenuity rather than any fault of the good inspector accounted for her escape.

Readers of the society columns may recall a startling announcement from that selfsame date when Mr. Sherlock Holmes, upon descending from a hansom delivering us back to Baker Street, fainted dead away in the road. As I have mentioned in the account titled "The Norwood Builder," this had happened upon no fewer than four occasions previously, although never before in public. I got him indoors, where smelling salts and brandy and hot broth were administered; but when all is said and done, I am grateful regarding the open-air setting in which this embarrassing predicament occurred. The fact it was well publicized gives me every cause to hope that similar disasters can be entirely prevented in future.

The Adventure of
the Mad Baritone

Mr. Sherlock Holmes of Baker Street, and I myself when in his estimable company, has been accosted by so many strange individuals that to list them would prove a task too Herculean for even the most dedicated biographer. The subject of operatic introductions indeed cannot even be called to my mind without a veritable eccentrics' menagerie flooding it. We had sat and listened to numberless wild appeals, impossible assertions, and nightmarish accounts, so many that during our busiest periods I wondered at the city of London itself—whether any other metropolis upon this colossal globe harbored such an array of skulking villains, and whether any other citizenry was so bedeviled by the goblins (all too human in nature) who lurked in its treetops and paving stones. Few other examples exhibit such an alarming commencement, however, as that of Mr. Horatio Falconer, whose introduction to our lives I still recall with a creeping chill.

The year was 1900, the November night a torrential one, lashing down sleet as if determined to drive out all inhabitants, saint and sinner alike, and begin afresh. I have mentioned before that, like any man of creative temperament, Holmes reacts to the weather almost as he would to a piece of musical accompaniment designed to alter the mood of the theatregoer. Thankfully, however, instead of succumbing to the storm's effects, my friend was engaged upon an eighteenth-century legal letter purporting to have been written by the estate's "ballivus," a man who served as a manorial lord's liaison with the reeve. This document, if genuine, could ruin a great family while making a disreputable one wealthy beyond imagining, and he sat at his desk poring over the parchment until well after midnight.

Despite being perfectly contented myself with a cigar, a glass of port, and a late edition, I had peered over his shoulder when emphatic grunts or exclamations issued. My curiosity had gained me nothing more than an indecipherable jumble of abbreviations, "VIIber" for September being the only one I could decipher, so for some twenty minutes I had left him to it. I was just beginning to nod when a sharp cry agitated the drink in my hand. I was on my feet instantly.

"Good Lord, Holmes, what's the matter?"

"Nothing whatever, my good man!" Whipping his head in my direction, he brandished the letter with far less care than he had previously used upon the delicate artifact, his torso fairly wriggling with restrained glee. "The Gascoyne family is quite safe from harm and I shall wire them on the morrow. The matter is settled."

"My dear fellow!" I gasped. "You are to be congratulated. But how did—"

"This paper represents one of the most unusual attempts at chicanery I've ever been privileged to witness. But it is without doubt a forgery. See here—no, you needn't worry over touching it; the clever rogues must have found an antique stock of parchment abandoned somewhere or other and experienced a malicious flash of inspiration. As I told you, the ink holds up under scrutiny and the penmanship is likewise masterly. But the historic word for a last will declared orally rather than written out is 'nuncupative,' and as you will astutely note, here they have used 'testamentary' owing to ignorance of antique legal terminology. There were five other indications which nagged at me terribly, but were too minor to send the interlopers packing. Thanks to this error in vocabulary, however, the Gascoynes can go on living as they always have lived—which I need not tell you will doubtless save the youngest daughter's engagement. Rather neatly managed, don't you think?"

So saying, Holmes released the forged document, allowing it to flutter to the floor. He crossed his arms and regarded me with the look of pure joy only evident when he has just exercised his formidable powers for justice, and before a trusted audience.

"Bravo!" I exclaimed readily, wringing his hand.

In the midst of a radiant grin, he yawned, and his glittering eyes drifted to the page now lying in disgrace upon our hearth rug. "That was a triumph of dedication over inclination near the end, Watson. I've a ghastly headache."

"I don't doubt it."

"You weren't present, but the Gascoyne patriarch was beside himself when he came to me, and small wonder, with his daughter's future prospects teetering upon the brink of imminent ruin. Frankly, I've better use for men who live by their wits or their sweat than for men who live by their pedigree, but it is pleasant to think that the innocent need not suffer from an opportunistic ruse."

"Hear, hear."

"Still." He shifted, one finger tapping against his long chin. "As a fellow professional in the field, I doff my cap to them, considering how much inventiveness, expertise, and daring this involved. The perpetrators were described to me as an impoverished family from a university town whose breadwinner had lost his position. This scheme is so outlandish that it would have worked in all likelihood, if not for me—a beautiful blend of craft and art, truly."

"You're a professional in the field of skullduggery, are you?"

His mouth twitched with merriment. "You'll admit that I'd be unmatched."

Shaking my head, I had turned away with the intention of fetching Holmes a headache powder from my bag when we heard a violent assault upon the downstairs bell, followed by equally brutish treatment of the door in the form of desperate pounding.

Holmes rubbed at his temples in pain. "Dear me. That is either someone come to take the house by force of arms at the midnight hour, in which case we should have to do battle with him, or someone who desperately desires us to wet our boots. Regarding either scenario, I am reluctant to—"

"I'll bring you something for your head in a moment," I assured him, hastening toward the staircase whilst blessing Providence that Mrs. Hudson was from home tending to an ailing relation.

As a medical man, and one who has long lived within the sphere of a finely honed scientific mind to boot, I cannot say that I endorse the existence of spirits who meddle in the affairs of men: so I do not believe in supernatural portents, no matter how clear they may seem to some. And yet, there is such a thing as common intuition, and mine that night pulsed with alarm at the cacophony upon our front step.

"Do have a care, Watson," I heard, and I glanced back to see that Holmes had appeared behind the banister rail with dressing gown hem fluttering, doubtless for the same reason my muscles were taut with alarm.

I released the lock and turned the handle, but before I could move back to allow our visitor entrance, a savage shape half-hurtled and half-pushed its way through the door. Thrown off balance, I glimpsed what seemed a bundle of rags with a revolver in its hands flying up the stairs two at a time.

"Holmes, he's armed!" I shouted, lunging in pursuit.

Mere seconds passed as I raced after the invader, but my heart was firing like a cannonade and my imagination was blackly poisoned with a single thought: Sherlock Holmes, of all London's residents, received perhaps the highest number and certainly the widest variety of death threats. Dozens of miscreants had at one time or another pledged themselves to the single-minded goal of his demise. Lacking other options, I was prepared to tackle this interloper, fling him to the hardwood, and be done; but the idea that a stray bullet might find its way to my friend turned the blood in my veins as cold as the sleet now spattering our entryway.

Time's flow slowed to a trickle when I crested the final step to discover Holmes with one foot neatly behind him in a fighter's stance, ready to dive or dodge as needs must. Before him stood a short, thick-shouldered figure with matted black hair, a streaming coat which looked as if it had been dredged straight from the Thames, and a gun clutched in one shaking hand.

"I'll do it," he boomed in a resonant baritone. "I swear to God I will, and then I'll have finished the business for good and all."

"You appear a trifle out of sorts, sir." Holmes's much higher voice was as smooth as a river stone, but I saw the way his agile fingers twitched and his eyes sent darting glances hither and thither as he tried to ascertain the wisest course. "Of course, I cannot blame you in the slightest, as no sane gentlemen cares to have wet snow poured down his collar, and I perceive you lack an umb—"

"Who says I'm sane?" the fellow demanded. "Who says I'm a gentleman, either?"

"Well." Holmes coughed politely. "I'll admit that both sanity and gentility are nuanced questions, but I perceive you originally come from respectable stock in the neighborhood of Colchester—Lexden, to be precise—and never having met you before in my life . . ." Here my friend paused and with a look ascertained I understood we faced not an old enemy, but something more volatile still. "It is a habit of mine to give the benefit of the—"

"I said I'll *do it*!" the visitor cried, raising the revolver and clapping its muzzle against his own head.

Horror contorted Holmes's features as I gasped. An instant later, he had transformed himself into the snake charmer I have described elsewhere, the man who gives the distinct impression that he could walk into the middle of a frothing mob and calm its spirits with a quiet overture.

"Oh, but you can't, you understand." Holmes struck a lilting, conversational tone. "No, I won't have it. See here, I think you came to Baker Street to tell me about yourself. Did you not? The only alternative explanation is that you came here so that I might witness your demise and vouch for it, which could suggest any of half a dozen motives that occur to me. But you see, I don't know who you are, and supposing you fire that weapon . . ." He shrugged sadly. "Perhaps I never will. My friend here—just behind you, the hearty chap with the moustache—is a doctor. If something ails you, he will do all he can to help. As for myself, I am criminally curious, you know, and I cannot have gentlemen from Lexden charging into my rooms and intriguing me only to watch them expire."

I had been confused, but though Holmes's words were glib, they were equally gentle, and already taking effect. The man appeared more cognizant of the terrible situation in which we found ourselves after hearing my friend make light of it. His trembling did not cease, however, and his rich voice when it emerged was knotted thickly with despair.

"I thought perhaps that you, only you, could help me. Foolishness! No one believes me."

"I might surprise you. I've been told I'm very unpredictable."

"This truly *is* the guise madness takes, coming here in the middle of the night and waving a gun in front of decent people—it's proof of everything they say! What I believe happened to me is impossible."

"But you see, I happen to be the world's foremost expert on what is possible versus what is impossible. So since you're already here, it would be a shame not to tell me about it." Holmes offered a tiny smile.

The poor fellow laughed and then collapsed to the floor as if someone had tossed a ragbag onto it, sobbing over and over, "God help me, God help me." Quick as a thought, Holmes had descended to his knees, pocketed the gun, and taken him squarely by the shoulders.

"All right," he said in a much more sober tone. "You've taken a spell, but whatever has happened to bring you here, nothing can harm you at the moment. You understand that all you must do is calm yourself, and my friend and I shall see to the rest? Very good. Some brandy I think might be in order, and I'll move the rack before the hearth so we can dry your coat, and we shall see what we can do."

"Brandy!" the fellow repeated after another anguished sound. "God have mercy. Some bread, thank you, and a cup of tea, and I'll do what I can to recover myself. I cannot express my shame over—"

"Tut-tut! Not another word of that nature, provided you allow me to retain your weapon temporarily in lieu of an apology. Do you call that a fair trade? All right, then. If you can make your way into the sitting room just there, I'll fetch the coatrack and some sandwiches. We must do for ourselves just now, as we've the most disloyal and frivolous landlady in Britain, who will insist on abandoning us whensoever one of her aunts is dying. It's extremely tedious. I am Sherlock Holmes, by the way, and this is my friend, Dr. John Watson."

When our guest perceived the hand proffered, he bent over it as if it were a lifeline. "Mr. Horatio Falconer, sir, and already a man forever in your debt."

"Not at all. Off with you toward the fire, and we shall see to housekeeping and return in a trice."

Mr. Falconer staggered to his feet and proceeded, still weeping hard, into the sitting room. On the instant he was gone, my friend fell back on his heels, looking thoroughly spent.

"Good heavens, Holmes, are you all right?" I demanded, approaching him. "That was an unprecedented performance. My dear fellow, can you stand?"

"Of course I can."

When I had helped pull him to his feet, I saw in the low light of the hall that he was indeed hale enough, though far more shaken than usual following a violent altercation. I could scarce blame him, feeling identically myself.

"If we never see such a display as that again, I'll give the universe top marks."

"It was, as you suggest, unusual, and not in a fashion that bears repeating," he conceded, seeming to shake the startlement from his limbs as he trotted downstairs.

"Holmes, I thought he was here to enact some terrible revenge on you."

"Yes, that likewise occurred to me. I saw that you were as ready as ever to fling yourself into the fray, and I humbly thank you for it."

"You've no need to thank me for anything, and you don't do anything humbly."

"Well, if that were the case, you'd have no notion of what it looks like, would you, and therefore cannot judge as to either the nature or the frequency of my humility," he teased, seeming fully recovered as he shut the front door and locked it. "My dear Doctor, I am going to make sandwiches, a task at which I excel as I excel at so many others. I request that you carry the coatrack upstairs and fix me a headache tonic, if you would be so kind. I find myself in direst need of one."

Some ten minutes later, Holmes and I sat in our respective chairs, listening to the coat drip as it dried, my friend's tonic swiftly dispatched, watching as our guest upon the sofa consumed his simple repast of cold beef and cheese. The interval gave us ample opportunity to observe him. Mr. Falconer seemed somewhere between the ages of forty-five and fifty-five, but his appearance made his reason for refusing brandy eminently clear. He had already been drunk when he arrived, for his movements were slow and deliberate, his craggy face was emblazoned with red veins, and his skin beneath the enlarged vessels was a sickly yellow hue. A hooked nose, tangled black hair that fell to his shoulders unrestrained, and a suit equally as decrepit as his coat completed this picture of total dissolution. His eyes within the wreckage, however, were of a clear, pale blue, and so artistic and lively despite their glassiness that I heartily pitied the fellow for having driven himself into such perilous territory as regarded his health. When he had finished, he sipped his tea and heaved an overwrought sigh.

"Gentlemen, I hardly know how to thank you, but before I take advantage of any more hospitality, I must embarrass myself still further. I cannot pay your retainer in cash, Mr. Holmes, though I can visit a pawn shop should you be willing to wait until the morrow."

So saying, he produced a small golden charm, obviously of enormous importance to him, considering it remained in his possession, and I passed it to Holmes. My friend had lit his pipe and sat smoking meditatively with his stork's legs crossed. He turned the shining object over in his fingers and tossed it in an arc back to our client.

"Saint Cecilia. Thank you, Mr. Falconer, but when a client lacks the resources to meet my entire fee, I prefer to leave the subject of money forgotten. Consider your own case to fall under the latter category. Which opera company was it sacked you?"

Mr. Falconer's jaw dropped. He rubbed at the short, wiry bristles on his cheeks. "How the devil did you know I was a singer?"

"How could I not know? You can't open your mouth to speak without betraying your extensive vocal training to the expert. As you are sleeping rough of late—either Hyde Park or St. James's, which both feature the loamy light brown soil which has attached itself to your coat—it is clear you are no longer employed, but a man of your obvious talent could find work at any time were your general condition improved. The scene just enacted in my hall, forgive my mentioning it, would not have occurred to someone lacking in creative sensitivity. Add to this the detail that Cecilia is the patron saint of musicians, and the matter becomes indisputable."

Our client winced at the reference to his earlier actions. "It was the Garrick Street Players, sir. I have played Morales, Guglielmo, Doctor Falke. . . . I had a permanent position in the company, but as you can see . . ." He gestured at himself. "Hyde Park is indeed my residence of late."

"What happened?"

Mr. Falconer shook his unkempt head. "The oldest tale ever told, Mr. Holmes. A love lost, a terrible habit gained—the triteness is almost as painful as the shame."

"But it is not this condition which drove you to such despair."

"No indeed."

"Consult me at your leisure, then."

"Mr. Holmes, I have been kidnapped."

"Indeed so?" Holmes puffed at his pipe. "And, having made a lucky escape, you wish to see your assailants brought to justice, I take it?"

"Mr. Holmes," our client said softly, "I have been kidnapped and released back into the streets of London unharmed three times."

As he frequently did when surprised, Holmes swept forward in his chair, grey eyes glowing like cinders. "Remarkable."

"Yes, hardly credible."

"The facts, if you please, from the beginning."

"I shall do as best I can." Mr. Falconer drew a still-unsteady finger around the rim of his saucer. "I am an only child orphaned at a young age and entirely alone in the world. You see me at my lowest tide, gentlemen, and have been subjected to an outrageous display to boot—no, no, I must speak of it, for the hopelessness I suffer has direct bearing on my case. After the first occasion on which I was abducted and set free, I half-thought it a grotesque joke and half a fevered nightmare, and when I told the story to my few mates at the only pub which offers me a rough bench any longer, The Fox's Tooth, they laughed it off as a dream. After the second, which was identical to the first, I went to Scotland Yard. They would have none of me, and told me I had best look sharp or end up in jail myself for telling the police outrageous tales. The third instance ended this morning, after which I pawned my father's watch—which had used to be decorated with my Saint Cecilia—exchanged it for a gun with which to protect myself or end myself, I hardly knew which; indulged in considerably more than I should have done, as per usual, for I cannot seem to stop; and then sought you out. If you fail to believe me, I shall run mad."

"Pray master yourself, then, and deliver your story with clarity and confidence."

"Can't you see, sir, that I have no confidence left?" Mr. Falconer protested, but immediately thereafter he snarled in disgust. "Very well. I have nothing save my life left to lose, after all.

"As you say, Mr. Holmes, I come from Lexden, and for some twenty years earned my living by my voice. In my youth, I traveled with various touring companies, but as I approached forty, I began to tire of the lifestyle, for all that it was gay and convivial, and joined the Garrick Street Players as a permanent fixture of their season. The glamorous habits of a life led flitting from city to city did not leave me, however, as I now regret beyond my ability to tell you. Thus, when a woman with whom

I had fallen abjectly in love treated me cruelly—indeed, had I been her bitterest foe, she could not have done a more thorough job—I fell from the tightrope upon which I'd been balancing for decades and landed as you see me: bereft, degraded, nigh-destroyed. I am embarrassed to say that I am not always in a state of awareness or remembrance, and it's difficult therefore to blame anyone for not believing me when I can barely believe myself.

"About a month ago, I made a few shillings by street-singing near to Covent Garden, which is how I earn enough for food and drink, and afterward made my way to The Fox's Tooth to drown my recollections in cheap gin. Unsurprisingly, the events of the night blurred after nine or ten o'clock, and I cannot tell you what time I left the pub, nor whether or not I made it to Hyde Park and the low line of shrubbery which has of late kept me reasonably dry and hidden from the constables. God, how little I'm sure of at this point! No doubt I am the worst client you've ever had the misfortune to address," he added bitterly.

Holmes's eyelids had drooped as he listened, and now he shut them completely. "Mr. Falconer, the worst clients want me to tell them whether their spouses have been unfaithful, or hope that I can locate lost railway luggage. Stop telling me what you don't know, and start telling me what you do."

"Quite right." Mr. Falconer nodded more decisively. "I will waste no more of your time, gentlemen. Yes, upon the night I just described, I fell into a stupor, only to awaken in completely strange environs. My head felt wooden, my legs weak, my vision full of stars—it wasn't like my usual symptoms at all, sir, and God knows they are plentiful. No, this was like emerging from an opium dream. The room in which I found myself spun, and I reeled from wall to wall in terror, not knowing who had put me there or why."

"Describe the chamber to me."

"The first time, I was so disoriented that I fear I didn't learn as much as I should have—but on the second and third, although rattled and sick, I examined the place thoroughly, and it was the same each time. It was a bedroom, Mr. Holmes. An ordinary bedroom with pale stripes on the walls, a walnut desk with an empty drawer, olive-hued curtains, a comfortable bed with a green quilt, and very queer light."

"How so?"

"Each time I have awoken there, the lamp has been off and the nocturnal atmosphere was bathed in blue. I should swear to it, though in my state I don't like to swear to anything."

"Well, well, let us assume you can swear to this or we shall have nothing to go on at all."

"True enough, and possibly it was a symptom of the drug I believe I was given. In any case, on every occasion, I shouted for help at the top of my lungs to no avail. But when I had quieted, hoarse and sick, I could always hear muffled arguing. A woman's voice, pleading, and a man's denying her request, or so it seemed. The words were indistinct and I might not have recalled them in any case, so porous is my mind, but I am certain the tone was that of an altercation. At times, I could hear the woman weeping, Mr. Holmes."

"Ominous."

"Extremely so. The sound filled me with dread. Every time, the urgency and passion with which they fought have increased. I am certain of it as I'm certain of little else, since other than listening to these quarrels, and shouting to the speakers for help, there was nothing to occupy me."

Holmes's eyes opened with a shrewd edge to their stare. "But you must have interacted with someone when they went to restore your freedom."

Mr. Falconer shuddered and carefully set down his teacup. "Yes."

"Well, come to the point, then! What sort of individual was your jailer?"

"I never saw him when he took me, for he always came upon me in my cups and snatched me up unawares," Mr. Falconer whispered. "But when he came to release me . . . He is a tall man, Mr. Holmes, nearly as tall as you, dressed all in black, wearing a hood like an executioner's."

My neck prickled with dread at the image.

"What was his eye color?" Holmes asked with clinical detachment.

"I am sorry, sir, but I could not say. He terrified me. Three times this man has overpowered me, though doing me no harm save to spirit me into a blue-lit bedroom. Once about a month ago, a fortnight after that, and finally last night. I flew at him when the door opened this time, but to no avail."

"What was his voice like?"

"He never spoke to me. He only entered with a rag and pressed it over my face. It confirmed to my mind that—assuming any of this is even true—I was dosed with chloroform, which explained my feelings of delirium."

"What did his hands look like?"

"I couldn't possibly tell you."

Holmes frowned in frustration. "Very well, leave the hooded man aside for now. What was across the street when you looked out the window? You must have done that much."

"Tumbledown brick row houses, Mr. Holmes. I could have been anywhere."

"It won't do, Mr. Falconer. I really think we can make progress if we only set our minds to the task at hand. What color?"

"Oh—red brick, Mr. Holmes. With grey trim."

"How many stories?"

"Three."

"You say they were not well maintained?"

"They were poor and plain, and some of the windows were broken and stopped up with newspaper. But there are many such places in London. The only truly unnatural aspect of the landscape was the blue light. It quite unnerved me."

"Where did you find yourself when you awoke?"

"At Covent Garden, sir."

"Ah, that is highly suggestive."

"How so?" I inquired.

"Mr. Falconer sings thereabouts for the odd coin. Likely the hooded man has heard him perform, and he associates the place with his victim, even if unconsciously. It seems natural to return him there. Have you encountered any strange audience members of late?"

"No one stands out to me."

"I am not surprised, but it was worth asking. You can tell me nothing more, I take it?"

Heaving an overwrought sigh, our client shook his head.

"I will take your case pro bono, Mr. Falconer." Holmes set aside his pipe and drummed his fingertips together. "It is remarkable, and therefore of its own intrinsic value to me. I must set one condition, however."

"Anything, Mr. Holmes!" he cried. "I should take heart, truly, if only I knew you believed me."

"I believe you, but owing to the lack of hard data, I cannot promise immediate results. You must swear that in the interim, you will do nothing tragic with this pistol. I should be very put out indeed if you ruined my investigation by wrecking your health in a permanent fashion."

Our guest's already red face colored still more deeply. "Nothing of the sort will happen, Mr. Holmes, I vow it will not. I already owe you my life, seemingly. It would be the worst sort of disrespect to discard it now."

"Then good night, Mr. Falconer, and I shall do all I can. I take it a note sent to The Fox's Tooth would find you if I had need?"

"Yes, Mr. Holmes." He took the gun my friend held out and hastily slipped it into his jacket pocket, going for his still-damp coat.

"Have you enough funds left over to find shelter tonight?" I could not help asking.

"Think nothing of my circumstances, sirs, or at least not those which I've brought on myself," he objected with a hollow expression that could not fail to painfully remind me of my late brother's. "Far more deserving men—aye, and women and children too—are out in the cold this evening. There's a cranny behind a statue in Newcastle Street not many know of that's mostly dry, and I'll make my way there. Good night, and thank you again for your extreme generosity. I pray you can find some answers for me."

When Mr. Falconer had gone, I rose and banked the fire, skirting the puddle left by his coat and attempting not to dwell upon the sibling I had lost untimely to his cups. "A highly disturbing account."

"And an absolutely unique one. I've been searching my memory for a parallel case to no avail. What do you make of it?" Holmes asked, tamping out his pipe.

"It is certainly nightmarish, and there may be nothing more to make of it than that—a nightmare. But I should abhor the feeling that I was in mortal danger and my story was not believed by anyone. We seem to owe it to him to investigate."

After a pause, Holmes swept his attention over me from top to toe. "You appear troubled, my dear Watson."

"It has been a troubling evening."

"Not generally troubled, specifically so."

Replacing the poker, I admitted, "My own history makes the matter more personal than it should be, perhaps."

"Of course," he acknowledged, his severe brows thawing. "But we encounter such examples of self-ruination all too often without your taking them to heart so."

"You may consider this a whimsical quirk of the softer emotions, then."

"Watson, for heaven's sake," he protested, concerned. "Out with it, man."

"If you insist, very well. Mr. Falconer is one of the last men on earth whom I should entrust with a gun."

"What else could I have done?" he appealed, worrying at his high forehead in energetic circles. "Stolen it from him? When his life seems in danger?"

"Of course not."

"My dear fellow, I thought you frowned upon my criminal tendencies."

"You misunderstand me."

"You imply I ought to have acted differently!"

"I am not suggesting that there was a better solution, Holmes. I am suggesting there was none."

"Oh, what's the use, I can't think like this, not when my head feels full of needles." My friend glided to his feet with a despairing huff. "Good night, Watson. If any other invaders with guns should happen to storm our gates, I beg that you will do me the favor of dispatching them without the necessity of consulting me."

Holmes slammed his bedroom door considerably harder than any man with a headache ought to have done, and I retired upstairs. When I had readied myself for sleep, listening to the wind shriek like a banshee and the slush spatter against the window, I wondered whether Mr. Horatio Falconer was fit to remember his promise when staring out from the bottom of a gin bottle. More despondently, I wondered whether it was the case that, even supposing he spared his own life so far as weaponry was concerned, he might destroy himself all too quickly simply by means of patronizing The Fox's Tooth, rendering my friend's assistance equally pointless.

The morning dawned clear and cold and I woke early, plagued by dreams of a gun pressed hard against Holmes's stark skull. As I washed and shaved, I thought again of Mr. Falconer and, in the broad light of day, could not give his tale nearly so much credence as I had granted it when sitting rapt before a midnight fireplace whilst the tempest without erased the rational world. By having been made his confidants, I could not help feeling, we might also have been made his dupes, even supposing his intentions blameless. A man of such unbridled passion, who admitted to extreme mental decay and who had invaded our home in such a shocking manner, could not be trusted, no matter Holmes's love of the inexplicable and bizarre. I made up my mind to tell him so.

When I reached the sitting room, however, I found a note indicating that Holmes had already departed but would return before luncheon. This was surprising, given the trials of the previous night, but Holmes better than any other man I knew was capable of thumbing his nose at fatigue. I was at my desk writing in my journal when my fellow lodger breezed in at a quarter to eleven whistling an air from *The Marriage of Figaro.*

"Heavens, Holmes, you can't have slept more than a few hours. I'm surprised to see you in such good spirits," I remarked as he shed his outer garments.

"Watson, how terribly uncharitable."

I laughed. "How is your head?"

"In perfect working order. And how are you faring?"

"I've been puzzling over the Falconer business."

"As have I, I assure you. I just took definitive steps."

"What if he is right to doubt himself so severely?" I argued, pressing my pen against my lip. "The room could be a fantasy associated with his childhood, the product of an imagination which has in some ways reverted to an infantile state."

Holmes smoothed a palm over his black hair as he approached me, returning it to its usual neat sheen. "You've been reading *Die Traumdeutung* again."

"Well, Dr. Freud makes some intriguing arguments."

"Watson, Watson, after all this time, I had hoped you might do a bit better," Holmes remarked, but his tone was jocular. "All right, let us suppose that everything we have heard was due to paranoid hallucinations brought on by hard living. Where does this leave us as far as the facts are concerned? Mr. Falconer dreams he has multiple times been assaulted, abducted, and freed by a hooded man. What do we make of the point that on every *single* occasion, he awakened with the sensation of having been drugged and not drunk? The gentleman has been drinking for a lengthy period, I think you'll agree—he ought to have a grasp on the sensation by this time. I am more inclined to believe the chloroform rag is real."

"Perhaps," I conceded doubtfully.

"You suggest his mind has deteriorated, which is a fair argument, but let me counter it with this one: if our client experienced fantastical nightmares in which ghouls of every variety set upon him and there was no pattern to the horror, I should agree with your suspicion of delirium tremens, and we should not be assisting him. If conversely he suffered from trauma which somehow created a tragic idée fixe regarding this room, and were it always identical, this morning I should have had my feet up before a roaring fire. But what do you make of the visions as he has actually told them to us?"

"They seem unlikely in the extreme."

"But not impossible! Mark that, Watson. None of it is impossible. Now, he claims to have been taken three times. The place to which he is spirited is very specific as he paints it: it is well furnished with a comfortable bed, a walnut desk, and dark green curtains. It is always night when he arrives, and the light is tinged with blue. He is locked within, and his cries are met with no reaction save when the hooded man arrives with the chloroform rag—and I think it apparent this same hooded man absconds with him in the first place. He always hears a woman pleading and weeping. Each time, she has grown more agitated, and the man's answering voice more insistent."

"All of this could be mere delusion. Why blue light of all things?"

"Does nothing suggest itself to you?"

"Apparently not."

"Well, well, never mind, then. It is perfectly clear to me, however. In fact, I made it the starting point of my investigation, though my search has not yielded results as of yet."

When he did not explain further, I understood that, as was most often the case, he had no intention of doing so. "You sound so definite. How are you sure of Mr. Falconer's story?"

"Because when he awakens, he is in Covent Garden."

"What bearing can that have?"

"If he were dreaming, would he not regain consciousness in Hyde Park, where he in his fashion resides?"

Pausing, I considered. "I hadn't thought of that."

"Granted, thinking is not your vocation, but you might have given it a touch more effort."

I knew better than to rise to such desiccated bait. "All you are saying may be true, but it remains unlikely that we'll ever get to the bottom of it unless we can comprehend what they want him for in the first place. Radical medical research? Some deranged idea of sport? Nothing can be answered before we understand *why*."

Laughing, Holmes clapped me on the shoulder. "A more dignified and logical response could be expected of no man save you to the best of my knowledge, Watson, though I admit I haven't met *everyone*. However, your perspective evinces a degree of pessimism I fail to share. We are not entirely helpless."

"Really?" I brightened. "What can we do? You said the clue of the blue light has come to nothing thus far."

"No, but it will come to something. And we can dog his steps. I've set an Irregular on the task with strictest orders to interfere in no way should he feel the smallest bit uneasy. I've dark misgivings regarding this case."

"Because it seems to be based upon the ravings of a lunatic?"

"No," he corrected me, slipping his hands into his pockets. "Because hooded men are dangerous when unmasked, and I aim to unmask one."

I saw little of my friend during the next few days, but often watched as a bushy-bearded worker with the thick leather gloves of an iron-smith vanished from our lodgings only to appear again after nightfall and emerge from Holmes's bedroom wearing his dressing gown and a guarded expression. Thus I heard nothing more of Mr. Falconer's case until one night when Holmes and I sat in a corner of a shabby café in Bethnal Green Road, sipping coffee following a simple repast. As to what on earth we were doing so far from Westminster I had no notion, for Holmes after sending me a telegram advising me of the appointment had done nothing save comment upon the occupation of Peking and praise the establishment's admittedly passable shepherd's pie. Since over the many years of our acquaintance I have taken diminishing pleasure in asking questions that will go unanswered, I expressed only mild surprise at our environs, and waited for Holmes to perform his conjuring trick.

"Do you find the night too bitter for a brief walk?" my friend asked, an impish smile playing at the edges of his mouth.

"No indeed. Doubtless it will lead us to whatever you mean to show me."

Holmes made a rueful noise as he settled the bill. "If you grow any more apt at observation and inference, I shall have no stock of surprises left. Come, we've only a few blocks to travel, and I admit I think this may interest you."

The night was frigid indeed, with creeping tendrils of fog crawling through the alleys and sinister ice crystals painted in the cracked windowpanes. I ducked deeply into my collar and Holmes did likewise, with only the high arc of his nose betraying his identity. Though Bethnal Green Road was exceedingly populous—indeed, notoriously so—as it was drawing close to ten o'clock, we were the only pedestrians save for hard-seeming men with bitter, cast-down eyes. We had been walking for only about two minutes when we reached Ainsley Street, and as we turned onto this narrower thoroughfare, I came to a halt with a low groan.

"Oh, what an idiot you must think me!" I lamented.

"Not at all. I reached the conclusion that Mr. Falconer's story seemed to you so outlandish and yet so distressingly familiar that a further stretch of the imagination was beyond your scope," he returned easily.

We faced a simple red brick house trimmed in peeling white, matching those on the other side of the impoverished street, exactly as Mr. Falconer had described them—but interrupting the moldering residences was a police station, its familiar beacon of blue light shining upon the filthy pavement and the mottled trunks of the plane trees.

"This is J Division," Holmes remarked. "Bethnal Green and environs, added by the Yard in eighteen eighty-six owing to the alarmingly rapid expansion of the city. I would have introduced you to it earlier, but I wanted to identify the exact house. It is this one, number forty-six Ainsley Street."

"How do you know?"

"Doubtless you have wondered where I've been for the past few days. As soon as I identified which police station's light Mr. Falconer observed, I made it my business to loiter here incognito. As Bethnal Green is an infamous slum, it wouldn't have done for me to lurk in respectable tweeds, you understand. The house immediately to the left of the station possesses an exceedingly tall resident, with a physician's sign in the front window. His name is Dr. Elijah Ashman."

"The hooded man?" I exclaimed.

"Such is my working hypothesis."

"But who would practice medicine in such a place?"

Holmes's eyes gleamed beneath the brim of his hat. "Who would practice medicine in a house no one calls upon, to boot?"

We stood across from the house in question, conversing—but we fell instantly silent when its door opened and a woman appeared, quietly but respectably dressed, the cobalt illumination lending her appearance an otherworldly quality. Holmes gripped my arm.

"Hullo!" he exclaimed. "And here we could well have the distraught female in question."

The strange woman's face was indeed pinched with worry. She walked at a brisk pace toward the main road and Holmes followed at a short distance, I at his side. When she reached the wider thoroughfare and seemed to cast about for a cab, Holmes slid up next to her and said, "Madam, I wonder whether I might have a word with you?"

"Oh!" she exclaimed, whirling.

She was small and thin, with dark hair and a petite upturned nose, wearing a good-quality grey cloak lined with red. I should have thought her pretty in an unremarkable fashion save for her blinking brown eyes, which were somewhat vacant and altogether haunted.

"Do I know you?" Her voice was tremulous. "This is not a part of London where I feel easy in my mind speaking to strangers."

"Nor indeed should you, but you are quite safe with us. I am Sherlock Holmes, and this is my friend Dr. Watson. We were, in fact, desirous to know whether we could assist you in any fashion. You appeared distressed when you exited that house, if you'll pardon my saying so."

"I see," she said in relief. "Well, that is all right then. I am Mrs. Sarah Pattison, but my husband has been deceased these five years—one of his ships was lost at sea—and he never did like my answering strange men, as he always called me too trusting by half. But I can tell that you are gentlemen and mean me no harm."

I glanced at Holmes during this rambling confession, but he did not appear the smallest bit impatient.

"You honor us, Mrs. Pattison," he said smoothly. "Ah! Here is a cab. Might we share it with you en route to more salutary environs, and might you tell us what a woman of your obvious good character is doing visiting a physician in Bethnal Green of all places? In your husband's absence, it would ease my mind to know you arrived home safely."

"An escort would be most welcome." She fretted at one of her gloves, glancing from side to side. "It's dreadful hereabouts, just *dreadful*. I'd not be here at all if my brother James were not friends with Dr. Ashman, who lives in poverty only because he practices such an obscure branch of medicine. He is a psychologist. He is trying to bring James back from the brink and—I'm sorry," she murmured as she dissolved in tears. "My brother has fallen into a life of terrible dissolution and hardly knows himself. It's too terrible to contemplate."

Holmes handed her up into the waiting cab. "You must tell us about it, and we shall see you safe home."

Mystified both at Mrs. Pattison's words and at her absent, almost childlike way of enunciating them, I followed Holmes into the four-wheeler. Mrs. Pattison gave her address as Cockspur Street near to Trafalgar Square, and we pulled away from the grim suburb, Holmes polite but intent and I determined to say nothing lest his powers of persuasion be interrupted and her steady flow of chatter stopped. The gas lamps we passed flickered wanly against our faces through the shaded windows, illuminating us in unnerving glimpses.

"James was always wild, but I never thought he should come to this pass," Mrs. Pattison lamented, drawing back her hood. "He fell in with a bad lot, Mr. Holmes, and entirely lost his self-respect—he has nearly ruined himself, and if Dr. Ashman cannot help him, I shall despair. Since my husband died, James was all I had in the world, and indeed he lived off an allowance I gave him inherited from the shipping concern. Now I write out the checks to Dr. Ashman instead, to settle my brother's debts, for it really wouldn't be appropriate for me to meet with such low types and James would only spend it all on drink. Oh, to think that he doesn't recognize his own sister any longer! It's heartbreaking. I shan't be able to bear it if he dies alone, in the cold, not knowing himself. He fancies himself an opera singer, Mr. Holmes. Can you imagine? His voice has always been stirring, but he is a clerk at a maritime warehouse."

My pulse sped significantly as she spoke. As for my friend, he appeared outwardly composed, but his entire posture vibrated with leashed energy.

"And you visit your brother periodically, at Dr. Ashman's practice?" he asked.

"Oh, yes. When James is there, the doctor sends me word. My poor brother is delusional—raving, sleeping out of doors—and it's quickly growing worse. I can't help feeling that if I saw him face-to-face, he might know me again, but Dr. Ashman insists that he has grown most violent, and in his medical capacity, he cannot allow me to actually enter the sickroom. When I hear James's voice, that beautiful voice that once brought me such comfort—oh, I can't describe how agonizing it is to hear him scream to be let out when all Dr. Ashman wants is to conduct sessions with him, to compel him to see reason. Perhaps try hypnosis or some other therapy. Anything which might do some good. But by the time James has sweated out the liquor, he is most desperate for more of it, and never has any difficulty escaping after Dr. Ashman has opened the door."

"An appalling situation, to be sure."

She nodded. "We are considering transferring him to a private asylum, which is the reason I was there tonight—I have met with my lawyer, and money will be no object as regards his care."

Nothing I had ever read of Dr. Freud's could have prepared me for Mrs. Pattison's statement, and my alarm must have shown on my countenance, for Holmes briefly pressed a warning hand to my knee.

"When came your brother to such a desperate pass that you could not be allowed in the room with him?"

"A little over a month ago."

"Did you observe him in Dr. Ashman's company previously?"

"Yes, many times—the two were very close, and though I had never before been to his practice, they had called on me at my home. At one point, he and James lodged together, so he was in the perfect position to note when my brother truly began to take leave of his senses, though as I said he has always been difficult to manage."

"And about a month ago is also when you began giving his allowance to his companion?"

"Yes. Oh, Mr. Holmes, it was such a difficult decision—but really, there was nothing I could do, for the first time I heard him shrieking to be released, I knew he could no longer be trusted with it himself."

"Did Dr. Ashman suggest this arrangement to you?"

"I can't recall. He may have done. It is good to speak to someone about this, for I have been nearly at the end of my wits. I am so glad you gentlemen were standing there, and offered to see me home."

She began to cry helplessly. Holmes leaned over and patted her gloved hand, and I could not help comparing her with her brother— his overabundance of emotions, his lack of control over them. When we had nearly arrived at Trafalgar Square, she had quieted, and Holmes's face was suffused with grave intensity.

"Mrs. Pattison, before your brother is committed, you must be given the chance to attempt to bring him back to some awareness of himself. Your instincts do you credit—perhaps when you set eyes on him, your familial bonds will work a form of magic that no one other than a sister could manage."

"Do you really think it possible?" she breathed.

"I do indeed. You must promise me you will insist to Dr. Ashman tomorrow that unless you can be convinced James truly would do you harm, you will not consent to pay for the asylum. If James is then intractable or sounds volatile, then of course you need not enter his chamber, but you owe it to your sibling to suggest the notion. I and Dr. Watson shall accompany you, so that you may feel quite safe."

"Oh, bless you, sir." Mrs. Pattison folded her kerchief after dabbing a final time at her cheeks. "You are right, I believe, and it is always best to consult the opinions of impartial parties. Yes, I shall do as you say, supposing you promise to meet me in Bethnal Green. It will be late, I fear—Dr. Ashman can never manage to lay hands on my brother until around midnight."

"Never mind the lateness," Holmes demurred, his voice a low purr that set my nerves sparking. "It is vital that you are firm and insistent, and that you make mention of the funds for your brother's care being absolutely at stake. You may trust that we will meet you outside the house in Ainsley Street without fail."

Promising us that she would do as Holmes asked, Mrs. Pattison stepped down from the carriage. Holmes's profile remained fixed on her until she had shut the door to her residence, and then he banged his fist against the wall of the hansom in what appeared to be triumph, crying out, "Baker Street, driver!"

"Holmes, what in God's name is the meaning of all this?" I marveled. "Has the man we know as Horatio Falconer lost his mind entirely?"

"I think we will find there is more to it than that, Watson," Holmes drawled, rubbing his hands together like a man who is about to commence a card trick. "I shall not be sorry to arrive home—the temperature has dropped a full seven degrees, I think, since we left the house, and it was low enough in the first place."

"You fear foul play," I insisted.

"Perhaps my nature is needlessly suspicious."

"I have at times known it to be so, but you are generally justified in your misgivings."

"You flatter me extremely, my dear fellow. Regretfully, I can confirm nothing until we reconvene with Mrs. Pattison, though tonight

I must write to Mr. Falconer—my Irregular confirms that he can be found daily at The Fox's Tooth, and a wire will surely reach him there."

"Do you mean to tell him we have seen his sister, Mrs. Pattison?"

"I mean to tell him by no means to use his gun no matter what may befall him tomorrow night," Holmes replied, smiling wolfishly. "Your own revolver ought to be quite enough firepower for our purposes, Doctor."

Tense as I am accustomed to being whilst awaiting the climax of some of Holmes's darker cases, on that occasion my anxiety was palpable. The dismal weather, the loaded gun in my pocket as we left Westminster, Mrs. Pattison's grief, and the so-called Mr. Falconer's pitiable confusion—all combined to unsettle me as we bounced and jostled our way back to Bethnal Green on the following night at around eleven o'clock. Holmes, for his part, seemed as imperturbable as a marble bust; but every so often, his excitement would betray him and he would cut glances at the shadowed streets, tapping his knuckles against his thigh in anticipation.

When we descended from the hack at Ainsley Street, I saw that we were not alone, for all that Mrs. Pattison had not yet arrived—our old friend Inspector Bradstreet stood in the road wearing an impassive stare, his bowler pulled low and his arms crossed against the daggerlike wind.

"Mr. Holmes, Dr. Watson." He nodded cordially. "Care to share with me what we're doing out in the cold tonight?"

"With any luck, arresting a truly audacious criminal mastermind," Holmes returned cheerily. "We have only to await his target to prevent an appalling instance of fraud—the second I've prevented in as many weeks, by the way. I ought to consider specializing. Ah, here is the lady herself."

Mrs. Sarah Pattison approached us with eagerness, her trusting expression turning to bewilderment at the sight of the plainclothesman. "Oh, goodness. I came to meet two allies, and find I have three."

"Mrs. Pattison, this is Inspector Bradstreet, who is here to ensure that the myriad evils of Bethnal Green do not get the better of us,"

Holmes returned. "We are in a dangerous neighborhood, as you've astutely noted yourself."

"An inspector! How decent of you—many thanks for your protection, sir."

"Well, now that we are all acquainted, shall we see what we can do about persuading your brother to mend his ways?" Holmes plunged into the street and we followed, I with my hand on the comforting weight of the gun in my pocket. "What is his full name, Mrs. Pattison?"

"Did I never tell you? Abergavenny," she answered. "I was Sarah Abergavenny, and he is Mr. James Abergavenny."

"Thank you, and might I suggest that you keep well back if anything untoward takes place?"

"Yes, Mr. Holmes, I shall be most careful."

Nodding, the detective rapped decisively on the door. Upon the instant it opened, we could hear a muffled wailing from upstairs which had been undetectable from the street. A tall, hatchet-faced man stood in the foyer, glaring out. His domed head was hairless, his eyes were dark and widely set, and his general appearance was suave and friendly enough save for a coldly appraising twist to his set of full, almost sensuous lips.

"Whatever have we here? Mrs. Pattison, as you can hear, now is no time to make personal appeals to your brother, though I quite understand and sympathize with your sentimental desire to set eyes on him. But what a crowd you've brought with you! Gentlemen, it should be apparent that I've a very sick patient upstairs, and one who cannot be cajoled or bargained with—this is no time for social calls, and I'll thank you to leave Mr. Abergavenny to my care."

"My name is Sherlock Holmes, and I am determined that Mr. Abergavenny's sister see him," Holmes declared, his foot firmly in the doorway. "I refuse to depart before my wishes in this matter are carried out—Mrs. Pattison *will* be allowed entrance, and I in her company as witness."

"You can do no such thing!" Dr Ashman snapped, bristling. "It would be perilous to all parties, quite impossible."

"I think you'll find he can," our friend of the Yard objected, show-ing his badge and a document. "I am Inspector Bradstreet, and I've a warrant to search the premises."

"How dare you, sir! On what grounds?"

"'Suspected kidnap' will do for the moment," Holmes replied, edging forcefully past the doctor, "although I shouldn't be surprised over additions to the list, so we shall keep an open mind. Hand over the key to the spare bedroom, if you please."

"You'll harm my patient, and my personal friend, if you upset him further," Dr. Ashman growled, though now his lofty cranium shone with nervous moisture. "I'll do no such thing!"

"Pity. But it won't delay us long." Holmes held up his set of adapt-able keys, jangling them, as Bradstreet and I elbowed our way inside with the lady well shielded. "Keep an eye on this one, Inspector, and don't let him budge. Watson, Mrs. Pattison, quickly!"

We rushed upstairs, then watched as Holmes crouched before the door. The whimpers and cries were much more audible here, and I easily recognized the voice of our client, though he sounded barely intelligible. Fright and despair had so overwhelmed him that he might have been a great hulking wolf, howling in the wilderness against the agony of a steel trap.

"Oh, my poor James," Mrs. Pattison fretted, tears springing once again into her eyes. "How I shall hate to see what he has come to."

"Yes, the sight of him may indeed surprise you. Just coming, Mr. Falconer, calm yourself!" my friend called, and the cacophony abruptly ceased.

When Holmes threw wide the door, the man I knew as Mr. Fal-coner staggered through it with a groan, holding both his dirtied hands to his coarsely matted head. Mrs. Pattison shrieked, shrinking back against the wall with her gloved hand over her heart.

"Oh! Oh! This is not my brother!" she cried.

"No, I rather thought not," Holmes said with evident satisfaction. "Steady on, then! Watson, will you do what you can for him? Though I rather think the best remedy will prove sleeping it off. Mrs. Pattison, your brother has been missing for over a month now, but his continued existence enabled this Dr. Ashman—supposing that is even his name, for the plaque in the window is quite new—to continue leaching away your savings, as no doubt he had previously done sponging funds off your brother when in his cups. I shall discover what truly happened to your sibling, on my honor. Just now, however, I need a word with Inspector Bradstreet. And the use of his set of handcuffs."

"There never really was any difficulty in the matter," Holmes said to me after I had revived poor Mr. Horatio Falconer somewhat and we had sent him, shaken but grateful, away from Bethnal Green in a cab (after eliciting the solemn vow that he would do his best to improve his state before being called upon to give testimony at the trial). "You were right to say that motive was everything, and I very much fear that Mr. Abergavenny will prove to have been long dead before this bizarre tale is ended."

"I cannot imagine how you worked it out," I confessed, whistling for a cab. Mrs. Pattison had gone with Bradstreet and his prisoner to give a statement—indeed, had not stopped hectically talking in circles ever since Holmes had revealed the substitution.

"You forget that I am the one who deduced that Mr. Falconer was an opera singer—he never told it to me, and I comprehended that his training was genuine." Holmes sprang easily into the cab and I joined him after giving directions. "I knew our client to be telling the truth when he came to us. Why should he have been taken only to be left in a room, then? His voice was remarkable, but his appearance was carefully hidden by his abductor. Mrs. Pattison's account was quite genuine, I believe. James Abergavenny truly had fallen upon hard times, his disgraceful habits doubtless greatly encouraged by his supposed 'friend' Ashman. Of course, I cannot yet tell you what became of this missing brother. But I can tell you that Dr. Ashman is a charlatan and a villain who probably could scarce believe his good fortune when he discovered a busker in Covent Garden who sounded just like Abergavenny—I told you it was significant that he was left there when set free."

"Yes, your reasoning is quite clear now."

"In the absence of Abergavenny, the money would vanish unless Ashman could keep up the illusion his friend had run mad. Mrs. Pattison is, you will agree, shockingly credulous, but Ashman took care that she should be exposed to the false brother only once a fortnight, and from behind a closed door. He likely didn't even allow her upstairs, further masking the true sound of Falconer's voice. I further surmise that he packed his drugged victim into well-paid cabs to transport him to Bethnal Green, with the excuse he had met with a beggar who needed medical care, or a fallen friend he was returning home, but we may never know that for certain unless Ashman confesses."

"It was masterfully done, Holmes—finding the house, working out the nature of the ruse, all of it," I averred warmly. "But those aspects are not even the most wonderful thing you have accomplished during the case."

"Whatever can you refer to?"

"Saving Mr. Falconer's life twice."

"Once," he corrected, a single brow swooping quizzically.

"Twice. Once at our flat, and once just now—he has promised to appear in court sober and sound-minded. Perhaps it is mindless optimism, but for some reason, I believe him. He will be a changed man, entirely thanks to you."

Holmes made a scoffing sound, though his cheekbones colored. "My dear Watson, you are the most incurably romantic chap I have ever encountered, and I do not mean that in a complimentary light."

Romantic I may well be, but on this occasion I was also correct. Mr. Horatio Falconer appeared at the assizes clean-shaven and well dressed, and not long thereafter we were privileged to see him perform in Bellini's *I puritani*. Sadly, however, thanks to Holmes's relentless investigations, it was discovered that Elijah Ashman had murdered James Abergavenny in a drunken dispute, killing his own livelihood by sheer accident and thereby necessitating the outrageous impositions our client had suffered.

Mrs. Pattison's fortune was thus saved, but her dear brother was lost to her, an outcome which did not dispose her to be grateful to my friend. She claimed to anyone who would listen that she would prefer to think her brother mad than dead, an illogical quirk of sentiment for which Holmes claimed not to blame her in the smallest degree.

Notes upon the
Diadem Club Affair

Excerpted passages from the personal diary of
Mr. Sherlock Holmes, consulting detective,
221B Baker Street, London W1:

Saturday, April 12th, 1902.

I can conceive of no greater torment than to be subjected to both Mrs.
Hudson's recipe for pork cheese and an audience with Lord Chesley
Templeton within an eight-hour period.

Surely I can be brought no lower than this. And Watson's absence
only confirms the fact that April, heralded by feckless poets throughout many nations (and doubtless at least three continents), is a ghastly
month and ought to be treated as such, rather than as a subject of
highly unscientific verse. The bards are in this case gilding a lump
rather than a lily.

My friend has determined against all good sense that he should
attend a symposium regarding modern pulmonary treatments, and thus
will return tomorrow from my own briefly attended alma mater, smelling of local ale and country air. That the man should keep abreast of the

latest advancements out of professional interest is perfectly natural, and a yen to learn more about poisons and bullet trajectories and types of stab wounds I should likewise understand. But an entire forum devoted to lungs, and outside London to boot? It isn't as if he needs to practice medicine. His wound pension is more than adequate to cover his modest gambling habit, his necessities, and the nominal sum I pretend is half the rent here. (The idea of Watson actually paying half of the exorbitant figure I dole out to prevent Mrs. Hudson from complaining about the unending stream of ruffians tramping in and out of her domicile would be absurd.)

If I am alive to see his homecoming, matters will have progressed better than they have done so far today.

Mrs. Hudson's pork cheese recipe is not even particularly offensive, if I am honest with myself—molded minced meat with what I've deduced are savory herbs, lemon peel, and nutmeg served cold, doubtless an orthodox methodology—but I cannot be expected to eat such a thing when I consumed a perfectly respectable luncheon the day previous. Neither can I pretend to patience when a wire arrives an hour after my rejecting the slice of congealed gravy, and rather than being able to request that Watson read the message aloud that I might allow the facts to filter effortlessly into their respective slots within my brain, I must accept that the doctor is *not present*, thanks to an intensive three days spent attempting to cure the *common cough*.

The telegram read:

> *MR. HOLMES.—I beg that you will meet with me today upon the quaint bench in Regent's Park which lies at the charming fork in the pathway opposite the weeping elm, nearly parallel to your own lodgings STOP The matter is most urgent STOP You will know me by the rather droll antique Masonic lapel pin I shall wear STOP From three o'clock until four, I shall eagerly await you STOP*

Of course this was curious, but there was nothing to be deduced from it save for the obvious facts that the gentleman was unused to intrigue, decidedly not a Freemason (they do not find their own sacred emblems "droll"), and born into the stratospheric upper classes, as he thought so little of presuming upon my time without an appointment and employing adjectives in telegrams. I rather balk at being summoned in such a peremptory manner. But I had nothing better to occupy my attention save for outlining the beginnings of a monograph upon spent bullet casings, so I silently agreed, not without a certain degree of pique.

That degree was nothing compared with the ire which visited my spirits this afternoon, however.

I know every inch of Regent's Park as well as I know the rest of London—better, because Watson will insist upon my taking comradely constitutionals. So I could picture precisely the locale my would-be client had indicated. The weather was nicely temperate, and a brisk breeze whipped about my coattails. After passing a duck pond, a copse of elms, a spinster (three months in mourning for a sibling, cat fancier, works as a legal typist), and a small fountain at 3:37 p.m. (it doesn't do to give too much leeway when a supplicant is both anonymous and presumptuous), I approached the bench in question and discovered that the identity of my client was not so much intriguing as alarming.

"Oh, Mr. Holmes, for so you must be, thank heaven you've come!" the delicately built man exclaimed under his breath as I sat beside him. "Dashed if I could have taken another *instant* of suspense, what, but then you consulting types march to the tick of your own clocks, don't you?"

Crossing my legs, I lit a cigarette to cover my annoyance. Lord Chesley Templeton was ludicrously attired in coarse tweeds which had obviously been ordered from an outrageously costly Jermyn Street tailor with specific instructions to use inferior cloth. The suit fit like a second skin and must have chafed like the devil. He did indeed sport an antique Masonic lapel pin, a five-pointed gold star with colorful enamel and the arcane emblems of the society, ringed with seed pearls and capped with a small brilliant no workingman could afford. (Whether it was droll I could not say—I could state for a certainty it failed to amuse me.) His thin mouth was quirked in a saucy smile, and he had clearly arrived long before I did, because his ears were pink from the wind. He had hidden his unmistakable high-browed and highborn features beneath a low cloth cap, rose-tinted glasses, and a beard which had been affixed with an overabundance of spirit gum, the smell of which was unmistakable. I could have told him he would have a wretched time getting the thing off without the proper solvent, but refrained.

"I am Mr. Jack Smith," said he, thrusting out a lily-white hand.

"Lord Chesley Templeton," I replied, taking it. "While I am no stranger to noble clients, I confess I find duplicitous ones tedious."

The gentleman goggled at me. Emitting a high yip of a laugh like the barking of a terrier, he swept his cap off and scratched his pale blond curls in astonishment. "By Jove! And there's me discovered already! Dashed if that wasn't middling clever, Mr. Holmes—do say how you did it, eh?"

"It was not even middling clever, I fear. I may not enjoy the society pages, but as any connoisseur of newspapers must, I do read them, and your face is printed next to every fashionable soiree from New York to Paris."

He grinned. "I suppose I am somewhat celebrated, eh?"

"Call it what you will."

"What a corker!" he crowed in that affected manner some men with twenty-four-karat accents have of employing popular slang. "Mr. Holmes, I knew you'd be perfect for this little lark I have in mind. The absolute toppingest of tops. You'll indulge me in keeping the matter absolutely secret, won't you, old chap, considering?"

My hackles were already rising, and we had not even spent a full minute in one another's company. "All my clients expect the same level of discretion from me."

"And from your doctor friend too, I trust, what's his name, Weston? Wilson? By gad yes, we'll want him for this. Your chum can keep his peace too, I fancy?"

"John Watson." Further nettled, I filled my lungs with smoke. "The good doctor probably knows more state secrets than most individuals in the state department."

"Capital fellow!"

"He is."

"Oh, I've no doubt, not a doubt in the *world*. It's worth a small fortune to the pair of you if you'll do as I wish."

"My fees are fixed, and I do as *I* wish whether a client has hired me or not. I beg of you to tell me why I am on this bench."

Lord Templeton's eyes, as blue and as empty as the April sky above, gleamed at me. "That's the ticket—straight to business, I like that in a man. It indicates a strong spine, and we don't want any of the flabby variety for this venture. Why, only yesterday I was saying to Sir Harry Eastmore, Harry, I says, when once you find a chap with some backbone, clasp him to your bosom, and never let go."

I made no reply to this. It seemed the best course.

"You probably wonder why I am incognito?"

"No, not especially."

"Come, sir, come! How could you not, a man of action like yourself, what? It would be deucedly unnatural if you didn't. Positively perverse. Well, Mr. Holmes, I am here to invite you to a secret meeting of the Diadem Club."

My jaw tightened, I hope imperceptibly. "And what is the Diadem Club?"

Absurdly pleased at the question, Lord Templeton clapped his hands in a manner my youngest Irregular would have found juvenile. "The Diadem Club is simply the *most* exclusive meeting of great minds this marvelous city boasts, Mr. Holmes, curse me if I exaggerate. *Strike* me down if I do, sir."

"Great minds," I reflected, not without a hint of tragedy in my tone. "And you are a member, you say?"

"Fair play, Mr. Holmes, fair play!" the terrible creature chortled. "You've the right end of the stick. I knew you'd catch on devilish fast. *Half* of the Diadem Club are members of the peerage—ministers and barons and how-d'ye-call-its, not the *absolute* cream when it comes to innate talents but frightfully rich you know, and dreadfully influential, which is why we must keep our meetings buttoned up to the neck, if you follow me. *Deathly* secret. Had things gone as I planned, you'd have learnt my true identity only when you attended our next meeting, but it's dashed difficult to pull the wool over Sherlock Holmes's eyes, eh? You'll make a ripping addition! The jewels in our diadem are our honored invitees, all the clever and famous folk we bring into our fold—hence the Diadem Club."

"You want me," I said slowly, "to attend a society meeting specifically because I am an internationally renowned criminologist?"

"Got it in one! Come, come, don't bother to thank me for thinking of you. The only Londoner more famous than Sherlock Holmes is Jack the Ripper, what?"

He tittered. I am not by nature a man disposed to violence, but capability is another thing to inclination. Watson takes prudent pains not to emphasize this fact lest the many malefactors who have cause to harm us grow emboldened, and I thank him for it, for I should generally rather outwit a man than be forced to knock him down.

And yet, I mused upon the park bench, idly flexing my fingers.

"Yes," the fop continued eagerly, "while half the Diadem Club are composed of bluebloods, the other half are our prized guests—better than collecting thoroughbreds or hounds or any of the usual creatures, eh? We meet under cover of darkness for fear of assassins, but don't think that stops us having a cracking good time. The founding members went in upon a private boat six years ago—perfectly innocent-looking little wreck, just sitting there, bobbing upon the waves as boats do and so forth . . . but inside! Curse me if the *Claire Wyndham* doesn't match the toniest club on earth, as they'd put the matter on Fifth Avenue. May lightning *strike* me!"

The thought of lightning striking Lord Templeton was not an unwelcome one.

"Russian china, Chinese silk, Austrian crystal, and a French chef, by gad," he prattled on. "I'm their newest member and so must make an impression, you see. These other bucks are always flaunting their latest painter or scientist or inventor, but if I bring them Sherlock Holmes and Dr. Watkins on a silver platter? Well, that would be a *proper* coup d'état, by Jove. The meeting is at midnight tomorrow. I only just hatched the notion of bringing you two hours ago and jotted off the wire posthaste. You'll say yes, of course?"

As I—seemingly ever more swiftly—approach my fiftieth year, I've had occasion to reflect that my manners are unlikely to undergo significant improvements at this late date. The horrid dandy was thrusting a sealed card under my nose. This I slid into my coat pocket while I pushed smoothly to my feet.

"Good day to you, Lord Templeton," I said as I strode back to Baker Street, swinging my cane as I went.

Saturday, April 12th, 1902 (continued).

I will have such revenges on Lord Templeton. I will do *such things*. What they are, yet I know not, but they shall be the terrors of the earth.

King Lear never much appealed to me, my own upbringing considered, but on occasion its language is enormously satisfying.

After leaving the ineptly disguised idiot in the park, I puttered about, smoked my pipe, sent dinner back fully a quarter consumed, and settled into my oldest dressing gown to review my preliminary notes regarding marks left on discharged shells. The sun sank low and the wind picked up. I shut all the windows and steeped myself in hearty shag fumes until my eyelids were abuzz and my mind was clear regarding the structure of my latest article. Greatly comforted at having passed the planning phase, I poured myself a brandy and read a recent treatise by the rising Inspector Jean-Pierre Beauchemin of the Sûreté upon similar lines. It was topical, and elegantly written, but hardly very informative. Further cheered, I refilled my glass. Mrs. Hudson knocked.

"There's been a boy, Mr. Holmes," she said with that air of long-suffering which indicates I have not been sufficiently fattening myself.

Raising an eyebrow, I murmured, "Young Rowan isn't due to deliver the Irregulars' weekly report until Monday."

"No, he was not one of your lads, but he left you this note. Reply unnecessary, he said."

"Ah. Thank you."

"Mr. Holmes, is there anything particular you'd like for breakfast?"

"My dear Mrs. Hudson, I should particularly like not to ruminate over the question at all." Recalling the date, I reconsidered. "On second thought, Watson returns tomorrow—just turn breakfast into an early lunch around eleven thirty and send up those tea sandwiches he likes."

"Oh, that'll be just the thing," she agreed, pleased. I seemed to have passed an obscure test of some kind. "Good night, then."

"Good night."

I stretched my slippers toward the fire I had just started and opened the envelope after a cursory examination born of habit. The address and brief letter were in an intimately familiar hand:

> *Sherlock,*
>
> *Do me the favor of falling in with your latest client's plans. Matters of some delicacy which recently arose at Whitehall require his indulgence. I have RSVP'ed on your behalf already. And do convey my regards to Sir Alderford Blythe when at the Diadem Club, whose work with me you are already familiar with.*
>
> *As ever,*
> *Mycroft*

Incredible. The British government in the form of my elder brother has just charged me with the task of playing prizewinning poodle to an anemic sap who makes the lowest commoner seem a towering force of mental energy.

But how, in light of king, country, and kin, can I possibly refuse?

There is one sole comfort in this debacle— since Watson is returning, the timing proves felicitous, as I hadn't any fresh case with which to occupy his thirst for action. These sudden medical urges must be nipped in the bud periodically and in the swiftest manner to hand. Thus shall I present this task to the doctor as a matter of interest and possibly even danger.

Something about the case—for a case I must now call it—truly does nag at me. Revenge apparently must be foregone and given place to starched collars and silk waistcoats.

Sunday, April 13th, 1902.

John Watson is a man greatly susceptible to expert staging. Granted, I have been known to plant important papers in curry dishes and leave duplicitous paint upon racehorses, and greatly enjoyed myself. A touch of the dramatic never fails to lend zest to any investigation. And yet . . . from time to time I find myself questioning how often I would perform such parlor tricks were my friend not so nakedly pleased by them. The answer eludes me.

Watson trudged up the stairs with restrained vigor near to lunchtime, as befits a hearty man of his age still in good training. He found me occupying the bearskin rug at my full and not inconsiderable length, with a few pillows arranged to make all comfortable, in shirtsleeves and a dressing gown, sampling my black clay pipe contemplatively.

This piece of theatre conveyed the impression that I was (1) possessed of an intriguing conundrum; (2) not excessively attuned to his return, at least not enough to worry him; and (3) exercising that not inconsiderable wit which he so admires and which prevents the necessity of his practicing medicine at present. Flicking my eyes over him from muddied shoe soles (which meant he had departed the campus on foot and not by trap) to sooty hat (which meant his train was not an express), I smiled briefly. The doctor looked well—revived by travel but happy to return. An answering smile tugged at his neat moustache and he set down his bag, clapping his hands to his knees as he perched on the settee next to my head.

"Something is afoot, or I'm no judge," he announced warmly.

It had worked, which meant it was best to delay further gratification. Shrugging, I slit my eyes at the ceiling. "There may be something in it, and then again it may be a shocking waste of my time. But you must be fatigued after a walk to the station and the myriad agonies of the local line. The tea and sandwiches are fresh—Mrs. Hudson left them ten minutes ago."

Watson shook his head with a rueful grin and went to hang his hat and coat upon the rack. "I would ask how you knew my mode of travel, but odds are near certain you'll reply with some detail involving dirt or dust."

"Then how do I know that they're tearing up the tennis courts and you were disappointed you couldn't borrow a racket and make use of them?"

This time he raised his expressive eyebrows. "I haven't the faintest."

"Have you cured phthisis worldwide yet?" I asked more nastily than I had meant to.

"Your medical knowledge is marvelously eccentric, old man. No, afflictions of the lungs plague us still. How did you know about their improving the tennis courts?"

As it happened, I knew from a combination of the quarterly university alumni newsletter and the fact he had packed his tennis shoes, but this elementary deduction did not merit public airing. En route to the dining table, Watson awaited a reply. When none was forthcoming, he adopted that strained look he cannot conceal when trying to ascertain whether I have been making too free with my constitution in his absence.

As this was not a tolerable expression, I raised myself onto one elbow with a mischievous twinkle. Watson, who is as receptive to arresting movements as he is to planned panoramas, relaxed visibly.

"I fear I must presume upon your time this evening, Watson. Will you allow it?"

"With great pleasure."

"Is your evening dress suitable for an outing at present?"

"We went to the opera a fortnight ago. I could have it aired within a few hours." Watson shook a napkin out and placed it on his lap. "Whatever for?"

Explaining to Watson about my abhorrent meeting and the still more abhorrent Diadem Club took five minutes. When this was through, I hinted that Brother Mycroft knew of strange storm clouds gathering—murky shadows which threatened the peerage, Whitehall, and possibly England. By the time I had finished, Watson had eradicated three cucumber sandwiches and two cups of tea and appeared equal parts annoyed (at our client), mystified (at his request), and intrigued (thanks to the combined persuasive powers of the Holmes brothers). His strong jaw tilted in contemplation as he passed his napkin over his mouth.

"What a distasteful prospect," he commented.

"Yes, it's ghastly."

"I should prefer running down a killer in some low den of iniquity, in all seriousness."

"The feeling is mutual."

"That you should be treated like a trophy in such a manner . . . I don't know how to stomach it, frankly."

"It's your own fault, spreading me so liberally across the pages of *The Strand* like some swaggering penny dreadful hero," I accused him, following the script of an argument almost as old as our friendship. "I loathe the notion, but ought I defy the Crown?"

"Of course not, forgive me. Our duty is clear." Drumming his fingers on the tablecloth, my friend sat back, emitting a weary breath tinged with anticipation. "I'll have my tails brushed. And my revolver cleaned," he added, winking.

Whensoever I think that my colleague is a volume long since memorized, I turn another page and he surprises me. In this instance, it was the candor and patriotism with which he replied to a remark about our monarch I had made with utter flippancy. At the best of times, I can be glib, and at the worst, unforgivably callous—to be taken seriously when I had not meant the sentiment at all was highly uncomfortable. I was abashed enough to redirect my attention to the mantel clock, for occasionally the doctor's sincerity is slightly overwhelming to a man of my reticence.

After all, despite my legendary prickliness, I am flesh and blood in addition to smoke and mirrors.

"You left yourself out, my dear fellow," I mentioned carelessly a few seconds later. "I've no wish to see you paraded like a circus tiger either."

"Your brother wouldn't have written if it wasn't important."

This recalled to my mind the unease I felt about something to do with Lord Templeton's account, something I could not put my finger upon which itched at the back of my brain. Having given the case so little thought save for detesting the prospect, I wondered what it was I had missed.

"Don't wind yourself up too tightly, Watson. If this matter involves nothing save wild geese . . ." I warned him.

"Then we'll have been paid richly to eat a lavish dinner. Where's the harm in that? I'll combine my funds with yours and you can send another set of your Irregulars away to school, the way you did with the Duke of Holdernesse's reward money last year."

My mouth dropped open, I confess. "You . . . I never . . ."

"Yes, you did. Don't lie to me, it's in poor form, my dear Holmes. I saw young Jenkins in the street the other day, who heard from Poole, who had it out of Jemmy, who spilled all."

This was most vexing. "Well, I must have a stern word with Jemmy, in that case, upon the subject of privacy."

Watson had the gall to laugh in my face. "Oh, come, I knew you were scheming to do *something* with the duke's six thousand pounds. Aside from your taste in wine, and your meticulousness with your tailor, you're the most frugal bachelor in existence, and how many times have I heard you repeat that your fees are fixed—save, of course, when you remit them? Anyway, do you suppose I don't notice when Irregulars vanish, are replaced, and one day reappear in the metropolis as clerks and solicitors? If I didn't already know you fail to consider me a complete imbecile, I should be insulted."

By this time, I was blushing furiously, a symptom of strong feeling long abhorred but uncontrollable nevertheless for a man of my waxen complexion. "Of course I don't, but—"

"Honestly, Holmes, what did you imagine I would conclude?" My friend's eyes sparkled. He was enjoying himself immensely. "That you suddenly bought a landed estate in Kent? That the price of shag tobacco had increased astronomically? Get up—I poured you tea and it's rapidly expiring."

Shutting my mouth, I obeyed, which was both more pleasant and simple than arguing. Watson is no genius, but I can personally attest that he owns a remarkable capacity for managing one. And half an hour ago, I found the emerald tiepin given me by our previous gracious sovereign, which I plan to wear this evening, and spent a wistful few minutes studying it.

Watson was a courageous soldier and remains one at heart, so why should it have surprised me that Mycroft's urges combined with my machinations moved him to undertake a repellent task so gracefully? I stopped to set this small domestic interlude down almost without knowing why, but I think I have it now.

Someday, God forbid it should ever prove necessary, I would like to think myself as ready to be of service to England as John Watson is to both the nation and its sole consulting detective. I would also like to think that he knows as much.

Monday, April 14th, 1902.

This diary belongs to the biggest fool ever to draw breath upon this island. Watson would not say so, in fact praised my quick thinking, but he may as well have complimented a prize cock for making an infernal racket. That would be very like him.

When we had donned white gloves and tall hats and called down for a hansom, and while Watson was making an adjustment to his cravat in the mirror above the sideboard, I finally opened the card Lord Chesley Templeton had given me with instructions as to the whereabouts of the *Claire Wyndham*, and suffered a profound shock.

"What the devil!" I exclaimed.

"Holmes?" Watson was peering over my shoulder seconds later.

The card was of the finest stock, deeply letterpressed with excellent ink, and read:

Mr. Sherlock Holmes & Dr. John Watson:
Please be at Cleopatra's Needle at 11:45.
The Diadem Club is honored to welcome you.

"Something about this alarms you?"

"Extremely."

Lord Chesley Templeton had been wearing a ludicrous suit impeccably tailored to fit him.

We meet under cover of darkness for fear of assassins, but don't think that stops us having a cracking good time, he had said.

I only just hatched the notion of bringing you two hours ago and jotted off the wire posthaste, he had also said.

Then, following my abrupt departure, the note from my brother. I cursed under my breath.

"Oh, Watson, Watson! I nearly made a farcical blunder, and we have been saved from my own stupidity only at the last moment. What a blind beetle I have been! Your revolver is loaded, I trust?"

"It should be of little use if it weren't." The doctor's eyes were wide. "May I ask what precisely we'll be doing this evening apart from attending a grotesquely snobbish dinner party?"

"Preventing a murder," I answered with unrestrained glee.

Watson's expression as I turned on my heel and trotted down the stairs following this pronouncement was worth every second I had spent in Lord Templeton's company.

The journey was uneventful and I kept my peace throughout. Both Watson and I benefit from these interludes—they stimulate his imagination and allow me time to focus my thoughts. We paid the cabbie and alighted to the street, walking unhurriedly to the Victoria Embankment. The night was quiet save for the occasional stroller, stately rows of trees along the gaslit walkway rustled in the cool breeze, lights danced over the Thames, there was bloodshed to be thwarted, and I reflected that I might be forced to reconsider my uncharitable opinion of April.

When we reached the looming and—under the circumstances—ominous-seeming Cleopatra's Needle, we found Lord Chesley Templeton leaning against its base like the most worthless titled rake in Christendom. He had suffered no injury from the spirit gum but was instead smooth-cheeked and debonair with his tousled pale curls jostling each other beneath his top hat, as I had anticipated. I bit down upon a smile and affected an air of supercilious irritation, which I admit comes naturally to me.

"By Jove, but here's the famous pair!" Lord Templeton cried. "Curse me if I'm not the prince of the Diadem Club after tonight. *Strike* me down if I am mistaken! Mr. Holmes, a pleasure to see you again. Dr. Watford, delighted to make your acquaintance."

Watson raised his eyebrows but, consummate gentleman that he is, he made no other sign as we all shook hands. I could not blame the doctor for his skeptical expression: the aristocrat wore a waistcoat of crimson velvet beneath a suit so expensive its price could have purchased a small country.

"This way!" He waved us along with a flourish, going so far as to execute a small jig as he set forth. "We've a private dock, of course, and the *Claire Wyndham* will arrive shortly. What a jolly night it is, to be sure!"

My friend knew better than to question me, but he did dart me a glance of such profound irony that I could not resist smirking in return.

At this point, were Watson writing the narrative, he would wax on endlessly about the quality of the fog tendrils beginning to creep along the turgid waters and the humble appearance of both the dilapidated private dock and the *Claire Wyndham*, with shabby black curtains drawn over its windows, bilge and barnacles crusting its hull, and chipped red paint flaking from its paddle box. And once we had been led inside the decrepit vessel, he would rapturously describe the sumptuous chandeliers, the champagne flowing into silver chalices, and the arch chatter of some two dozen aristocrats and their pet prodigies, all gushing effusions at each other as we progressed along the Thames.

I shall retain silence on the subject save for the fact it was every bit as beastly as we had both anticipated.

We were introduced to all and sundry; grotesque levels of enthusiasm were expressed at our presence; and I was seated adjacent to Lord Templeton for dinner, Watson next to a baroness with a wide, pleasant face and plentiful ropes of pearls (fiction writer, Hungarian origins, obviously from a musical family). Turning to my left after the soup had been cleared, I shook hands with Sir Alderford Blythe. A short man with a waxed moustache and thin black brows, he brought to mind a rather skittish beetle. His shoulders were stiff with tension, but his eyes remained determinedly neutral, and he had touched neither food nor drink.

"Your work with Brother Mycroft has been greatly appreciated by many parties," said I softly. "How go the negotiations?"

"Better than we could initially have hoped, Mr. Holmes," he returned under his breath. "If we are successful, a Japanese alliance may yet be procured, and would have the profoundest consequences upon our international relations."

"So I have been told."

"Your brother is a brilliantly farsighted individual."

"My dear gentlemen, take a turn upon the deck with me before the fish course?" Lord Templeton piped merrily to Watson and myself, gripping our shoulders. "I'm positively dying for a smoke. I shall simply *expire*. You must accompany me lest I succumb to *boredom*, which is the very last affliction which should plague us on this of all nights."

Pressing Sir Alderford's forearm reassuringly, I rose and the three of us exited. Secluded in the shadow of a smokestack, Lord Templeton passed us slender French cigarettes and said in an incisive tenor, "Thank you for coming, Mr. Holmes, Dr. Watson. Your brother explained the mission, I trust?"

All pretense of dandyism had dissolved like so much steam. Watson's square chin dropped before he abruptly closed his lips again, bless the fellow.

"Your suit and the card had already shown your hand rather neatly," I demurred. "You deliberately told me you had only just thought of inviting me to the Diadem Club two hours previous, yet somehow you managed to procure a fully tailored Jermyn Street suit for that admirably preposterous disguise and a letterpressed invitation with our names at the top. I was meant to take notice, and Mycroft's hint clinched the matter. Post me up, if you please. There will be an attempt on Sir Alderford's life tonight?"

"You don't disappoint, Mr. Holmes." Lord Templeton nodded gravely. "Indeed so. I was lucky to have secured a place in the club, and had your brother not intervened . . ." He shook his fair head. "One of the invitees, masquerading as a pioneering physicist, is in fact the spy Louis La Rothiere."

"Of Notting Hill? You mean the tall fellow with the pomaded hair and the brocade waistcoat?"

"Why, yes, I do. You have encountered him before, I take it."

"Never, but the chap who was introduced as a Sussex-born poly-math remarked upon the vintage *Veuve Clicquot Ponsardin* they were so liberally serving as only a native Frenchman could ever accomplish. Accents and their origins are a hobby of mine. I've had my eye on him all evening."

Lord Templeton smiled, though he remained grave. "For obvious reasons, I cannot myself intervene—all my value to England relies upon my maintaining this persona. The stalwart duo of Sherlock Holmes and John Watson, however? No one will so much as blink. The accent in remarking on the champagne—brilliant! Our cover could not be more perfect. The quarry is in our sights, and the trophy entirely yours, gentlemen. Whitehall thanks you for your service."

Just then, a rustling which was not the susurration of waves met my keen ears, and I stepped out of the shadows. Watson's dining companion the baroness stood there, likewise smoking, wearing a look of great attentiveness.

"And *that's* the stunner, Mr. Holmes, the knockout punch!" Lord Templeton exclaimed, instantly a pretentious peacock once more. "Oh, Baroness, what luck you're there! Did you hear my proposal about the play I mean to write about Mr. Holmes and Dr. Whitson here? I shall play the role of the canny spy late of the Boer Wars, India, the Irish conflict, and the Chinese court. It'll be a smash hit, nothing less, eh? I'd stake a thousand pounds it will. I'd put my *life* on the line, to be sure. Well, we had all better get back to the fish, what?"

Few words are required to detail what remains. As midnight neared, I identified a concealed knife about La Rothiere's person. In the ensuing struggle, which was *most* invigorating, I suffered a slice to the palm, the punch bowl and its entire contents were sacrificed to the cause of justice, and Watson's revolver finally settled the matter. My explanations were met with actual applause, which was gauche but hardly avoidable. Watson clucked over my injury but finally allowed that his handkerchief would do to stanch the wound until after we disembarked. (While both of us relish danger, we each tend to rather abhor the sight of the other actively bleeding, a paradox I do not wish to have cause to marvel over ever again.) When we docked once more near to Cleopatra's Needle, a trio of Yard detectives awaited us, and La Rothiere was carted away.

"Simply smashing to meet you, Mr. Holmes!" Lord Templeton rejoiced, clapping his hands and then clasping them adoringly under his chin like a music hall ingenue. "And Dr. Waldron. A *joy*. Best to your brother, Mr. Holmes, and tell the *Strand* illustrator to stop putting you in that tragic hat. It's an affront, I tell you, a travesty of justice. You look *much* better in city togs, curse me if I lie. *Strike* me down if that isn't my heartfelt opinion. Farewell!"

We bade him good night, Watson with an air of amazement and I struggling not to laugh until another, better thought sobered me.

"I would do the same, if I were asked," said I, my gaze on Lord Chesley Templeton's slim back as he flounced away.

"Beg pardon?"

Watson inspires a dreadful habit in me of blurting out whatever thought comes into my head, supposing I urgently want him to know its contents, and these slips require me to tell stories backward, which is nigh-impossible to accomplish in any elegant fashion. I blame the doctor for this failing unequivocally. His florid syntax has infected my much more methodical approach to language.

Mentally cuffing myself, I explained, "Lord Chesley Templeton is a consummate performer—he lives and breathes the role whilst recording every scrap of data, making deductions, planning his next moves. I would not be inexpert at this task. In fact, I daresay it would fall directly under my purview as a specialist, and if called upon by the Crown to perform such a duty, for years if necessary, I should instantly agree. I don't know that I'd excel at marching through deserts or returning enemy fire or ordering men to their deaths, but at *that* . . ." I nodded at the disappearing silhouette. "At that I could succeed. And I would say yes."

"Holmes," Watson huffed, frowning in the solicitous way he has, "do you suppose I don't already know that?"

When I made no answer, for I could think of none suitable, he chuckled fondly. "Let us presume you shan't be required to, all right? It would mean the country was headed for certain disaster. Your theoretical talents as a spy will keep, for the rest of our lives I hope. Right, I'm finding us a cab. I expected to be done in following a night at the Diadem Club, but admittedly not in this fashion, and I've yet to patch you up again."

Sunday, April 20th, 1902.

"What's the matter, Watson?" I asked without turning my head after the second post this morning. He was not in my line of sight where I sat at my worktable organizing academic references upon bullet casings (scant though they were), but my chemistry apparatus was, and I always keep my flasks polished to a high sheen.

"It's terribly disconcerting when you do that, you know." The doctor's voice was even, but still his knit brows betrayed perplexity at the letter in his hand.

"When I do what?"

"Deduce me without looking at me."

"It's efficient, my dear fellow. Anything amiss?"

"Not precisely." Watson tossed the paper to his desktop before him. "I've had a letter from the baroness at the Diadem Club that night—apparently she's a writer. She asked whether I would mind her appropriating the details of our adventure aboard the *Claire Wyndham*. Admittedly you played a minor enough role, and I can't reveal the smallest hint of Lord Templeton's involvement, so since I won't use it myself, I am bound to say yes."

I swiveled, appalled. "If another spinner of fanciful tales even dreams of—"

"Pray calm yourself. No, I'm your biographer, and I'll tell her as much." Watson smiled in a lopsided manner, tapping the desk with his pen. "I can't think what she'll make of it without either mentioning you or betraying Whitehall. Of course, I'll advise her on the subject."

"What is her name?"

"Baroness Emmunska Orczy."

"I've never heard of her."

"Well, neither have I. But I can't see the harm so long as I give her fair warning as to the difficulties."

Watson set to penning a return correspondence at once. A curious addendum to a curious case, I thought it. Happily, however, a new scientific treatise upon the art of detection will shortly make its way into the world, the quality of which I hope will balance out the endless stream of sentimentality flowing from the pens of loosely factual biographers and adventure authors alike.

Acknowledgments

There are a number of admirable Sherlockians who made this collection possible, including my "Good Old Index" Mr. Leslie Klinger, m'colleagues Dr. Ashley Polasek and Timothy Greer (who help keep me sane), and my fellow Baker Street Babes and Adventuresses and Irregulars (many of whom will recognize their names throughout these pages). Many thanks to Josh Getzler, Dan Lazar, and Kerri Kolen, who shared responsibility for pulling my first novel, *Dust and Shadow*, from the vast unwashed pile of unsolicited manuscripts. After its publication, all sorts of kindly people began allowing me to inflict further adventures of the Great Detective and the Good Doctor on the universe. I'm grateful to the editors of those anthologies, and in particular to Andrew Gulli of *The Strand Magazine*, for whom I've been thrilled to write ten mysteries from 2009 to the present.

As always, I'm endlessly thankful for Erin Malone, Tracy Fisher, Cathryn Summerhayes, and all the folks at William Morris Endeavor who take such meticulous care of me. Thanks to my family, friends, and Sherlockians of all stripes for their ceaseless support, and to my husband, Gabriel, for assuring me that if Sir Arthur Conan Doyle was allowed to entirely fabricate various scientific facts, then I was as well. Using exclusively real science would not have been a suitable tribute to the brilliant writer whose swamp adders and monkey serums have given us such grand scope for debate over the years.

Finally, my most heartfelt thanks to Otto Penzler, and not just for believing in this collection—he has helped my career along in myriad ways, he recommends my work in the most generous terminology, and I'm endlessly honored that one of the most widely read pillars of the mystery community appreciates my writing. I'll be launching my novels from The Mysterious Bookshop until Manhattan Island is swept away into the sea.

Credits